DEAL
WITH THE
DEVIL

DEAL
WITH THE
DEVIL

A MERCENARY LIBRARIANS NOVEL

KIT ROCHA

TOR

A TOM DOHERTY ASSOCIATES BOOK
NEW YORK

This is a work of fiction. All of the characters, organizations, and events portrayed
in this novel are either products of the author's imagination
or are used fictitiously.

DEAL WITH THE DEVIL

A Tor Book
Published by Tom Doherty Associates
120 Broadway
New York, NY 10271

www.tor-forge.com

Tor® is a registered trademark of Macmillan Publishing Group, LLC.

The Library of Congress Cataloging-in-Publication Data is available upon request.

ISBN 978-1-250-20936-8 (trade paperback)
ISBN 978-1-250-25629-4 (hardcover)
ISBN 978-1-250-20935-1 (ebook)

Our books may be purchased in bulk for promotional, educational, or business use.
Please contact your local bookseller or the Macmillan Corporate and Premium
Sales Department at 1-800-221-7945, extension 5442, or by email at
MacmillanSpecialMarkets@macmillan.com.

First Edition: 2020

Printed in the United States of America

0 9 8 7 6 5 4 3 2 1

For our fairy godmother, who can turn a pumpkin
into a coach with a single text message.
Thank you, Ms. Bev.

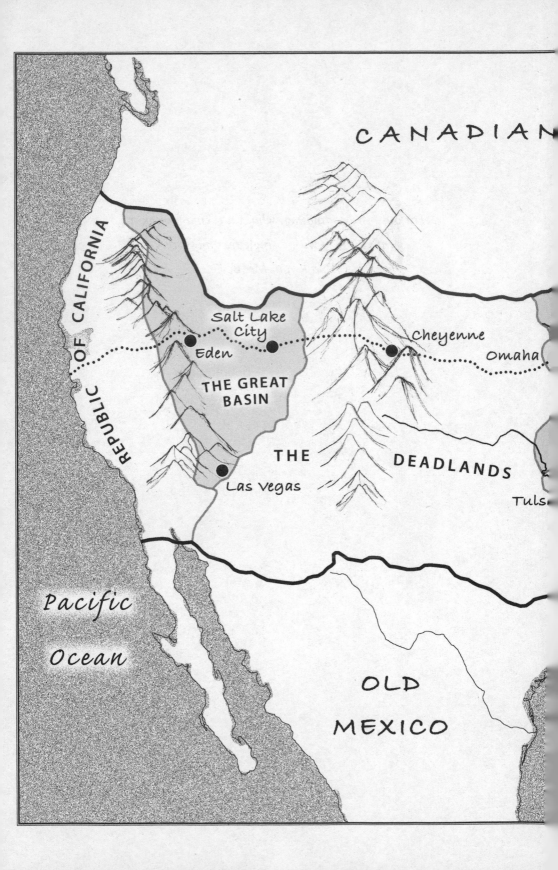

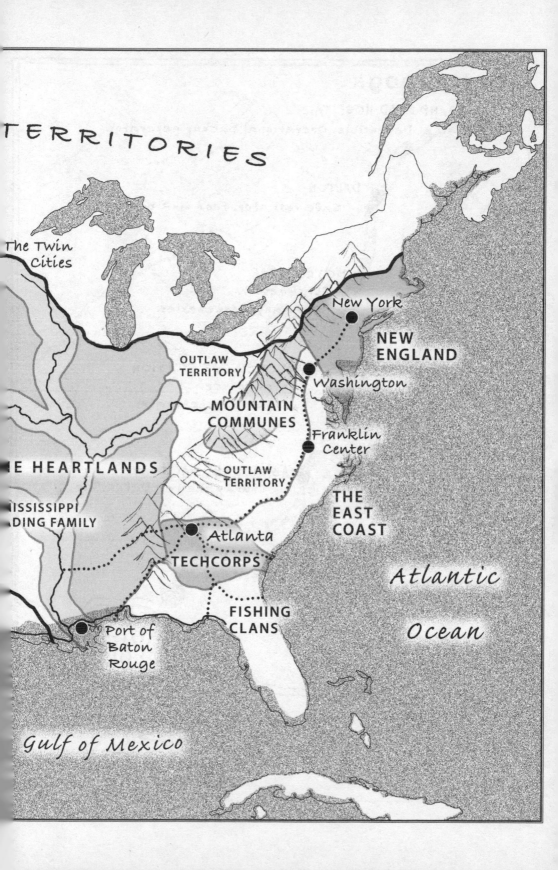

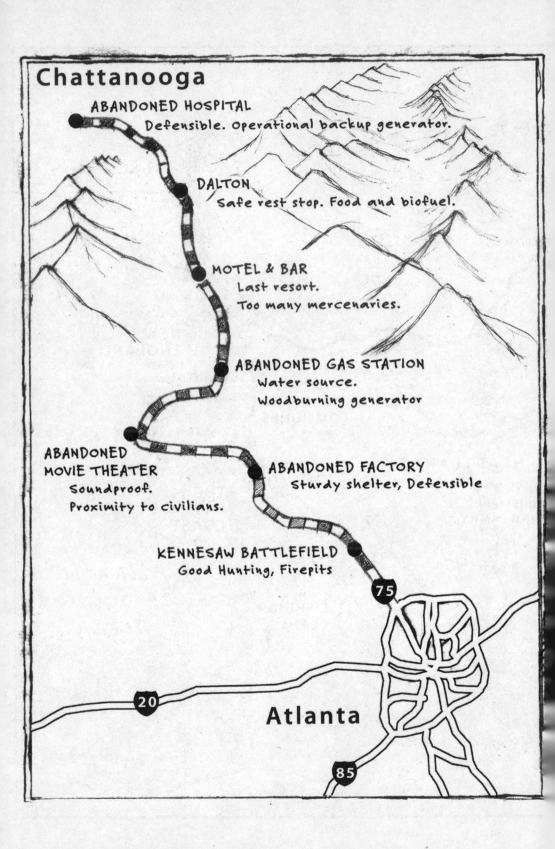

DEAL
WITH THE
DEVIL

CLASSIFIED BEHAVIOR EVALUATION

Franklin Center for Genetic Research

Subject HS-Gen16-A is the first candidate to achieve perfect marks on the eight-year physical benchmark tests. HS-Gen16-B and HS-Gen16-C show equal promise in intellect and empathy, respectively. I recommend we accelerate their training, with a specific focus on exploring the limits of their endurance.

Dr. Baudin, February 2060

ONE

Nina had broken the cardinal rule, and now she had to kill someone.

Four someones, actually. She counted the shuffling footsteps behind her as she eyed the stack of crates and scrap blocking the alley's exit. Razor wire glinted in the low light, heading off any thought of climbing over the mess. The only route of escape was back the way she'd come.

A brutally effective trap. Under other circumstances, she might have admired its elegance. Right now, it just pissed her off.

Never go out alone after dark. Dani's admonition—or did it qualify as an order?—echoed in Nina's head as she turned to face the men who'd blocked her in. The obvious leader stepped forward, brandishing a cheap pistol, as the three others fell into loose formation around him. The tall man on the left stood with his hand hovering near his hip, like he was getting ready to reach for a weapon tucked into the back of his waistband. The two on the right carried knives.

Surprisingly expert grips on all the weapons. The tall one was favoring his left knee. And one of the men wielding a knife was *built,* with the kind of bulk that made close contact a bad idea. Four men, two guns, at least three knives.

She did not have *time* for this.

"The bag," the leader grunted. "Now."

Nina's hand tightened around the black strap slung over her shoulder. She didn't like fighting if she could avoid it—too many variables—but she couldn't afford to comply. She might have, if the satchel had held her usual haul of scavenged books or random data. But this was a commission, specially sourced information collected for a specific purpose—and a specific client.

Losing it would cost her more than money.

"Walk away," she advised flatly.

One of them snickered.

Oh well, she had to try. Not that the world would suffer by losing these assholes, but because her conscience demanded it. Of course, they'd laid a trap in a dirty alley, and they didn't seem too broken up about going four-on-one to rob her.

Maybe she was actively doing the world a favor.

The leader stepped forward, his index finger trembling as he pulled the trigger. Nina ducked, and the bullet went high, shattering a window that was probably already cracked or broken to begin with.

Everything in Five Points was.

When she came back up, she was inches from the man's face, close enough to see flecks of spittle fly as he opened his mouth to yell at the others. She smashed the heel of her hand under his chin, snapping his teeth shut on his tongue.

He screamed, and she ducked again, this time to put herself on the other side of his outstretched arm. A hard blow to his shoulder spun him around, away from her, and she pressed close to his back, turning him into a shield.

Then she locked one hand around his, turning him into a weapon, too. She squeezed off two more shots, each finding its target in the dead center of an attacker's chest, before the gun jammed.

Shit.

The third man returned fire. The bullets slammed into his friend—so much for honor among thieves—and sent Nina stumbling back. She recovered just in time to dodge another shot, but she heard the razor-sharp whistle of its path as it cut through the air near her head.

Too goddamn close.

She launched herself at her last attacker. She kicked out, feinting as if to disarm him, only to target his weak leg at the last second. Her boot crashed into his knee, and she felt the joint give as he crumpled. The gun fell and skittered across the grimy asphalt, lodging itself under a mangled crate butted up against a length of chain-link fencing.

Just as well. They'd undoubtedly drawn enough attention already. She reached into her jacket, drew her pistol, and slid her thumb over the biometric scanner embedded in its grip. The weapon activated, chambering a round with a soft click.

The two shots she fired exited the elongated barrel just as quietly, silencing the man's shrieking and groaning.

Nina stood over him for a moment, watching the dark blood as it began to pool beneath his head. "You did pretty well," she muttered. "You never really stood a chance, that's all."

A chill swept over her despite the relatively warm spring night, raising the fine hairs on the back of her neck. For a moment, it felt like someone was watching her. Not just observing, but staring at her hard enough to bore holes through flesh.

Right into her soul.

She shook it off and holstered her pistol. There probably *were* eyes on her—the pickers waiting to crawl the place when she was gone. They would wait for her to take first pass at the bodies, out of grudging respect as well as self-preservation. As victor, she had the greatest right to claim the spoils.

She knelt beside one of the bodies, and spent shell casings bit into her skin through her pants. They weren't even from this firefight, just scattered detritus. Another testament to this area's legacy of violence.

Once upon a time, this had been a nice neighborhood. The building on Nina's left used to house city offices, and the one across the street—now a highly trafficked brothel—was an old warehouse that had been converted into chichi lofts catering to the young and wealthy. A faded sign still hung on the side of the building—*Now leasing for Spring 2043.*

They never finished the construction, and no one but squatters ever got the chance to move in. Not after the devastation of 2042.

Not after the Flares.

It started with a solar storm. For two days, a huge blast of magnetic energy surged toward earth, headed straight for southern Europe, exciting scientists and doomsday preppers alike. In the end, huge areas of France, Spain, and Italy were impacted, though the long-term damage to their power grids was minimal.

No, the worst thing about that storm was how it interfered with satellites, scrambling their signals so that no one noticed the much larger coronal mass ejection in its wake.

The second solar flare hit North America head on. By that time, the United States' utility infrastructure had been crumbling for decades, ignored or worse by politicians with other priorities—tax cuts for corporations and new fighter jets and the same old fossil fuels that had driven them into the Energy Wars to begin with. The flare struck a killing blow, pushing the weakened government to its knees as it plunged the country into darkness and chaos.

This used to be a nice neighborhood, not that Nina knew any of that firsthand. But there were plenty of old-timers down at the local bar who'd tell you all about the world that once was—the shining city of Atlanta, back before the desolation of the Flares—for the cost of a few highballs.

Nina's stomach twisted. She could still feel the hungry weight of those stares on her as she rose and backed away from the corpse at her feet.

Tonight, the vultures could have it. All she wanted was to get home.

The scavengers were already converging.

Perched on the rooftop where he'd been doing recon, Knox watched the gang of kids creep out of the darkness. They moved like shadows themselves, wraith-thin and nearly silent. The shitty streetlights dimmed and surged as the kids spread out in the bloodstained alley, swarming the dead bodies with tragic efficiency.

They worked fast, gathering up everything Nina had left behind. Bloodied clothes, worn boots, even the shitty gun wedged under a broken crate. A girl who couldn't have been more than sixteen popped the magazine to check it before tucking the handgun through her belt. Before long, the group had stripped the men down to their underwear and melted back into the gloom.

The whole thing had taken only minutes. The men who'd tried to jump Nina lay sprawled and exposed on the cracked asphalt, their pale skin washed out by the flickering metal-halide lights. They looked even sadder like this. Naked, abandoned.

And dead. Very, very dead.

Knox eased back from the edge of the roof and rolled to his feet, ignoring the warning ache in his muscles. He got a running start and made the leap between buildings. The impact of the landing stabbed through his knees, and he rolled to disperse the shock of the force—something he wouldn't have had to do a week ago.

Time contracted around Knox. He could *feel* each second that slipped away. He swung out onto the rickety fire ladder and slid toward the ground, ruthlessly forcing his mind back to the job.

But he kept seeing those dead bodies. Nina had killed four armed men in the time it had taken Knox to draw a deep breath, then walked away from the encounter without a scratch.

Of course this job couldn't be easy.

His safe house was a mile-and-a-half hike through the shittier parts of Atlanta. This far south of the TechCorps HQ, security was lax, and Protectorate forces wouldn't venture out without a direct order. There were no checkpoints like the ones lining the streets that wound their way up the Hill, where the TechCorps sprawled like a brooding dragon sitting on its hoard. There, disciplined squads made regular sweeps amongst the posh high-rises that housed elite scientists and distinguished executives. Farther down the Hill, haphazard patrols guarded the more modest homes and businesses that catered to the fortunate families who'd found a way to make themselves useful to the TechCorps.

None of that existed here. The southern half of the city could be on fire, and the Protectorate wouldn't stir itself to piss in this general direction in a feeble attempt to put it out. Sure, they swept in every few months to remind people that the TechCorps still had one boot pressed to their necks, ready to come down. But the rest of the time, they didn't give a shit if the people in the poorer neighborhoods tore each other apart, as long as the TechCorps had enough warm bodies to fill their support staff jobs and their experiment rooms.

People so desperate for money they'd do damn near anything for it? That was the only resource no one was running out of any time soon.

Knox knew that better than most.

Still, he hadn't realized just how bad it had gotten until the Protectorate had pulled them in to deal with the growing labor uprisings. For years, Knox and his team had been deployed outside of TechCorps' territory, entrusted with delicate missions that required a certain amount of discretion and finesse. Knox had advanced corporate interests and forged connections in dozens of regions—from the fiercely competitive shipping clans in Florida and the Gulf Coast to the warring crime syndicates that had taken over Washington, D.C.

Not that the word *crime* had much meaning anymore. The only rules left were the ones you were powerful enough to enforce.

Knox had seen lawless places that had descended into swirling chaos, as well as cities with rigid laws that made military discipline seem lax. He'd even seen towns where people had come together, pooling their resources to restore comfort to everyone. The mountain communities dotting the Appalachians, the close-knit neighborhoods ringing New York City's boroughs, the cozy communes in New England—all were places almost idyllic in their relative peace.

Somehow, Atlanta had become a combination of all three. Though the TechCorps held the city in its brutal grip, their control didn't extend to support, so the outlying neighborhoods had fallen into neglect. But within those neighborhoods, you could find sparks of light. Communities coming together. Workers fighting for better pay, for better lives.

Hope. That was why the Protectorate had recalled the Silver Devils. Hope had been bubbling up through the cracks in the TechCorps' power, and they'd wanted Knox to snuff it out.

In those orders, Knox had finally found a line he couldn't cross.

He broke free of the final line of buildings and left the streetlights behind. Darkness wrapped around him, another layer of safety, and he relaxed slightly. No one was likely to be wandering out this way after dark. The Devils had set up shop in West End, in an abandoned warehouse overlooking the reservoir. The crumbling remains of the old interstate rose beside it, dwarfing the squat concrete building. A huge chunk of the overpass had caved in over a decade ago, wiping out the community below and discouraging resettlement.

After the Flares, weak infrastructure had been their downfall. The federal government had been held together by tissue paper by that point, unable to function effectively, and state governments had filled the void with varying levels of success. Atlanta had been doing better than most of the rest of Georgia, with strong citywide leadership that might have rallied, given time.

Except that the infrastructure was already so fragile. And the TechCorps were right there, a monolith of recently merged medical and tech companies with the latest and greatest of *everything*. How generous they must have seemed in those first dark days, reaching out with their seemingly unlimited supplies of solar power, water, food, and medicine.

TechCorps offers were always too good to be true, and the hooks they sank into you went bone deep. Atlanta's swiftly displaced city government had no doubt learned that lesson as harshly as Knox had.

Knox approached the abandoned warehouse they'd taken over. It was truly off the grid, not even hooked up with power or water. They had to procure or process both for themselves. Not the most comfortable place to crash, but it didn't matter. They wouldn't be here long.

Besides, the Silver Devils had stayed in worse.

Knox approached from the north and stopped precisely five feet from the back door. His embedded communicator beeped, and he activated it with a low command. "Knox here."

"Gotcha, Captain. Disabling security."

Conall's reply echoed inside Knox's head. They'd had the subcutaneous comms for almost a year, and Knox still wished they'd carved them out along with their trackers three days earlier. Conall swore he'd modified the frequencies to be unique and untraceable, but the things still creeped Knox the fuck out.

Implants to make him stronger and faster? Fine. To moderate his biochemistry to make him the perfect soldier? Okay.

Conall's voice serving as his inner monologue?

Too far.

It took nearly a minute before Conall sounded the all clear. Knox crossed to the door, which popped open just as he reached it. Conall greeted him with a grin and an outstretched hand. "Glasses."

Knox slipped off his glasses and relinquished them. "Pull the last thirty minutes of footage first and get it up on the wall. Everyone needs to see it."

"So you caught up with the mark?"

"Yeah." Knox eased past Conall and let the tech worry about resetting the security measures. The cavernous main room of the warehouse was well lit, with bright solar-powered LEDs hanging from the bare beams. Rafe and Gray sat at one end of the trestle table, the remains of a meal as well as one of Gray's ever-present disassembled guns spread out between them.

Knox stopped at the other end and stripped off his tactical vest. "We have a problem."

"How bad?" Rafe asked, his rice-laden spoon hovering in the air. "She got a security team or something?"

"She *is* a security team." Knox shrugged out of his shoulder rig and dropped it on the table. His backup pistol followed, as well as the knife sheath strapped to his leg. "Watch the footage."

Rafe obediently picked up his chair and turned it to face the white-washed section of wall at the back of the building. Gray looked up without moving—or taking his full attention from the rifle components in front of him.

After another few seconds of fiddling and some muttered curses, Conall flipped his handheld projector upright, and the surveillance footage from Knox's glasses appeared on the wall. The video from the night-vision camera was tinged with green, though Conall color-corrected it with a few keystrokes.

On-screen, Nina arrived in the alley. The video washed out the gold undertones of her skin, and the angle of the shot left her face in shadow. She surveyed the trap she'd walked into with no apparent alarm as the four men drifted into the frame.

Knox had almost intervened then. The instructions he'd received had been *very* specific—if he wanted his biochem hacker back, he was to deliver Nina to the designated coordinates, alive and unharmed.

He'd seen so much death in those four shadowy outlines—first Nina's, when they overpowered her. Then Luna's, when Knox failed to provide her ransom. Then each of his men, one by one, as their degrading enhancements slowly poisoned their bodies. Without a biochem hacker to regulate their implants, the Silver Devils might as well put bullets in their heads right now. Or go crawling back to the Protectorate.

Knox would prefer the bullet.

"Holy shit!" Conall's shocked exclamation drew Knox's attention back to the surveillance footage. Four bodies were already on the ground. It had happened that quickly—so quickly Knox hadn't even had time to vault off the roof to help.

Rafe shoved his spoon into his bowl of rice and braced his elbows on the table. "Go back and play it slow."

Conall obeyed. Even at half speed, Nina was *fast*. She dodged a fuck-ing bullet before commandeering the man who'd tried to shoot her as a human shield. Then she used his gun to fire on two of his friends while the weapon was still in his hand.

Knox was good, the best the Protectorate had ever turned out. And even he wasn't sure he could have pulled that off.

Gray sat back in his chair and rubbed his chin, his brows drawn together in a contemplative frown. "Who is she?"

"Fuck that," Conall retorted. "*What* is she?"

"Trouble," Rafe rumbled. "Hot, sexy trouble. Does this mean we go with plan B?"

Rafe always wanted to go with plan B, where he deployed his charming smile and his big, beautiful brown eyes, and everyone melted for him. Knox had relied on the man's natural charisma on plenty of missions, but the thought of Rafe using sex to lure Nina into a trap . . .

"No," he said, too curtly. "Plan A was to pick her up off the street. That clearly won't work. Plan B would be to sedate her, not seduce her, but we don't know what she is or whether our tranqs will work on her. So we go with plan C. She's an information broker. We're going to make her an offer no broker could refuse."

Gray scrubbed one hand over his face with a rough sigh. "Maybe we should focus on figuring out another way to get Luna back." He gestured toward the makeshift screen. "I already wasn't crazy about kidnapping someone. I'm really not crazy about getting killed during the attempt."

Knox wasn't wild about the kidnapping, either. When he'd first joined the Protectorate, it had been with wide eyes and dreams of heroics. He'd decided that he would accept the biochemical enhancements. He'd train day and night, if that was what it took. And then he'd go back out into the world and do some damn good. Help people like his father, who'd died protecting a neighborhood store from petty thieves. Make things better instead of worse.

His eyes hadn't been wide in a long time. The world wasn't interested in being saved. And the only allegiance Knox owed now was to the men in this room, men who'd followed him into battle and the depths of hell and now into treason, where a ticking clock was counting down to their slow, painful deaths.

"We don't have time," he reminded Gray. "Conall couldn't trace the communication. We don't know who took her, or what they'll do if we show up at those coordinates without the payment they requested. And every day we stall, our side effects are getting worse."

"It's Luna," Rafe declared, as if that answered the moral dilemma. "Helping us is what got her into this mess. And sure, the lady is hot and all, but . . ." He waved a hand at the paused video, showing Nina frozen in the act of delivering her silent coup de grace. "You don't get that good at killing by being a sweet little pussycat."

Gray relented, holding up both hands in surrender. "Understood. Still not too keen on dying, though, so this ruse of yours had better work, Knox."

It would, because Knox had been saving this weapon since the day Conall had offered it to him. His game-winning ace. An information broker's ultimate fantasy.

"Conall?"

"Hmm?"

"How thorough are those files you have on the Rogue Library of Congress bunker?"

Conall tipped his chair on two legs so he could snag a small data pad off his workstation. "Old Uncle Aiden was a little cracked, but he was fucking meticulous. So I'm guessing pretty thorough."

"You're guessing?"

"I never actually decrypted most of them. Seemed a little reckless."

"How long would it take you to decrypt it and redact any references to location?"

Conall tapped his leg as his eyes darted back and forth and his lips moved in silent calculation. He'd always sparked with barely restrained energy, but now he was restless and fidgety all the time.

"Twelve hours?" Conall said finally. "Maybe twenty-four, if some of the files have multiple encryptions."

Too long, but it was still the best chance they had. Knox slid an empty tablet down the table. Conall caught it. "Do it. We need schematics, paper trails. Proof. Redact anything that would lead her to the real location. Load it all on there."

Conall raised one brow. "Wouldn't it be easier to just throw together some dummy shit? I can make it look good enough to sell the con."

Knox turned back to the video frozen on the wall. He'd underestimated her physical strength. He wasn't about to make the same mistake with her mind. "This isn't the time to take chances. Use the real data."

"Yes, sir."

And that was that, as far as Conall was concerned. He settled into his task, trusting that Knox would spend his family secret wisely. That he'd save Luna, save *them,* keep them all out of TechCorps torture cells, and probably score them enough credits to settle down to blissful lives of leisure.

Knox had worked hard to earn that trust. To *deserve* it. Somehow, he had to pull this off and be worthy of it.

TWO

Nina got up early the next morning. She started the coffee, cracked the last of their eggs into a bowl, and reached for a whisk. Her best chance of avoiding a lecture—albeit well deserved—from Dani was to pretend she'd crashed out early and slept for ten hours.

Maya came down first, her booted feet thudding on the iron stairs. She was still clad in her pajamas, a worn gray T-shirt and soft black pants, but she'd already twisted her dark braids up on top of her head. Her wireless earbuds were firmly in place, and the faint throb of pop music reached Nina before Maya tapped her watch to shut it off. "Hey."

Nina pulled Maya's favorite mug from its hook beneath the cabinet. "Good morning."

"I guess." Maya slid onto a stool at the kitchen island and rubbed her eyes. "At least there's real coffee. I could smell it from my room."

"Savor it, because we're almost out." She filled Maya's mug and pushed it across the steel countertop. "We need more eggs, too. I'll talk to Mrs. O'Dell this afternoon."

Maya dragged the little tin of synthetic sweetener toward her and dumped a heaping spoonful into her coffee. "I finished listening to that engineering manual you found before we went out last night, so let her know I can take a look at her solar converter whenever she wants."

"I will. How was the club?"

"Loud." Maya sipped her coffee, and some of the tension eased from her face as she sighed with appreciation. "Dani didn't break any fingers, though, so it was a good night. Or a bad one. Guess it depends on your perspective."

"That it does." There were dark circles under Maya's eyes, like she hadn't slept well. "Dancing it out didn't work, huh?"

"It helped a little," Maya lied.

Nina pressed her hands to the cold steel counter, then busied herself with pouring the beaten eggs into the waiting skillet. It was the only way to stop herself from making suggestions about other ways Maya could deal with her condition.

Maya had thought of everything. *Tried* everything. She wasn't getting worse, but the stress had to be wearing on her. The human brain just wasn't built to process and commit to memory every bit of auditory stimulus it received.

Finally, Nina broke. "You know, there's one thing we haven't—"

"Where the hell were you last night?"

Fuck. Dani stood on the top landing, both arms crossed over her chest. She was dressed for a workout, in stark shades of black and white that seemed to mirror her disapproval, and her blond hair was drawn back in a tight ponytail as severe as her expression.

"Wait, what?" Maya squinted at Nina over the rim of her coffee mug. "I thought you were asleep when we got home."

"She wasn't." Dani descended the stairs slowly, her stare growing more focused and stern with each footfall. "I checked her bed."

Nina stifled a sigh as she stirred the eggs. "That's very creepy, you know."

"Whatever. Where were you?"

"Dead drop." Nina handed Maya a stack of plates and silverware. "The Professor came through last-minute on the Carver job. Had to do the pickup without you."

Dani's jaw tightened. "It couldn't wait?"

"C'mon, Dani." Maya juggled her mug and the dishes on her way to the scarred wooden table. "You really think the material would still be there this morning?" She distributed the plates in front of their chairs. "But you could have swung by the club for us, Nina."

"I didn't want to ruin your night." Nina dished the eggs onto the plates, put the skillet in the sink, and pulled the pitcher of orange juice from the refrigerator.

Silence fell as they sat down to breakfast, a lull that went on for so long Nina started to think maybe she'd gotten away with it, after all.

Then Dani spoke again. "Did you have any trouble?"

Nina kept her gaze fixed on her plate and wished—for the millionth time—that she could lie worth a damn. "Eat your eggs before they get cold."

Dani's fork clattered to her plate.

Maya leaned across the table to poke Nina with the tines of her fork. "Whatever happened, just tell us."

There was no avoiding it now. "I got jumped. But the good news is that you just hurt me worse than any of those guys did. And they're dead now. End of story."

"Shit. Who was it?"

"They didn't introduce themselves, Maya." Nina wrapped both hands around her mug. "They just shoved knives and guns in my face and demanded my bag. Which was obviously not going to happen."

Dani studied her. "The small-time gangs are getting bolder. It's been too long since the Protectorate smacked them around."

Because the Protectorate didn't care how many thieves and gangs roved the city, as long as they stayed off the Hill and didn't interfere with business as usual. "So we'll pick up the slack," Nina said firmly. "Maybe we should train after breakfast."

Maya groaned. "Again? *Seriously?*"

"You just stabbed me with your fork for going out by myself, so hell yeah, you're going to train. Because if you try to argue now that training isn't necessary, I'm stabbing you back."

"That's not fair." She pointed her fork at Nina and then Dani. "Superpowers. Superpowers." She turned the fork toward herself. "*Nada.*"

It was a gross oversimplification. "That's not accurate," Nina observed. "You may not have been rewired or custom-crafted on a genetic level, but you have your thing."

"*Yeeeeeeah.*" Maya drew out the word. "But remembering literally everything I hear isn't exactly a combat skill. And I'm not about to armwrestle someone if I can just shoot them in the head instead."

"Uh-huh." Dani propped her chin on one hand. "So what do you do when you can't?"

Maya made a face at her. "Rest easy in heaven knowing you're gonna avenge me?"

"Not if you give up without a fucking fight." Dani snorted. "Haunt me forever, see if I care. I'm not embarking on a dark path of vengeance and death because you skipped cardio."

Maya waved a grumpy middle finger at her before shoving the last of her eggs into her mouth. She chewed, swallowed, and sighed. "Fine. I'll let you guys throw my ass around."

Dani might live for a good endorphin rush, but Nina would rather have gone back to bed. It wasn't a luxury any of them had. "You said it." She gestured to herself and Dani. "Superpowers." Then she indicated Maya. "Has to work twice as hard in case shit gets bad."

"Yeah, yeah, yeah." Maya picked up her coffee. "Y'all are really gonna regret this next time trivia night rolls around."

"At least you'll be alive to give us hell." Nina rose. "Come on."

Maya began to clean up her dishes, but Dani waved her off. "I'll do them. See you in a few."

Nina and Maya climbed the stairs and headed down the hall to their training room. Support beams crisscrossed the high ceiling, and the bare brick walls had been left exposed, but everything else was the latest, most expensive tech they could afford. Bioresponsive weight machines and other equipment ringed the perimeter of the room, leaving the center clear except for a thick foam sparring mat.

Nina stopped by the control panel and activated one of the treadmills. It chirped, a bright, cheerful sound, and slowly began to fold out of its recessed space in the wall. "You shrugged it off, but Dani had a point. What do you do when you can't shoot an attacker?"

"Run," she responded obediently. "Run like hell."

"Yep, so hop on."

Nina watched Maya's form as she stepped onto the treadmill's rolling platform. She wouldn't be able to do a full workout, not without changing out of those heavy boots, but this wasn't about the cardiovascular workout or even her endurance.

This was about thinking.

With that in mind, she waited until Maya had jogged half a mile before speaking again. "And what if you can't run?"

"I fight dirty," Maya replied, only a little breathless. "I crush balls, poke eyes, scratch faces, smash knees."

"With?"

"Whatever I can find. Or my bare hands if I have to."

"Bare hands are a last resort." Nina wiggled her fingers. "They tend to break."

"So, whatever's closest to me that has some heft. Break a plate across their head. Throw hot coffee at them. Fork them in the face."

"You're obsessed with forks." Dani strolled in, shaking her head, and went straight for the pull-up bar mounted on the wall between the leg press and the ab board. "What is that about, anyway?"

"They're everywhere, they're unassuming, and no one expects it." Maya glanced at Nina. "That's the point, right? Using everyday shit?"

"Mainly," she admitted, "but it's also about improvising the right weapon at the right moment, and in the right situation. Let's say . . . you're running a hustle at Clem's."

At least she had the decency to flush. "I don't *hustle*. It's not my fault that men underestimate my pool game."

"You're running a hustle," Nina repeated, walking around the treadmill with her hands on her hips. "Your mark doesn't take kindly to losing all his credits, so he starts some shit."

"I assume Clem doesn't shoot him in this scenario?"

"Nope. You're on your own."

Maya frowned, her boots still thumping on the treadmill. "Well, start with a pool cue. I'm already holding one, I assume."

"Sure." Nina prodded Maya in the side. "Go on."

Maya swatted at Nina's fingers. "Smack him with it, jam the end into his balls, crack it over his head."

Nina stopped in front of the treadmill. "Armpits."

Maya almost missed a step. "What?"

"She said armpits." Dani paused, her chin hovering just above the steel bar. "Something as long as a pool cue telegraphs, so you probably won't land a shot on some guy's balls. He'll just twist out of the way. But if you jab him in the armpit—"

"He won't see it coming, so he won't guard," Nina finished. "And it fucking *hurts*."

"Okay, armpits. Check. Or I'll just kick a chair into his legs. If he goes down, I get to go back to plan A and haul ass out of there."

"Hey, you know what you need?" Dani looped one arm over the pull-up bar and swung from it. "A sock in your pocket."

Maya burst into breathless laughter. "Did you spike your coffee with something?"

Dani scowled. "It's for the billiard balls. Pop one in there, and boom—instant improvised flail. I knew this lady who would put *anything* solid and heavy into a sock and whup your ass with it. I saw her break a guy's arm with that trick once."

"Okay, so I put the eight ball in a sock and start breaking arms with it. That'll definitely cut down on people trying to buy me drinks. Might be worth it for that alone."

Nina thumped one of the treadmill's handrails. "Focus."

"Better idea." Dani dropped from the pull-up bar, her athletic shoes slapping against the polished wood floor. "Lose the boots and back up all those glib words, Maya. Spar with me."

Maya smacked the treadmill controls. When the belt whispered to a stop, she hopped off and settled on the edge of the mat to pull off her boots. "As long as we all know this is totally unfair."

Maya had a point. Her brain may have been altered to give her perfect auditory recall, but Dani had modifications of her own. Her entire nervous system had been rewired in an experimental procedure that granted her superhuman reflexes and reaction times. Fighting her at full speed was like fighting a blur.

"Don't worry." Dani stretched her arms across her chest, one after the other. "I'll slow it down, just for you."

"Uh-huh, sure you will." With her boots stripped off, Maya resecured her long braids on top of her head, mimicked Dani's stretches, and stepped warily onto the mat.

They circled each other for only a few seconds before Dani lunged, coming in for a shot to the gut. Maya blocked and spun away, and Dani barely gave her time to recover before throwing a right hook directly at her jaw.

It didn't land. She might complain about having to train more than once a week, but Maya was making progress. If some asshole off the street started hassling her, she'd probably be able to handle it, even if she wasn't armed. Of course, all it took to end your life—or, at the very least, to grandly fuck up your day—was a single lucky shot.

So, she had to keep training.

Dani and Maya continued to throw punches and kicks, to block and parry, while Nina circled the mat, studying them. Once or twice, Dani had to move at her normal speed to avoid having Maya's feet or fists connect, and every time Maya let out a well-deserved laugh of triumph.

The slap of blows being deflected. The scuffle of feet on the padded floor. The sounds were hypnotic, lulling Nina into memory. She'd practically grown up in rooms just like this—bright lights and the smells of sweat and disinfectant. Brusque trainers demonstrating throws and yelling out corrections.

Dani's back hit the mat with a thud, and the all-too-familiar noise reverberated through Nina as if *she* had been the one to fall. The training rooms at the Franklin Center had been larger, so sound echoed more, and lined with mirrors on all four walls, so that every person was reflected off the surfaces and multiplied.

An especially dizzying effect in a scientific facility full of clones.

Her cluster had consisted of the standard three, and they may have looked identical, but their differences had gone far deeper than superficial physical attributes. Ava was the cool, logical one, the brilliant tactician who could instantly size up a situation and outmaneuver any enemy. Hotheaded Zoey, on the other hand, had felt so sharply and so deeply that she made every single breath seem like a magical gift from some benevolent god. And Nina had been somewhere in the middle, solidly caught between her brain and her heart, ruled by neither. Combining aspects of both while coming up decidedly short.

The Center had called them clones, designations A through C of HS-Gen16. But to Nina, Ava and Zoey had simply been her family.

And if she'd worked harder—trained more, *been better*—then they might still be alive.

Another thud dragged her out of the past, and she looked over as Maya rolled stubbornly to her feet, shaking off the takedown with a scowl of concentration.

"That's enough." Nina's throat ached, and her voice nearly cracked. "For today, anyway. We have things to do. Maya?"

Maya backed away, grinning at Dani. Then she slumped to the mat and sprawled out on her back with her arms flung wide. "I did the books last night before we went out. It's not looking great."

Well, shit. "How not great?" Nina asked.

"The Carver job will help. We're not gonna, like, run out of food or anything." Maya tilted her head to meet Nina's gaze. "But if you want to finish the basement and get heaters in there before it gets cold, we're going to need to take more retrieval jobs."

The back of her neck ached, and Nina rubbed at it. Insulating the basement and installing heat and beds before the weather turned cold had been her main goal for the year. Every winter, a lack of adequate heating and shelter killed at least a dozen people a week—and that was just in this neighborhood. They froze to death because they didn't have anywhere to go. She had to get it done.

Then there was all the other stuff that kept getting shuffled aside—more shelving for the books they scavenged or traded for, another combination printer and binding machine, more activities for the community . . .

The list always seemed to grow instead of getting any shorter.

"Okay," she said finally. "Okay, I'll go out and make it happen. Maya, you handle the freeze dryers. Everything is prepped already, it just has to go in for the next cycle. Dani, you're on food delivery. I'll try to drum up some business."

Dani pursed her lips and rocked back on her heels. "You know, I still have some active contacts. It wouldn't be hard to land a couple quick jobs—"

"No. Jesus, Dani. You agreed—no more assassinations."

"I'm willing to concede that killing people to earn money in order to save people may seem a little counterintuitive." Dani shrugged. "But I only kill *bad guys*."

"*No.*"

Maya rolled upright and started to stretch. "If we get that desperate, I can do another brain dump. People love TechCorps secrets."

That was a terrible idea for entirely different reasons. If Maya let the wrong secret slip, it could clue the TechCorps in to the fact that she was not, in fact, as dead as their records seemed to indicate. "No way. Look, I'll handle it. You just have to trust me."

"I do," Maya said immediately. "We both do. You know that. We just want to help."

"You will—by delivering food and preserving more." The rest was Nina's responsibility.

Nina stayed out so long that it was full dark by the time she made her way back to the warehouse. Despite grabbing a quick lunch at the market earlier, she was *starving*—which made the sight of the pot of soup still warming on the stove particularly welcome.

She'd just filled a bowl when someone knocked on the front door. Dani and Maya were probably upstairs somewhere, or maybe not even home, so Nina abandoned her food with a sigh.

The first floor of the converted warehouse was mostly one big, open room, and Nina muttered a couple of blistering curses as she crossed it. She disengaged each of the bolts on the front door, including the biometric one near the top—

Then she opened it to a Greek god and forgot all about her rumbling stomach.

He had to be one of Dani's hookups. He was vaguely her type, tall and broad, with the kind of exquisitely defined physique that came from conditioning, not just work. His clothes—jeans, boots, T-shirt—were casual and unremarkable except for the loving way they fit. He had blue eyes, brown hair that was a bit too long on the top, and a beard short enough for Nina to see the strong jaw beneath.

How odd. Though he wasn't dressed like one, he carried himself like a soldier. And soldiers were *not* Dani's style.

Nina kept a tight grip on the edge of the door and smiled. "Can I help you?"

"I'm looking for Nina." His voice was low and clear. "Someone said I'd find her here."

"Someone like who?"

"An artifact dealer up on Centennial Hill. Janos."

Word that she was looking for work must have spread fast. "Janos must not like you very much. Showing up at someone's house uninvited is considered pretty damn rude in this business. It gets people shot." *Or worse.*

He reached into his back pocket and slowly drew out a palm-sized data tablet. "Trust me. What I have on here is worth it."

Dealing with him was a gamble, which was unfortunate, because she'd never been able to resist a good gamble. "What's your name?"

He paused for half a beat. "Garrett."

"Then come on in." She swung the door wide and stepped back. She watched him assess his surroundings, taking in all the exits, available cover, potential weapons. He studied the open kitchen, the seating arranged in the living area, the back hall, and the stairs to the loft overhead.

Definitely a soldier.

"I was about to have dinner." She headed toward the kitchen again without turning her back on him. "Would you care to join me?"

His gaze flicked to the bowl of soup. "Thank you, but I'm not hungry."

"Coffee, then?" Nina offered politely.

"No, thank you."

"Are you sure? It's real."

His brow furrowed. "It's not necessary."

Most people in Five Points hadn't tasted real coffee in so long they would have tripped over themselves getting to the carafe. But this guy was unmoved. "Not impressed, huh? You must be doing all right for yourself. So what are you, Garrett? A smuggler?" She arched an eyebrow as she sat down at the table. "A soldier?"

"I'm a guy with a score that'll make the Crypt look like pocket change." He placed the tablet on the table and slid it toward her.

Nina caught the tablet before it slid off the edge, and kept her smile in place. Not many people outside the recovery business knew about the Crypt. Hell, it had been lost and forgotten even before the Flares, before all the satellites had gone dark and power grids across the nation had been fried to a crisp.

The Crypt of Civilization was a time capsule, an assortment of items and books on microfilm that had been gathered and interred in the early part of the twentieth century. It had taken Nina two years to find it and one more to surreptitiously empty it. The money she'd made from selling off most of the artifacts had bought her this building, and digitizing the microfilm had kick-started her information library.

She didn't try to hide the fact that she'd pulled that job, but she didn't advertise it, either—and she wasn't about to talk about it with a stranger who couldn't quite manage to scrub off the smell of military police.

Instead of activating the screen, she held the tablet out to him. "Not interested."

The furrow between his brows deepened, and a frown curved his full lips. "You're not even going to look?"

"I may be a thief, but I don't deal with liars."

"What, exactly, do you think I'm lying about?"

"I didn't say you were lying. I said you're a liar." She blew on a spoonful of soup to cool it. "I see where the distinction might be confusing."

His jaw clenched. Frustration flared in his eyes as he stared down at her, chasing away the last of his feigned harmlessness. Of course, since nothing in her life could be easy, he was even hotter like this. A little angry. A little flustered.

Slow heat began to unfurl in her belly as she stared back—until the soft brush of boot soles on the loft landing broke the spell.

Nina spoke without looking up. "Who is he?"

"Captain Garrett Knox." Maya's voice was ice. "Leader of a special squad called the Silver Devils. Protectorate golden boy. The TechCorps' favorite bully. Can I stab him?"

"You're too far away." Dani stepped out of the shadows of the back hallway, a pistol in her hands. "Besides, Captain Knox is leaving now."

The man stiffened, pivoting to put his back to the wall. His gaze jumped from Nina to Maya to Dani, lingering on the pistol. Then he slowly raised his hands in a placating gesture of surrender. "Your intel is out of date. I may lead the Silver Devils, but we left the Protectorate."

The throb behind Nina's eyes was either irrepressible curiosity or the beginnings of a headache. "Entire squads don't leave the Protectorate, Captain."

"Trust me, they're not happy about it." He turned his head and lifted the hair at the back of his neck, where an angry red scar cut a path across his tanned skin. Med-gel had done its healing work, but the original incision must have been deep. "We cut out our trackers four days ago. Before that, my hacker used his intranet access to download this data." He smoothed his hair back into place and gestured to the tablet. "Our retirement plan."

Ignoring Dani's pointed look, Nina activated the screen. The top half displayed a map, while the bottom was covered with a vault schematic. "What am I looking at, and why should it excite me?"

He took a single step closer. "Have you ever heard of the RLOC?"

The skin on her arms prickled as she rose. "Of course—the Rogue Library of Congress. When the U.S. government was faltering toward the end of the Energy Wars, they cut the Library of Congress loose as dead weight. So a handful of federal employees banded together with a group of hackers to make their own digital backups. At least, that's the story."

"It's more than a story." Now that he wasn't choosing his words so carefully, his voice flowed like smooth whiskey. "Supposedly, there are seven bunkers in cities around the country, each one containing the entire digitized contents of the Library of Congress on multiple servers. Most of the bunkers have never been confirmed. But my man found a paper trail on one in Chattanooga."

"It's bullshit," she shot back. "Every treasure hunter and his grandma has been looking for those RLOC bunkers since the Flares. It's a folktale. They don't exist."

"Just *look* at the files." Though his tone stayed even, stress carved lines around his eyes, and his muscles were so tight her own body ached in sympathy.

He was desperate, all right, but *why*? More out of pity than anything else, she skimmed the documents. The intel looked good, almost good enough to make her believe in the fairy tale.

Almost—but not quite.

So why wasn't she showing him the door yet?

She deactivated the tablet and pressed it into his hands. His fingers trembled, a fine tremor that vibrated up her arm and made her skin tingle again. "Why is this so important? You could head south to Florida, run security ops for one of the shipping cartels. There's plenty of work down there for a man with your training and skills."

"He can't." The grudging admission came from Maya as she descended the stairs, her gaze never leaving Knox. The chill hadn't left her dark brown eyes, but there was something else there, too—a hint of empathy. "Protectorate soldiers get their abilities from implants that adjust their biochemistry, and the implants are programmed to degrade without periodic maintenance. It's a dead man's switch. Keeps their weapons in line."

"I have a lead on someone who can help us," Knox said quietly. "But it doesn't come cheap. I have a team depending on me, and this job is our best chance."

He definitely wasn't lying now. "You should have led with that," Nina told him, her resolve weakening. "Why us? You're the Silver Devils. Just go get it yourselves."

"We're a mercenary squad. We fight people." He flashed the schematics at her again. "This? It's beyond my pay grade. I don't have a safe cracker, and none of us have experience with old file formats. Even if we manage to access the servers, I don't know what data will sell or who might buy it. We'll clear twice as much, easy, by partnering with an experienced broker. Even after we split the take."

"Okay. Then why do *we* need *you*?"

"Because I didn't put all the details on here. I'm not stupid." He tucked the tablet back into his pocket and crossed his arms over his chest. "It's a week's drive, at least, straight through outlaw territory. Maybe you do okay in the city, but the wilds are a whole different game. You need security."

Oh, the *ego*. "I can handle myself."

"Yeah, I noticed that last night." His lips quirked in a smile, one imbued with enough heat to draw her closer against her will. "You didn't catch me following you, though."

There it was. Nina waved away Maya's protest and Dani's outraged growl, torn between being impressed and being pissed off. She went with both. "Not many people could follow me halfway across the city without getting made. You have my congratulations."

He inclined his head, graciously accepting the praise. "You're good, I'm not denying that. But outlaws attack in force. You need real protection. You need me and my team."

"We'll see." She brushed past him, careful not to touch him again, and crossed the living room—though she couldn't resist a tiny smile as she pulled open the door. "Bring your crew to Clementine's in two hours, Captain. Let's see how well the kids play together before we decide to get hitched."

"Fine." He stepped over the threshold and turned back. "But if you're on board, I want to leave tomorrow. We don't have time to waste."

"I haven't agreed to anything. Yet." She leaned her cheek against the edge of the door. "Thanks for helping me out last night, by the way. Sure was nice, not having to fight all those bastards by myself."

"I was on my way," he retorted. Then, unexpectedly, he smiled at her, a real smile that lit up his blue eyes and made her knees wobble. "Next time, save me a few."

"Uh-huh. Bye, Knox." She closed the door in his face and turned around.

Dani was so far beyond disapproval that she'd wrapped around to amusement. Her eyes gleamed as she shook her head. "This? Is a terrible idea."

"Not denying it," Nina admitted. "Maya, what do you know?"

Maya slumped into a chair, her fingers tapping lightly on the table in the pattern she used when she was sifting through her memories for a specific conversation. The first three fingers, followed by two taps of her pinkie, a ritual that lasted only a few seconds before she straightened, her eyes unfocused.

When she spoke, her cadence had changed. Instead of her usual wry drawl or warm excitement, the words were clipped, cool, enunciated almost to the point of parody.

She sounded like Birgitte Skovgaard, the TechCorps vice president who had raised her.

"I received the final psychological profiles of the Silver Devils," she said, still staring at nothing. "Captain Garrett Knox troubles me. The way he executes his mission objectives shows . . . a certain kind of honor. Under normal circumstances, I'd suspect he might be sympathetic to our cause. But Protectorate Command trusts him, and there must be a reason for that. He may not show the same blatantly psychopathic tendencies as some of the other squad leaders, but that isn't exactly a glowing character reference.

"As for his squad . . . Conall is brilliant, but eager to please. He'll remain loyal to Knox as long as he receives positive reinforcement. The sniper, on the other hand, concerns me deeply. He's an effective killer, so the Protectorate higher-ups protect him despite his antisocial personality, but I suspect his obedience is conditional and unreliable. The final two—"

Maya's voice resumed its normal rhythm. "And then someone sneezed in the hallway, so Birgitte stopped. We didn't usually talk about seditious activities in her office, but it was late and she wanted me to memorize the details of the report before she destroyed the hard copy." The tapping resumed, and Maya's gaze lost focus again, as if she was fast-forwarding in her mind.

"We talked about her meetings the next day. And then—" She swallowed hard, and her eyes tightened. "Simon came in to see if we were going back to the penthouse soon. Then he guarded the door so she could finish."

Maya fell into Birgitte's cadence once again. "The final two have potential. If it weren't for their unfortunate association with Garrett Knox, I might have already approached one or both. Rafael Morales is charismatic and *very* popular, and not just with his peers. The staff and menial workers respect him and show signs of intense loyalty. In my experience, being beloved by the powerless can be an indication of strong moral fiber.

"James Mason, their medic, is the same—though there are fewer reports of him charming his way through the barracks. Rumor has it he uses his leisure time to assist at pop-up clinics in poor neighborhoods, directly contravening the Protectorate ban on moonlighting. He also gives free consultations to L-10 workers whose benefits packages don't include medical treatments for their families. He clearly recognizes the flaws and abuses in our current system.

"Final analysis—there's a strong case to be made for any man capable of winning over Morales and Mason. Garrett Knox could serve as a potential ally. It's worth continuing to watch him. But his file shows plenty of red flags, and he's been one of the sharpest weapons in the Protectorate's arsenal. The fact that he accomplishes their aims without overt cruelty may simply make him a more insidious danger than we presumed. For now, I'm not willing to trust him with our secrets. This is a delicate time for our movement. We have to proceed with caution."

Maya blinked and focused on Nina. "Then she burned the file, and we went home. I think she had watchers set on Knox, but if they discovered anything, they didn't get it to her before . . . Before."

Before Birgitte's quiet revolution had been uncovered.

Before Birgitte had been killed for it.

Nina cleared her throat. "So what do you think?"

"The Silver Devils are legendary killers. Going on a road trip with them is a fairly shitty idea." Maya shrugged. "But a wheelbarrow full of cash would solve a *lot* of our problems."

"Agreed. All in favor?" Nina raised her right hand.

Maya copied her without hesitation.

After a moment, Dani holstered her pistol and followed suit, her head hanging low. "It's a wild-goose chase," she proclaimed. "And that's the *best*-case scenario."

"No, the best-case scenario is it's real, and nobody in the neighborhood freezes to death this winter." Maya shrugged. "Worst case? The dumbasses try to murder us in our sleep and get a real big surprise when they find out you and Nina don't need any damn bodyguards."

"Then it's settled." Nina engaged the locks once again, just to be safe, and leaned against the door. "We'll get there early tonight, see if Clem's heard anything about them. Fair enough?"

"Fair enough." Dani shook her head. "It's still a bad idea."

Of course it was. That was the part that could make it so much fun.

TECHCORPS PROPRIETARY DATA, L2 SECURITY CLEARANCE

Recruit 66–615 continues to exceed expectations. If he out-performs the predicted benchmarks during his next evalua-tion, I recommend we waive the two-year oversight period and transfer him immediately to Protectorate training, prefer-ably on the officer track.

Recruit Analysis, August 2061

THREE

Clementine's was the kind of dive bar Knox had mostly seen in pre-Flare vids.

When their jobs required meetings of this sort, Knox usually sent Rafe. He slid into places like this like a knife into a perfectly oiled sheath, like he *belonged*. Knox, on the other hand, had never been able to look or act like anything but a soldier.

He still couldn't. The second they stepped across the threshold, gazes swung toward them. Knox slouched his shoulders and deepened his scowl, but it didn't help. Eyes began to narrow in suspicion as the chatter closest to the door halted.

Rafe swaggered into the sudden silence, slapped a crinkled handful of cash on the counter, and laid his most charming smile on the aging bartender. "Got anything that bites back there?"

Her weathered cheeks turned pink under her white-streaked ginger hair, but she frowned as she slammed a fresh glass down on the counter. "Just my shotgun."

"A girl after my own heart."

The bartender's frown wouldn't last long. They never did. Rafe had a knack for understanding what made people tick, a knack that had brought them to this dark, cramped little bar packed with obvious criminals.

He'd been the one to coach Knox on how to approach Nina. *No one in this business comes in on the level, so tell a little lie first. The one you want them to catch. Then, when they think they have you on the ropes, lie with the truth.*

Vaguely, through layers of ruthless pragmatism, Knox could remember disliking deception. When he'd been all shiny and new, fresh off the supersoldier assembly line and convinced you could fight evil with good.

Evil wasn't afraid of good. Because good people always expected evil to play by the rules, and by the time they realized the game had changed, evil had won.

Knox was only interested in one game now, and Conall's unusually subdued presence next to him was motivation enough. The muscle cramp that had seized their tech just before they left hadn't incapacitated him, but it was a useful reminder.

When the Protectorate had withheld treatment from Mace, the team's medic, to educate them on the importance of obedience, his downward spiral had started with muscle cramps, too.

Gray nudged Knox with his elbow. "Back left corner."

Knox turned his head and felt a kick to his gut.

Nina fit here. She reigned over her corner booth like a queen surveying her court, her big brown eyes missing nothing. He'd been close enough to her to know they were rimmed with gold, and that her hair smelled like fruit. Her thick eyelashes and full lips and sharp cheekbones couldn't be described by a word as prosaic as *beautiful*.

The physical impact of just *looking* at her was so sharp that Knox jerked away, as if he'd touched a hot stove. Out of sheer self-preservation, he shifted his gaze to her two companions.

Maya was short, compact and curvy, with warm brown skin and black hair that cascaded over her shoulders in a mass of sleek braids. Street gossip had given Knox her name, though he doubted it was her real one. Conall hadn't been able to find any trace of a Maya matching her description in any TechCorps system, but she'd spoken about his implants with the confidence of an insider. Maybe she was one of the rare genetic modification experiments to slip through their fingers.

That was the problem with creating people with superhuman abilities—they were *hard* to contain, which was why the TechCorps tended to build in contingency plans. Like the kill switch counting down to detonation in Knox's brain.

Dani was even more of an enigma. The pale blonde had an icy quality that made Gray seem downright cuddly, and something about the way she moved made Knox's instincts scream. She felt like a snake coiled to strike, and somehow he knew he wouldn't be fast enough to get out of the way if she did.

Even if Maya hadn't been modified, this one *definitely* was.

Reluctantly, he returned his attention to Nina. She was staring at him now, her eyes sparking with challenge from all the way across the bar. She was dressed simply, in utilitarian cargo pants and a black T-shirt not so different from his own. The rich color of her leather jacket complemented her golden skin, dark hair, and warm brown eyes.

She was hot. Hell, they were *all* hot.

And dangerous. They had to be, because in a bar full of drunk thieves, con artists, and thugs for hire, no one was giving them shit or trying to hit on them.

Nina waved them over with a nearly full bottle of whiskey. "They're with us, Clem."

The bartender snorted and shoved a few more empty glasses at them before pinning Rafe with a look. "Guess our love just wasn't meant to be."

"Don't give up on me yet." He used one giant hand to sweep up all four shot glasses. "I'll be back for a bottle to go. Pick me out something real good, eh?"

Knox shot him a quelling look before threading his way through the jumble of tables. He felt the eyes on him as he passed rough men and women decked out in leather and chains, their weapons on prominent display, but Nina's loud claim had dispersed the worst of the tension.

Whatever she was, they trusted her in this neighborhood.

He stopped a few steps short of her table. "Nina."

"Knox." She lifted her glass in salute. "Any trouble finding the place?"

"Nope." He inclined his head. "Maybe we should do official introductions this time."

"By all means." She pointed carelessly. "This is Maya, and that's Dani."

He gestured to his men. "Rafe, Conall, and Gray."

Dani flipped a knife from one hand to the other, then pointed the tip of the blade at each of them in turn. "Let me guess—muscle, tech, and bullets."

Rafe quirked an eyebrow at her. "Charm, brains, and taciturn silences. But you were close."

"Hmph. I think I was right." She stabbed the tip of the knife into the table. "And save the flirtation for Clementine, would you? No one here is interested."

Knox fought a smile at the affronted expression on Rafe's face. But the brawler shook it off and set the glasses on the table. "Have a drink. Maybe I'll get prettier."

"Pretty isn't your problem," Maya grumbled. "You're *too* pretty. No one around here trusts too pretty."

"Or too quiet, or too fidgety," Dani added with pointed looks at Gray and Conall.

Gray broke his silence with a low chuckle. "So what *do* people around here trust?"

"For starters?" Dani flipped the cap off the bottle and started filling their glasses. "A voice like that."

Nina rolled her eyes and jerked her head toward the other side of the bar—and an empty pool table. "Do you play, Captain?"

Their old barracks had a pool table. Knox had spent hours running the table, as the clack of the balls served as his own brand of meditation, a way to sort through possibilities and outcomes and nail down his backup plans. "I dabble."

"Sounds like a yes." She slid off the cracked vinyl seat, grabbed her drink, and murmured, "Mind your manners while I'm gone."

Knox wasn't sure if she was talking to her people or his—and it didn't matter. He gave Gray a significant look that was their long-standing code for *keep those two under control*. Gray nodded once, and Knox followed Nina back through the maze of tables to where the pool table stood with its chipped balls and scratched felt.

"So." She lifted the cue ball and tossed it in the air a few times. "We checked out your story."

A tiny chill crawled up his spine. If they'd poked around in the wrong places and tipped someone off . . . "Which part of it?"

"The part where you told the Protectorate to fuck off and die."

"Subtly, I hope." He found the battered rack and dropped it on the felt. "No one's going to have a good night if the Protectorate busts up in here to execute us for desertion."

"Relax, no one's getting shot tonight." She tossed the ball on the table and peeled off her jacket. Instead of the T-shirt he'd expected, she was wearing a tank top with tiny straps that bared smooth shoulders, well-muscled arms, the upper curves of her breasts—and way too much sun-kissed skin.

Lock it down.

He'd watched Rafe play this game enough times to recognize when someone was trying to steer him around by the dick. The mischief in her eyes as she bent over to retrieve the rest of the balls—and gave him an excellent view of her pants hugging her perfect ass—drove the message home.

Nina was a dangerous woman.

That made him feel a little better about playing her.

"So what's the plan, Captain?"

Ah, yes. The plan. "We have two retrofitted military trucks stashed just outside the city. The old interstates are mostly shit, but there are some navigable stretches left. Can any of you drive?"

She arranged the pool balls in the rack with quick, efficient movements. "Mm-hmm."

"Then we go north. Conall has GPS coordinates. When we get there, we dig. Then you crack the vault."

Nina made a soft noise and leaned her hip against the table. "Won't it be kind of hard to use satellite navigation without satellites?"

So she didn't know *everything.* Knox swept up the cue ball and rounded the table. "Most government satellites were destroyed by the Flares," he agreed, setting the ball carefully in place. "The feds always were shit at keeping up with technical innovations like enhanced solar shielding. You know who wasn't?"

"The Russians?"

He doubted anyone else in this bar under the age of sixty even knew what Russia was. Another piece to add to the mental puzzle of Nina. When the networks had gone down and the lights went out, most people's worlds had shrunk to a few miles in any given direction. Unless you were rich, lack of access placed education firmly out of reach. Your only chance was to ace a TechCorps aptitude screening and get funneled into one of their specialized study tracks. Even Knox's knowledge of pre-Flare countries was mostly limited to a brutally intense crash course on military history.

Nina had clearly received a more comprehensive education.

He lined up a shot and snapped his arm forward, sending the cue ball zipping across the felt. It clacked loudly against the balls, scattering them and sinking two. "Thirty-seven," he told her, moving around the table to line up his next shot. "That's how many private-sector TechCorps satellites survived the solar storms. Thanks to Conall, we still have access to them."

"Sneaky," she said approvingly.

"GPS is easy. We can even use them for some limited communication." He tilted his head back toward the booth, where Conall was gesturing to Maya's wrist. After a wary moment, she unbuckled her watch and held it out. "Conall's the best," he said, not bothering to keep the pride from his voice.

"I'm sure he is." Nina squinted at him, curiosity radiating off her. "What about you? What's your story?"

Lie with the truth. He bent over the table again, but she was so close he could feel her along his skin. He hit the cue ball a little off-center and sent it careening straight into the back corner pocket. "Not much to it. I joined the Protectorate to help people. Ended up hurting them. Got out."

She retrieved the cue ball and placed it on the felt once again. "How long were you in?"

Forever.

Knox didn't want to do the math, even in the safety and solitude of his own mind, but he couldn't help it. The number came to him immediately, and with damning clarity.

Nine thousand, five hundred, and fifty-one days. It had been more than twenty years since he'd marched up to a Protectorate recruiting station, still burning with the kind of anger only grief could sustain, and he'd spent every day since being broken down into smaller and smaller pieces.

How long had it taken him to realize that the Protectorate wasn't made up of the shining heroes from glossy vids and propaganda bulletins? How many days before he'd understood that the Protectorate was just another efficient subsidiary of the TechCorps, the perfect combination of obedient test subjects and private army?

"Too long," he grated out. When she slanted a look at him, he struggled for a casual tone. "I thought if I climbed high enough in the ranks, I'd be able to make a difference. For a while, it seemed like I was."

"That's not how the Protectorate operates." She leaned down, stretching out over the felt to study the angles. "Maybe that's easier to see from the outside."

"Maybe." Her tank top slipped up, revealing a narrow strip of skin on her lower back. You'd have to be three days dead not to imagine gripping those lush hips and dragging her back—

Fuck. A clock ticking down to his inevitable death was apparently hell on his self-control. It had been so long since he'd actually feared death, he'd forgotten what that fear could do to his body. More specifically, what it could do to his dick.

His dick wasn't interested in the mission. It was interested in immediate, enthusiastic gratification.

He dragged his gaze from her ass. "Do you want to look at the vault schematics again? See if you need any special equipment?"

"Hydeker Millennial, 700 Series, with a modified hermetic seal." She took her shot, her cue gliding easily over the worn felt. "Not much to it, really."

She'd barely glanced at the files earlier, but apparently she'd retained plenty. He ignored the clatter of the pool balls and slotted that into his sparse mental profile. Enhanced reflexes, superior strength, and impressive recall, but none of the obvious side effects that went hand in hand with most of the TechCorps' experiments.

What the hell *was* she?

She straightened slowly, flashing him an eyeful of cleavage, and he cleared his throat. "Does that mean you're signing on?"

Instead of answering, she turned her attention back to the corner booth, where Rafe sat, unflinching, his fingers spread wide on the table, while Dani stabbed her knife between each one in turn. She picked up speed, moving faster and faster until even Rafe's easy smile grew strained.

Nina chuckled. "They seem to be getting along fine. You know what? I think we can—"

Only a few feet away, an obvious disagreement exploded into violence. The clatter of wood on wood burst through the smoky air as a chair hit the floor, its recent occupant on his feet and seething. He held a knife to his companion's throat, the wicked tip already piercing skin to draw blood.

Knox's instincts took over.

He planted one hand on the edge of the pool table and vaulted it. Nina was still turning toward the source of the commotion when his boots hit the grimy floor. He put his body between her and the scuffle, his pistol out and ready, his entire being fixated on one truth.

Without Nina, every man on his team was going to die.

A blast shook the room. The armed man went down, gasping for breath and clutching his chest, while Clementine stood behind the bar and calmly began reloading her shotgun.

"That was your warning." Her gnarled hands were steady about her task. "Next round won't be rubber, so you'd better *move your fucking ass.*"

The man half scrambled, half crawled to the door, where he disappeared into the night.

All around the bar, people shrugged and went back to their conversations. It took Knox a second longer to choke back his chemically augmented adrenaline high. He holstered his gun and checked on his men—Gray was as inscrutable as ever, Conall looked shocked, and Rafe was still ready to upend the table and dive to Knox's defense.

He urged the man to stand down with a tiny shake of his head.

Nina didn't look tense or worried. If anything, she looked *amused* as she tossed back the last of her drink and studied him. "Are you going to be this jumpy on the road, Captain?"

His title rolled off her tongue like she'd been taking lessons from Rafe on how to make innocent words sound as filthy as possible. All the adrenaline raging through him without an outlet simmered beneath his skin like unquenchable fire.

"Yeah, *sweetheart,*" he rumbled, packing every bit of that heat into the endearment. He couldn't tell if it sounded like a curse or a threat or a prayer. "I'm gonna be this jumpy."

A slow smile curved her lips, and she pressed her empty glass into his hands. "You provide transpo, supplies, and watch our backs. We'll take care of everything else. For that, it's a sixty/forty split—and I'm being generous, so don't try to negotiate with me. Sound good?"

Rafe would have haggled. He would have sold the con by working Nina around to a fifty/fifty profit share. But Knox had lied with the truth a little *too* well. He was desperate, and Nina knew it. She could smell it on him.

As long as she didn't figure out why, this would work out just fine.

Silently, he held out his hand.

"You'll have to take my word to seal the deal. I'm not real big on touching strangers." Still smiling, she leaned past him and retrieved her jacket. "And Captain? If your plan is to burn me, don't. My team and I can make you wish you had just let the Protectorate execute you when you had the chance."

With that, she left him standing there, his hand dangling in the air, his body a riot of thwarted violence and simmering need—and a thrilling edge of fear.

It had been a long time since he'd faced someone he wasn't sure he could defeat in single combat. He'd forgotten what *that* did to his body, too.

So it was probably for the best she hadn't touched him. He'd gone down some dark roads since the Protectorate had ground the hope out of him, but he wanted to believe he wasn't the kind of asshole who'd fuck a woman he was about to betray. But maybe they'd beaten that last scrap of goodness out of him, too. Maybe there wasn't anything left in him worth saving.

He sought out Gray's somber face in the crowd. Rafe's easy smile. Conall's jittery intensity.

Knox was doing this for them. And for Luna, who'd been snatched out of her apartment because of her connection to them. Four reasons to do the job, no matter how much of his soul it consumed. If he could buy them all a second chance at life, Knox would follow the devil himself straight down into hell.

He was already headed there, anyway.

RAFE

Rafe had always liked people.

It was an admittedly weird trait in someone who'd met as many ass-holes as he had. Even weirder for a Protectorate soldier. Most folks who joined the Protectorate were either damaged or desperate, and that was *before* the TechCorps started playing with their biochemistry and cultivating their most violent instincts. A decade-plus of living with that violence had honed some of Rafe's edges, but it hadn't sliced out that fundamental aspect of his character.

Rafe liked people. And people liked Rafe.

He hoisted the case of nutritional supplements up into the truck and did a final count of the neatly wrapped bars. He'd had to be careful gathering supplies this time. At least a third of his contact network could probably be persuaded to sell him out to the Protectorate. Another third wouldn't do it for money, but they had family that could be leveraged.

The only ones Rafe could really trust were the folks with bigger bounties on their heads than his. Luckily, he'd spent the last decade pointedly not turning any of them in, so they all owed him favors. A *lot* of favors.

He'd spent the last week cashing in.

Now the trucks were stocked for a long trip, and Rafe had found everything he wanted except for the shelters. The tents waiting to be packed away were sufficient for good weather—barely—but they wouldn't hold up to a real storm, and they offered no other protection. When the Devils had deployed on missions for the TechCorps, they'd requisitioned lightweight antiballistic carbon-fiber composite shelters that expanded into structures sturdy enough to keep out both the elements and feral animals.

He'd tried to get his hands on a few, but the technology was proprietary. And the quartermaster was probably the only Protectorate officer who couldn't be bribed. After all, the TechCorps kept their equipment on tighter lockdown than its personnel.

They'd always considered people easier to replace.

"Anything left for me to do?"

Rafe turned to find Gray leaning against the side of the truck. He was as tall as Rafe and almost as built, but the bastard moved like a wraith. "You got their supplies packed in?"

"I did." But he shook his head. "I told Knox it was a waste of time. They're going to show up kitted out with all their own shit, you know they are."

Yes, Nina was that type. Meticulous, prepared, competent. But Rafe hadn't bothered to argue with Knox. The more events slid out of their captain's control, the more ruthlessly he would tighten his fist around the details still within his power. Knox planned for contingencies the rest of them had never considered and could barely imagine.

"So we'll have extra supplies." Rafe tucked the last of their hunting gear into the back of the truck and slammed the door shut. "What do you make of them?"

"Does it matter? They're collateral damage." Gray pinned him with a knowing look. "Don't forget that part, Rafe. I mean it."

"Hey, Luna's *my* contact. I'll do whatever it takes to get her back." Especially when guilt over her capture was a knife lodged between his ribs.

Rafe must have led the kidnapper to her. He'd been so careful but, somewhere along the line, his security precautions had failed. Someone had connected Luna to the Devils. Someone who wasn't interested in turning in rogue soldiers for bounties, or in the sizable finders' fees the TechCorps handed out for "discovering" new talent.

Whoever was after Nina had to be one scary fucker.

Gray just snorted. "How's the hand?"

Rafe glanced down. Med-gel worked fast. The tiny scar just above the knuckle of his middle finger had almost healed. But he was convinced that Dani's slip of the hand had been very deliberate. She'd stabbed that knife between his fingers with such pinpoint precision that she'd left four perfect divots in the table where she'd hit the same spot over and over.

Except for the one time she'd stabbed *him*. "I'll live."

"No shit. But are you going to get distracted?"

"Because she stabbed me?" Rafe snorted and hefted his bag over his shoulder. "Unlike the rest of you sad-ass hermits, I'm not hard up for com-pany."

"Hey, those ladies might be a little rough on other parts of you, but not a damn one of them is hard on the eyes."

They weren't, for sure, but Gray was the last one Rafe had expected to hear comment on it. Conall appreciated pretty girls, even though he tended to lose his good sense over surly boys. And Knox might be the next thing to a monk, but physical allure was a tactical consideration he would never ignore. Gray, on the other hand, liked his privacy. And when they were in the field, he kept his mind on business.

Maybe he was thinking about the tactical considerations, too. "Is this still about me? Or are you worried we're all going to get stupid?"

"Look—" Gray reached for the pocket where he used to keep his cig-arettes. He'd quit, but he still reached for the nonexistent pack a dozen times a day. Sighing, he ran his hand through his hair instead. "The mis-sion's solid, and we have the upper hand. For now. The best way to lose it is for us to grow consciences. Or, yeah, start thinking with our dicks."

"How kinky do you think I am? The woman *stabbed* me."

Gray arched one eyebrow.

"Okay, but she did it without asking permission first." Still, he had to admit it was a *little* hot. Not the nonconsensual aspect, of course—Rafe had some *very* strict personal rules about keeping everything cheerfully consensual—but the degree of control she had displayed. That blade had been driving toward his hand hard enough to plunge straight through it and into the battered wood below, and Dani had somehow pulled its downward momentum precisely enough for the tip to barely pierce his skin.

Rafe could lift a car. He could probably throw one, too, if he was really desperate. But his raw strength felt clumsy compared to that woman's sur-gically exact reflexes.

"Just watch yourself." Gray's normally serious expression had pulled into an even more severe frown. "This is going to be a tricky job."

"You mean it's going to be shitty." Rafe kicked at a crumbling piece of concrete. "I don't particularly want to get cozy with these chicks and then have to stab them in the back. But I said all I have to say already. It's Luna. To keep her safe, I might stab *you* in the back."

"That's different. I'd let you."

Rafe huffed out a laugh, but he couldn't give it much real humor. Rafe could deflect all he wanted, but Gray's point would still be there, its jagged edges digging in.

Rafe liked people. And he had a sinking feeling that mysterious Nina and scowling little Maya and even the homicidally inclined Dani were something far worse than attractive. There was every chance they were also highly likable. Gray could talk all day about not growing a conscience, but the truth was that Rafe didn't *need* to grow one. It was already there, writhing beneath the pragmatism he wore like armor.

He made hard choices to protect his people. His family, hidden away where the TechCorps could never find them. His squad, who had become his brothers.

And Luna. Wary, brilliant Luna. A childhood that could inspire nightmares had left her with scars that went deep. It had taken him years to earn her trust. At some point, she'd become a stand-in for the sister he rarely got to see. Or maybe a reminder of the pained shadow his sister might have become if Rafe hadn't made so many hard choices.

Luna had rebuilt her life, brick by brick. Sometimes Rafe had even been around to help. And all that work would be for nothing if he didn't deliver Nina into the hands of whatever evil-fucking-genius person had drawn the connection between them.

Rafe liked people. Now, for the first time, he almost wished the Protectorate had managed to beat that out of him.

CLASSIFIED BEHAVIOR EVALUATION

Franklin Center for Genetic Research

Subject HS-Gen16-C has been showing signs of emotional distress since clusters KJ-Gen2 and LN-Gen3 were decommissioned. Her strong attachment to the flawed C-designations in both clusters shows a predilection toward being protective of the weak. Recommend psychological intervention and behavioral reconditioning.

Dr. Zima, July 2062

FOUR

Nina was accustomed to packing light and moving fast. At one point, she'd traveled with everything she owned tucked carefully into a single pack. Now, planning to leave her home base for two solid weeks, she realized just how far she'd come from those solitary days.

And it wasn't just that she had so much *stuff* now. She had responsibilities that were harder to leave. She glanced over at the corner, where Maya was showing one of the building's tenants how to operate the book printer.

"You load the paper here." Maya hauled open the printer drawer, which was stacked with crisp pages tinged gray from the recycling process. "Wait until they've paid you, though. Most people are on the level, but some assholes figure once you print up some random book, you're stuck with it, and they can haggle you down. Paper's too pricey to fuck around with."

"Payment first," Tai echoed obediently, and Nina had no doubt that the woman would remember. She was a scavenger by trade, perfectly well aware of how precious raw materials could be.

Paper was the biggest expense associated with operating the printing machine. There was also a roll of thin cardboard inside that the machine would cut to size to form the covers and spine, but that lasted a long time, as did the glue that bound the pages. The paper went *fast*.

Tai pushed her heavy-rimmed glasses up her nose and scribbled in her little notebook. "What if I run out?"

"You shouldn't. We have about a month's supply out in the warehouse." Maya bumped the drawer shut with her hip and picked up a tablet. "This is the list of printable books . . ."

In a perfect world, they could print all their books and lend them out, just like a real library. They had the space to store the volumes, but they couldn't afford to do the printing. Especially since Maya wasn't wrong—

some people were assholes. They'd tried lending out some of the physical books Nina had recovered, but half of them had never been returned.

At least they'd had the presence of mind to digitize those volumes before they vanished. They could replace them—if they had the money to do it. Maybe, if they managed to pull off this job, they would. They could even buy more items to lend out, like heavy equipment and tools necessary for proper do-it-yourself repairs to shelters, appliances, and vehicles.

But that was one giant fucking *if*.

Nina checked her drill bits, then tucked her last borescope into its slim case and joined Dani at the kitchen table. Her friend's main pack was zipped and ready, propped against one table leg, but the duffel she used to carry her weapons was still open on the table, surrounded by a mountain of firepower.

Dani looked up, a frown of consternation creasing her brow. "I can't decide which pistols to take."

"Which ones do you want to take?"

"Honestly? All of them."

Of course. "You know, the Devils are supposed to be handling security."

Dani barked out a laugh, shook her head, and added four more handguns to her duffel.

Maya came over and dropped her hiking pack on the table. "Tai went to check out the projector. The neighborhood kids will have their nightly movies while we're gone."

"Good." Nina nodded to her pack. "You have everything you need?"

"I think so. I wouldn't mind bringing some extra lotion. You know, if Dani has any room between her rocket launcher and her armored tank."

"Got plenty of room for you right here." Dani raised her middle finger.

At Maya's laugh, Nina pushed Dani's hand away. "Just remember that we have to haul this shit to the rendezvous point. And we might end up carrying it on the road if things go sideways."

Dani zipped her duffel bag with a flourish. "If this job goes that wrong, we're ditching the soldiers of fortune. They'll manage without us."

Maya headed for the cabinet where they stored their freeze-dried food. "Rafe will be heartbroken that you don't care."

Dani scoffed. "First-name basis already? Don't tell me you fell for his Romeo act."

"Better him than the other one." Maya shuddered as she sorted through the shiny silver packets of food. "The techie's not so bad, but that sniper . . . There's something *dark* in his eyes."

Dani flashed Nina an *are you hearing this shit?* look and hefted her pack. "That's it, Maya. I'm confiscating your tablets. You read too many Gothic novels."

"Fair point," Nina allowed. Then again, so was Maya's. There *was* a darkness in Knox's men—and in Knox.

Oh, he'd tried to hide it. Maybe he thought he had to now that he was outside the Protectorate, where they probably ate darkness for breakfast. But if he thought the people who lived in the TechCorps' shadow would be all sweetness and light, he'd be sorely disappointed.

Maya returned with their rations, only to dump the whole armful on the table with a curse before reaching for Dani's arm. "Shit, you're bleeding."

Dani glanced down at the blood welling from a ragged but shallow gash across the back of her forearm, then shrugged. "It's nothing. Just a scratch."

The sight turned Nina's stomach. She could deal with bloody injuries, but this was different. Dani's failure to notice the wound had nothing to do with its superficial nature. The experimental procedure that had altered her nervous system had left her with a single, potentially deadly side effect—an inability to feel pain.

Nina swallowed her tension. "We need to dress it."

"I already packed the medical supplies," Dani protested.

"There's an extra tube of med-gel in the basket on top of the fridge." When Maya turned to retrieve it, Nina met Dani's eyes and lowered her voice. "You have to be more careful. You *know* that."

Dani smiled. "Don't worry about me, Nina. Worry about your captain and his pretty eyes."

Nina looked away.

"He's up to something," Dani persisted.

"I'm aware." She just hadn't figured out his game yet. "He's no Protectorate double agent. If he was, we'd be in custody already."

"Agreed. So what *does* he want?"

If they were lucky, to get his hands on 40 percent of the haul from a fabled RLOC server. If they were slightly less lucky, to double-cross Nina and get his hands on all of it, leaving her team lying in a ditch somewhere.

"Nothing we can't handle" was all she said.

Dani squared her shoulders, visibly gearing up to press the issue, but Maya came back with the medical supplies. She groused at Dani as she laid out the med-gel and a sterile dressing, and soon they were bickering like—

Sisters.

Automatically, Nina's hand flew to her throat, but encountered only bare skin. "I left something upstairs," she muttered. "I'll be right back."

After taking the stairs two at a time, Nina held her breath as she scanned her surroundings for the glint of silver. The floor was clear, as were her small wooden dresser, her bedside table, and her small jewelry box.

She found the necklace in the bathroom, dangling from the hook she'd screwed into the brick wall next to the sink. She snatched it up and put it on, finally exhaling as its familiar, comforting weight settled around her neck.

Nina didn't have much left to remember her sisters by. Even some of her most vivid memories were beginning to fade, worn thin by the passage of time. But this pendant—three interlocking rings on a simple chain, identical to the ones her sisters had worn—was concrete. As long as she had it, she would always have a piece of Ava and Zoey.

She turned to leave the bathroom, and her breath nearly left her again as she caught a glimpse of herself in the mirror above the sink. No, the necklace wasn't the only reminder of her sisters. It couldn't be, not when their faces stared back at her from every reflective surface.

But sometimes the pendant was the only reminder she could bear to look at.

Dani bellowed Nina's name, snapping her out of the past. "I'm coming!" she called back, then braced her hands on the sink and took another, harder look in the mirror.

It didn't matter what Garrett Knox wanted, whether he was telling the truth or not. Nina had to be prepared for the worst. If she let him catch her off guard, Dani and Maya would be the ones paying the price.

And then Nina's sisters wouldn't be the only people she'd gotten killed with her carelessness.

———

Nina was late.

Knox locked down his nervousness and distracted himself by recheck-ing the supplies packed into the truck's secure storage area. His team gave him shit about his exhaustive lists and endless contingency plans, but Knox couldn't count the number of times they'd come home intact because he'd been prepared for something no one could have seen coming.

Weapons. Med-kits. Hunting gear. Emergency rations. Survival sup-plies. He flipped open a box of tasteless, nutrient-dense meal bars. Game was plentiful where they were going, but he still counted the rations, enough for five men to survive two weeks—

His fist clenched, crushing the cardboard box top.

There were only four of them now.

"Hey, Cap."

Knox forced himself to release the box and turned to block Conall's view of it. "What've you got?"

"Not what I wanted." Oblivious to Knox's mood, Conall leaned against the truck's bumper and opened his tablet. "I got clear pictures of all their faces at the bar, but facial recognition isn't bringing up much in the Tech-Corps database."

Conall was usually more precise in his phrasing. "Much?"

"Nothing on Nina or the blonde. They might as well be ghosts." He skated his finger over the screen and pulled up a file. "Pretty sure this is Maya, though."

The screen displayed a TechCorps employee profile for a Marjorie Chevalier. The black band across the top denoted executive-level access. The red band indicated something far worse.

She'd gone AWOL.

He studied the picture. The girl featured was so young that her cheeks still curved with childlike fullness. Her black hair had been shorn close to her head, and her face was devoid of the heavy makeup Maya had worn to the bar, but the brown skin, tilted nose, and dark, wary eyes were all the same.

"Why are you only pretty sure?" Knox asked as he skimmed the sparse status details. Most employee files were written in obscure, coded lan-guage. *Special Executive Assistant* meant someone who'd been altered to serve a specific purpose, that was simple enough. But the two words on the next line chilled Knox's blood.

Data Courier.

Knox skimmed back up to the red bar and tapped it. Text filled the space, bright white and stark. *CONFIRMED DEAD. 2,000,000-credit reward unclaimed.*

The familiar rhythm of Conall's voice had faded to a distant hum, but one word caught Knox's attention. "Wait, what did you say?"

Conall heaved an aggrieved sigh. "I *said* that coders back at the dawn of the twenty-first century were lazy. And racist. And cheap. Facial recognition was designed by white people who tested it on other white people, and even after everyone knew it was all kinds of fucked up, most of the private sector had been building on those flawed algorithms for so long they didn't want to go back and start from scratch. Too expensive."

"But you found her."

"Not with their system. But the employee database is mirrored on the GhostNet. I used a better algorithm to start my search, then crossreferenced with presumed age and—"

If Conall got going, Knox would be on the receiving end of a tenminute monologue on data filtering. "Good work." He waved the tablet. "Can I keep this?"

"Sure." Conall pushed off the vehicle. "I'm going to go make sure everything's ready in their truck."

When he was gone, Knox went back to Maya's profile. Dragging the red bar down expanded the specifics of her supposed death. A Protectorate squad leader's brief report detailed his team's discovery of skeletonized remains while out on an unrelated mission. They'd followed protocol, collecting DNA and scans of the teeth before continuing to their objective.

Knox knew what was coming without having to scroll down. But he did it anyway, with a sick twist of recognition. As soon as the lab had processed the results and matched them to Marjorie Chevalier, the squad leader had been hauled before his superiors and ordered back to retrieve the body.

By that point, scavengers had done their work. There was nothing left to further confirm identity or cause of death. The squad leader had been severely reprimanded, and his team punished, even though they'd followed regulations and their orders to the letter.

The Protectorate had a way of only caring about the rules and regulations that suited them in the moment.

His gaze snagged on Maya's designation again. *Data Courier.*

No wonder she'd known who he was. She'd rattled off his name and rank with the confidence of someone reading *his* profile—which she probably had been, in her own way. Data couriers were chosen and modified as children, then trained to be the ideal receptacles of important data. Perfect auditory recall.

And perfect loyalty. The TechCorps didn't treat their data couriers the way they treated grunt soldiers. Brainwashed from childhood, couriers lived in luxury, every desire and whim indulged . . . until the stress of perfect recall began to unravel their minds. Then it was the Gold Star retirement package—a quick bullet in the back of the head and a trip to the incinerator.

Maya had clearly gotten out before that. And Knox would bet every last credit of that unclaimed reward that Nina had been somehow responsible for faking the girl's death.

He shouldn't find that level of ingenuity attractive.

He shouldn't find that level of stupidity *honorable.*

Two million was a lot. It was live-soft-up-on-the-Hill money. Never-worry-about-food-or-shelter-again money. Knox couldn't think of many information brokers or treasure seekers who would have passed up that opportunity to cash in.

Unless they had just as much reason to avoid the TechCorps as Maya did.

Gray's sharp whistle alerted him, and he turned to see Nina and her people clearing the barricade at the end of the access road. All three were weighted down with packs, and Nina's alone looked bulky enough to contain two weeks' worth of supplies for all of them. She moved effortlessly with it, though, confirming his suspicions that speed and brains weren't her only enhancements.

And that she still didn't trust him or his promise to provide supplies. He couldn't blame her. He wouldn't have trusted his men's safety to someone else's planning, either.

"Captain." She smiled as she shrugged out of her pack. "Beautiful day, isn't it?"

It was hot and sunny, two states he'd noticed because the heat increased the need to stay properly hydrated, and the sun would allow them to rely on solar power for the trucks and reserve their biofuel. The weather was an important variable in his plans, but he rarely ascribed subjective value to it. "It's fine."

"Mmm." She eyed him expectantly, then nudged her pack with her boot. "Where should I put this?"

He nodded to the second truck, where Conall was making one last check of its solar panels. "We already loaded food and survival supplies for you, but there should be room for your gear. Which of you is driving?"

Nina arched an eyebrow and turned to Dani and Maya. Silently, they lifted their left hands flat, palms up, and smacked their fists against them. On the third count, Nina and Maya each splayed two fingers out, while Dani kept her fist closed.

Dani did a little victory dance, then shoved past Knox and slung her duffel and her pack into the second truck.

Nina sighed. "I don't know why we bother."

"She always wins," Maya grumbled in agreement as she unstrapped her heavy backpack. She dragged it away, leaving Knox and Nina alone.

He was painfully aware of the life story still displayed on the folded tablet in his hand. The easy democratic ritual and cheerful rivalry between the women didn't match the dark violence and ruthless efficiency laid out in Maya's troubled life and manufactured death.

None of them were what they seemed. He had to remember that.

He tucked the tablet into his back pocket and nodded toward the truck. "We'll be good on power as long as this weather holds. Just follow close behind us. There are short-range radios in the trucks if you see anything. We should be clear of raiders for at least a day, but it's still smart to keep an eye out."

"It's your show," Nina said amiably. "I'm just along for the ride."

"Then let's get moving. We have a long way to go before dark."

She stopped just short of rolling her eyes and tossed him a wave as she headed for the truck. While her crew settled into the vehicle, Gray stepped up beside Knox. "I don't like it."

"Which part?"

"Her." Gray's frown turned into a scowl. "I can't tell if she's clueless, or if she fully expects you to try and murder her in her sleep."

She definitely wasn't clueless. Nina moved through the world with a lazy confidence Knox recognized on a gut level—the confidence of someone who knew she could handle whatever trouble came her way. "I'm guessing it's option B."

"Then she'll want to strike first." Gray hesitated. "Watch yourself, okay?"

"Watching my back is your job."

"Sure, but it won't do much good if she's attached to your front."

Knox refused to let the words conjure any naked mental images. Lust could be compartmentalized just like any other unnecessary emotion. He'd already packed it away, along with hope and guilt and honor and everything else he couldn't afford to indulge if he wanted to see Luna alive and his men healthy.

So it wasn't difficult to flash his second a flat, unamused look. "Not an issue, Gray."

"Yes, sir." Gray climbed into the passenger seat to ride shotgun—literally, since he had a loaded 12-gauge propped against the console, waiting for him.

Conall and Rafe were already folded into the backseat, where Conall was fiddling with another tablet. "I've got the signal from the bug on their truck. Want to listen in?"

Knox started the engine, which hummed almost silently as he turned the wheel and pulled off the edge of the access road. "Put it over the speakers."

"I'm not sure," Dani was muttering. "They're trained to respond to threats, so proper elimination order isn't just important, it's vital. And I don't know their skill sets well enough to choose. Yet."

"Uh . . ." Conall leaned forward between the seats. "Are they plotting to kill us? *Already?*"

Gray shushed him.

"Hey, I've made it clear who's the most trouble," came Maya's voice. "And don't give me any shit about Gothic novels. The sniper has to go first."

"True," Dani answered, "but misguidedly narrow thinking. We could do three at once. More if Nina lets me break out the explosives."

"No explosives," Nina countered. "Clean kills."

Dani sighed. "All right—the big one first. Rafe. Then, whoever comes at me next."

"At least the blonde appreciates me," Rafe said cheerfully from the backseat, as if this was all hilarious. As if Knox wasn't wondering if he should risk the tranqs, after all.

"Your turn, fearless leader," Dani said.

Nina laughed. "I thought you already had me pegged to go one-on-one with the captain."

"*I'm* not getting within arm's reach of him," Maya stated firmly. "They don't pick nice guys to command Protectorate squads. If I have to take him down, it'll be with a bullet in the back of the head while he's taking a piss."

"Better bring a buddy along on your bathroom breaks," Conall muttered, sounding far less amused than Rafe. He always *had* had better survival instincts.

"Use your imagination, Maya." Nina's voice dropped an octave, smoothing into something low and seductive. "It doesn't have to be unpleasant. You don't come at a lion head on, but you don't have to sneak up behind it, either. You can pet it until it lets down its guard."

Knox gripped the steering wheel tighter and stared at the uneven road ahead. He could feel Gray staring at him. He could feel them *all* staring at him, waiting for a reaction.

He refused to give it.

But she kept going. "If you play your cards right, it won't matter that he knows about the knife under your pillow. He'll crawl into your bed anyway. And by the time you have that blade at his throat, he won't care anymore. It's all been worth it."

The steering wheel creaked. Adrenaline throbbed through him. Knox didn't know what was more dangerous—the blunt violence in her words or the sultry heat in her voice.

Dani snorted. "And how do you know that would work?"

"Because Garrett Knox likes a little danger. Don't you, Captain?"

"Oh, *shit*," Conall breathed. "They found the bug."

Nina's voice cooled. "If you have concerns, voice them. If you have questions, ask me. Don't eavesdrop on my team. It's over the line." She paused. "Maya?"

"Bye, boys."

A squeal of static blared through the speakers. Conall bit off another curse and slapped at his tablet until the truck fell blessedly silent.

Gray exhaled slowly. "Okay, so she's definitely not clueless. New question—what kind of person retains a chipper disposition even when they know their personal safety is in jeopardy?"

"The kind of person so dangerous, you blackmail an elite mercenary squad into retrieving them," Knox replied. "Which is why we need to focus on this job and get it done. Luna's life depends on it."

TECHCORPS PROPRIETARY DATA, L2 SECURITY CLEARANCE

Recruit MD–701 is responding well to the new cognitive enhancement regimen. There's been no apparent degradation in strength or stamina, but cognitive processing speeds far surpass those of the average soldier. His medical training should be accelerated.

Recruit Analysis, February 2063

FIVE

The roads were a little rough, but nothing the vehicle Knox had provided couldn't handle. Dani managed to avoid the worst of the potholes and jagged cracks in the asphalt, and they made good time and distance, over twenty miles before Knox's truck shuddered to a halt in front of them.

They followed suit, and Nina climbed out of the passenger seat, shading her eyes against the midday sun. Knox's men had already exited their seats and spread out in the middle of the overpass, and as she crested the gentle rise leading up to their position, she saw why.

A section of the bridge had collapsed. Craggy bits of concrete jutted from its shattered edge like broken teeth, shot through with twisted steel rebar. A yawning chasm stretched out, fifty feet across, impassable and mocking.

"Well, fuck." Nina stopped beside Knox, who was frowning in consternation. "I thought your boy wonder mapped this route with satellite imagery."

"I did." Conall glared at the tablet in his gloved hand. "But it's not like I can get instant images. There aren't *that* many satellites left up there. My last recon sweep was about a week ago."

"So this is new." Nina sidled up to the precipice. An armored truck emblazoned with a discreet version of the TechCorps logo lay crumpled on the ground below, its bulletproof windows shattered but intact. Blood painted two of them, radiating outward from central impact points. The locked doors in the back had broken open, and crates used to transport cash spilled out of them.

It was a tempting picture. Too tempting.

Dani kicked a loose chunk of concrete over the edge as she peered down at the truck. "Well, this is a trap."

Maya inched up on Dani's other side and let out a sharp laugh. "Holy shit. It's not even subtle."

Maybe not, but it *was* sophisticated, the kind of thing that took skill and resources to set up. Going down to check it out could be worth it for the intelligence alone.

Knox crouched and tugged off his glove. He dragged his fingers through a small puddle of liquid on the cracked pavement and rubbed his fingers together. "Low-quality biofuel made from vegetable oil. There's an old pre-Flare air base not far from here where raiders have set up camp."

"Dobbins-Crenshaw AFB," Nina murmured. "I know."

He rose and wiped his hand on his cargo pants as he pinned her with a serious look. "I hope you're not considering something stupid."

"That's the one thing you can *always* count on, Captain." She leaned closer. "You're not the tiniest bit curious?"

He arched one eyebrow. Without breaking eye contact, he held out his hand. "Rifle."

Silently, Gray handed it over. Knox lifted the rifle and peered through the scope. "The Dobbins crew prefers clean kills. They use motion-activated taser mines."

"Taser mines?"

He gestured toward the truck. "They set up a detector grid around the bait and wait for their prey to electrocute themselves. Explosives might destroy anything useful on the bodies, you see. The sensors are set up . . ." He looked through the scope again. "One on that rock, another next to the tree, the third three feet south of the lowest case, and the fourth over by the overpass sign."

Nina held out a hand. "May I?"

With an appraising look, he passed her the rifle. With the scope's magnification—and Knox's direction—she spotted the motion detectors, each flashing minuscule green lights that almost blended into the lush overgrowth surrounding the wreck. She couldn't see the tasers at all, though she could just make out a painted metal box that must have been their power source tucked behind one wheel of the truck.

She relinquished the rifle. "I guess you don't have to be curious, then."

Knox slanted a look at her. "No. Because I'm experienced."

He bit off the word, four clipped syllables that were anything but seductive. Still, the casual competence behind them sent a thrill shivering up Nina's spine.

She covered with a half shrug. "I'm impressed. Might still be worth going down there, though. I don't have any taser mines, and they seem useful."

Gray stepped forward. "With all due respect—"

"—we don't know how often they check their traps," Dani finished for him. "I love a good scavenger hunt, but they could be headed this way right now. The smart thing to do is get the hell out of here."

"I agree." Knox handed the weapon back to Gray and tilted his head toward the trap.

The sniper nodded and stretched out on his stomach at the edge of the drop-off. Using a bent piece of rebar to steady his weapon, he fired off four precise, quiet shots, destroying the motion sensors. Finally, he put three bullets in the power source, disabling the mines.

Nina watched, her mind whirling. The man who'd taught her ambush tactics class at the Franklin Center had been a veteran of three brutal pre-Flare conflicts, each successive one dirtier and nastier than the last. He would have called this trap an inefficient, incomplete use of resources. If Nina had presented this to him, he would have made her not only rebuild it, but start over completely.

"You're thinking," Dani muttered. "What is it?"

"Nothing. Just making it better in my head."

Knox glanced at her, that appraising look back in his eyes. "How would you fix it?"

There was that *thrill* again. "It's a greedy trap for greedy people. Which is perfectly serviceable, I guess. There are a lot of those out here."

He nodded.

Nina could almost hear her teacher's gruff voice as she continued. "But they could cast a wider net with some recorded audio—cries for help, screams of pain. It wouldn't deter anyone who just wanted the money, but it would turn the situation into an emergency. Emergencies are good. They make people move faster, pay less attention to safety." She shrugged again. "Isn't that what you soldiers spend so much time training to prevent? Tunnel vision?"

"In part, yes." He turned to stare down into the chasm. "A ticking clock can force a person to take inadvisable risks, no matter how much training they have."

He spoke with the sharp certainty of personal experience, and it cut. Nina stepped back from the broken edge and held both arms out at her sides. "Let's go, then. Make your inadvisable risk in teaming up with me pay off."

"All right." He gestured south as they turned back to the trucks. "We'll have to backtrack, but I still want to make it to Kennesaw before dark. The old battlefield is a good place to camp. Raiders don't like it. People swear it's haunted."

Nina smiled. "Let me guess—Captain Garrett Knox is too practical to believe in ghosts."

"Why?" he asked. "Do *you*?"

"Yes." But not the kind he was thinking of. Nina wasn't afraid of the damned souls from some bitter, long-ago civil war. Even if those phantoms lingered, they had nothing to do with her. They were probably busy reliving their last days of futile conflict, over and over.

She touched the pendant at the hollow of her throat. Her ghosts, the ones she believed in with all her heart, were a little more personal. Closer to home. And she carried them with her always.

Their rough camp on the haunted battlefield turned out rather cozy.

The picnic area had seen better days. Most of the old wooden tables had succumbed to time, the elements, and the insidious, persistent creep of vegetation. The Silver Devils had camped here a few times over the years, but each time they arrived to find the kudzu they'd previously cut back had wound its way back over grills and around fire pits.

It hadn't taken long to clear it again, and the stone picnic tables were as sturdy as ever. The hunting had been good tonight, too—barely thirty minutes after Conall and Rafe had disappeared into the woods, they'd returned with two massive wild turkeys.

The scent of the second one roasting still filled the air. The fire in the pit Gray had dug crackled and spit sparks from the green wood, but even that was a boon, as the smoke had driven away the worst of the bugs. Knox's men were wrapped in their bedrolls, the first hour of his watch had passed in peace, and the instant coffee in his travel mug wasn't exactly *good*, but it was hot and much improved by the powdered cream Maya had offered him.

Everything was going according to plan. Everything was goddamn perfect.

The back of his neck still itched like there was a target painted on it.

A twig snapped to his right, and he spun on the bench, his pistol already halfway out of its holster. Nina stood there, a steaming cup in her hand. After a moment, she pointed to her feet. "I did that on purpose, so I wouldn't startle you. Didn't work, did it?"

"No." He stowed his weapon and nodded to the opposite side of the table. "Want to sit?"

"Thank you." She slid onto the rough stone bench, set her cup in front of her, and wrapped both hands around it. "I came to offer a truce."

Her voice was light and easy. The firelight gilded half of her face and left the rest in shadow, turning her expression enigmatic. She was hard to read anyway. Sharp where he expected softness. Amused where he expected anger. "What kind of truce?"

"The kind where we stop poking at each other all the time." She laughed a little. "The kind where I can stop coming up with creative ways to talk about murdering you because I know you're eavesdropping."

Knox didn't want to like her. Liking her would make all this a hell of a lot worse. But he couldn't help his grudging smile. "Fair's fair. We had it coming. But old habits are hard to break. My men are alive because I'm meticulous."

"I don't doubt it. And yes, you had it coming." She hesitated. "But it's exhausting, all the same."

"Can't argue with that." He lifted one hand from his mug to offer her a handshake before remembering she didn't like to touch strangers. He dropped it awkwardly to the table instead. "A truce would be good. I think you've already wooed Conall to your side, anyway. I've never seen rations like those potatoes you made. Tasted like real food."

"It *is* real food," she corrected. "We have machines at home that freeze it, then remove the moisture. After that, it can keep for decades. So people from the community bring us things to preserve, and we keep a small part of it in return. A woman in my building grew those potatoes on our roof."

He thought back to the bar, to the way people had moved around Nina and her crew. The way they'd watched them. He'd marked it up to the rational fear anyone with brains showed for a dominant predator, but that hadn't quite fit, because no one had actually seemed afraid of them.

Maybe Nina was something even more dangerous than a predator.

Maybe she was a *leader*.

Knox cleared his throat. "Did you mean it? That I can just . . . ask you what I want to know?"

"Yes." She held up a hand. "But only about myself, not my crew. Their stories aren't mine to tell."

"Of course." He gripped his mug and considered his approach. Directly to the question he most wanted to ask, or a circuitous route? He bought time by building on the current topic. "I admit, I was wondering what you did with all the money from the Crypt score. But tech like that couldn't have come cheap."

Nina sipped her drink—not coffee, like his, but a fragrant herbal tea. "We work hard, and the investment was worth it. If people can't grow and preserve food, they have to buy it from TechCorps suppliers. Not only is that stuff heavily processed, it's expensive. And it tastes like shit. This way, everyone wins." She smiled slowly. "Well, everyone except the TechCorps."

Losing wasn't something the TechCorps did often, and food had always been one of the main levers of force they used to keep the population under control. Most people either bought food directly from a company grocer or paid for access to a cafeteria. Some clever folks always tried to cut out the middleman and grow their own food, but the very reasonably priced seeds the TechCorps sold were deliberately modified to offer subpar yields. And farmers who saved seed from the harvested fruits and vegetables to sow the next year discovered they wouldn't grow.

The TechCorps had elevated plausibly deniable scientific sabotage to an exquisite art form.

Nina wouldn't reward those machinations. She and her neighbors undoubtedly sourced their seeds from the smugglers who brought in illegal heirloom varieties. Unlike the modified hybrids the TechCorps pushed, the heirloom seeds could be harvested, saved, and used again the next season. A sustainable solution.

Hell, Nina probably shouldered the risk of obtaining the seeds herself. It seemed like the sort of thing she'd do. The TechCorps couldn't know about it, or about her food preservation collective, or they already would have come after her. When people started trusting each other and working together at the community level, areas stabilized. And stable families didn't strike devil's bargains with the TechCorps.

Knox had the destruction of more than one would-be organizer on what was left of his soul.

Not a pleasant turn of thought, and he hoped it didn't show in his eyes. "Do you do other things for the neighborhood?"

"Some. Not enough." She braced her elbow on the table and rested her chin in her hand. "We have activities to keep the kids out of trouble. Clothing drives, job postings, recycled tech, community meals. When it's very hot or very cold out, we open a floor for shelter. And then . . . there are the books."

"The books?"

"Books, Captain. Things you read?" Her playful smile returned. "We can distribute digital files for free, but we also have a machine that can print copies for cost. And Maya helps the people who have material they want to turn into a book."

He liked her smile. Not just because it softened the forbidding angles of her face, but because of the careless edge of challenge in that mischievous expression. It was rare to see someone confident enough to challenge him.

He sipped his coffee and eyed her over the rim of his mug. "So . . . you're like a pre-Flare library."

"Exactly." Her voice dropped. "But is that *really* what you want to know?"

"It's part of it. You'd be surprised how much I just learned."

"Would I?"

"Mmm." Knox set down his mug and leaned forward. "The Crypt could have set you up in a nice apartment with all the luxuries, especially if you'd sold everything in there as exclusives to rich collectors. I'll bet you didn't, though. You digitized all those old books and movies, all that music, and you hand it out to people for free. You sank your liquid cash into expensive technology, but now that you have the market cornered on supply, you barely demand anything for access. You print books at cost. Preserve people's food for next to nothing."

She tilted her head in expectation of his judgment.

He leveled a finger at her. "You're an idealist. You think you can put good out into the world and make things better."

"Sort of." Her dark eyes bored into his. "You didn't have to interrogate me for that. I admit it."

He leaned closer, and even though everyone else was asleep, he low-ered his voice to a soft rumble. "You've tangled with the TechCorps before. I've seen Maya's file, and Christ knows what they did to Dani. You know that's not how the world works."

"Maybe." She finished her tea in one gulp and turned the cup over on the rough tabletop. "But I'm going to keep trying. Even if it changes noth-ing."

There was no bleak cynicism in her warm brown eyes, none of the hopeless nihilism of a soldier still fighting a losing war simply because they didn't know how to stop. Nina could entertain the possibility of fail-ure, but she didn't really believe in it. Not yet.

One question hung in the silence between them. She was waiting for him to ask it, and he hated having to. He wasn't used to stepping into a sit-uation without a full biographical and psychological profile on every per-son involved. Knowledge was power, and in this arena, and with Conall's help, Knox had always been very, very powerful.

He curled his fingers around the tin mug until he felt the soft metal bend under his punishing grip. "Where the hell did you come from?"

"I believe they used to call it North Carolina."

Not what he'd meant, and she knew it. "If you don't want to answer the question . . ."

"Not everything is a matter of preference, Knox." She paused. "Hon-estly? I'm not sure I know *how* to answer it. It's complicated."

It was the first hint of vulnerability he'd seen in her. She turned toward the firelight, offering a profile lit with flickering shadows. Sharp cheek-bones, a sculpted jaw, dramatically tilted eyebrows, a straight nose above full lips . . .

She was an exquisite trap. He knew it, and he still couldn't stop himself from stepping into it. "It's okay," he said softly. Anything to banish that helplessness from her eyes.

"Is it?"

"Everything's complicated these days."

Her brows drew together in a curious frown. "Your situation seems pretty simple. I mean, the hard part's past you, right? Now all you have to do is survive."

"You think survival is simple?"

"Sure. It's the most straightforward thing that exists. The strongest drive we have." She shrugged one shoulder. "Everything else can get sticky. But survival is what it is."

Said the woman who'd faked Maya's death instead of claiming a two-million-credit reward. Maybe she'd never been desperate enough to understand. "Survival's simple. The complicated part is deciding what you're willing to do to survive."

She rocked her overturned cup onto one side of the rim, then let it settle to the table once more. "Philosophy isn't my strong suit. But I do have two rules that have worked for me so far. You're welcome to borrow them."

"And what are those?"

She held up a finger. "Number one—nothing that seems impossible ever really is. You just haven't found the right answer yet. Or the right question."

For the first time, he wondered how young she was. Her blithe optimism made him feel *ancient*. "And number two?"

"No matter what I think I have to do, I also have to look at myself in the mirror tomorrow."

It was a well-placed kick to the gut, and he'd asked for it. His coffee didn't taste as good now that it was growing cold, but he drained his cup to buy some time. When he set it down across from hers, he'd mastered his expression.

Mostly.

"Protectorate soldiers don't spend a lot of time looking in mirrors," he said finally. "It doesn't end well."

"I know a little something about that." She smiled, warm and encouraging. "But you're not a Protectorate soldier anymore. Baby steps."

That smile was a trap, too. Even more dangerous because he didn't think she meant it as one. She'd gotten cagey about her origins, but *this* was real. Her bright, sunny smile. Her relentless optimism. All this reckless, deadly hope.

She was good. Fast, tough, smart. A fearless warrior. But her strength was also a weakness. Nina was willing to throw herself at the world because she was so damn competent, she'd never lost. She had overcome every obstacle and out-thought every opponent.

Until him.

No satisfaction came from identifying the cracks in her defenses, no pleasure. The balance of power had tipped ever so precariously in his favor, and he would take strategic advantage of it. Knox would be the bastard who shattered all that hope and optimism. Lives depended on his ability to complete his mission.

Mirrors were overrated anyway.

CLASSIFIED BEHAVIOR EVALUATION

Franklin Center for Genetic Research

HS-Gen16-A continues to exhibit strong leadership abilities. Her tendency to develop strong bonds with others could prove problematic if not curbed. I suggest instructors employ standard psychological methods—i.e., favoritism—to cultivate conflict and set her at odds with her classmates.

Dr. Baudin, June 2066

SIX

Maya had taken over driving duties, which was just as well, because Nina's head was pounding, and Dani was just *cranky*.

Abandoning the interstate for the smaller back roads meant slower going, even under the best of circumstances. But a storm had apparently blown through the area they were traversing, and it must have been one of the region's deadly tornadoes. The damage was singularly recognizable—not only had the tops of trees been twisted off, leaving bare crowns of bright, splintered wood reaching toward the sky, but debris and downed trees littered the roads. They could drive around most of them, but every few miles, they reached a blockage they couldn't navigate.

Even with laser saws, clearing them was hot, sweaty, frustrating work. And the constant wobble of swerving to avoid potholes and branches and rock slides was taking its toll on her equilibrium. Nina leaned her head against the car window, but the sensation of the uncomfortably warm glass against her cheek only made her stomach roil harder. She wanted a drink. She wanted a bath. More than anything, she wanted to stop moving for a while and just be *still*.

A moment later, she got her wish. The truck slowed, and she opened her eyes to another roadblock, this one a gigantic pine that could take them hours to clear.

"Shit." Maya exhaled roughly as she shifted the vehicle into park, but made no move to open the door. "I was not born to be a damn lumberjack."

"Come on." Dani patted her shoulder. "The sooner we get out there, the sooner we'll be done."

Maya sighed again. Then she glanced at Nina, sympathy furrowing her brow. "You okay?"

"I didn't sleep well last night." An understatement. After the conversation with Knox, she'd spent half the night waking up every fifteen minutes, her heart pounding. It was an old habit drilled into her during combat training, the ability to snap awake every quarter hour, but it only happened these days when she was distressed.

Which was exactly why she'd eventually given up on sleep and lain awake, staring at the stars, so tense and fidgety that not even counting the stitches in her sleeping bag had helped. She'd almost said too much to Knox. *Revealed* too much.

It wasn't just that urge to confide in him, though, or even the near-constant urge to touch him. The whole interaction had been strangely charged in a way that went beyond the physical. Every time he looked at her, she swore he was about to open his mouth and tell her something *vital*. The words never came, but they were there, all the same. Loud enough to echo between them.

She didn't know him well enough to read him that closely, and that was the most unnerving part of it all.

She pushed open the door and climbed out. Conall and Rafe were already examining the tree trunk, and Gray was busy assembling the saw at the back of their Jeep. That left only Knox standing alone, and Nina found herself both eager and also strangely reluctant to speak to him.

But she had to. "This is the biggest one yet."

He had his arms crossed, one hand scratching idly at the stubble on his cheek. "Hopefully there won't be too many more. We should be back on the interstate in another ten miles."

She watched his fingers as they moved and tried not to think about them stroking over her skin. "Right."

Knox slanted a look at Maya, who was still seated behind the wheel and glaring balefully at the fallen tree. "If any of your team needs to sit this one out, it's okay. We're built for this."

A fact that was impossible to miss—or ignore. Rafe was already limbing the trunk, his muscles bulging as he tore off branches as big around as Nina's arm with nothing more than his gloved hands. And Conall, who seemed more at home with tech than physical exertion, had stowed his ever-present tablet to help.

"I noticed," she told Knox dryly. "But someone has to run the saw while we clear the wood."

At her signal, Maya and Dani exited the truck. Gray fixed the expandable frame of the saw, with its two articulating lasers, around the tree trunk and locked it in place. He placed it about a third of the way up the portion blocking the road, something Nina noted with approval. If they could buck it into three huge logs, they might be able to roll it aside. Maybe they wouldn't be there all day, after all.

But Knox didn't seem pleased. His shoulders were tight, and his narrowed gaze was fixed on some far-off point in the woods.

Nina moved closer, even though the proximity made her skin prickle with something she *wished* was warning. "What's wrong?"

He turned to stare back down the road, his lips pressed into a tight frown. "Something's off."

She dropped her hand to the comforting weight of the pistol at her hip. She didn't spend a lot of time this deep in the forest, and she was far more accustomed to the noises of the city—the crashes and bangs of people and machinery, laughter and catcalls and the occasional scream. This was . . .

Quiet. There were soft sounds here, like birds chirping and the breeze stirring through the trees. But the breeze had died down, and even the birds had fallen silent. Like the entire world had drawn in a deep, bracing breath and was holding it.

Before Nina could say anything, Dani darted across the road, slammed into Maya, and shielded her against the relative safety of the truck. "Incoming!"

Instinctively, Nina looked up. Dull gray grenades the size of her fist sailed through the air only to fall and skitter across the pavement. One by one, they slid to a stop and opened, tiny metal spider legs steadying them as deadly arcs of electricity streamed forth.

Not grenades. Mines.

She was still pulling her pistol when Knox tackled her. By the time they hit the cracked asphalt, they had each squeezed off a shot, impacting the mine closest to them.

It exploded in a shower of smoke and sparks, and Nina pushed up on her elbows, dizzy with adrenaline. "Time to see how good you are, Captain."

"Take the ones on the left." Knox rolled to his feet and fired again.

"Your left or my—Oh, fuck it."

Raiders streamed out of the woods on either side of the road, dressed

in faded military fatigues and rough leather. There were *dozens* of them
by the time Nina jumped to her feet. She dispatched three as she spun
around, part of her attention focused on surveying the controlled chaos
of the fight.

Gray's rifle was useless at this range. Conall tossed him a large automatic pistol with a huge magazine instead, but he still mainly used it to
bash his attackers in the face. When they stumbled back far enough to
allow him clear, clean shots, he took them.

Maya stuck close to the shelter of the truck, gun in hand. No one could
get close to her without going through Dani, anyway. Dani took every
punch with stoic aplomb before lashing out in response. She was a verita-
ble blur as she kicked and whirled, and Nina thought she was only punch-
ing the raiders until they started to fall, bleeding and wailing. Only then
did she catch the sharp glint of the knives in Dani's hands.

Rafe favored hand-to-hand, as well, but his style was dirtier. He swept
one raider's feet out from under him, then followed him to the ground,
pausing only to activate the laser saw. It whirred to life as Rafe shoved his
opponent's head directly into the deadly beam's path.

Nina turned away before it made contact.

Knox was at the center of it all, blocking attacks and dodging shots
with absent-minded and enviable efficiency. As with her, half of his attention was on the bigger picture, on making sure his people were safe.

He was better at it. While Nina was distracted, watching Knox easily toss aside his attackers, a pair of heavy arms locked around her from
behind, lifting her off her feet. Another raider rushed at them, head on,
his eyes gleaming with murderous rage. Knox yelled something, and Dani
pivoted, but there was nothing either of them could do to reach her.

Time contracted, slowing as Nina's focus narrowed. There was one
mine left that hadn't been disabled yet, behind and just a little to the left
of the man running at her. The one holding her had his face close to hers,
close enough for his fetid breath to gust against her cheek. He still had
both arms around her, his hands free of weapons.

She could work with that.

The world snapped back into place. Nina lifted her legs and kicked the
raider in front of her hard in the chest. He sprawled back, landing on the
last active mine, and his body arched as the current surged through it.

At the same time, she slammed her head back against her captor's face.

Bone crunched as his nose shattered, and his arms tightened painfully for a breathless moment.

Then he dropped her.

As she braced herself to hit the asphalt on bent legs instead of her face, Knox passed by in a blur. He crashed into her attacker, carrying the man back with one hand locked around his throat. With a roar, he heaved the man off the ground and flung him at the reinforcements rushing toward them. All three men went down in a tangle of limbs, and Knox finished them off with six precise shots.

"Heads up." Gray took cover behind the fallen tree. "Their friends are here."

A personnel truck rumbled around the next bend in the road, headed their way. It barely slowed before men began spilling out of it and firing on their position. Nina dove for cover as well, sliding across the asphalt as bullets whizzed overhead.

"Now aren't you sad I didn't bring the C-4?" Dani muttered.

A little, though that rocket launcher Maya had teased her about might have come in handy, too. Nina tried to peek over the log, but the fresh wave of raiders was laying down too much suppressive fire. All she caught was a glimpse of piecemeal armor, better than what the last guys had been equipped with. And these attackers had proper weapons, ones they actually carried like soldiers.

So the first group had all been expendable grunts, cannon fodder, and these raiders were the real deal. Too bad, because it would only take them moments to reach the tree, and then Nina and all her friends would be in a world of trouble. "Ideas?"

Knox ended up on Nina's other side. He pressed his back to the tree and closed his eyes. "Those are Mark 15s," he said, his eyes popping open again. "Older military issue. The first models to use biometric access. They're battery operated."

"On it." Conall dragged a heavy duffel toward him and pulled out a squat black gun with copper wire twisted around the barrel. He flipped a switch on the side, turned it on the advancing raiders . . . and waited.

"Any day now, Con," Gray muttered.

"The pulse has to charge," he hissed back.

Oh, none of this was funny anymore. Nina tensed as bullets pinged off the trucks, and the hair on her arms stood on end as the scrape and shuffle of heavy boots grew closer. Pretty soon, the fuckers would be standing right over them, and the scant cover offered by the fallen tree wouldn't matter anymore.

Knox released a shuddering breath. "*Con—*"

The gun in Conall's hand beeped, and he pulled the trigger. The incoming gunfire abruptly ceased, replaced by a breathless moment of silence.

"*Now,*" Nina said, her voice blending with Knox's as they both gave the order. Everyone rose in unison and returned fire in a deafening volley.

When it ended, the raiders lay dead or dying.

Rafe and Gray joined Dani and Maya as they went to check the bodies, and Nina holstered her weapon. It was an ignominious end, dying in the middle of the road in a well-timed hail of bullets, but Nina had precious little sympathy to spare.

The raiders had chosen their path.

Gray nudged one of the fallen men with the toe of his boot. "Fatigues. Military weapons that belong in a museum. It's definitely the Dobbins crew."

Nina rubbed a hand over her face. It came away streaked with someone else's blood. "How many of them *are* there?"

"Enough." Knox walked to the opposite end of the tree and bit off a curse as he gripped one massive shredded root. "It's another trap. They brought the tree down with explosives."

"They must have been pretty pissed about us disabling the last one," she noted. Pissed enough to track them and set up an ambush. "Are they old friends of yours?"

"No." With a frustrated twist of his wrist, Knox snapped off the root and tossed it away. "Just nasty and prone to grudges."

"Well, their mistake." Rafe grabbed a boot and hauled one of the corpses out of the way. "C'mon, Conall. Help me clear the road."

Conall's face was flushed. He started toward the closest fallen raider, his movements stiff and unsteady. After two steps, he tripped over nothing and pitched into the fallen tree with a grunt of surprise.

Then he hit the asphalt, seizing.

"Shit!" Rafe vaulted the tree and skidded to his knees next to Conall. "*Knox.*"

Knox was already moving. He sank down beside them, his face pale and tight with worry. "Get the med-kit. Con—come on, man. Come on."

They were freaking out, but not shocked. Whatever was happening, they knew exactly what it was. Nina stood back, giving them room to loosen Conall's tactical vest and brace his head. "What's wrong with him?"

Gray unzipped the med-kit with a vicious jerk. "Neural overload."

Her blood chilled. "His implants are malfunctioning?"

"Yes." Knox bit the word out like a curse. "He's gone the longest without having them adjusted. It's hitting him first."

Nina knelt above Conall's head, cradling his neck so that Knox had his hands free to dig through the kit. "How do we treat him?"

He surfaced with a nasal syringe and gripped Conall's chin. He administered the liquid up the man's nose, then tossed aside the applicator and brushed the hair back from Conall's sweaty forehead. "This should stop the seizure. That's all we can do."

It took less than a minute—forty-seven seconds that Nina ticked off to distract herself from rising panic—but it felt like an eternity before Conall's spasms began to slow. They lessened in intensity, as well, growing less and less violent until he finally lay still. Sweat soaked his clothes, and his eyes, though half-open, were dull and unfocused.

Gray slipped a small monitor onto Conall's fingertip and frowned at the tablet in his hand. "Oxygenation and heart rate are okay. He got lucky."

"This time." Knox framed Conall's face with his hands, the miserable weight of responsibility—and failure—darkening his features. "I'll get him to the truck. Gray, find us someplace secure to stay the night."

Rafe scooped up Conall's abandoned tablet and tossed it to Gray. "I'll clear the road."

Nina moved to Conall's feet. "Let me help you carry—"

"I've got him." Knox rose, Conall's bulk cradled easily in his arms. Nina hurried to open the truck's back door, and Knox settled him carefully on the backseat.

Dani had joined Rafe in dragging the raiders' bodies out of the road. But when she reached for the fallen tree, he waved her off and gripped the trunk with his massive hands.

"You're going to hurt yourself," she protested.

"Hurt's relative," he growled, then hoisted.

Rafe's entire body strained as he lifted the trunk in agonizing increments. Nina held her breath, waiting for it to crash back down on him—but it didn't. With a roar, he hefted it onto his shoulders, the rough bark catching on his clothes and in his hair, and began inching it aside. When he'd cleared enough of the roadway for them to ease the trucks around the tree, he dropped it with a loud noise and a shower of pine needles.

With the adrenaline of the fight and Conall's subsequent medical emergency pounding through her veins, Nina's headache was a full-blown throb now. She pushed it aside as she faced Knox again. "Later, you and I are going to have a talk."

He held her gaze for only a heartbeat before turning back to Conall. "As soon as he's settled, I'm all yours."

Somehow, she doubted it. If the day had proven anything, it was that Captain Knox and his people had secrets, secrets that ran just as deep as hers.

Deeper.

Maya was tossing the last of the equipment she'd stripped from their attackers into the truck. "Hey," she called to Dani. "A little help here?"

Dani had wandered closer, but her attention was still on Rafe. "Can you believe that? It goes beyond macho pride. It's idiocy."

"It's useful," Maya retorted. "He could have tossed the last three trees out of the way, too."

"Or not." Dani's voice was dark as she closed up the back of the truck. "What happens to you when you have too much noise coming at you? Overload, right?" She shook her head. "If Rafe keeps carrying on like that, he'll wind up like Conall."

She would know. The TechCorps experiment she'd been a part of was meant to be the next stage in the evolution of their supersoldier program— by physically altering the nervous system, their scientists hoped to attain all the speed and strength with none of the drawbacks of the implants. They'd discovered too late that the rewiring procedure came with its own set of complications.

Dani was more like the Devils than Knox and his crew realized, and if *she* was worried about them, they really were in deep shit.

And it was Nina's job to make sure they didn't drag her team down with them.

SEVEN

Shelter turned out to be an abandoned warehouse with four solid walls, a roof, and not much else to recommend it.

It was enough. Knox sat with Conall, who seemed to have recovered from his seizure, as Rafe and Gray cleared enough space for their bedrolls. By the time Conall agreed to eat and take another sedative, Rafe had also helped the women set up their own area.

And Nina had vanished.

Logic said she was walking the perimeter. It was the first thing Knox usually did when they set up someplace new, even if someone else had already done the necessary recon. It wasn't that he didn't trust his men to recognize danger or perform the task—each one of them knew the price of inattention. But Knox needed to walk the terrain himself, to evaluate the strengths and weaknesses of their defenses, to fix a mental map in place so he could plan for a range of scenarios. He couldn't rest until he'd set his contingencies in place.

Though his relentless attention to detail wasn't new, the desperation with which he clung to it was. Every day, his thoughts felt a little slower, a little more . . . muddled. He should have *known* the fallen tree was a trap, and a clumsy one, at that. The shredded roots on that damn tree had been about as subtle as fireworks.

Instinctively, he'd known something wasn't right. But his brain had failed to make the proper connections in time, and Conall had suffered for it. Knox's cognitive enhancements were degrading, and the worst part was knowing that next time, the consequences could be even worse.

The second-worst part was knowing he didn't have much edge left to lose. Nina was smart, not to mention devastatingly capable. So far, Knox's only real advantage over her was a deeper understanding of the terrible ways people could betray one another.

It wasn't enough.

He couldn't relax with Nina out of sight. After catching Gray's eye and receiving a silent nod in response, Knox set out down an aisle of towering metal shelves.

The warehouse had obviously been looted, probably dozens of times over the decades, with people carrying away anything they could use or sell. Half of the racks were stripped bare, with overturned boxes littering the floor. As he kicked one out of the way, a bright pink shoe spilled out.

Knox crouched to pick it up. It was child-sized, more cut-outs than actual material, and made from a thin, glittery plastic that seemed wildly impractical. Most of the shoes left behind were like that—remnants of a softer world, a more whimsical one. A world where children didn't worry about broken glass or rusty nails or all the things that could hurt or kill them every time they walked outside.

Not many people had the luxury of being soft and whimsical anymore.

He abandoned the shoe and paced to the end of the aisle. The soft scrape of boot soles and a partly open door gave him a direction. He winced at the loud squeak as he pushed open the heavy door to the loading dock, but Nina didn't turn around.

She was staring down at the loading area. Once upon a time, massive trucks had backed into the space, sunken so that their trailers would be level with the dock, to deliver or load thousands of boxes of shoes. Now, it was flooded—permanently, judging from the algae that slicked the concrete. Moonlight glinted off the water, and the breeze made it lap against the dock walls in tiny little waves.

After a moment, Nina gestured to the water. "There's a creek behind the warehouse. It must overflow in this direction when hard rains come."

He was about to ask how she knew when the moonlight caught silvery scales flitting through the water. "There are fish?"

"Nothing for eating. Just little minnows." She shoved her hands in her back pockets. "*Notropis chrosomus*. Rainbow shiners."

She kept surprising him. "You have a special interest in fish?"

"Not particularly." She glanced over at him. "How's Conall?"

"Better."

"Good. Then we can jump right in on how you lied to me."

The muscles at the back of his neck tensed with warning. He kept his arms loose by his sides, half expecting an attack. "Lied about what?"

"Your team's ability to protect mine." She turned toward him while taking a step closer, and just like that, she was in his space, her face dangerously close to his. "You're not just desperate. You're dying."

Instinct straightened his spine, but he couldn't rely on looming over her for physical intimidation. She was tall, she was pissed, and he still wasn't sure which of them would win in a fight.

It was perversely exhilarating.

"I never told you we weren't dying," he said evenly. "And we protected you just fine. Conall overdid it today, that's all. We'll adjust our strategy."

Her eyes widened in disbelief. "And the next time one of you *overdoes it*?"

"That's my problem." Knox leaned closer. "I said I'd take care of security. I'll take care of security. Or do you have some complaints about our efficiency in dispatching the enemy today?"

"Just one." Before he could step back, she grabbed his wrist. Her fingers dug into his flesh, all her deceptive strength on full display. "The part where a member of your team almost died right in front of us. Which makes it *our* problem, Garrett. So don't brush me off."

She was upset. If she gripped him any tighter, she'd leave bruises on his skin, ugly marks in the graceful shape of her fingers. The logical part of his brain analyzed the naïveté of her response, the weakness it revealed, and the best possible response: calm de-escalation.

The darker part of him, three days into a steady diet of anxiety and thwarted adrenaline, overrode logic. In the still moment just before his self-control snapped, he judged the firmness of her grip, the strength of their respective stances, the distance to the wall, and the improbably clean scent of her hair.

It still smelled like fruit. Impossible, after two days on the road.

Intoxicating.

Fuck, this was all a terrible idea.

He twisted his hand lightning fast, breaking her grip to catch *her* wrist, reversing their positions. But Nina didn't flinch or struggle, just flexed her hand almost absently.

She was busy staring at his mouth.

"You should fight back," he rasped, irrationally irritated by her lack of concern.

"Why?" Her voice was velvet, low and secret and dark. "Are you trying to hurt me?"

"Everyone's trying to hurt you." Her skin was warm under his palm, and he could feel her pulse beating strong and fast. "That's the one thing in this world no one can ever afford to forget."

"Right." Slowly, she used her free hand to peel his fingers away from her wrist. For a moment, their hands were locked together, an unexpected, maddening intimacy. Then she stepped away, breaking the contact. "If time is of the essence, maybe we should keep driving at night instead of camping. Anything to reach our destination faster."

Knox rubbed his thumb over his fingers, where her touch lingered like an electric charge. A simple chemical reaction, or a warning sign that he was skating dangerously close to the same neural overload as Conall? "We can't," he said softly. "Forgoing proper rest will only hasten our biochemical decline."

"I see." She turned once more toward the small pond that had established itself in the loading dock. The moonlight reflecting off its surface lit her face, which was set in a carefully neutral expression. "It's not too late to go back."

Oh, it was far past *too late*. Loyalty aside, Rafe had spent years carefully cultivating Luna as a contact. Even if they could find another biochem expert with her skill and familiarity with TechCorps implants, said expert would probably bolt at the sight of a Protectorate soldier. Or try to kill them all.

Knox had been sent to "recruit" enough geniuses to know how those visits usually went.

"This is our best shot," he said, lying with the truth again. "We should move faster once we get back on the interstate."

"Should. If. Maybe." She huffed out a soft, unamused laugh. "Not my favorite words. I like to gamble, but not with people's lives."

"Gambling with my life is my job. Don't worry about it."

"Is there anything I can do?" Nina paused. "Would you even tell me if there was?"

The crack in his self-control fractured along the fault lines of his sudden guilt, and he reacted the way any wounded creature backed into a corner would have—he snapped at her. "I don't need any fucking help. All I need is food and some sleep."

She went still, her only visible reaction to his rough outburst. "Understood." Her voice was mild, but when she turned away from the water, her eyes were flashing fire. "I'll leave you alone, then."

He'd gone too far. He couldn't afford to antagonize her, not when she was already thinking about ditching the trip and heading home. Knox reached out to grab her elbow. "Nina, wait—"

It was as far as he got. She slapped his hand away and went on the offensive, launching into a flurry of punches. He had to back away to block them without hurting her. Too late, he realized that was her plan. His back slammed into the wall, and *she* slammed into *him*—one arm pinning his chest, her other hand holding a knife so close to his throat that the blade would nick him if he swallowed too hard.

A violent and abrupt explosion. Every sleek line of her body promised menace, but she was still staring at his mouth, so maybe he wasn't the only one getting stupid.

Knox licked his lower lip.

Her chest heaved, and she shoved away from him. "Don't worry, Captain. I get it." The blade slid back into her thigh sheath with a whisper. "Distance. You do your thing, I'll do mine, and we'll be sure to keep a little space between us."

"Sounds like a plan," he replied, hoping the low volume of his voice would hide the betraying rasp of arousal. "I'll take first watch."

"Fuck you."

She strode away, fury still etched in every stiff movement. A better man, a *decent* man, wouldn't have watched her denim-clad ass until the shadows swallowed her whole.

Knox was starting to think *damned* was too good a word for him.

He rubbed his hand against the rough fabric of his cargo pants to banish the feel of her, but she was everywhere. A burning line of fire across his chest where her arm had pressed against him. A thinner, harsher sting where her knife had kissed his skin. It was so sharp it had barely hurt, and that was the part he had to remember.

Nina was that blade, honed to such a seductive edge you wouldn't realize she had even cut you until you were bleeding to death.

The greatest danger she represented wasn't that knife. It was the insidious way she kept erasing the boundaries he tried to draw. That relentless *kindness*. The fact that, contrary to the rules of survival, after only two days in his presence she seemed to genuinely care about Knox and his men.

Borderline suicidal for her. And potentially lethal for him.

He dragged in a breath of sticky, humid night air. The brackish water carried its own scent, pungent and earthy. The landing dock would have been crawling with bugs without the fish, whose silver scales reflected the moonlight as they surfaced to catch mosquito larvae.

Arousal still simmered under his skin. So did guilt. Frustrated at himself and furious with his unraveling control, Knox spun and slammed his fist into the wall.

He didn't pull the punch. The impact of it rattled up his arm as the brick cracked. Crumbled. Pain bloomed, bright and immediate, as his skin split, but he didn't care. Pain was a distraction, a reminder, a lover he'd embraced for most of his life.

And, in the end, it was a warning he didn't need anymore.

Knox pulled his hand back. His fist had driven deep, shattering the exterior wall. His blood smeared the brick in dark shadows. He wiped the debris from his knuckles and stared down into the open wound, where indestructible polymers had protected his joints from damage. Beneath that, where his bones had once been, a shiny titanium alloy glinted in the dim light.

The holding cells the TechCorps had locked them in had been built of materials far stronger than brick and mortar. But they hadn't prevented his teammates from seeing each other. Hearing each other.

Knox imagined that was at least part of the point.

Mace had gone through the muscle cramps first. Through his agonizing pain, the medic had reassured the team. Mace had always been calm in a medical emergency, and he was calm during his own. Even when the cramps turned to seizures like the one that had struck Conall. Even when those seizures had intensified.

Mace had stayed calm as death wrapped dark, hungry hands around him.

His suffering was meant to be an abject lesson to his teammates, especially Knox, who hadn't stayed calm at all. That last day, as the convulsions had claimed Mace and his weakened groans took on an edge of fear, Knox had tried to batter his way out of his cell. It was unthinkable to watch one of his men die, and intolerable to see him do it alone, afraid. Senselessly. *Needlessly.*

He'd beaten at the reinforced polycarbonate walls of the cell until his hands bled. Until his skin was scraped raw. Until his bones shattered.

Until *he* shattered.

And then he'd fallen to his knees, his mangled, bloody hands hanging uselessly at his sides, and begged for mercy. Not for himself. For Mace.

But mercy wasn't a TechCorps directive.

They had broken something inside Knox that day, something that couldn't be repaired. It didn't matter that they'd taken him from the holding cell straight into surgery and replaced his shattered bones with the latest tech. He'd been numb as they rushed him through regeneration therapy. Dead inside.

They put him in the testing facility and exclaimed excitedly as he punched what they told him to punch, as he split the skin over his knuckles again and again, pulverizing everything they put in front of him. He endured the painful regeneration and imagined driving his newly indestructible fists through their chipper, triumphant faces.

He mouthed the promises they wanted him to make and gave them the loyalty oaths they wanted to hear. And he'd meant them. For the three weeks after Mace's heart had finally stopped, nothing had mattered to Knox except perfect compliance. He'd valued his conscience too highly and had disobeyed an order. As a result, they'd tortured one of his men to death. So the rest of his squad's lives had depended on his ability to acquiesce.

It wasn't until the TechCorps reunited him with his team that the spark of defiance had kindled again. Not for himself—he couldn't afford to have a conscience anymore—but for his men, because the safety you bought by selling off bigger bits of your soul every day was nothing but an illusion.

His team deserved a chance to break free before this life shattered them as completely as it had Knox. Their only chance—their only tiny, futile chance—lay at the rendezvous coordinates. In delivering three presumably innocent people, possibly to their deaths.

His crew was on board with the plan now, but Knox could already see the fractures forming. He'd chosen his men not because they were good at their jobs, but because they were good people. He'd seen his own simmering need to help reflected in each one. Maybe they didn't aspire to be heroes—the Protectorate wouldn't have tolerated that—but they absolutely wanted to minimize the hurt, to soften the cruelty.

Conall would break first. Rafe might hold out longer, what with Luna's life hanging in the balance, but the clock was already ticking. Knox had to get them to the rendezvous point and secure their futures before their own innate senses of decency overrode their survival instincts.

He had to be hard enough for all of them. Merciless enough. They might hate him before the end of this, and Knox wouldn't blame them.

But he couldn't care. Not about that and not about Nina, with her alluring smiles and irrational compassion. She could be the best damn person in the world, and it wouldn't matter to Knox. If betraying her could buy his men their futures, he'd do it in a heartbeat.

He couldn't watch another one of them die.

DANI

Nina came back from her perimeter sweep silently seething, and a frisson of alarm raced up Dani's spine.

Trouble. So much about this job was plain old, straight-up *trouble*.

It made more sense when Knox strode into the cavernous main room of the warehouse a few minutes later, looking just as pissed. He shot Nina one irritated look before pointedly turning his back on all three of them and stalking to where Conall lay, stretched out on a bedroll. Nina ignored him, every ounce of her attention focused on pouring herself a cup of coffee.

Dani nudged Maya with her foot. "Guess the honeymoon's over."

"Good," Maya grumbled softly. "I feel better about life when she's a little mad at him."

It wouldn't last. It never did—Nina could get angry or irritated, but she always seemed to burn through the emotions like flashfire. She just didn't possess the bitterness that fueled and sustained grudges. "She likes him."

"Nina likes everyone." Maya settled more comfortably on her bedroll, her legs crossed, a little silver packet of freeze-dried peaches in one hand. "She can afford to give people the benefit of the doubt. If they try to fuck her over, she can just flatten them."

"Yeah." That was the easy part. Dealing with the fallout, that was another thing entirely.

Dani opened her bag and set out several soft, folded pieces of cloth and her gun oil. She grimaced when she pulled her knives from their sheaths—she'd wiped them down after the fight earlier, but she'd missed some of the blood, which sucked. She liked 1095 carbon steel for fighting, but it rusted like a motherfucker.

She started the slow, meditative process of cleaning and oiling her blades. She could do it without thought. Hell, she could probably do it in her sleep.

The TechCorps trained their executive bodyguards well.

Dani let her hands move about their task and looked up as Nina joined them. She was still tense, though her breathing had steadied, and she no longer looked like she might snatch one of Dani's blades and go after Knox. She sipped her coffee, grimaced, and made a soft noise of frustration.

Maya held out her bag. "Hungry? I can reconstitute something for you."

"No, thank you." Nina sighed. "It's just . . . been a day. And Captain Knox doesn't seem to want to play nice."

No shit, he didn't. He had something up his sleeve, and only a sociopath would *want* to smile and laugh with someone before jamming a knife into their back. It was a special kind of hellish mind game, and, for all his faults, it didn't seem to be Knox's thing.

But Dani had already voiced her opinions about him, and about the mission, so she only shrugged. "Some people don't want to get close. We don't need to be buddies with them. Let's save that for the people back home."

"Yeah. Though the nerdy one is growing on me." Maya ran a finger over the edge of her battered watch. "He fixed the crackle in my left earbud. Is he going to be okay?"

Nina's fingers tightened around her mug. "I don't know. I hope so."

Dani glanced past her. Conall kept trying to reach for his tablet. Every time he did, Knox snatched it away with an admonition she could clearly read on his lips: *Relax.* Judging from the painfully tense set of his shoulders, he didn't seem to be taking his own advice.

Gray had another gun broken down—*how* did he have more than her?—and was cleaning the barrel. Rafe was reading an actual book, his long, nimble fingers toying with the corners of the pages long before he actually needed to turn them.

That figured. He seemed like a tactile sort, one of those touchy-feely types who were always rubbing up on people and things, exploring the world through physical perception instead of using their other, easier senses. Nina was the worst, but this guy was coming up a close second.

Touchy-feely people liked to touch and feel. It got to be a habit, which was probably why Rafe was so flirtatious, and why Nina found the Silver Devils' captain so fascinating.

Dani set her blades aside. "When's the last time you got laid?"

Nina choked on her coffee. "Excuse me?"

"You heard me. Was it that fling you had with the Professor?"

"No, it was . . . Dakota, wasn't it?" Maya waved her bag of peaches to punctuate her point. "The seed smuggler. She always brought Nina impossible-to-find fruit. I miss her."

Dani did too, but not as much as she missed the mechanic, or the burly bouncer from Clem's place, or the baker. At least Nina tended to stay on good terms with her exes, even after their time together ended and she moved on to her next relationship.

And she always moved on. It wasn't that Nina didn't care, it was that she cared *so much,* and about everybody. She was earnestly interested in people, could find something to love in just about anyone. The mere thought exhausted Dani, who preferred to keep a small handful of people close.

Another thing the TechCorps had taught her—to care about as little as possible. It was difficult, after all, to convince a bodyguard to die for her charge if she had anything left to live for. So step one was always, *always* to isolate a new recruit.

It was another lesson that had stuck with Dani. It suited her, being alone except for Nina and Maya. She didn't need to date someone to have sex. She didn't need to *like* them.

Nina, on the other hand . . .

Dani lowered her voice. "Knox is hot. A little boring, if you ask me, but you tend to gravitate toward that. It's been a while since your last hookup, and you're getting antsy. That's all this is. Maya, help me out here."

"It's a bad idea." Maya shrugged. "I mean, you already know that. But I get the appeal. It's a thing, you know. The bars close to the Protectorate barracks are always crawling with groupies. All that stamina and shit."

Nina's flush deepened, and it didn't look like embarrassment.

"Don't mention the stamina," Dani advised Maya. "I mean, I get that *you* don't find it hot, but—"

Maya pulled a face at her. "It's hot in *theory.* But some of us don't want strangers all up in our personal space for more than five minutes, much less all night. I'll stick to the safe option of my fabulous imagination and nice, long baths."

"I don't want anyone all up in my anything," Nina insisted firmly. "Captain Knox and I have to work together. To that end, we need to maintain a measure of civility between us."

Civility was the last thing on Garrett Knox's mind when he was staring at Nina's ass—but pointing that out would be counterproductive as hell. "There you go. And when the job is done? Whatever happens, happens."

It was an empty promise. Assuming they managed to finish the job without getting royally fucked over, Knox and his men would vanish so fast the rest of them would be left sucking on dust. Nina might be sad for a while, but sad was better than brokenhearted.

"I have my head on straight," Nina whispered. "You don't have to worry about me."

Those were two vastly unrelated statements. Dani never worried because she thought Nina was fucking up, just like she never fretted over Maya for that reason. They could both get their shit done. The real problem was everyone else, all the people who could—and would—hurt them, out of malice or carelessness or greed or—

Yes, even necessity.

"I'm just doing my job." Dani gave her knives one last wipedown, stowed them, and obediently held out both hands for Maya to check.

She turned them over, meticulously studying Dani's skin for undetected cuts. When she didn't find any, Maya smiled and dropped a packet of fruit into Dani's hands. "Eat something."

Across the room, Rafe set an empty med-gel applicator aside and started wrapping one of Knox's hands. Whatever had happened between their team leaders outside, it had ended in bloodshed.

If that wasn't some fucking inauspicious sign from the gods, Dani didn't know what was.

TECHCORPS PROPRIETARY DATA, L2 SECURITY CLEARANCE

Recruit TE–815 received the highest score in the history of the program on his most recent aptitude assessment. His technological training will be accelerated, and every effort made to cultivate his loyalty. If the cognitive enhancement program progresses as planned, TE–815 is a prime candidate for the first cohort.

Recruit Analysis, September 2070

EIGHT

They'd chosen the warehouse to shelter because it was close to the spot where Knox had planned for them to hit the interstate again. But when they got to the elevated, sun-bleached stretch of road, Nina could see instantly that the massive concrete pillars that supported it were crumbling away. It wouldn't have been detectable from an overhead satellite shot, but only luck had kept the wide lanes from buckling already.

Back to square one—the close, claustrophobic two-lane back roads.

When they climbed back into the vehicles, Nina took over driving. She thought it might help, having something to focus on besides her own whirling, contentious thoughts. Instead, she spent the day staring at the truck ahead of theirs, berating herself because, even through the tinting, she could tell exactly which dark blob was Knox.

Just from the way he moved.

They passed through long-abandoned ghost towns, where every structure had been reclaimed by the Georgia jungle, swallowed by kudzu and young pines. They also drove through a few small enclaves where children played in dusty side yards and clean laundry fluttered on clotheslines.

They didn't stop at any of them. They had no business there, disrupting the fragile peace of people who only wanted to get by. As dusk began to deepen, the Silver Devils' truck rumbled past a larger settlement. The cluster of lights cut through the shadows and gloom, then receded behind them as they continued on to the darkness at the edge of town.

They pulled over at a movie theater. While everyone else dropped their gear and headed into the depths of the building to do recon, Nina lingered in the lobby. Some of the movie posters remained, locked behind plexiglass frames too high on the wall to be easily reached. Most had the staged, overly patriotic stiltedness of state-sponsored propaganda, but there were a few titles she recognized.

When she was growing up at the Franklin Center, movie night was a big deal. After a week of seemingly endless classes and training, the kids would crowd through the doors of the in-house theater with their drinks and snacks, jockeying for the best seats, even though every view was a good one. But it was something Nina's sisters had especially enjoyed.

Nina's gaze caught on one of the posters. If she closed her eyes, she could still see Zoey's animation as she raved about the love story at the heart of the movie. That memory sparked another one—Ava's pensive frown as she discussed whether the central theme of the story was the one the filmmakers had meant to convey, or something else entirely.

Nina's chest *hurt*. Nothing as vague or pretty as an ache. This was like a dropkick she hadn't seen coming, with no time to guard against the attack.

There was a reason she didn't watch many movies anymore.

Maya came back, having shed her pack and stripped down to her jeans and a strappy tank top. "The roof's a little iffy on the west side, but most of the building seems sturdy enough. The soundproofing is intact."

"It's fine," Nina said automatically. "Anyplace is fine."

Frowning, Maya stopped next to her and stared up at the poster. After a few moments, she murmured, "You okay?"

"Yeah, of course." Nina hefted her bag and tried to smile. "My ass is numb, and so is the rest of me. You'd think not running into trouble would be great, right? Turns out, it's boring as hell."

"We can survive a little boredom." Maya leaned her head against Nina's shoulder—a rare moment of physical affection. "This place is fucking surreal."

"How's that?"

"I mean, look at it." She gestured around at the cavernous lobby. The concessions displays had long since been broken and looted, but the signs offering to deliver snacks and drinks and even full meals straight to your seat remained. "All this, just to watch a vid you could see on your tablet or toss up onto the wall."

It wasn't the same, at least not in Nina's experience. She'd never gone to a proper theater, surrounded by a bunch of strangers, but she'd sat with all the other kids from the Center and felt . . . kinship. A camaraderie that had nothing to do with who managed the best time on the 10K run that day or scored the highest on a math test. For two hours, they weren't competitors, they were *friends*. Normal kids with normal lives.

They could even forget they were locked in a laboratory.

The pain in Nina's chest surged again, and she cleared her throat. "You've seen the little ones back home when they're really looking forward to whatever movie you're showing. They practically vibrate with excitement. There's an energy to it."

"True." Maya squeezed Nina's arm before pulling away. "I never got to watch movies with other kids. We had a five-foot vid wall right there in the penthouse, and I could watch any movie in the TechCorps databanks whenever I wanted. But I think the kids back home have more fun watching on the side of the warehouse than I ever did."

"There's one way to know for certain," Nina suggested. "If any of these screens are still standing, that is."

Maya's face lit with a familiar combination of excitement and determination. "I'll see what's left for equipment."

She rushed off, intent on her new task, and Nina set off to explore the building.

It was one level, except for the projection rooms and a single central office that rose high above the two-story entry, with shattered windows looking out over the musty lobby below. Nina tried to go up and look around, but the questionable structural integrity of the stairs dissuaded her.

Whatever was up there, it wasn't worth a broken leg.

Instead, she moved on, peeking in vast screening rooms and tiny cleaning closets. She avoided the wing where the roof had collapsed, passed by the open theater where almost everyone else had congregated—and realized that she wasn't just exploring.

She was looking for Knox.

The moment the thought formed in her mind, she rejected it, physically turning back to join the others. It didn't matter that she had legitimate reasons for needing to talk to Knox, eminently practical ones. Her desire to see him had nothing to do with logistics. It was all about the tingle of awareness she felt in his presence, or the way a few scant points of contact between them had left her aching.

If she talked to him, she might forgive him for barking at her the previous night. And she desperately needed her anger, because the only other things left were lust and temptation.

Both were luxuries she couldn't afford right now.

When she got back to the screening room, Dani was staring up at the projection booth, both hands on her hips. Climbing ropes dangled down the wall from the small aperture, and a quick check of the remaining people in the room told Nina exactly who was up there. "Maya and Conall found a projector, I assume?"

"Yep. Trying to get it operational now." A frown creased Dani's brow. "Where have you been?"

"Nowhere. Just looking around." Nina avoided her gaze. "I wanted to set up the camp shower, but I couldn't find a place to pump water. Looks like we'll have to wait another night."

"At least." Dani snorted. "Could have had our showers last night, if you hadn't been determined to save a few fish."

Nina shrugged.

"Doesn't matter anyway." Dani brushed the issue aside, as if she herself hadn't raised it. "With the kind of heat we're running into? It won't be long before the skies open up and give us all the water we could ever want, and then some."

The storms were definitely coming. Since they were traveling, and solid, safe shelter was by no means a guarantee, the thought should have worried Nina. But all she could think of was relief—from the heat, the humidity. From the electric pressure building in the air.

She smothered a laugh. There was something building, all right, but it had nothing to do with the weather. And the culmination of it had the potential to be even more dangerous than a lightning strike.

CLASSIFIED BEHAVIOR EVALUATION

Franklin Center for Genetic Research

Subject HS-Gen16-B has successfully breached the decoy server. She seems satisfied for now to decrypt the data she acquired, but I suggest immediate Code Yellow data compartmentalization for sensitive files.

And flag HS-Gen16-B's network activities.

Dr. Keller, March 2072

NINE

The door that led to the movie theater's roof was on its east side. The keypad that controlled the locking mechanism was useless without electricity, so Knox opened the door the less subtle way—with a firm grip and a heave of muscle.

Metal rusted by decades of neglect groaned and gave way. Knox left the door propped against the wall and stepped out into the humid night.

Gravel had covered the roof at one point. It spread out beneath a vast array of empty solar mounts, showing the paths of a dozen scavengers who'd scaled the building over the years and absconded with those precious panels.

This far from town, the night was dark. The stars shone bright enough to touch overhead, and it only took him a moment to use them to orient himself to face south. He withdrew his tablet and the tube that held his portable satellite dish.

An irritating necessity. Before they'd gone rogue, they'd had a permanent dish attached to their transport truck, wired into an onboard modem with a wireless signal amplifier. They'd had instant access to the Tech-Corps network and the CityNet from anywhere within line of sight of the vehicle.

And the TechCorps had had instant access to their current GPS coordinates at any moment.

The new uplink was anonymous. Clever, too. The cylindrical case broke apart to form a base and stand for the antenna within—a parabolic dish made of a composite fabric so light it could be folded down to the width of two fingers. When freed from the tube, it snapped open without a single wrinkle or crease. It only took a few minutes to assemble and connect the slim solar battery.

Knox still resented it. A few minutes was too long, given Nina's habit of wandering.

His tablet unfolded into a smooth screen that glowed softly in the darkness. Conall's irreverent sense of humor was to blame for the cartoonish outline of a ghost in the bottom corner of the tablet. Tapping it launched a simple window with a blinking white cursor.

Knox watched it, counting the blinks that seemed to keep time with his thudding heart. After eleven beats, text rolled across the screen.

connected to the ghost network . . .

Nobody knew how the GhostNet had started. Nobody knew how it persisted. The best network specialists in the TechCorps had spent years trying to snuff it out, but every Protectorate raid had yielded only abandoned buildings and baffled neighbors. Conall was convinced that its mysterious architect was someone high enough up in the TechCorps' tech admin ranks to protect their creation, but who that benefactor might be was a mystery.

It didn't matter. Black market dealers, criminals, and revolutionaries all over the city paid for access to untraceable communication. The fee was outrageous, but it came with a satellite uplink and a secret back door through the TechCorps' satellite system. Conall had tried to explain how it worked once, but the details didn't matter to Knox.

Only the access did.

He had one message waiting for him, a clickable IP address. He tapped it and waited for the connection to open.

It didn't take long.

Provide proof of acquisition.

Knox found the digital footage Conall had surreptitiously shot that morning of the three women loading gear into their truck and sent it to whoever was waiting. Within a minute, he received a reply.

Relay your GPS coordinates.

The demands were stark, unblunted by greetings or small talk. Not that he expected a kidnapper to be polite, but something about the terseness of the messages bothered Knox. Every sentence had been stripped down to the bare bones of communication. There was nothing to indicate who was on the other side—where they came from, who they were working for. Why they wanted Nina.

Nothing grated on Knox's nerves like incomplete data.

First provide proof of life, he sent back. *I want to talk to Luna.*

No response.

His heart was beating faster than that blinking cursor now. Finally, a picture appeared. If there had been anything left inside him but numbness, it would have broken his damn heart.

Luna's light brown skin was sallow, and her dark hair hung in tangled strands. The pink stripes framing her face were incongruous, too bright and cheerful for her tight expression. Smudged eyeliner enhanced dark circles under brown eyes that sparked with barely contained rage.

Desperately glad that Rafe wasn't here to see it, Knox took a steadying breath. She looked disheveled but unharmed, but there was no way of knowing how long ago the picture had been taken—or what could have happened to her in the meantime. *Not good enough. Video or the deal is off.*

Another endless pause. Knox was starting to hate that blinking cursor, along with the helplessness it implied. If the kidnapper called his bluff—if they retaliated against Luna—

The tablet beeped. *Incoming video request.*

He accepted it.

Luna's face appeared on his screen, looking the same as in the picture. The camera's focus was so tight he could only see a foot on either side of her head, nondescript concrete walls with no identifying features. The light came from behind whoever was holding the camera, shining brightly on Luna's face and casting everything else into shadow.

She squinted, half covering her eyes with one hand as she peered at the camera. "Knox?"

"Hey, Luna. Are you all right?"

"Typical Thursday night." She bared her teeth. "A few more armed men than usual. You?"

He added mercenaries to his mental list of things to worry about. "The typical number of armed men, more or less. We're coming to get you—"

"*No.*"

"We're coming to get you," he repeated firmly. "Conall needs you, Luna. And if you think anything could stop Rafe . . ."

She grimaced, but didn't argue. "Whatever they want, I'll repay you, Knox. I swear."

"I know you will—"

The screen plunged into darkness before he could finish, leaving her final words roiling through him. Her life alone would be worth sacrificing for. And Luna would save Conall. She'd save all of them.

She wouldn't be the one who owed a debt at the end of all of this.

Relay your GPS coordinates immediately.

The words flashed onto the screen. Still unsettled, Knox flipped to another tab to copy their location, then sent the information to the kidnapper. As soon as it had transmitted, the connection terminated.

Knox folded the tablet. He disassembled the satellite equipment, focusing on the minutiae of the activity to steady himself. The way the pieces of the cylindrical tube *clicked* together as he slid them back into place. The smooth texture of the parabolic dish as he rolled it tight enough to fit into its case. The warmth of the solar battery against his thigh after he slipped it into his pocket.

Maybe he could break every part of this mission down into pieces so small, he wouldn't have to think about the whole they formed. A mindless, efficient task list. Assemble. Disassemble. Drive. Walk. Eat. Sleep. Lie.

Betray.

No, Knox had always survived by being able to focus on the bigger picture as well as the details. There was no switching off his brain. No comfortable, unthinking complicity. He would always end up back here, fighting to convince himself he was okay with what he was doing. That it was worth it.

It wasn't. But he was going to do it anyway. *That* was the truth he needed to embrace.

He thought his mood couldn't get any fouler. But when he got back inside, a muffled *boom* rattled down the darkened hallway. He followed the sound to a theater with the door propped open and Gray standing just inside.

And a movie playing on the screen.

"How the hell did this happen?" Knox demanded as a spaceship zipped across the massive screen with a roar that echoed out of half the speakers with only a mild crackle.

"Conall and Maya got one of the old projectors running." The corner of his mouth tipped up. "Damn thing must have been too heavy to steal."

God knew scavengers had stripped away everything else. A few dozen reclining chairs were strewn across the risers that formed the floor of the theater, but the empty space showed there must have been five times as many to begin with. Bits of fabric clung to the wall, but most of it had been torn down. Even the carpet in front of the screen had been cut up in places.

Conall was perched halfway up the risers with Maya. The light from the screen illuminated their faces, both alight with pure enjoyment as the fictional space battle played out before them. Even Rafe, stretched out on Conall's other side with a rifle across his lap, seemed to be enjoying himself.

Nina and Dani were huddled on the opposite side of the theater, a mirror to Knox and Gray, though maybe it was his own guilt that painted their expressions as wary. "I don't know if spending time with them is a good idea," he murmured.

"Oh, it's terrible. Really fucking stupid."

It was. He thought he'd have more time before his crew's commitment to their present mission began to waver, but Maya was a grenade tossed into their precarious situation. She was young and guarded enough to provoke Rafe's incurable big-brother instincts, and brilliant and mechanically inclined enough to win Conall's rarely proffered respect.

Desire would have been easy. Well—not *easy*. One glimpse at Nina and the inevitable crackle of electricity under Knox's skin was enough to disprove that.

But desire was *manageable*.

Friendship? That would get them all killed.

"Nina asked me to find you, by the way. She suggested we all fend for ourselves for dinner." Gray shook his head. "What happened last night?"

Knox forced his gaze away from the woman in question. "I was an asshole. Because I'm *not* stupid."

"It's a fine line to walk. Piss her off too bad, and we'll all be fucked." Gray stroked his chin thoughtfully. "Want me to handle it?"

Knox's entire body tightened, and he tried to control his tone. He really did. "Handle what, exactly?"

"Distraction." Gray huffed out a low laugh. "Come on, man. I know I'm no Rafe, but that might work to our advantage. The lady seems to prefer her men a little rougher around the edges."

Gray had been the closest thing Knox had to a friend for nearly a decade, the first man he'd brought onto his team when he formed the Silver

Devils. The man he depended on to tell him ugly truths and have his back on increasingly dangerous missions.

Knox had never wanted to punch the bastard quite this much before.

"No." His voice sounded harsh to his own ears. Maybe he'd never had as much self-control as he flattered himself to possess. "I have a . . . connection to her. I understand how she thinks now. I can manage this."

Gray hummed and turned his attention back to the battle playing out on the screen. "I can't tell if you're lying to me or to yourself. That's new."

"I *have* to manage this." Their words were all but swallowed by the booming from the speakers, but he still lowered his voice. "I just talked to Luna. She's okay. For now."

That put Gray on edge. "You told her we're on our way, right?"

"Yes. It shouldn't be more than a few more days to the exchange coordinates if we can keep moving. We just have to keep our shit together and focus on her."

"A lot can happen in a few days," Gray muttered.

Conall's whoop of laughter rose above the sound of the movie. The truth of Gray's words sank like a rock to settle in Knox's gut as he watched Conall offer Maya half of his nutrition bar. She wrinkled her nose and crossed her hands in front of her in an X, the universal sign of *no deal* in the outlying neighborhoods. Then she picked up a silver packet and tossed it to him.

Knox couldn't tell what was in it in the dark. They seemed to have a million of those little packets, each one representing some friend or neighbor who had come to them for assistance and left a little bit of their harvest behind.

What would happen to those people when Nina didn't return? Someone would probably take over her building, someone without her idealistic streak. They'd charge for all the things Nina offered for free, and life in her corner of Atlanta would get a little harder, a little darker.

God, he was a son of a bitch. "Yeah," he agreed, embracing the bolt of pain. He almost missed the numbness, but doing something this shitty *should* hurt. "A lot can happen in a few days."

TECHCORPS PROPRIETARY DATA, L2 SECURITY CLEARANCE

Request to promote 66–615 to rank of lieutenant conditionally authorized, effective immediately. He should be assigned to a pragmatic captain who can assess if his persistent idealism is an affectation or a character flaw.

Recruit Analysis, January 2073

TEN

The oppressive heat didn't abate as they continued north. If anything, it grew heavier, sinking down until Nina felt like it was pressing her into the earth, and even the truck's air conditioning struggled to counter it. Rolling down the windows didn't help. Along with the heat came smothering humidity. It had to be hovering upward of 80 percent, the kind of level that turned everything into soup. The kind where even sweating didn't help, because the moisture just sat on your skin, refusing to evaporate into the already saturated air.

But, still, it didn't rain.

They stopped in the middle of nowhere this time, at a quaint, old-fashioned filling station with a small attached garage. It was the kind of place that used to be common in minuscule settlements that barely qualified as towns, a place for people to grab a drink or some gasoline, then catch up on the gossip while some affable man with his name embroidered on his shirt saw to that pesky Check Engine light.

The store had been cleared of anything useful, its shelves standing empty and sharp like the metal spines of long-dead creatures, stretching out into the darkness. The solar lanterns they brought in chased away the gloom, but the stifling stillness remained, closing in on Nina.

At least the stewing heat outside came with the occasional puff of wind. And it didn't feel like a tomb.

By unspoken agreement, everyone dropped their gear in a loose circle at the edges of the glow cast by the lanterns. But something had shifted the night before in the movie theater—instead of carefully separating themselves into *us* and *them,* her team and Knox's mingled together, with Maya carelessly dropping her gear beside Conall's as they carried on an animated conversation. Even Dani seemed heedless of where she placed her belongings, most of her attention focused on arguing with Rafe and Gray about—of all things—the transition metal molybdenum.

Only Knox kept his distance, but Nina was getting used to that. He had a routine for when they stopped to camp, a checklist he progressed through with deliberate thoroughness. Supplies inside. Interior surveyed. Tasks assigned to his men.

While everyone else scattered to secure the perimeter, Maya and Conall tried to get the central air going. It wasn't the most efficient use of their charged solar batteries, but Nina's shirt had been plastered to her back all fucking day. She would have sacrificed *blood* at that point for a little comfort. Maya and Conall poked at it, but the system was shot. Without maintenance, the rubber hoses had succumbed to dry rot, allowing the refrigerant to evaporate into nothingness.

Nina went in search of the next best thing—her shower. The water faucets in the small bathroom were dry, but she found a cistern out back. She set up the pump and the frame for the camp shower without looking too closely at the pool of rainwater in the huge concrete well. The pump's microfilter would take care of any contaminants, and she was better off not knowing what those contaminants might be.

She was nearly finished when Gray popped his head out the back door. "Do you need batteries for that?"

"Just one. Small capacity."

"I'll get it hooked up." He gestured. "Maya and I found a couple of industrial fans in the garage. We're working on them."

"Good." Nina rose and stretched her back, groaning when her spine cracked. "If you get them going, I'll marry you. Both."

He snorted. "Knox is out front. If you want to tell him about the shower."

She really didn't. But a quick pass through the filling station yielded no distractions. As promised, Maya was tinkering with a large, round fan that looked capable of moving blessedly copious quantities of air. Dani had set up the camp stove for a real meal. Conall was sweeping dust, debris, and more than a few dead bugs clear of the cement floor, while Rafe pilfered through an abandoned tool cabinet.

"I'll be outside if you need me," Nina murmured, but no one was listening.

Someone had rolled up the giant bay door at the front of the garage. A rhythmic thudding sound drifted in on the thick night air. Nina followed it around the side of the building and froze.

Knox was chopping wood. He'd stripped to the waist, and his sweat-beaded skin gleamed in the light from a magnetic solar lamp he'd affixed to a massive generator. As she watched, he brought the ax down in clean, precise strokes to split a massive log.

"What are you doing?" Her voice sounded too high to her own ears. Breathless.

The ax thudded into the stump he was using as a base. Knox straightened and turned, revealing his bare chest and vivid strokes of black ink over his heart. "It's a wood-burning generator. We can save the batteries."

On closer inspection, the bulk of the machine's mass was dedicated to the burner box, where Knox had already laid a fire. If it worked—and they kept it fed—it could power everything they needed. "That'll come in handy. There are a few fans inside, and I set up a shower out back."

He ran a hand through his damp hair, and her imagination took over. It was easier than breathing to picture his skin slicked with water instead of sweat, the rivulets sliding down the changing contours of muscle like the hands of a lover. But the fantasy stopped with her field of view, right there at his low-slung tactical belt.

Nina resented every square centimeter of cloth and leather.

"A shower would be nice."

"Hmm?" The statement dragged her from her lascivious thoughts, but not far enough. "Oh. Right. It won't be hot, but at this point, you'll probably wish it was cold."

His lips twitched.

Dammit. "Because of the weather, I mean."

"Mmm." He ran his fingers through his hair again with a grimace. "I hope this front breaks soon. I'm not used to having to sleep in conditions like this."

"It can't last forever." Having an entire discussion about the weather—nope, not awkward at all.

Nina was accustomed to awkward. Some of the other trainees in her classes at the Franklin Center had been much worse, barely able to carry on a conversation that wasn't centered on magazine capacities. A few had been uncomfortable with any kind of social interaction, while others were simply all business. They could debate the merits and drawbacks of various martial arts with capability and grace, they just didn't give a shit how your day was going.

This was something else entirely, a new, bewildering unease that had sprung up after that moment on the warehouse dock. Nina had pushed, Knox had snarled at her, and now they had . . . this.

There was a lesson somewhere in that. She just wasn't sure what it was.

She busied herself with gathering some of the wood he'd already cut, stacking it beside the generator's burner box, just so she wouldn't have to look at his gleaming chest. He retrieved the ax, but before he resumed chopping, the soft strains of a violin began to drift out of the open garage.

Knox paused, his brow wrinkling in confusion. "That doesn't sound like anything Conall listens to."

"No, that's Rowan, a musician from the neighborhood." The music swelled. "Maya's been working with them, making recordings of their compositions."

His eyes tightened. *Something* flashed across his face, gone too swiftly to recognize. He fixed his expression into pleasant curiosity, but all trace of warmth was gone. "Do you guys do a lot of that? Record new things?"

"We wouldn't be proper archivists if we spent all our time digging up the past. People didn't stop creating after the Flares." She dropped the last piece of wood on the pile. "We didn't stop *living.* That's an important thing to remember, I think."

"Is that how you define living?"

"Not for everyone." Not for her. She didn't create anything. Her job—her life—was about preservation, making sure the creations of others persisted. "But for people in general, for society? Yes."

Knox leaned down for another log and set it in place. He split it in two with one smooth stroke of the ax, and she really had to stop watching him do this. "Right now? I can't see past keeping my men breathing. Might be nice to think they can have more someday."

Assurances hovered on the tip of her tongue, automatic and empty, considering Conall's worsening condition. So Nina remained silent, closing her eyes to let Rowan's music wash over her instead. The rhythm lulled her, and every lilting note spoke of hope, of dreams.

She wondered if Knox could hear it, too.

A harsh mechanical whir interrupted the song, followed by a whoop of sheer, exultant victory. "Sounds like the gods have blessed us tonight."

The firm set of his mouth softened into something that was almost a smile. "Go cool off. I'll finish up."

Her heart stuttered. "In a minute. First, I owe you an apology. For what happened on the loading dock."

"No, you don't. I was being an asshole."

"Yes, you absolutely were. But so was I." She shrugged. "You don't owe me anything. Least of all your innermost thoughts."

He flexed his fingers around the ax handle. "You know them, for the most part. Getting Conall safe. Getting all of them safe. I can't—there isn't anything else. They trust me."

She could almost taste the lie, and it made the roof of her mouth itch. Garrett Knox had plenty going on in that head of his—but none of it was her business. She *had* to remember that. "Okay. I'll see you inside."

By the time Nina made it into the garage, both fans were running, and she flashed Maya and Gray a well-deserved thumbs-up as she took her place in front of one of the huge metal drums. She knew the blast of air was no cooler than the ambient temperature, but it felt like *heaven* as it flowed over her skin and through her hair.

Maya grinned at her from in front of the second fan. "Think those mechanical manuals have paid off yet?"

"In spades." Nina lifted the tail of her thin tank top so the airflow could reach more bare skin and sighed. "I promised Gray I'd marry you both if you pulled this off. Will he hold me to it?"

Maya's gaze drifted to the far side of the garage, where Gray had shed his jacket, but nothing else. He seemed unbothered by the heat. By *anything*, for that matter. "I don't know. Maybe? He doesn't talk much. I think I'm going to downgrade him from Gothic villain to uncommunicative brooder."

"Probably a solid plan."

"Don't tell Dani. She'll get *ideas*."

The lights flickered to life before Nina could reply, casting the oil-stained concrete floor and dirt-filled corners of the garage into unpleasantly stark relief.

And illuminating Knox as he materialized out of the darkness.

He was as rough around the edges as the gas station. Sweaty and dirt-smudged, with little chips of wood clinging to his tight jeans and ash from the fire darkening his fingers. One hand curled around the handle of the ax balanced recklessly on his bare shoulder, and that shoulder—

The light revealed scars that hadn't been visible outside. Most were healed slashes, but there were a few bullet holes and even one small burn. He was a fighter. He wore the proof of that on his skin.

And there was *so much skin*.

Nina shivered, and immediately decided to blame it on the cooling effect of convection.

"Okay," Maya murmured. "Maybe I'm upgrading *him* to Gothic villain."

Smart move, kid. Nina tried to say it out loud, but her tongue felt like it was glued to the roof of her mouth. Knox was still standing there, exuding enough sex appeal to power all their equipment without the generator's help.

He leaned the ax against a metal rack that had once held tires. Nina edged over to give him room in front of the fan, though she kept her gaze carefully averted as a last-ditch attempt to save her sanity from the vagaries of her libido. It didn't work. She could feel his presence like a physical touch, as if every inch of empty space between them simply didn't exist.

And her body reacted accordingly. Goose bumps rose on her arms, the back of her neck prickled, and her skin felt heavy and tight at the same time, like the tense milliseconds just before a full-body shudder.

A dozen conflicting urges tore through her, each one more primal than the last. She needed to start a fight. She needed to find someone to fuck. She needed to *run*.

She needed that cold shower more than ever.

CLASSIFIED BEHAVIOR EVALUATION

Franklin Center for Genetic Research

Subject HS-Gen16-A completed the advanced survival training test. There exists, however, some disagreement over whether she earned a passing grade. Her orders were to return to base camp within the allotted time, assuming acceptable losses. But rather than abandon an injured subordinate, she carried him over nineteen miles of mountain terrain, further damaging her own fractured ankle. When I questioned her, she said no loss was acceptable if she could prevent it while still satisfying her mission objective.

Her belligerence regarding her orders is unacceptable. She has therefore been remanded to solitary custody, to remain for a period no shorter than three weeks.

Dr. Baudin, December 2073

ELEVEN

Gray gripped the steering wheel and peered through the windshield at the motel's pitted, dingy façade. "You sure about this?"

Knox didn't have an answer. Not an honest one, anyway. He *wasn't* sure about this. He'd weighed risk against danger for the last hour of the drive, periodically using the rearview mirror to assess the angry storm clouds roiling in the distance and the terrifying pallor of Conall's face.

The storm had been moving slowly, but it was almost on them now. A mean storm, a treacherous one. It would split the sky and let loose a deluge, and the fact that it was slow moving only made it more perilous. Most of the shelters they'd stayed in recently would be hail-strewn and flooded by morning.

They needed real walls and a solid roof. And Conall needed a bed. Knox had always known that the techie's biochemical modifications emphasized sharpening his mind and enhancing his ability to rapidly process information, but he hadn't realized how that tiny difference would manifest once their implants started misfiring.

Conall was a heartbeat away from neural overload now, all the time. Even while he slept, his eyes shifted restlessly beneath his closed lids— though even that was rare. Without sedatives, Conall wasn't sleeping much anymore.

There were no safe moves left. Just varying levels of risk.

Knox stared at the motel. It might have been nice before the Flares. Each room had a balcony with a few rusty chairs, and a pool containing six inches of sludge sat between the two wings of the building. Neglect had run it down, but lights shone through the curtains of most of the rooms, and plenty more spilled through the glass doors of the dirty little lobby.

It was a dump. It was full of people. And it was better than a tent in a thunderstorm. "You guys wait here," he said, and slipped from the truck.

Thunder rolled in the distance. It was still swelteringly hot, so humid that sweat slicked his skin before he'd taken two steps. The evening air pressed down on him, and his joints twinged like he was an old-timer in a bar bitching about his weather knee.

Nina was already standing outside the motel office, her hands in her pockets, staring up at the sign proclaiming vacancies. "Ready to turn on the charm, Captain?"

She sounded dubious. Probably wondered why he wasn't sending Rafe in to do battle with his pretty brown eyes and perfect smile.

Charm wasn't Knox's best weapon, but he had enough for an emergency.

It took a second to sink into it. To push all the reasons he shouldn't smile at her into a dark corner and slam the door. After that, it was easy. The smile curved his lips without effort, because she was the kind of woman he'd always liked, back when he had the luxury of liking people. Dangerous, smart, and earnest.

Knox pulled open the door for her, unable to hold back a relieved exhalation when a puff of cool air hit him, and gestured her inside with a playful bow.

With a roll of her eyes, she shook her head. "Smartass."

When she edged past him, her arm brushed his with a static charge more dangerous than the coming storm. A lock of her hair tickled his cheek. He inhaled the impossible floral scent of it and allowed himself one reckless, dangerous moment to wonder what the masses of it would feel like wrapped around his fingers.

He didn't have time for fantasies. The old man behind the desk was straightening up, one hand still behind the counter in a way that screamed *I'm pointing a gun at you.*

If Nina noticed—and she *must* have noticed—she didn't let it show. "The sign outside says you have rooms available."

The man's gaze bounced back and forth between the two of them. "This isn't that kind of place."

She arched an eyebrow. "Not the kind of place where people sleep?"

Sleeping wasn't the implication under the old man's scowl. If the stakes had been a little lower, Knox might have asked the old bastard which of them was supposed to be paying the other, and for what kind of sex, but he had a feeling he wouldn't like the answer either way. And he couldn't afford to knock the man's teeth out.

The proprietor leaned to one side, peering around them and out the window. "Those your trucks?"

The man's shifted position made his ragged T-shirt sleeve ride up, revealing a lovingly cared-for tattoo, the black ink still as vivid as the green and blue at its heart—a stylized rendering of the earth. The symbol of Clean Earth First, a radical ecological group that had transformed into a fierce militia during the energy crisis. What had started out as bloodless corporate warfare had devolved into a messy civil war that the faltering federal administration had tried to deny was happening.

Not many Clean Earth Firsters had come out of the 2030s alive. The man in front of them had to be a tough son of a bitch who had seen not only violence, but the bone-grinding horror of all-out war.

And no one with that tattoo was likely to be a fan of the TechCorps.

Knox inclined his head. "Yep, our trucks. We're headed north. Not looking for trouble, just some solid walls and a roof before that storm breaks. We can pay credits or trade. I've got solar chargers, a water filter . . . Real cigarettes and bourbon."

After a long moment of tense silence, the man shrugged. "I like money. And bourbon." He reached beneath the counter and retrieved an old-fashioned key on a worn plastic fob. "It's one-fifty for the night."

"We need more than one room," Nina countered. "At least four."

"I got three. Take 'em or leave 'em."

Nina sighed, then turned to Knox. "You guys can have two. We'll be okay in one."

"That's fine." Knox moved slowly, aware that the gun under the counter was still in the man's reach, and placed several TechCorps chits on the counter. "I'll throw the bourbon in extra."

"Extra, my ass. This is a discounted rate." The proprietor reached for the chits.

Nina swept them up first and shoved them back at Knox. While the man sputtered, she laid out three credit sticks. "Three hundred for three rooms. Clean credits. You could spend them on the moon, if you could manage to get there."

The old man stared at the credit sticks, but he didn't argue. Instead, he slapped his hand down to cover them before anyone could take them back.

Every city that had survived the Flares had their own form of currency these days, but you could only reliably expect to spend them *in* those cities. TechCorps credits were better. Since the conglomerate sprawled across the Southeast, you could usually use TechCorps chits to buy fresh fish in the insular communities that dotted the shores of the Gulf of Mexico or pay for a night of sin and self-indulgence up in D.C. as easily as you could buy goods in Atlanta.

Usually.

Only one type of money had more value—clean credits backed by the powerful trade association that operated out of Baton Rouge and dominated the Mississippi with their river boats and barges. Those credits could get you anything, anywhere, no hassle and no questions asked.

The man pulled out a reader and checked the balance on each stick. Apparently satisfied, he retrieved two more keys and tossed them on the counter. "No food. No ice. We got running water. You want anything else, get it at the bar down the road."

"That'll do." Knox swept up all three keys and turned toward the door, waving Nina out in front of him. As soon as they were back outside in the thick night air, he cast her a look. "What happened to charming?"

"Roll over too easy, and you look desperate. Desperate means no other options. No other options means trouble." She grinned. "Plus, I don't like being cheated."

Knox bit back a snort, but the urge to laugh died when he glanced at the trucks.

"Hello, Lieutenant Knox."

For a horrible moment, Knox wondered if full neural degradation had crept over him. Surely he was hallucinating the grizzled old soldier wielding a sawed-off shotgun and a smug smile. There was no reason for a piece of his past like Sergeant Benjamin Boyd to be standing in this tiny speck of nowhere, eyeing Knox like a prize that had fallen into his lap.

But a hallucination wouldn't have dragged their teams from their vehicles. The mercenaries gathered in a loose circle around them weren't pointing their guns at Nina's team or the Devils, but tension crackled through the air, and it wasn't from the gathering storm. Knox could feel the potential for violence like a sudden gust of wind.

Then Boyd's gaze slid to Nina, and Knox's shock splintered. He stepped between them, dragging Boyd's attention back to him. "Actually, it's Captain now. A lot can change in seven years."

"Right, right. Command of your own squad." Boyd's eyes gleamed. "How'd that work out for you?"

The mockery underlying the question might not be evident to Nina, but Knox felt it in his bones. He and Boyd had always scraped each other's tempers, all the way back to Knox's earliest days in the Protectorate. At first, the friction had been the natural result of Knox's idealism clashing with Boyd's pragmatic cynicism. But as the Protectorate slowly beat the hope out of Knox, Boyd's resentment had shifted to something deeper.

Neither of them had *fit* in the Protectorate. Neither of them liked the job, but Knox had figured out a way to play the game, climb the ranks, and carve out a little bit of control. Boyd, on the other hand, had never been able to stomach taking an order he disliked. His attitude and his mouth had held him back while Knox excelled.

Until seven years ago, when a mission had gone sideways and Boyd had turned up presumed dead.

Seven years. Seven fucking years, without the benefit of implant maintenance.

Fuck, Boyd *should* be dead.

The fact that he wasn't jackknifed hope through Knox, along with apprehension. Boyd was fully capable of denying him answers out of spite. Knox had to be careful, play this just right.

And, like Nina had said, he couldn't let Boyd sense his desperation.

Planting his feet, Knox hooked his thumbs through his belt and gave the man a lazy once-over. The years hadn't been kind to him—he looked *old*. Plenty of Protectorate soldiers looked a decade or more younger than their biological ages, thanks to the benefits of constant metabolic maintenance and cutting-edge medical care.

Boyd looked like the decades had caught up with him—and then run another lap around him. Deep grooves bracketed his eyes, his skin was sallow and leathery, and his hair had gone almost completely silver. There was a glassy, glittery look to his eyes, the look of a man on his third or fourth whiskey of the evening. Maybe a man who chased away his morning hangover with another bottle.

But he still looked tough, lean and wiry and wound tight enough to turn this situation violent over any slight, real or imagined. Knox dragged his gaze back up to the man's eyes and quirked an eyebrow. "You look better than I expected."

Boyd stared back at him. "Are you finished?"

"You wanted me to loosen up. Isn't that what you always said?"

"This isn't a social call, Knox. I'm not here to catch up with an old training buddy." He paused. "It's business."

"What sort of business?"

"A proposition for you and your boys." He gestured for one of his men to take his shotgun, then held out both open hands as he stepped closer to Knox. "I got a little place down the road—drinks, girls, the usual. But fights are the real moneymaker."

The shape of the trap clarified. Boyd wanted ringers for his dirty fights, men who could take enough of a beating to make it look good before going down hard—or putting someone else in the dirt. "Doesn't seem fair, does it?"

"Fair's just like everything else—open to interpretation." Boyd shrugged. "I'll give you a decent cut, for old times' sake. We're talking about a lot of money here."

"I'm not interested in money." Knox held the man's gaze. "We need a decent night's sleep, not a beating."

"Yeah?" Boyd glanced over, presumably at Conall, who was likely ashen-faced and swaying on his feet. "I don't think any amount of shut-eye is gonna fix your boy, there."

Knox didn't let himself look. The sight would only stoke his anger. "And you think a fistfight will?"

Wordlessly, Boyd jerked up his sleeve. The inside of his scarred forearm bulged where something had been implanted beneath the skin. Knox watched, uneasy, as the sick green glow of a flashing light bled through the man's flesh.

"It's not pretty," Boyd admitted. "It burns. Itches, too. But it gets the job done."

Knox tightened his fists until his nails dug into his palms. A bootleg implant was a blunt instrument, flooding the body with drugs to mitigate the most common effects of degradation without precision or discernment. The sustained release was easier on the body than just pumping your veins full of the shit people traded on the street, but not by much. And not forever.

No wonder Boyd looked like a man who'd climbed into a bottle. The bottle had climbed into *him*.

As a long-term solution, it made Knox's skin crawl. But for a couple of weeks, to hold them over if they started to fall apart . . .

He jerked his chin at the implant. "Where'd you get it?"

"I know a guy. Are you in?" Boyd's wide grin made it clear he knew the answer already. "Two fights should do it. Don't want to get greedy."

For Conall, Knox would fight. Hell, for Conall, he'd lose, if Boyd demanded it. "How long do those things last?"

"Two weeks, give or take."

"We'll do it for ten of them."

Boyd laughed. "I can't even get my hands on ten at once, Knox. Two."

"Four," he countered. "For four, I'll fight. And I'll get one of my men to do it, too."

Boyd pretended to consider it, then nodded. "That's fair. You better put on a damn good show, though."

"You want us to win or lose?"

"Haven't decided yet." Boyd turned away, and his men fell out of formation. "My place is just down the street—the Loaded Barrel. Be there in an hour. Bring your ladies along, too."

"It's a deal."

Boyd's satisfied grin as he looked back was far from comforting. He melted into the dark, his men like shadows following him, and Knox turned to his team.

Gray let out a low growl. Conall leaned against Rafe, who was holding him up with one arm braced around him.

Rafe's dark eyes were furious and determined. "I'll do it."

"Or we could split." Dani already had a knife in her hand, running her thumb along the hilt as if the repetitive motion soothed her. "With a short pit stop to stab your old friend in the face and cut that implant out of his arm."

"*Dani.*"

"What, Nina? Some people need stabbing, and that guy's a prime example. I can tell."

"She's not wrong." Knox rubbed a hand over his face. If they still had

Mace, he might have risked it. Though if they still had Mace, Conall never would have gotten this bad. "But we don't know how long he's had that thing implanted already, and we can't exactly stop and ask for a medic on our way out of town if we cut our way through him and his men."

Nina stepped closer and pitched her voice low. "Will he keep his word? Come through on the deal if you and Rafe fight?"

"Probably. He can't risk us ratting him out to the Protectorate. He'd have to abandon everything he's built here."

Maybe she wasn't as idealistic as she seemed, because she shook her head. "That's not what I'm asking. Still, we'll be there. We can watch your back."

She was *worried* about him.

It was a terrible time for guilt to surface, but it broke over Knox like a rogue wave. He weathered it. Wallowed in it. Maybe the right move would be to snatch at the shallow hope these implants offered, consign his men to the desperate half-lives of addicts, always two weeks from dying without their next fix.

But even if he did, there was still Luna, waiting somewhere out there for a rescue that would be a thousand times more dangerous if he showed up without her ransom.

Actually, maybe this was the perfect time for guilt. He was the exact sort of scum who should have to endure the punishing brutality of an underground fight.

He might even enjoy it.

**TECHCORPS PROPRIETARY DATA,
L2 SECURITY CLEARANCE**

Recruit 66–793 is our top sniper. His marksmanship is unmatched. We are aware of Behavior's continuing concerns about his emotional reticence, but we submit that if fourteen years of aggressive monitoring has uncovered neither troubling pathologies nor questions of loyalty, the issue should be considered resolved pending further developments.

He's an extremely useful tool, Birgitte. Stop trying to throw him away because he creeps you out.

Internal Memo, May 2075

TWELVE

The Loaded Barrel looked like every other rough-and-tumble roadhouse Nina had ever seen. The floors were scuffed and sticky, littered with cigarette butts, and the scents of cheap liquor and even cheaper perfume hung heavy in the air, mingling with the smoke.

A massive chain-link cage dominated one side of the room, built around a raised platform with a concrete floor. Bare bulbs hung above it, illuminating the interior with harsh light almost bright enough to wash out the rust-colored bloodstains on the rough concrete below.

Almost.

Two men were fighting in the cage, the din from the crowd drowning out the sounds of fists against flesh and cries of pain. More fighters were lined up to enter the cage, stripped to the waist and vibrating with restless energy—or drugs. Some had medical patches affixed to their torsos or upper arms, recognizable from a distance only by the vague outline of the TechCorps logo. One man even had a continuous injection pod on the side of his throat, an oval disc meant to flood his bloodstream with a steady supply of . . . something.

Judging from his twitching, it wasn't loaded with sedatives.

On the other side of the room, near the busy bar, Boyd had settled into a corner booth with a drink in one hand and a redhead in the other. Several heavily armed men flanked the booth, taking bets and paying out winnings, while more men looked on.

"Even the armed guards have armed guards," Dani muttered. "I guess killing Boyd's out of the question, after all."

"I bet we could do it," Rafe replied, his usual humor edged with something darker. "You take the dozen on the left, and I'll take the dozen on the right."

It sounded like a joke—mostly—so Nina answered in kind. "Not until we have what we came for."

Knox was studying the bar in careful, deliberate silence. His gaze drifted around the room, taking in everything from the spectators to the exits, breaking down the space into quadrants. He kept his expression carefully neutral, but she could see the moment he came to the same tactical conclusion she'd already reached.

If this went sideways, they'd be in a world of hurt.

But all he said was, "Keep an eye on Conall for me."

"Hey." Nina touched his arm, and he tensed as he turned to face her. "We have an advantage, Knox. That asshole looked straight at my team, and all he saw was arm candy. If he starts any shit, he'll regret it. I promise."

"I know." He lowered his voice. "If something happens . . . you and Dani get Conall and Maya out. Gray will help. Rafe and I will buy you time."

He had to know her better than that by now. "Uh-huh."

Before Knox could argue, Boyd lifted a hand and beckoned. Rafe and Knox headed over, and Nina went back to cataloguing exit routes to quell her rising sense of unease.

There was something brewing in the crowd, a lust for violence that cranked higher when one of the men in the cage went down. Someone passed his opponent a crude wooden baton through the cage wall, and even the raucous din couldn't drown out the sound of the savage beating that followed.

Next to Nina, Maya went rigid. "Are they fighting to the *death*?"

Nina didn't think so. It would be a hell of a stupid way to make money—then again, Boyd had done nothing so far to convince her he was particularly smart. "Put in your earbuds, okay? You don't need to—"

The bar's patrons quieted as Boyd rose. For a moment, he remained silent, relishing the attention, then he waved his hand. "Break it up. And find the medic."

The hush broke into whoops and jeers, then lapsed into laughter and conversation as the spectators broke away and surged toward the bar. As they cleared, Nina got a good look at the carnage in the cage. The defeated fighter lay sprawled in a spreading pool of blood, the wooden club abandoned at his side. More blood and spittle flecked the concrete around him, along with what looked like a few of his teeth.

Knox and Rafe headed back, moving against the tide of customers determined to grab a drink before the next fight. Nina met them halfway. "What did he say?"

"We're fighting to win. Rafe is up next," Knox said. "And then I'm fighting Boyd's champion."

"What, you don't rate the champ?" Dani patted Rafe's shoulder. "It's all right. We'll work on it. I'll help you."

Rafe responded by stripping his T-shirt over his head. His dog tags followed with a jingle, and he handed all of it to Dani. "Hold these. I'll be back for them."

She rolled her eyes and shoved the bundle of fabric at Gray before prodding Rafe in the chest. "They fight dirty, but so do you. How long does asshole over there want you to drag it out?"

"He wants a show. I'm gonna give him one." Rafe closed his hand over Dani's with a wicked smile. "Don't worry, babycakes. I'll be fine."

She snatched her hand away. "Guard your head, and don't get cocky. The big ones like you always go down hardest."

"Yeah, I do. Every chance I get."

Dani muttered something unintelligible under her breath and brushed past him, heading in the direction of the bar.

Rafe shrugged one big shoulder. "She doesn't get my sense of humor."

"Because this isn't funny." Knox gripped Rafe's arm, his expression tense. "Don't take risks just for Boyd and his fucking show."

The steel in Knox's order seemed to subdue Rafe. "I won't," he promised. "I got this."

"I know you do."

The referee—if you could even call him that—banged a pipe against a corner post of the cage, and it almost sounded like a bell. Rafe headed toward the cage door, leaving Knox to rub a hand over his face.

He was more worried than he had let Rafe know, and Nina didn't blame him. Sometimes, luck just wasn't on your side, and even the best training and the greatest advantages couldn't save you from defeat.

Still . . . "It's not a battle," she whispered. "It's just a cage match."

"I know." Knox rubbed at the knuckles of his right hand and lowered his voice. "I can handle the danger in a fight, but it's hard to just stand here and . . . watch one of them get hurt."

If it hadn't been tactically inadvisable, Dani would have volunteered to fight. And then Nina would have been the one helplessly watching someone under her protection march into danger. "I understand. But you have to trust him. *And* yourself."

"I do."

Two little words, but they prickled over her skin with the metallic scrape of a lie. "Knox—"

"Boyd hates me." Knox watched Rafe climb into the cage, his eyes shrouded. "But I don't think he's smart enough to use Rafe against me. Boyd has never cared about anyone else as much as he does himself, so he can't fathom it."

Sadly, you didn't have to understand something like that in order to use it as a weapon. From what Nina could see, Boyd understood the situation perfectly—if he really wanted to hurt Knox, he'd hurt the rest of the Silver Devils. But the man seemed strangely reluctant to do it. Perhaps, buried somewhere beneath all the greed and bravado, Boyd actually possessed a shred of honor.

Or maybe they just hadn't yet reached the part of the night when Boyd decided to exact his *real* revenge.

Rafe's opponent peeled away from the crowd of fighters to a chorus of cheers. He may not have been Boyd's champion fighter, but he was clearly well known—and well liked by the audience. He stood tall, almost as tall as Rafe, though his build was lean, with a wiry kind of hardness. He was pale, with a bit of a sunburn across his shoulders and the top of his shaved head.

He didn't seem to have any of the modifications some of the other fighters boasted, not until he turned around and Nina caught sight of the continuous injection pod on his back. It sat squarely between his shoulder blades, right over his spine.

Nina shuddered. The pods were typically used for subcutaneous or intramuscular injection, with relatively short, slim needles. From what she knew of human anatomy, it would take a longer, more robust needle to penetrate the spinal cord for drug delivery. The kind that would hurt.

This guy didn't seem to mind the pain.

Rafe wasn't bothered. He lazily stretched one arm across his body, smiling at his opponent's audible snarl.

With another ringing crash of the pipe, the match began. Rafe and the bald fighter circled slowly, sizing each other up. Both had impeccable form, stances that hovered right on the line between loose and ready.

The stranger took the first swing, but Rafe landed the first hit, a quick jab that caught his opponent on the chin and snapped his head back. The man recovered quickly, getting in a jab of his own before taking another blow to the side of his head.

Nina started to breathe a little.

Beside her, Knox's tight stance began to ease. "Whatever he's on, he's not as good as Rafe."

Before Nina could reply, the man in the cage surged toward Rafe again. Lightning quick, he struck, and struck *hard*. The blow sent Rafe spinning, and he slammed against the chain-link wall of the cage with a force that rattled Nina's bones.

Knox went taut, as if consciously tightening every muscle was the only thing keeping him from recoiling in horror—or diving into the cage to intervene. Stricken, Nina reached out.

She half expected him to pull away, but he let her wrap her fingers around his. For a mere moment, a fraction of a heartbeat, he squeezed her hand.

Nina's stomach clenched.

His fingers were warm and strong around hers. Tension sparked from the contact, and the noise in the room faded a little, replaced by a low buzz in her ears. She'd thought that touching him before, with lust driving her, was affecting. But this, the intimacy of comfort, was a hundred times worse.

Or better, depending on how you looked at it.

Rafe rebounded, swinging his fists toward his opponent. They circled and jabbed, testing each other. The first time Rafe dropped his guard and took another solid hit, it looked deliberate.

The next three . . . didn't.

"What the hell is he doing?" Gray muttered.

"Making it look good," Knox growled. "Letting this guy kick his ass. I'm going to kill him."

Maya made a harsh, choked sound in the back of her throat. "I can't—" The words cut off abruptly, and she turned and darted off into the crowd.

Nina's stomach twisted again, this time with worry. "Maya, wait!"

Gray shook his head. "I'll go after her. You two watch the fight."

He melted into the throng of bodies, and Nina bit back a curse as she turned back toward the cage. More than anything, she wanted to rush to Maya's aid. But sometimes it seemed like Maya tried so hard to save face in front of Nina, to be strong for her, that she couldn't express herself, or even feel what she needed to feel. She was so busy *being okay* that she was never truly all right.

Maybe Gray could give her the space she needed without smothering her with overprotective concern.

Nina squared her shoulders, planted her feet, and fixed her gaze on Rafe's bloody face. She couldn't be the one to help Maya right now, but she had a whole different job to do. Soon, Knox would be the one in that cage.

And Nina had to be ready for any dirty shit Boyd might pull.

MAYA

Maya couldn't breathe.

Her earbuds blasted music into her ears. The FlowMac Pop revival of the 2060s had produced a lot of music with thudding bass and catchy rhythms, all with lyrics so cliched and empty that Maya had seen bar fights start over the question of whether the songs even qualified as music. After all, they'd been composed by retro AI software trained on music produced by then-modern AI software, a bit of recursive nonsense that Maya had always loved.

Purists swore that the older software roughened up the pristine edges of the music produced by newer algorithms. Critics retorted that making the music *worse* didn't make it less rote. Art was supposed to convey the soul, and so far no one had created an algorithm with one of those.

Maya mostly agreed with the critics. But that was precisely why she loved the safe, pounding beat and the empty lyrics that melted away into meaningless sound. FlowMac Pop was predictable. It drowned out the noise of the world, it didn't surprise her, and it never overwhelmed her with unexpected, unwanted emotion.

Sometimes, the last thing she could tolerate was being forced to *feel*.

The air in the bar stank of sweat and blood and cheap moonshine. Not being able to breathe might have been desirable, except that her body was screaming for oxygen. Every shallow breath she dragged in made the panic churning in her gut worse. She reached for her watch, her fingers finding the tiny volume button on the side from tactile memory.

Already as loud as it would go. Her earbuds could reduce the crowd's shouts to a background rumble, but the sound of fists striking flesh seemed to slice straight through her. The barest hint of it was all it took for the memories to bloom, bright and vivid and terrifying.

She could feel the rope around her wrists. The scrape of it on her skin. She could still smell blood, but the sharp, antiseptic scent of the regeneration drugs and the metallic chill of the penthouse's air conditioning overrode the filth of the bar.

Most of the time, Maya's memories were of sound. She could replay any moment in her life like pulling up a track on her earbuds. But the bad ones, the ones that hurt—

Oh, she could feel those. See them. *Taste* them.

And she couldn't *breathe*.

Something brushed her left shoulder, and she lashed out. Too late, her scrambled brain identified the large form next to her as Gray, but she couldn't pull her punch fast enough. Her fist crashed into his arm, leaving her fingers aching from the impact.

"Hey, now." His mouth formed the words, though she couldn't hear him through the upbeat drone of music in her ears. "It's okay."

Maya fumbled for the Mute button on the side of her watch. The sound of the fight roared up around her, echoing with all the memories she was trying to escape. The press of bodies around her constricted until bright little lights flickered at the edges of her vision.

She didn't care that Gray was brooding and dark and possibly the most dangerous man in the fucking bar. She cared that he was big and scary enough to clear a path to the door. She gripped his jacket, the leather improbably soft under her clutching fingers. "Out. Get me out."

"Come on." He grasped her arm and led her in the opposite direction—no doubt toward the nearest exit. He was a man who only operated efficiently, as if he didn't know any other way. All that deliberate precision set her nerves on edge most of the time.

Right now, it was glorious.

So were those dark, Gothic villain eyes. People who turned to snarl at them took one look at Gray's face and skittered out of the way like rats scenting a predator. Maybe it was the flickering lights encroaching on her vision or the lack of oxygen, but hysterical laughter tried to claw its way out of Maya's throat.

Shit, it must be nice to look as dangerous as you were.

Gray finally reached a dented steel door Maya hadn't even seen because it was covered with scratched and peeling paint the same shade as the wall. He pushed through it, and a hot gust of wind hit her in the face.

The night was swampy as hell. She stumbled out into it, grateful even as it closed on her skin, humid and claustrophobic. The heavy door swung shut behind them, dampening the sounds of the bar to a distant, blessedly unintelligible roar. She inhaled until her lungs burned and let it go in a gushing breath.

The pinpricks of light receded. Maya slumped back against the soot-stained brick wall, wanting desperately to slide to the ground but terrified of what sort of trash, broken bottles, and fluids she might land in.

She braced for the inevitable—more words that would wash over her, sinking into her brain like nails driving this moment home. But when she forced her eyes open, Gray was simply . . . *watching*. Not leering or staring. Even the number of steps between them seemed like more of his efficiency—close enough to catch her if she tipped over, but far enough away to give her space.

Weird. He was so damn weird.

Maya rubbed at her wrist. The phantom pain had faded, but prickles remained just under her skin. Her heart still pounded like she was trapped. The memories hovered, an itch at the base of her skull. It wasn't this bad in the heat of a fight, when she had adrenaline pumping through her veins. But hovering, frozen, *listening* to the sound of fists slamming into flesh—

We can beat him until he's nothing but pulp. We can grind his bones to dust. And then we'll rebuild him and start from the beginning. The only way to stop it is to open your mouth—

Torture didn't work on data couriers. Maya didn't know exactly what the TechCorps had done to her brain—a fact which was its own sort of nightmare—but excess physical pain short-circuited her memory. If it lasted too long, her brain would shut down entirely, neatly locking away all the precious, secret intel she contained.

But that wouldn't stop them from torturing people she loved.

—give us the names and we'll stop—

—we'll stop hurting him—

"Say something," Maya gasped, bracing her clenched fists on her legs. "I don't care what, just—"

"Storm's coming." Gray interrupted her with a steady, unhurried cadence, as if he'd been planning to speak instead of responding to her plea. "At least we'll be indoors tonight."

Dani was right about his voice. The rest of Gray might be scary and cold, but his voice was like warm molasses, dark and sweet. The words didn't even bother her, because they were harmless and nonthreatening. Nothing she'd regret remembering forever, and worth wrapping herself in the blanket of his voice. "Keep going."

"I don't mind storms," he continued. "Some of the guys from the Protectorate have problems with the thunder, but it doesn't bother me. One thing I don't like, though? How everything gets really calm and still just before it hits. It's eerie."

She clung to the smooth, steady words. Her hysterically inappropriate sense of humor resurfaced, and she closed her eyes and imagined how much she could make if she talked him into letting her record him while he read some books. Hell, maybe her wheelbarrow full of money had been standing right here the whole time.

"What's even worse is the eye of a storm." Fabric and leather rustled, and his voice moved closer. "We ran an op down near the Gulf once. While we were there, a hurricane hit, and we had to hunker down. In the middle of the storm, everything got quiet. The whole sky was the strangest green I've ever seen. I thought it was all over, but Mace—" His voice hitched, and he cleared his throat. "Mace said no, it was just the eye of the storm. The middle. Sure enough, after that, it started right up again. Like it had never stopped."

The name pinged something. A different memory. No tactile sensation or visual accompaniment, just her VP's clear, brisk voice. *James Mason, Medical Corps.*

The thought brought another echo—Birgitte's voice, hot with frustration as she slammed things around on her desk.

It's inexcusably reckless. Mark my words, Marjorie, that sniper is trouble. He's utterly cold. Nothing touches him. They think they have him under control, but they're wrong. Someday, we'll find out he has a body count we knew nothing about.

Birgitte had always insisted on using names instead of serial numbers or job titles when talking about TechCorps employees. Names were humanizing, she always said, which had turned her refusal to use Gray's into its own damning statement.

Maya forced her eyes open again. Gray was close now, so close that she could have reached out to touch him. She didn't—the last thing she needed with her senses rioting toward overload was more stimulation. But she met his even gaze, and saw . . . something. A ghost of loss. *Pain*.

He might be dark and cold, but some things touched him.

She wet her lips nervously. "Mace was your medic, right? What happened?"

Gray looked away.

"I'm sorry," she whispered. He didn't have to answer. She knew how far the TechCorps could go when they wanted to pull obedience out of someone by force. "They fucked me up, too."

Gray ran a hand over his empty shirt pocket and shook his head. "Are you square now? Not going to puke?"

She managed a weak smile. "Probably not. But I can't go back inside. The sounds . . ." She flexed her fingers, which were stiff from being clenched into helpless fists. "I can't forget things I hear. And I don't need any more bad memories."

"Then we'll stay out here." He leaned against the wall beside her.

It was almost nice. The distant rumble of thunder shivered through her, and she could feel the crackle of static in the air. It wouldn't be long before the sky tore open and relieved this sweltering, miserable heat.

Too soon, the silence swelled into a void so empty that it begged for memories to fill it. "Can you tell me more about the hurricane?"

After a long moment, he grunted softly. "The winds get high. They look scary, but hurricanes aren't like other storms. It's not the wind you really have to worry about. It's the water . . ."

The tension in her muscles slowly melted. She let her open hands hang limply at her sides, afraid that even pressing them against the brick would be one sensation too many. But his words rolled over her, stroking and soothing, beautiful blissful nothingness. Just the weather. He was telling her about the weather, and she wanted to drown in it.

FlowMac Pop had nothing on this.

TECHCORPS PROPRIETARY DATA,
L1 SECURITY CLEARANCE

One week post 55–312's procedure, and the unexpected results persist. As far as we can ascertain, 55–312 is either indifferent or insensitive to pain. More interestingly, she fails to exhibit the detrimental complications typically seen in congenital sufferers, such as chewing injuries and corneal infections secondary to abrasion.

The department has requisitioned regeneration equipment in order to test the nature (indifference vs. insensitivity) as well as the limits, if any, of her condition. We anticipate prompt approval.

Recruit Analysis, February 2077

THIRTEEN

Watching Rafe take hit after hit shouldn't have reminded Knox of watching Mace die.

There were no similarities between the sterile, impersonal TechCorps cells and Boyd's grimy dive of a bar. No one had laid a finger on the Silver Devils' medic. No one needed to. Mace's body had consumed itself from the inside, just like Conall's was beginning to do.

And Mace had had no control. As bloody as this fight looked, Knox could see the strategy in Rafe's choices. He took hard hits, vicious, bloody ones. But he always twisted to avoid any incapacitating blows. He controlled the fight so skillfully that even a trained soldier like Boyd might not see it.

In order to see what was going on, you'd have to understand how much punishment Rafe would willingly take to achieve his endgame.

Watching that punishment shouldn't have reminded Knox of Mace. But it was one of his men, bleeding and hurting while he was helpless to stop it, and owning up to how badly the TechCorps had broken him meant owning up to this.

Knox couldn't put the mission above his men anymore.

His gut churned. His muscles burned from the tension of holding himself still. The only part of him that didn't ache was the hand gripping Nina's. Sweet warmth burned where their palms met. Every brush of her fingers was the gentlest of electric shocks.

He almost talked himself into letting go when Boyd cast a look at them, his red-rimmed eyes lingering on their joined hands, but releasing her now would look like he was trying to hide something. Besides, Nina had been right. Boyd considered all the women arm candy—and reinforcing that idea would keep them safer.

It was getting too easy to rationalize touching her.

Dani returned with two drinks. She offered one to Nina, who refused. With a shrug, Dani drained them both, one right after the other, then pressed the empty glasses into the hands of a confused passerby.

Then she crossed her arms over her chest and glared at the cage. "He should have ended this by now."

"He better do it soon," Knox rumbled. Rafe had a swollen eye, a bloody face, and so many bruises he'd be thankful to fall into a proper bed to-night. If it got much worse—

Between one heartbeat and the next, the fight shifted. A punch that should have taken out a few of Rafe's teeth swung wide as he ducked with impossible speed and came up under his opponent's guard. With a roar of rage, Rafe hoisted the man off his feet and flung him bodily against the side of the cage. The rattle of the impact was swiftly drowned out by shocked gasps and new screams from the crowd.

The other man slumped to the concrete for a charged moment while Rafe danced back. He spread his hands to his sides, his lips moving in a clear taunt that the crowd swallowed up. Whatever it was got his opponent back on his feet, his face contorted in a snarl of rage.

"Come on, Rafe," Nina whispered.

Rafe twisted out of the way at the last moment. The fighter couldn't stop abruptly enough, especially when Rafe planted a hand at his back and helped him slam face-first into the cage. Knox tensed, because he knew what was coming next.

Boyd had told them to give the people a show, and Rafe delivered. He curled his fingers around the injector at the back of the man's spine and tore it free with a roar. His opponent howled in agony and crumpled to the concrete, his body jerking.

Rafe held his gruesome prize above his head as the fickle crowd switched sides, screeching their approval of the violence and destruction. Even Boyd seemed pleased, grinning in his booth as he waved a hand like a king and gave them permission to clear the cage.

Knox was probably the only one who knew Rafe well enough to see the rage seething in his eyes. He'd given the crowd their show, but he would never forgive Boyd for forcing the brutal display.

Appreciative fans tried to mob Rafe when he stepped out of the cage. He kept his expression easy, and his charming smile probably fooled most of them. In moments, though, he'd extricated himself, strolling back to meet Knox's gaze with all that anger and more than a hint of challenge.

"You didn't have to take that many hits," Knox murmured.

"I know." Rafe glanced at Dani, clearly trying to raise one eyebrow and not doing a great job with his eye rapidly swelling. "You gonna critique me too?"

"Would you listen to me if I did?"

"Maybe. Where's my shirt?"

"Talk to Gray." Dani wiped a smudge of blood from Rafe's cheek. "I'm not sure all your new fans want you wearing one, though."

"Too bad." Rafe tried to smile and winced as his split lip started bleeding again.

Boyd sauntered over from his booth in the corner. He climbed up onto a platform next to the cage, where two men were busily hosing blood off the concrete floor. He raised his arms, and a relative hush fell over the bar.

"You all know our undefeated champion." He spoke with all the gravitas of a king addressing his court. "Every week—sometimes every night—you come here. You drink, you have fun, and you watch Diesel *kick some ass*." The cheers rose again, deafening in their volume, until Boyd cut them off again. "Tonight, someone came here, thinking he could beat Diesel. A stranger."

His gaze cut to Knox.

Heads swiveled in his direction. Knox let his emotions drop away, a ritual so familiar it might as well have been muscle memory. He shed his feelings as he shed his shirt, stripping it over his head without any particular concern for the heavy, hungry stares from the crowd.

They wanted his blood. His pain. They wanted a good show.

Knox had to give them one.

Nina turned to face him. "Knox—" *Don't do this*. The words were unmistakable, blazing in her eyes, but she held them back. "Be careful. And . . ."

The soft worry on her face threatened to shatter his comforting blankness. "Yeah?"

"Remember what you're fighting for."

His gaze stole to Conall. Rafe stood next to him, making a face as Conall prodded his various injuries. The techie's face was drawn, stress lines digging grooves into his forehead and around his eyes.

"I won't forget," Knox murmured. The crowd parted before him, and he stepped forward.

Nina pulled him back. She folded her hand around the back of his neck, her fingers trembling on his skin, and drew his mouth down to hers.

The shock of it shattered his calm.

Heat roared through him. Her lips were softer than he'd let himself imagine, warm and full and parting before his brain had time to catch up with what was happening.

His body didn't wait. He took advantage of her offer on instinct, licking her lower lip to drag a small, muffled moan from her. He drove one hand into the tumble of loose hair at the back of her head and spread his fingers wide, and then it was his turn to groan as she licked his tongue.

Not shy. Not restrained. Her kiss was as bold as she was, fearless and intense, hot enough to pull a man under and make him beg to keep drowning.

Nina broke away, her fingertips trailing down his shoulder as she stepped back. Her retreat was as abrupt as her kiss, leaving him swaying toward her before he caught himself.

It was just part of the cover. Nina was playing arm candy to the hilt, sending her man into battle with a kiss. He repeated the reminder over and over in his head, as if repetition could drive back the simmering hunger she'd kindled in his blood.

Sweet, merciful *fuck,* she was dangerous.

Knox turned toward the cage, his body still rioting, and found Boyd watching him with a far too appraising look. No—watching *Nina.* Knox didn't like the look in his eyes, but the quickest way out of this place was through the champion, so he walked forward to meet him.

Diesel was already climbing into the cage. He was so big he had to duck to get through the opening. Straightened to his full height, he stood a head over Knox. He was bulky in a way that didn't come from hard work or even hours in a gym. When he flexed for the roaring crowd, his muscle groups looked like they had their own muscle groups.

The obvious answer was confirmed when he reached for a metal cylinder someone passed through the chain-link fencing. He held up the jet injector and slammed it against the side of his neck. The onlookers screamed as he doped himself up and then hurled the empty container into the crowd. Pure theater, just like the way he flung his arms wide and snarled, the perfect picture of a frenzied warrior on the edge of sanity.

Diesel was playing to his fans, but whatever he'd injected himself with was likely to make Knox's night unpleasant.

Knox swung up into the cage. The clang of the door behind him settled his emotions. The need pulsing through him didn't vanish. It . . . transformed. This time, his focus felt feral, dangerous, and it was hard to remember he was fighting for Conall.

It would be easy to pretend he was fighting for Nina.

Boyd's chosen fighter was good. Between the drugs, his size, and Diesel's skill, Nina could understand how this guy had gone undefeated for so long. He was almost a match for Knox.

Almost.

Perversely, the realization settled her nerves. Knox didn't have to *let* Diesel hit him. He still had the edge over Boyd's champ, but the gap wasn't as wide in this fight as it had been in Rafe's. Whereas Rafe had had to split his attention between winning and showmanship, Knox could throw the full weight of his effort into beating his opponent.

It wasn't as difficult to watch as Rafe deliberately getting his ass kicked. But Nina watched anyway—every jab, every feint. Every blow, glancing or solid. Every gap in the cage, where spectators' eager hands grasped the chain links.

But no weapons were passed through. It seemed unthinkable, Knox's bout staying clean and aboveboard when Boyd had already proven he wasn't opposed to dirty tactics. But then she spotted the man walking her way, a predatory gleam in his eye, and comprehension washed over her.

He had another plan up his sleeve. A whole different way to fuck with Knox.

Boyd stopped a few paces away, and he didn't bother to hide his lazy, appraising look. "So, the teacher's pet finally found someone willing to put up with the stick up his ass."

The man was as transparent as he was revolting, and as revolting as he was predictable. Still, Nina couldn't deny that she'd encouraged Boyd's conclusion by not correcting his assumptions. She'd even cemented it by planting that kiss on Knox.

That impulsive, delicious, earth-shaking kiss.

So she swallowed her sigh. "Don't you have scads of money to count, or something?"

"Some things are better than money." Boyd grinned. "I came over to see if you're interested in a little wager."

Dani's stance shifted, and Nina surreptitiously flashed her a signal to stand down. "The fight's already begun, Sergeant. Betting window's closed."

"Window closes when I say it closes." He hooked his thumbs in his wide belt. "What do you say, girl? Wanna hedge your bets? Put your money on our champion? That way, if you lose your boyfriend, you'll still have a nice stack of credits."

He wasn't talking about money or bets. A slimy implication underscored his words, made even more uncomfortable by the fact that it wasn't even motivated by sexual interest. That, at least, would be understandable. But this asshole simply wanted to stick it to Knox, and he wanted to use her to do it.

The more time she spent in Boyd's presence, the more seriously Nina considered letting Dani stab him, after all.

"I have a little to spare." She had one credit stick left in her pocket that she hadn't given the motel's proprietor in their negotiations. She tugged it free and held it up, then jerked it back as Boyd reached for it. "One hundred. But I'm betting on Knox, not your boy."

"Bah." Boyd shook his head and turned to scowl at the cage. "Everyone always does, and fuck if I know why. He's always been a sanctimonious little prig, staring down his nose at the rest of us like he wasn't out there sucking up to the TechCorps and screwing over the little guy just like everyone else."

It took a special kind of mental gymnastics to hate someone else because they'd done all the same terrible things you had. "What do you care what he thinks?"

"I don't," Boyd spat. It might even have been convincing, if his scowl hadn't deepened. "I just don't get why people keep falling for his righteous, noble do-gooder act. Did he tell you all of his *hero* stories? About how he stopped a riot with his precious diplomatic skills? Or when he parachuted into a battle zone to save some kids?" Disdain dripped from every word. "That time he delivered a damn baby during a siege? Such a fucking hero."

Knox hadn't mentioned any of it. Of course he wouldn't, though Nina couldn't quite put her finger on why she knew that. Did he not view any of it as particularly heroic? Was he simply modest? Or did he, for whatever reason, just not want her to know anything *good* about him?

She told Boyd the truth—such as it was. "Knox and I don't talk much about the past."

A roar went up from the crowd around them. Diesel had charged Knox, the momentum driving them both up against the side of the cage. Knox took a brutal hit to the jaw, but he managed to get one hand up between them. His fingers locked around Diesel's throat, squeezing with such strength that the man's face turned red as he broke off his attack to claw at Knox's hand.

With a roar, Knox hoisted the huge man off the ground and threw him with enough strength to send him crashing into the opposite side of the cage.

Boyd frowned.

"Knox is going to win," she told him. "You know it's true. You must have known before the fight even started. But you want him to lose, even if it costs you. Why?"

"I win either way. I get rich, or I get to watch someone finally beat the smug smile off that bastard's face. I'm having the best night of my life." He gave her another of those skin-crawling looks of appraisal. "It could still get better, though."

Nina's composure cracked—just for a moment, long enough for her to grimace before she schooled her expression.

Boyd didn't seem to mind her disgust. If anything, he *enjoyed* it. "Whatever Knox is giving you, believe me. I could give it to you better."

The vague sense of unease tightened around Nina like a vise. "I'm not interested."

"Mmm. We'll see." He held out a hand. "Still wanna bet on the boy?"

"Damn straight." She dropped the credit stick on his outstretched palm and pulled her hand back before he could get any bright ideas about touching her.

His seedy laugh slithered over her as he tucked the credit stick into his pocket and resumed watching the fight.

It didn't last long. Bloody and battered, Diesel couldn't keep up. His reaction times slowed, and his clumsy blows failed to land entirely. By the time Knox got him on the floor, the man was swinging and kicking desperately, trying to roll away and climb to his feet.

Knox ended it by clenching his fingers in Diesel's hair and slamming the man's head against the rough concrete.

Diesel stilled, and a hush fell over the crowd. Then everything exploded, cheers and screams of everything from disbelief to dismay. Their champion had fallen, and to a mysterious stranger, no less.

It was the kind of shit people wrote songs about.

Boyd didn't look like he was in the mood for a good ballad, though. He'd gone a little green, and Nina pressed her lips together firmly as he scowled and turned on her. "I guess we're both rich tonight," he muttered. "Come to my table and get your winnings."

She had one chance here, one safe card to play. "Keep them. It wasn't a properly placed bet, anyway."

His bloodshot eyes narrowed. "What are you playing at?"

"I don't want anything from you," she assured him. "Nothing you haven't already promised, anyway."

"Nobody wants *nothing*. That's not how the world works."

"It's how *I* work." She took a step closer so she could lower her voice. "Knox held up his end of the bargain, and now it's your turn. Help Conall, and then leave us all the hell alone."

"Fuck." Boyd spat on the floor—and on Nina's boots. "You're just like that motherfucker. You righteous assholes deserve each other."

He stomped away, and Dani snorted. "He seems nice."

"I'm still open to murder and mayhem," Rafe said, holding a cold beer bottle to his eye. "The captain's probably hoping for a lower profile, though."

Low profile was out of the question for Knox. People swarmed him as he exited the cage—brand-new fans, dazzled women and men looking for a hookup, even the other fighters. They didn't know him, but they wanted to.

Nina understood the feeling.

CONALL

There were seventeen water stains on their motel room's ceiling. The peeling wallpaper was printed with a subtle geometric triangle pattern. Triangles were harder to count, because if you stacked a few of them together, they made more triangles. There was a trick to it that Conall could never remember—something about the base number of triangles?

It didn't matter. No one would be coming behind him to check his work. He wasn't racing the clock and his fellow recruits, tense with the knowledge that whoever solved the problem too slowly might not be there tomorrow.

Of course, disappearing didn't mean they were *dead*. The aptitude it took to be drafted into the TechCorps' elite computer division made a kid too valuable for disposal. But their teachers also made it clear that washing out into a lesser program would result in the revocation of the privileges and perks that came with being the best.

The techs who lived chained to their little desks, crunching numbers for the scientists and sleeping in assigned bunks, weren't *exactly* indentured, but there was no way to repay your education on a tech's salary. You'd be eighty by the time you had a hope in hell of breaking free of your debt. The only way to breathe free air again was to push your brain to its limits, to go faster and harder than all the brilliant kids around you.

To be the best.

No, to be *second* best. Second best would have been smarter. If he'd stopped before hitting the peak of his world, Conall would probably be in a high-rise somewhere, doing home security for TechCorps board members and taking baths in champagne flecked with gold dust. But he couldn't resist clawing his way to number one.

And the TechCorps couldn't resist seeing how much higher he could go if they hacked his brain.

Conall couldn't remember the trick to counting triangles, but he didn't need it. His brain never stopped working. There were eight thousand, six hundred, and forty-seven triangles on the wall in front of him. Once upon a time, knowing that would have given him a soothing rush of satisfaction. A blissful chance to catch his breath.

Now, he couldn't remember bliss. He needed something new to count.

The man in the clean—well, *mostly* clean—white coat beside the chair rubbed something cold on the inside of Conall's forearm. "Normally, I'd use a general sedative for this," he said flatly, "but your condition won't allow it." He paused. "I'd advise you not to watch."

Not very encouraging. Conall's wired brain skittered in sixteen different directions, instantly compiling an anxiety-driven list of everything that could go wrong if he let some backwoods butcher cut him open and hop him up on unregulated drugs.

He could go into neural overload. He could die. He could *wish* he'd died when the high hit him wrong and amped up the world to a brilliant Technicolor so out of control that his sanity cracked under the pressure. He could crash. He could burn out half his brain cells and never be the best at anything ever again.

That last one scared him the most.

Mace would have handled this better. Mace would have sat down with Conall and laid out the possible side effects. He would have given Conall a sense of control over what was about to happen, even if that control was a mere illusion.

"Conall?"

Mace would have understood what was happening to Conall in a way the others couldn't, because the medic had been like Conall—calibrated for genius. Always thinking just a little bit faster.

No wonder he'd declined so rapidly in that shithole prison cell.

"Conall."

Conall dragged his ragged attention toward the sound of his name. Knox swam into focus, wearing the deep groove between his eyebrows that meant he was worried. For the first five years Conall had been a part of the Silver Devils, he'd seen that forehead crease half a dozen times.

Every one had meant they were in shit so deep they'd be washing it out of their hair—if they survived.

Now it seemed like it was there all the damn time.

"Are you ready?" Knox asked, low and intense. "If you want to wait—"

"No." Conall's eyes unfocused. There was a cheap, crooked painting on the wall behind him. More geometric shapes. Rectangles inside rectangles. Thirty-seven of them. "No, this needs to happen."

"Okay. Do it." Knox's voice drifted by, rough around the edges with emotion the captain pretended he couldn't feel. Knox always worried too much about Conall. He'd wanted a tech for his squad, and the Protectorate had requisitioned him the best available man for the job. Conall hadn't grown up training for combat like the rest of them, and Knox thought that made him vulnerable. The born-and-bred soldier boys never seemed to understand that brains would always outmaneuver brawn in the long game.

The short game? Well, that could get a little uncomfortable.

Vague pressure pinched his arm. The local anesthetic had numbed him from shoulder to elbow, but the alien tugging and the *sound* of the blade—whisper soft, sharp, wrong—dragged his meandering focus straight to what was happening to him.

Mistake. Mistake, mistake, oh *fuck*. Mistake.

Blood welled up on his skin. *Out* of his skin. The doctor—no, not a doctor, whatever else he was, he was definitely not a doctor—had the implant gripped in a pair of forceps and was—was

Pain exploded through Conall. His brain scrambled to fill in the blanks the anesthetic had muffled, unhelpfully bypassing the numbness with vivid, agonizing detail. Conall sucked in a breath and jerked his attention back to the wall. Triangles. Triangles—*fuck,* who gave a shit about triangles when a madman was flaying open his flesh and he was just letting it happen?

"Conall." Knox's face appeared, blocking out the triangles. The groove between his eyes was so deep it looked painful. Every muscle in the man's forehead had to be aching. What muscles did that, anyway? The *corrugator supercilii*? *Occipitofrontalis*? Mace would know.

Mace was dead.

Knox gripped the shoulder attached to the arm not currently being stabbed. "I thought you were going to numb that. He's clearly in pain."

"Not his fault," Conall ground out. "Brain's too smart to fall for stupid tricks. I know what it should feel like, so I feel it."

"Almost done with placement," the medic said. "All I have to do is wire it in."

Conall started to look, but Knox grabbed his chin, his fingers damn near digging bruises into skin as he kept Conall's head turned away. "Tell me what you're going to buy once we're free and clear. I know you have a list."

Of course he had a list. When they'd bolted, they'd had to do it with the scant amount of tech Knox could requisition without arousing suspicion. There were a hundred things Conall had left behind. A permanent satellite dish. Tiny camera drones with a twenty-mile signal radius. His entire case of smart lenses—contacts that could record, analyze, and display results like they were floating in front of him.

Hell, he missed those the most. His brain hadn't scrambled in so many restless directions with that constant low-level input.

"C'mon, Conall. Talk to me."

He met his captain's dark, worried eyes. Poor Knox. So bad at sucking it up and letting other people hurt. "Crab dinner," he rasped. "When we're really free, I want to go down to the Gulf and spend a year's worth of wages stuffing myself on seafood."

The words did what he intended. That groove between Knox's brows almost vanished. His lips twitched up. Not quite a smile—the captain didn't do a lot of smiling—but close. "All right, Con. It's a deal. All the seafood you can eat. My treat."

Knox would never have to pay. Conall wasn't making it to the Gulf. He was pretty sure he wasn't making it to the end of this mission.

That was the problem with being the smartest guy in the room. Sometimes, you were the only one who knew the odds were terrible and your time was nearly up.

CLASSIFIED BEHAVIOR EVALUATION

Franklin Center for Genetic Research

The HS-Gen16 cluster failed its final examination. As feared, HS-Gen16-A was unable to operate under the assumption of acceptable loss. HS-Gen16-C was confirmed dead on test site. HS-Gen16-B is in critical condition.

Per established procedure, the cluster will be decommissioned, and the Center's investment recouped as applicable.

Dr. Baudin, June 2077

FOURTEEN

Nina stood outside of Knox's motel room, her fingers clenched around the neck of a tequila bottle, her hand upraised to knock on the garish orange door.

The plan had seemed so *easy* when she'd formulated it in the shower—they could share a bottle of booze, talk, and see where the night went. No strings, no expectations. No worries.

So why was she hesitating? The worst he could do was shut her out again . . . and maybe that was the problem. Getting shot down didn't usually bother her—nothing ventured, nothing gained, and all that—but this was different.

Knox was different.

Thunder rolled, heralding the storm that had been brewing for days. Part of her wanted to flee back to her room. Instead, she knocked. Seconds dragged by, enough to make her rethink fleeing—

Knox opened the door. Shirtless.

Bruises were already rising from his fight. Not as many as Rafe would have, but the patchwork of red and slowly purpling skin still left her fighting a sympathetic wince.

Knox's gaze dropped to the bottle in her hand. In silence, he stepped back and held the door wider.

A med-kit lay open on the scarred dresser, and Nina spun to face Knox. "Are you hurt?"

"It's not bad." He closed the door and turned his back to her, craning his head to peer at the back of his shoulder. "I think there was a broken link in the chain. Ripped me up a little when I hit it."

He had a ragged gash in the skin over his left shoulder blade. It wasn't deep, but it was in an awkward spot that would pull every time he moved his arm. "I'll have to close it, or it won't heal. Have you cleaned it yet?"

"Yeah." He crossed to the dresser, standing close enough that his bare arm brushed hers. "I have some zip sutures, but the angle's tough. If you don't mind—"

"Sit." She handed him the bottle and gestured toward the bottom corner of the bed. When he had complied, she moved the med-kit from the dresser to the mattress behind him. "If you like tequila, now would be a good time to indulge."

He took a healthy swig, his face twisting in a scowl as the liquor hit him. After a moment, he took another, longer drink. "It's not terrible."

Nina hid a smile as she swabbed med-gel on his wound. "The cut or the booze?"

"The tequila." He tilted the bottle and studied the label. "Maybe you should give Rafe some."

"He and Gray are busy looking after Conall. Who is fine, by the way. I checked in on him just now." There was a staple gun in the med-kit, but that was overkill for a cut like this one. She reached for the adhesive clips he'd mentioned instead. "They said they sent you down here to clean up and get some rest. But I thought, after a night like tonight . . . Well, I thought you might not want to be alone."

"Maybe not." He rubbed his thumb against the bottle. "Your girls okay? Maya looked a little spooked when we came outside."

"Wouldn't be here if she needed me. But your concern is noted."

"I didn't mean—" He huffed out a laugh and took another drink. "I'm shit at this, you know."

At small talk, or at talking to *her*? "Relax. I'm just messing with you."

"People don't *mess* with me. They obey me or they try to kill me. There's usually not much of a middle ground."

Nina peeled the adhesive clips away from their sterile backing and placed them at regular intervals on either side of the laceration. Threading the thin plastic ties came next, and finally she pulled them taut. The effect was something between tying a shoe and zipping a zipper, closing the wound efficiently without sutures or staples.

She admired her handiwork for a moment, then began to dress the wound. "All done. You know the drill, I assume—twelve hours, and you'll be good as new. I'm pretty decent at this, so you probably won't even scar. I guess this is your lucky day in more ways than one."

"Is it?" He held the bottle out to her. "I guess we all came through in one piece. That's something."

There was something unbearably intimate, almost erotic, about lifting the bottle to her lips with him watching her. She gulped the liquor to wash away the sensation, but the shuddering burn only made it more intense. "Boyd shouldn't bother you anymore."

One of those dark, stern eyebrows swept up. "That must have been a hell of a conversation you had with him. Boyd would crawl over broken glass to bother me."

"Oh, there's something he loves more than watching you squirm— money." She shrugged. "I bribed him."

That won her a swift frown. "You shouldn't have given him anything—"

"We made a bet," she cut in. "He lost." She lifted the bottle to her mouth again and took a lingering sip this time. She imagined she could taste him on the glass—impossible, with the deep, jagged flavor of the tequila cutting through everything. "Do you really want to keep talking about him?"

"No," Knox conceded. He rubbed at his knuckles, his gaze tracing the bottle as it hovered close to her lips. "But that's another thing I'm shit at. Doing what I want."

The air in the room squeezed tight around her. "Maybe you need some practice."

He reached out, and time itself seemed to slow. His fingers closed over hers as he folded them around the bottle. He tugged, pulling her with him as he lifted the tequila to his lips and took a sip. "You know I'm a terrible idea, right? There's nothing good inside me. Nothing about me that ends well."

She could think of a few things, and they all started and ended with those hands. That mouth. "I'm not trying to break you to ride, Knox. Fixing you isn't my job. But . . ."

"But?"

Saying it out loud felt like a tiny betrayal—but leaving the words unspoken didn't stop them from being true. "Don't you ever get sick of being the steady one? The one who's never allowed to fuck up? Don't you ever get *tired*?"

He stared at her, those dark eyes so close. The air between them crackled. His fingers flexed over hers, his grip a hair short of painful. When he finally spoke, his voice rasped over her like sandpaper. "All the fucking time."

The confession hung between them, heavy with something caught between desperation and pain. Something that echoed deep in Nina's gut.

"We're here right now." Gently, she disengaged their hands and set the tequila aside. "We can forget about all that, just for tonight, and take what we want. Or I can go back to my room. Either way, no harm, no foul. But it's up to you. It has to be."

He studied her in tense silence, all his secrets piling up behind his eyes. His fingertips brushed her cheek, trailing heat as he rubbed his thumb over her lower lip.

Nina froze. One wrong word or move might make him turn away from her again . . . but she couldn't spend all her time being so *careful*. Either he wanted this—wanted *her*—or he didn't.

She licked his thumb.

A growl rattled up from his chest. A moment later the thunder echoed him, cracking loud overhead and rumbling through the room. Knox slid his hand around the back of her head, plunging his fingers deep to tangle in her hair.

And then he kissed her. *Hard.*

It was nothing like the kiss before his fight. That had been for show, and Knox had been too startled to react. That brief contact didn't compare to his mouth moving over hers, open and hungry, or the way he pulled her closer. He released her hair, only to curl both hands under her thighs and drag her up his body.

Everything about him was rigid and unyielding, from his trembling self-control to his muscles. Even his dick pressed against her through their clothes, stiff and insistent, tempting her to wrap her legs around his hips and grind closer.

He moaned into her mouth, his grip on her tightening. He finally broke the kiss, but only to close his teeth on her jaw in a teasing nip. "Take off your shirt."

Caged in his arms, Nina could only drag it halfway up. She squirmed, trying to ease the fabric over her breasts without sacrificing a single millimeter of contact, but that only chafed the worn cotton over her nipples. "Help me."

He hoisted her higher, bracing one arm around her lower back. "I've got you. I'm not going to drop you."

She leaned back and dragged the tank top over her head, not caring where it fell, then clutched his shoulders as he took advantage of the vulnerable expanse of her throat. His mouth blazed hot, his tongue a shuddering tease before his teeth closed over her pulse in a primal, dangerous claim.

Not a savage bite. Just hard enough to skate that sweet, giddy edge, and she knew when he lifted his head and she glimpsed his wild, almost feral eyes that he was no stranger to dancing along the line between pleasure and pain.

Then his gaze dropped, skimming over her collarbone to linger on the bare curves of her breasts. "You're fucking exquisite."

"Don't tell me." His beard rasped under her palm as she stroked his jaw. "Show me."

He whirled them around. The room dipped and swayed as he sank a knee onto the bed and lowered her with such a perfectly controlled flex of muscle that she drifted lightly to the mattress. He braced a hand on either side of her head and stared down at her with a feverish glint in his eyes. "Just how strong are you?"

She arched against him. "Can we arm-wrestle another time?"

"Maybe." A lazy smile curved his lips. "Some people chase after Protectorate soldiers. They think they're getting a wild night with an out-of-control warrior. Some guys play to the fantasy, but it's a lie. We can't let go with human lovers. Too easy to hurt them."

For a moment, Nina wanted to laugh. Then the true import of his words hit her, washing away any hint of amusement. How long had it been since someone had wanted him for *who* he was, not what he was? Judging from the hesitation that lingered just beneath his casual, easy words, too long.

It broke her heart.

She braced herself and shifted their positions, flipping him smoothly onto his back before sitting up over him. "It's not so easy to hurt me."

Relief transformed his face, and she realized that she'd never seen him without a subtle *tension*—the beginnings of a frown, or fine lines around his eyes, or muscles stiff with unease. All of that vanished as he ran his hands up her abdomen and splayed his fingers wide just beneath her breasts. "You have no idea how hot that is."

"What, throwing you around a motel room?" She rolled her hips against his and shuddered through the jolt of pleasure that raced through her. "Cheap date."

"You're the only person who's ever done it." His thumbs swept up, teasingly close to her tight, aching nipples. He watched her intently as he pulled one hand back and licked the pad of his thumb.

When he pressed it to her nipple, she had to bite her lip to hold back a moan. She moved, desperate for the slick heat to continue, and it did—until he pinched her.

Nina grabbed his wrist, but not to pull him away. To dig her fingernails into his skin, silently begging for more. Obedient to her silent command, he tugged gently at her nipple, testing her response as he pushed her to the edge of pleasure and edged across the line into pain.

She breathed his name, a fervent sigh of anticipation and shivering approval.

"That's it." He sat up in a graceful flex of muscle, coming face-to-face with her for a charged moment before arching her back over his legs. It thrust her breasts up toward him, and he closed his lips around her nipple, chasing the kiss of pain he'd given her with the sweet, soothing stroke of his tongue.

It was unbearable, and Nina never wanted it to stop. She gripped his head, threading her fingers through his hair as he ground his hips up against hers with slow, unhurried movements.

She picked up the rhythm. But just as she was losing herself to the heat of his mouth and the hardness of his body beneath hers, he tipped her to the bed and scraped his teeth over her collarbone. He kissed a path between her breasts, nipped at her ribs, and tickled his tongue around her belly button.

Then he rose above her and slid his hands down her legs until his nimble fingers caught the laces on her left boot. He worked the knot loose and pulled off first one boot, then the other, all without looking away from her. His gaze was hot, his every movement precise. Efficient. Determined.

By the time he reached for the button on her jeans, Nina was ferociously glad she'd packed a couple of pairs of nice underwear. The sheer black mesh wasn't fancy, but it was less utilitarian than her usual choices.

Knox didn't seem to notice—or care—as he stripped every scrap of fabric from her body with single-minded focus. Her underwear joined the growing pile of clothes on the floor as he stretched out over her, his jeans rough against her inner thighs, his body trembling with tension.

For a charged moment, he simply stared at her as thunder roared and the lights flickered under the force of the unleashed storm. The same storm seemed to be raging inside him, held back by the finest of threads.

Holding his gaze, barely even *breathing*, Nina unbuckled his belt.

He shuddered, and his hands fisted in the blankets on either side of her head. He let her work the leather free, but when she reached for the button on his pants, he snapped.

"*Wait.*" He grabbed her hands with a growl and dragged them up over her head. His fingers formed a gentle, implacable cage as he pinned her wrists to the pillow. He settled next to her on the bed, his bare chest blazing hot against her bare skin, and trailed his free hand down between her breasts. "My turn first."

"I'm not one of your men, Captain." She fought to be still, but her body arched to his touch anyway. "What makes you think I'll follow orders?"

"What makes you think I want you to?" He dragged his finger in a taunting circle on her abdomen. "A leader who relies on mindless obedience gets what they deserve. I have subtler methods of persuasion at my disposal."

Oh. "Such as?"

Knox slid a leg over hers and used it to edge her thighs wider as his fingers drifted even lower—implacable, relentless. His first touch was maddeningly gentle, just the soft brush of his fingers between her thighs. But his eyes fixed on her face with that *look* he got when they settled into a new place for the night, the one that meant he was memorizing every detail and committing it to memory for use in some future battle plan.

Recon had never been hotter.

He touched her slowly, tracing fire over her slick, swollen flesh until she clenched her fists in sheer frustrated anticipation. She tried to buck up, to meet every careful caress halfway, but Knox kept her hips pinned to the bed.

A satisfied smile tugged at his lips, and Nina shuddered through the realization that he was playing with her. Teasing her.

Did he understand yet that his turn really would come? Or was he *counting* on that?

The careful, teasing stimulation built, twisting tighter until Nina's legs were shaking and she ached to feel the graze of his nails or his teeth on her skin—something, anything, to kick-start the slow, inexorable swell of pleasure.

Something hard enough to get her off.

Then, just as she was sliding into desperation, opening her mouth to beg, Knox pressed his thumb firmly against her clit.

"Fuck!" She arched again, galvanized by the blinding heat. His grip on her wrists broke, and she drove her fingers into his hair and pulled.

His groan shattered on a curse as he kept his thumb moving in firm, demanding circles, keeping time with the pleasure pulsing through her. Nina gasped with every fresh wave—and whimpered when he didn't stop. She tilted her hips in invitation, and he eased one finger inside her.

"Look at me." The desperation seething beneath the command was what drew her gaze like magnetic north.

He wasn't just watching her, gauging her reactions. He was utterly focused, every tiny shred of attention dialed in like he wanted to drown in her. And maybe he did. Whether he crawled into that bottle of tequila or into her, Nina didn't blame him for wanting to escape for a little while.

Whatever this was, the scant space between them seethed. Nina fell into it, closing the distance between them to capture his mouth. He met her kiss, then took control of it, rough and deep, as the fine edges of his perfect control began to unravel.

He nipped her lower lip and sank another broad finger into her. Nina broke the kiss and rubbed her cheek against his, hungry for as much sensation as possible, even the rough chafe of his beard on her face.

His breath fell hot on her ear. His whisper was a low rumble. "I can do this all night, you know. My hands aren't just flesh and bone. They don't get tired."

"Never doubted it." Shivering, Nina rubbed her hip against his erection. "Your dick might start to feel left out, though."

His warm chuckle flowed over her like honey. "If you want it, you're gonna have to ask nicer than that."

"What, bat my eyes and—" His fingers crooked, stroking inside her, and her words splintered with a cry.

He chuckled again, his thumb resuming those taunting circles over her clit. "Somehow I doubt you bat your eyelashes. I bet you just take what you want."

She'd never been able to resist a challenge. She grabbed his wrists and flipped him over again, pinning his hands beside his head as she straddled his stomach. "Like this?"

He pushed up, testing her. She held firm, drinking in the sight of his flexing muscles as he strained against her grip. A slow, reckless smile curved his lips, one of hunger and discovery. "You can take all of me, can't you?"

"Everything." Nina indulged herself as she released him, drawing her fingers slowly down his arms, across his shoulders. She molded her hands to his chest, smiling when his pectorals clenched at her touch. "What about you?"

"Can I take all of you?" With his hands free, he moved her back until her hips were over his, and the hard line of his erection ground up against her exposed pussy. "Let's find out."

"Let's." She slipped free of his grasping hands and knelt over his thighs instead. The coarse fabric of his pants abraded her skin, but that was part of the appeal. Soft and rough, dominance and submission.

Power and pleasure.

She lingered over the buttons on his fly before loosening each one, watching his expression tighten with every passing heartbeat. "Problem?" she asked innocently.

He growled in response. "You have about five seconds before I get you back under me."

"Come on, Captain. It's my turn—your rules, not mine." She leaned over him as she eased his pants and underwear down, so close that his cock sprang free to nestle between her breasts as she licked a path over his ribs.

He groaned and thrust up against her. "Fuck the rules."

Sure, he said that now. Nina swallowed a laugh and nipped at his abs as she wrapped her hand around his shaft. "Give me three minutes."

His muscles trembled with tension, and his gaze . . . She didn't have words for what she saw there. Danger, lust—and barely a hint of his beautiful self-control. "Three minutes," he agreed.

She started with a slow, light stroke. Knox had had to relearn his body after his TechCorps experimentation; Nina had lived in hers for thirty-four years. She knew exactly how to exert precise control over the strength and speed granted by her genetic modifications.

It was *all* she knew, and she put it to good use. She pumped her hand over him, squeezing and releasing, varying the pressure and the rhythm until the head of his cock was slick with arousal and Knox was gripping the blanket so hard it tore. *"Fuck."*

A single minute could have passed, or a whole hour. Touching him created some kind of vortex where nothing else existed, not even the basic concepts of time and fucking space. She leaned over him again. "You have a contraceptive implant, right?"

He stared at her, panting, for so long that she wondered if the words had penetrated. Then he jerked his head in an unsteady nod. "Yes. Yes, I do."

Of course. Even if it hadn't been standard issue for Protectorate recruits, Knox was too conscientious not to get one anyway—and realizing that she knew that about him, knew it the way she knew her own name and lab designation . . .

It felt strange, an intimacy deeper than his naked skin pressed to hers. His eyes locked with hers in a single moment of connection, and she knew he felt it, too.

The thought dissipated like smoke when he reached for her, his big hands grasping her hips just a little too hard. Her back hit the bed, and he kicked free of his pants and slid over her, hot and hard, rocking his hips against her in taunting promise. "Your three minutes is up."

"Fair's fair," she gasped.

"I won't even make you beg." His hips forced her thighs wide. He braced his weight on one hand next to her head and watched her face as he pushed into her—slow, relentless.

It wasn't enough. Nina gripped his sides, digging her nails into his flesh as she arched to meet him. His control wavered, his hips jerked forward—

Then he froze, released a shuddering breath, and stared down at her. "Do you know how easy it would be to fall into you?"

Giddy satisfaction cut through the searing pleasure. He'd spoken of holding back, locking down, keeping control. A hundred different ways to say *self-denial*—and one way to encourage him to let go.

"Give it to me," she whispered.

He did, in one swift, uncontrolled thrust so hard it drove her an inch up the bed. He groaned and dropped his forehead to hers. "Too much?"

She raked her teeth over his earlobe. "More."

He groaned again.

And he let go.

Each powerful thrust streaked through her like the lightning outside. But instead of discharging the tense connection that had built between them, it only made it more intense. Nina clung to him, swept away by something deeper than lust or pleasure.

Swept away by *him*. Knox, unrestrained, his caution stripped away. Not the soldier. Not the captain.

The man.

His mouth seized hers, hot and desperate, as he urged her legs higher up his sides to wrap around his back instead of his hips. The new angle turned the lightning into fire, and Nina came *hard*. She bit his shoulder to stifle her cries, but the thunder outside drowned them out anyway.

She was still shaking when he rolled them again, urging her over him. Too far gone to tease, she picked up a new, faster rhythm, dragging her nails down his chest as she rode him. He hissed his approval of the pain and pressed his head back against the pillow, the muscles in his neck tense and trembling.

Then he planted his feet on the bed and drove up to meet her rocking thrusts, harder and harder, until the force of their bodies coming together slammed the headboard against the wall. Knox spoke to her, low, encouraging whispers lost to the sound of the storm raging outside, drowned out by the blood pounding in her ears.

Just a little more. Maybe he said it, or maybe the thought swirled up out of the lust driving her. Either way, Nina obeyed. She shifted her hips, leaning forward, her hands slipping on the sweat-slicked skin of his chest with every desperate thrust. A heartbeat later, he went rigid beneath her and choked out her name—

His expression reflected the deepest agony and the most incandescent pleasure. Just looking at him might have been enough to get her there, but then his grip on her hips tightened past the point of pain, and Nina lost it. She shuddered above him, every muscle clenching so hard it hurt, and it felt so good she never wanted it to end.

But it had to. Nina collapsed on his chest, shivering as he panted roughly against her neck. His arms came around her, one hand sinking into her hair, the other splaying across the small of her back, as if holding her in place.

As if he thought she might leave.

"Relax, Captain." Nina lifted her head and grinned down at him. "We're just getting started."

FIFTEEN

The patio door squealed a quiet protest, jolting Knox from sleep.

Disorientation claimed him for a dizzy moment. His body was a riot of conflicting sensory input—pain in his shoulder, aches in his muscles, bruises that would no doubt be glorious by morning. But lazy pleasure and bone-deep satisfaction competed with the discomfort, a sated feeling he hadn't experienced in years. The sensation of having fucked so deep and hard and *good* that he'd worked a decade of holding back out of his system.

When he decided to screw up, he didn't do it by half.

The blankets tangled around his legs. The sheet next to him was still warm from Nina's body. He turned his head just enough to squint through the darkness. Lightning forked across the sky, illuminating her silhouette where she stood at the open patio door, watching the storm rage outside.

Something inside him had broken tonight. His instincts. His common sense. He'd fucked the woman he was going to betray, and then he'd fallen asleep in her arms. A pin dropping thirty feet away usually jerked him from restless sleep, but he'd slept so deeply she'd disentangled herself from him and slipped from the bed without waking him.

He could keep lying to himself, but his body was done playing along. He wanted her—no surprise there, but the depth of his craving startled him. The sex should have worked her out of his system. He'd satisfied his curiosity about so many things—the feel of her hair wrapped around his fingers, the way her hips fit the curve of his hands. The noises she made, desperate and playful, needy and demanding, and everything in between.

He'd taken his time, because somewhere in the back of his head he'd still been rationalizing, telling himself this was just another mission objective. Give in to the inevitable. Give them *both* what they wanted and prove that lust and danger and terrible decisions were an explosive combination that burned hot, but burned out fast.

Knox turned his face toward the pillow. The bed smelled like sex, the pillow like the impossible floral sweetness of her hair. His body's swift, fascinated reaction to the combination made a liar of him.

Danger and bad decisions might burn hot, but they were nowhere close to burning out.

Lightning flashed again, revealing the outline of Nina's naked body. Thunder cracked almost immediately, proof that the storm was right on top of them. Most people huddled in interior rooms or deep in their basements when storms like these swept the South. The TechCorps had made some investments into weather radar and storm predictions within the city itself, but out here . . .

When tornadoes hit Georgia, they usually came wrapped in rain. You might not know it was coming until the lightning lit up the sky just long enough to show you that smudge on the horizon . . . and by then it was too late. He'd seen entire settlements swept away in mere seconds of terrifying destruction. Even more disturbing, he'd seen buildings cut in half, part of them reduced to rubble, the rest pristine and untouched, dishes still on the table, paintings hung straight—like a giant knife had carved off the fronts and turned them into macabre dollhouses.

People down here respected the weather. They feared it. And there was Nina, naked and letting the storm inside.

Reveling in it.

Maybe that's all he was to her, a storm passing through her life. Excitement and danger and the thrill of something forbidden. Maybe all of his self-indulgent brooding over his impending betrayal was the arrogance of a man assuming he had the upper hand, when he was really nothing more than her latest adrenaline high.

And maybe he was just trying to rationalize fucking her because he already knew he was going to do it again.

"Did I wake you?"

He could barely hear her over the sound of the rain slapping on the pavement outside, but her husky tone still stirred his blood. "If you hadn't, the storm would have."

"That's too bad." She turned her head just enough for him to see her smiling profile. "You seemed like you needed the rest."

Hard to argue with that. Knox pushed himself upright and swung his legs off the bed. The tequila was still open on the bedside table. Since it was a night for reckless decisions, he snagged the bottle. It burned going down. He knew his body would metabolize it before he could get a good buzz going, but it *felt* decadent and irresponsible.

God, how long had it been since he'd let himself be irresponsible? "Do you like storms?" he asked after taking another swig.

"No. But my sisters did." Nina's smile vanished. "It was the only thing they could ever agree on."

Sisters.

He paused with the bottle halfway to his lips. He'd built all his assumptions around the idea that Nina was part of some rogue military project. Most of the military bases east of the Mississippi had been privatized during the tumultuous runup to the Energy Wars, liquidated for the cash flow the faltering government needed in order to bring the West Coast—with its vital food supply—back under control. But some of those newly minted private mercenary companies had retained access to information on military genetic projects, and they had no doubt resumed experimentation once the Flares had wiped out any pretense of oversight.

As far as Knox knew, what had remained of the actual military after the Flares had focused on consolidating power in the West. Rumors drifted back across the Mississippi River, whispers of genetically altered soldiers who were born possessing all of Knox's implant-gifted strengths. Knox had also heard rumors about the brutal brainwashing protocols they used to keep those soldiers loyal, a regime of torture and conditioning that stripped away emotion and empathy and made Protectorate training look like a cheerful slumber party.

It was a lot of work, keeping your supersoldiers in line. The TechCorps had always preferred the elegance of a kill switch. Even knowing that the biochemical bomb ticking down in his brain would eventually destroy him, Knox couldn't say he'd trade places with one of those emotionless killing machines. At least his mind had always been his own.

So he'd heard some strange things over the years, but he'd never heard of any military genetics projects that utilized siblings. Strong bonds of loyalty like that were inconvenient and dangerous, especially in soldiers who didn't come with off switches.

Or maybe her sisters *were* the off switches. Built-in hostages.

Brutal.

"There were three of us." Nina's voice sounded vaguely detached. A little distant. "There were always three in every cluster. That's how the Franklin Center operated."

The Franklin Center. The words tugged at a vague memory, but he couldn't follow the path. It didn't sound military, though. "That's where you're from?"

"The Franklin Center for Genetic Research." She leaned against the wall, as if she needed it to hold her up. "Trios of genetically engineered clones as far as the eye could see. That's where I grew up."

Clones.

He shifted uneasily. The TechCorps' public stance on cloning was that it was an ethics quagmire, and of *course* they'd never do such a thing. Their public stances often differed greatly from their private ones, but Knox was pretty sure they wouldn't have created Nina. He had no doubt they'd violate their ethics mandates in a heartbeat if the money was good enough, but someone like Nina—someone with power built into her and nothing to check her reckless, unrelenting *decency*—

They'd never take that risk.

But someone *had* created her. Someone who'd left her with shaky knees and that vague detachment. A sick weight settled in his stomach. "What was it like there? Was it . . . bad?"

"I don't know," she admitted. "It's all I ever knew. We worked hard, trained hard. But they didn't keep us isolated from each other, and I don't remember being sad."

He needed to know why she'd left. What had happened to her sisters, who might be chasing her, how dangerous they were. What they'd do to get her back. A dozen questions piled up in his throat, each fighting to get free.

It was the lost look in her eyes that stopped him. The fact that she didn't know how to answer a question as basic as *what was it like?* That the best she had to offer was the lack of sorrow.

He rose silently, crossed the space between them, and held out the bottle.

She stared up at him, unmoving. "You feel sorry for me."

"A little," he admitted. "Maybe not too much. I know a lot of people who can definitely remember being sad."

"No." She finally reached for the tequila. "That came later."

He waited until she'd taken a generous sip of the liquor. "What happened?"

Her cheeks were wet. It might have just been the rain, but Knox couldn't be sure. She moved slowly, as if she had been the one to take a beating in the cage. One more drink, and she set the bottle on the battered dresser.

He'd laid out his clothes for tomorrow. Nina picked up the worn white T-shirt he'd left folded on top of the stack and hauled it over her head. He waited until she'd crawled back onto the bed and curled up, then moved slowly, like she was a wild animal he might startle.

The bedsprings squeaked as he slid onto the mattress. He settled next to her—close, but not touching—and asked the question again. "What happened, Nina?"

She took a deep, shaky breath. "We each had different skills. Ava was the brains. Zoey was the heart."

He could guess what she must have been, but something told him she needed to say it. "And you?"

Her fingers slid over his, tracing the rough bumps of his knuckles. "I was the fists. Combat, soldier, brute force—whatever you want to call it."

"You were their leader."

"I was the muscle," she corrected. "Anyway, when we finished our training, we were going to change the world. Save it. It didn't exactly turn out that way."

She fell silent, and he waited. After a few moments, she shifted on the bed, moving closer, and continued. "Our first mission was a simple rescue. A pharmaceutical company had kidnapped one of the Center's neuro-geneticists. You know how it goes—they tried to woo him with money, then blackmail. They'd moved on to torture by the time we got the assignment."

"*Torture?*" Knox had brought in his share of "recruited" scientists over the years, but the TechCorps typically employed more subtle methods of persuasion—for very practical reasons. "What kind of work could they possibly be getting out of him like that?"

"I don't know. And I couldn't ask him." She swallowed hard. "We infiltrated the building easily enough. We had a clean window of operations. It should have worked. But when we found him . . . he was in bad shape. Not the torture—they'd regenerated all the damage—but the strain. I think he'd had a stroke. Ava called it, said we should abort, but Zoey refused to leave him there."

He knew all about hard calls, and he had no doubt what Nina would have chosen. "You still tried to get him out."

"We almost succeeded. We were close to our extraction point when the fire teams caught up with us." Nina's gaze focused on a spot on the wall, and the words kept tumbling out, faster and faster, until they were almost running together. "We were pinned down, and they had all the advantages. High ground, home field, numbers. The scientist went down first, and then Zoey—" Her voice broke. "And then Zoey."

He finally touched her, wrapping an arm around her shoulder to tug her against his chest. "I'm sorry."

She didn't seem to hear him. "Ava and I kept fighting. I don't know when she got hit, but after I took down the last soldier, I turned around and—" Her eyes squeezed shut. "Zoey was gone, and Ava was bleeding out. I managed to get her back to the Center, at least, but . . . she didn't make it."

He pulled her closer, his heart raw from how deeply he understood. How many missions had almost gone sideways because of something as simple as a choice between brains and heart? He could imagine too easily how her sisters had responded to the fallen scientist. Ava would have been like Gray, ruthlessly pragmatic, always focused on the bigger picture. Willing to leave the man behind for the sake of the mission. And Zoey would have responded like Rafe, unwilling to give up on *anyone*, even if it meant gambling her life on a hopeless cause.

And Nina would have been caught in the middle, her idealism at war with the need to keep her sisters safe. A no-win scenario.

It was a miracle she'd gotten out alive.

Nina clung to him, breathing in slow, deep, deliberate measures. "Clusters only function as a unit, and two-thirds of mine was dead. I was officially decommissioned. The Center offered to find me a job, and they did—with a private security force just like the one that killed my sisters."

Knox stroked her hair, the silken strands wild beneath his fingers. Fine shivers trembled through her body. He felt like he'd torn away her smiling, carefree mask and found a well of pain deep enough to drown in.

"You didn't take it." He didn't make it a question. He knew she couldn't have.

"No. I used what Ava and Zoey had taught me, and I left. In the middle of the night, with the clothes on my back. And this." She lifted the silver pendant she wore from the hollow of her throat.

He hooked a finger under the thin chain. It wasn't so different from the one his dog tags hung from, but instead of cool steel and identification numbers, hers was threaded through three interlocking rings. "For your sisters?"

She nodded. "Zoey made them. A set of three for each of us."

He rubbed his thumb over the delicate rings. They wove in and out of each other, distinct but intertwined. A more elegant memorial than the one he had.

Releasing her necklace, he twisted off the bed to snag his jeans. His Protectorate-issue dog tags were in the back pocket, three little rectangles of metal.

Two for him. One for Mace.

Silently, he held them out to her.

She shuffled through the tags, pausing at the third. The damning one. Then she looked up at him. "What happened?"

"Do you remember the strike at the microchip factory?"

Nina sucked in a breath. "A couple of months ago. Half a dozen people were killed, five times that injured. The Protectorate said the workers rioted, but that's not what I've heard."

"The Protectorate tasked me with inciting a riot and using it as cover to eliminate the ringleaders who were trying to force better working conditions." If he closed his eyes, he'd see the orders, crisp text scrolling across his tablet. He'd feel the dread and rage all over again. "One of the perks of commanding the most elite squad in the Protectorate was that I usually had some . . . discretion with my orders. I'd done plenty of shit that was bad. Unforgivable, even. But nothing like that. Nothing that was just . . . evil."

"What did you do?"

"I submitted a modified mission objective. With a little time for recon and permission to negotiate on the TechCorps' behalf, I was sure I could end the strike. We were *good* at what we did. Those people probably still wouldn't have gotten everything they deserved or needed, but they would have been alive."

"That was your mistake, I guess?" she asked softly. "Assuming that your superiors *wanted* them alive."

"No, I knew they didn't care." He reached out for the dog tags and pressed his thumb to Mace's. "My mistake was thinking I was important enough to change their minds."

She touched his hand. Touched the tag. "They killed him?"

Hoarse, bitter laughter shredded his throat. "Depends on your definition of *killed*. They locked us up. All five of us, each in our own separate cell. Polycarbonate—so we could see each other. Then they stopped servicing his implant."

Knox couldn't think about it, couldn't let himself remember those agonizing weeks. Not with Conall upstairs, drugged and woozy and falling the fuck apart. Knox curled his hand into a fist. "Mace was our medic. His implant is—*was* like Conall's, more geared toward intellect than just physical enhancement. The neural overload hits them first. You've seen the start of it with Conall, but Mace . . . By the end . . ."

Nina peeled Knox's fingers away from the tag, and he realized the metal edges had begun to bite into his skin. She made a quiet noise as she slid into his lap, and another as she cupped his face, her thumbs stroking over his cheeks. "I'm sorry," she whispered. "I'm here."

It was wrong to accept her soothing. Wrong to accept her tenderness, as if he'd ever done a damn thing to deserve it except hurt everyone he was supposed to protect.

As if he wouldn't hurt her.

But the pain had cracked open. It burned as he clenched his fists again, wondering if he could break his own unbreakable hands with the pressure. "It took him weeks to die. Weeks of agony. In the end, he was alone, and hurting, and *scared,* and I couldn't get to him. All I could do was beat my fists against those fucking walls until I shattered every bone in my hands. And I remember thinking—I remember thinking at least I'd made myself useless to them."

She shuddered. Tilted her head. "They regenerated them?"

There was that laugh again, the one that cut like shards of glass. "They couldn't regenerate the kind of damage I did, so they replaced everything. They broke me and rebuilt me and sent me out to be a good little soldier again." He exhaled on a shudder and held her gaze. "That's why I'm an asshole. That's why you can't trust me. They ripped all the good out of me, Nina. All that's left is making sure what happened to Mace doesn't happen to the rest of my men. There's nothing—"

He bit down on the words, on the *truth*. She was straddling his lap, petting him with soft fingers, stroking a damn confession out of him. He could taste the warning on his lips. He could hear it as if he'd spoken it.

There's nothing I won't do. No one I won't destroy.

Even me.

Even you.

He held the words back with the shredded remains of his self-control. Sweet merciful *fuck*, she was dangerous. And he couldn't even say she hadn't warned him. She'd predicted this moment on their first day out, laughing as she and her girls played games with the Devils over their own listening devices.

You don't come at a lion head on, but you don't have to sneak up behind it, either. You can pet it until it lets down its guard.

Nina whispered his name, then pressed a soft, lingering kiss to the corner of his mouth. Even knowing how close he was to burning down everything he'd sacrificed for, his body thrilled at the touch. He turned into the kiss, catching her mouth, distracting them both with the heat that flared up at the first brush of their tongues.

She pulled away, but only long enough to drag his shirt over her head and toss it aside on the bed. Then it was skin against skin, her breasts pressed to his chest as he wrapped both arms around her and surrendered to the need.

He told himself it was just sex as he plunged both hands deep into her hair and tangled his fingers tight, holding her in place for an endless kiss that had her panting and squirming in his lap, begging silently for the erection he ground up against her.

He told himself it was just sex when he tilted her back onto the bed and worked his way down her body with soft kisses mixed with softer bites, a combination that made her yank his hair and gasp his name like a curse, especially when he reached his destination.

He told himself it was just sex as he spread her thighs wide and let her ride his tongue, the jerky, desperate lift of her hips providing primal, necessary proof that he held *some* of the power here. That he could make her writhe and whimper and even beg when he added his fingers and twisted her second orgasm into an abrupt, brutal third, her body clenching wildly as he drove her to the edge of sanity.

He told himself it was just sex when he crawled up her body, indulging himself by lingering over her breasts and licking her nipples until her fingernails broke the skin of his shoulders and her gasps turned to husky, implacable command.

He told himself it was just sex until he was inside her, each thrust a reckless display of enhanced strength that she met with strength of her own. She scratched and bit and wrapped her sleekly muscled limbs around him, reminding him with every moan, every sigh, every whisper for *more* that she could equal him. Match him. *Take* him.

When she came around his dick the final time, shuddering, and then closed her teeth over the hammering pulse in his throat with a growl of possession that shot straight to the base of his spine, Knox stopped telling himself it was just sex.

This was heaven and hell. A tormenting glimpse of the life he could have had, the life he could never have now. All because he'd brought her *here,* to this dump of a town to swim through the grime of his past with betrayal in his heart. He could never deserve the way she softly stroked his cheeks and murmured his name in that pleasure-drunk voice.

He came with a wrenching cry, and the pleasure *hurt*. Not just because nothing this bad should feel so good. Not just because he knew this should be the last time.

It hurt because in that moment, staring down into her flushed cheeks and tender eyes, his muscles trembling with the strength it took not to collapse into her arms, he realized the truth.

Knox didn't think he could betray her, after all.

And he had no idea what the *fuck* he was going to do.

TECHCORPS PROPRIETARY DATA, L1 SECURITY CLEARANCE

All attempts to replicate 55–312's resistance to pain have met with failure. We reached the suggested mortality threshold of 80.7 percent this morning. If you wish for the experiments to proceed, I'll need an administrative override and access to a fresh batch of test subjects.

Recruit Analysis, June 2078

SIXTEEN

Light had just begun to stream through the cracks in the crooked blinds when Nina slipped out of Knox's bed. Just like the night before, he stirred, his fists clenching around nothing, but didn't open his eyes.

He looked so young when he slept. Unguarded, like the world didn't weigh on him as much. She wanted to sink back into his arms and kiss him awake, keep kissing him as the sun clawed its way into the sky, until necessity and hunger drove them from the bed.

And that was exactly why she had to leave. So she dressed in the darkness and slipped out into the still, misty morning, closing the door silently behind her.

The covered walkway that led to the other wing of the motel was deserted except for the birds that chirped from the nests they'd built in the corners of the awning. Nina surveyed the storm damage as she walked—a few fallen branches, some debris scattered about the cracked parking lot, and leaves stuck to the sides of the cars.

Minimal. Good.

Shivering, she rubbed at her bare arms. The rain had washed away the worst of the oppressive heat, and a cool breeze teased at her hair. Goose bumps rose on her flesh, but she welcomed them. After spending several sweltering days wishing desperately for this respite, she wasn't about to take it for granted.

When she reached the room she was sharing with her team, Nina dragged the old-fashioned key from her pocket. It stuck in the lock, and she had to finesse it open.

Maya was alone inside, seated on the rumpled covers in her shorts and a bra, her hair still covered by her silk sleeping scarf. She had her legs crossed, her earbuds in, and a gun in one hand.

She lowered it when Nina stepped inside. "Well, good morning."

Nina tossed her key on the dresser with a clatter. "Dani in the bathroom?"

"No, she went out last night." Maya set the gun aside and cut her music with a tap on her wrist. Then she studied Nina's face. "You seem more . . . relaxed."

"*Maya*." Nina's cheeks burned as she dragged her bag to the foot of the untouched bed and searched for some fresh clothes. "I'm sorry. I wouldn't have gone anywhere if I'd known Dani planned to. We shouldn't have left you alone last night."

"I can take care of myself, you know. And I kinda needed some space anyway." Maya's eyes narrowed. "Also you're changing the subject."

"There's a subject? I thought you were just making a random observation." She pinned Maya with a look. "You certainly didn't ask a question."

"Because I was kind of hoping you'd say, 'Yeah, I rode that ride and I'm over it.' Or something about scratching an itch."

No. Nina didn't have any expectations, and Knox didn't owe her anything. But if her attraction to him had been that casual, nothing more than mere curiosity, then she would have kept her damn pants on. "You know me better than that."

"I know." Maya sighed, and her voice dropped to a gentle whisper. "I just worry, Nina. Not about the mission, or about us. I know you'll protect us. But you're not always as careful with your heart."

She'd never had to be—or maybe she didn't know how. Pain was a constant for her, as much a part of her daily existence as breathing. And she'd decided a long time ago that embracing that pain was better than locking herself away from feeling anything at all. If she had, she may as well have curled up and died along with her sisters.

She just couldn't let things go too far.

Nina slipped off her shoes, exchanged her shirt for a clean one, and unbuttoned her jeans. "I'll be okay, Maya."

Usually that would have been the end of it. But Maya shifted up onto her knees and reached out to touch Nina's arm. "It's in your voice, when you talk to him. Or about him. I haven't heard it since Sergei."

Hearing his name, thinking about him, didn't hurt the way Nina anticipated. When had that stopped? Probably as gradually as it had begun.

It had started with a chance meeting in the Southside market. Sergei was a fisherman by trade, and he'd come in from the coast with his skipper to sell their catch. He wasn't really Nina's type, but she liked his face, and he had a laugh that made her smile. Still, she'd never expected their fun, casual flirtation to turn into anything more than equally fun, casual sex.

Until the day he told her he was leaving. Winter was coming, and the Gulf was better than the blustery Atlantic when the cold weather descended. Shocked and numb, Nina had somehow managed to smile and nod as Sergei told her how great she was, and that maybe he'd roll back around with the spring.

He probably never even realized he'd broken her heart.

Knox knew he would, if she let him. He was living on borrowed time, but his warnings to her seemed to have nothing to do with the threat of his deteriorating physical condition. When he pushed her away—which was hard and often—he spoke only of how ruined he was in other ways.

I'm an asshole.

You can't trust me.

They ripped all the good out of me, Nina.

All that's left—

She stripped off her jeans and pulled on a fresh pair of dark green cargo pants. "That was years ago. I'm not that young anymore."

Maya sighed softly. "If you're sure. Just be careful, okay? If he hurts you, I'll have to fork him in the jugular. And I am *not* as fast as he is."

Another key jangled in the lock, and Dani stepped in. "Who are we forking?"

Nina frowned. Dani wore a short, tight black dress and lace-up heels. Her makeup was smudged, and her hair was disheveled—though it could have looked that way on purpose. On anyone else, the outfit would have screamed *I'm looking for a good time, and you're going to show me one.*

On Dani, they may as well have been tactical fatigues.

"Oh, yeah," Maya said with a wince. "I, uh, forgot that part. She went out hunting."

Shit. "Where?" Nina demanded. The answer would determine how much time they had left to get the fuck out of town.

"Back to the bar." Dani yawned. "I paid Boyd a little visit. Someone had to do it."

"Aww, shit." Maya rolled off the bed and grabbed for her bag. "I guess I better get dressed."

"Don't insult me." Dani sniffed. "He's still alive—for now. We have plenty of time."

Nina stifled a sigh. "Poison?"

"Only the finest." Dani slipped a thin metal tube from her clutch. It was a spring-loaded injector, the kind used to administer tiny grains of slow-acting poison. "Piece of cake."

"Was it really necessary? I paid him off."

"I had a sneaking suspicion that wasn't going to stick." Dani sank to the bed and began to unlace her shoes. "Besides, you wouldn't ask me that question if you'd heard some of the foul shit that came out of his mouth once he thought I was down to party."

"I'm sure he's trash." Maya's voice was muffled as she pulled her shirt on over her head. She swept her braids free of the fabric and pinned Dani with an annoyed look. "But you could have *told* me. Aren't you the one always harping on how we don't go out on jobs alone?"

"Right. But this was a decidedly extracurricular activity, so."

A dangerous one. But it was hard to worry too much after the fact, and Nina couldn't deny that part of her was relieved. Not just that Boyd wouldn't be a concern as they continued their travels, but that he couldn't hurt anyone else.

That he couldn't hurt *Knox*.

Nina pushed the thought away. "I should have been informed. You might have needed backup, whether you wanted it or not."

"You? Were busy." Dani peeled off her dress. "How was it, by the way? I've never boned a Protectorate soldier before. Is walking difficult this morning?"

Nina threw a pillow at her head.

The pillow bounced off Dani and landed on the floor. Maya nudged it into place with her foot, then sat on it to pull on her socks and boots. "Are you going to talk some sense into our fearless leader, or what? Because she's not listening to me."

"Yeah, I think that ship has sailed." In no hurry to get dressed again, Dani pulled her knees up on the bed and rested her chin on them. "Also? Rafe said last night that he thinks Nina and Knox fucking is a terrible idea, so I suddenly find myself much more open to it. I officially support you, Nina. *Get it.*"

"Oh, for *fuck's sake*." Maya groaned and jerked on her boot laces so hard she snapped one. "Maybe you should just hate-fuck Rafe and get it over with. I mean, if we're gonna make terrible life choices, we should commit."

Dani pursed her lips in thought. "Hmm. I'm not ruling it out. Have you *seen* his thighs? He seems a little high-maintenance, though."

Nina picked up Dani's bag and tossed it to her. "You're never this chipper in the mornings. You're high on murder."

"*Almost* murder," Dani corrected. "Boyd's still kicking. Call it impending murder. Murder-to-be?"

"Imminent vigilantism." Maya rose and kicked the pillow back toward the bed. "I mean, is it really murder if he has it coming?"

More like justice. "Whatever you want to call it, can we keep it to a minimum for the rest of the trip?" Nina asked. "I'm going to have to tell the guys about this, and they're already scared of you."

"Terrified." Dani's eyes gleamed. "Isn't it great? They're—" The words stopped suddenly and she straightened on the bed. "Hold on, you changed the subject. Maya, she changed the subject."

"Yeah, it's kinda her thing today."

Dani sat up straighter, every trace of amusement replaced by a solemnity that shadowed her delicate features. "Nina, seriously. You know you have to pull it back, right? Playing with a little fire is fun, but you can't douse yourself in vodka and strike a match."

If they were both this worried, Nina couldn't shrug it off. "It was one night. One really, really *good* night," she admitted. "But even if I wanted more, I'm pretty sure Captain Knox . . . doesn't."

She stood there awkwardly as sympathy filled Maya's eyes. Then Dani slid off the bed and wrapped both arms around Nina.

"Then he's stupid," she whispered. "Smart, but stupid. Right, Maya?"

"A fucking idiot," Maya agreed, rising to hug Nina from the other side. "Maybe I'll fork him either way. After we have our wheelbarrow full of money."

They were right—and Knox would have been the first to say so. Still, the idea of pulling away from him now kindled a bittersweet ache in the center of her chest. They'd shared so much, and she wanted to do it again. The sex, sure, but more than that, the *intimacy*.

Which meant she didn't have a choice. She had to distance herself. Fucking was one thing—one very understandable thing—but feelings were dangerous. Knox knew that, and it was time for Nina to follow his lead.

No matter how much it hurt.

Nina's eyes stung, and she disentangled herself from the group hug before either of her friends could notice. "Maya, do a sweep of the room, please. If we accidentally leave anything behind, it's gone forever. And Dani?"

"Yes, ma'am?"

Nina didn't bother stifling her sigh this time. "Please put some clothes on before the man you poisoned drops dead and we all get killed."

Dani grinned. "You got it, boss."

GRAY

There were a select number of things Gray knew for certain. Unassailable, incontrovertible truths that he could revisit whenever the noise in his head got too loud, and he needed the steady comfort of concrete reality.

The sun rose in the east, for example.

The perfect pull weight for a trigger was 4.7 pounds of pressure.

His captain was incapable of distraction.

That last fact was carved in stone, more cosmically sound than any of the rest of it. It had saved their entire team more times than Gray could count.

And it was falling apart.

Knox was brooding. Not thinking or planning—Gray knew how Knox looked when he'd turned inward to map out possibilities and variables. Right now, he was staring into the back of the truck with a deep furrow between his brows, even though nothing back there required such fierce contemplation.

Brooding.

"I don't think any of it is going to bite you." Gray flicked Knox's collar, exposing a rising bruise on his neck that he definitely did not get in the cage at Boyd's place. "Looks like something did, though."

Knox's jaw clenched. He shoved his bag on top of the supplies and slammed the truck's cargo door. "I have the lecture coming, so bring it on."

"Yeah, you'd like that, wouldn't you?"

"Not really, to be honest."

"Sure, you would. A little extra punishment to go along with your self-flagellation. Well, I'm not playing."

Knox pivoted to face him. He was wearing his *stone-cold captain* face, but Gray had known him long enough to see the cracks in the mask. "You don't think I deserve the punishment? After the last week?"

Gray had his opinions, but he wasn't sure they counted for much, if anything. "Doesn't matter what I think. Every man has to reckon with his own conscience, Knox."

"That's what I'm trying to do." Knox crossed his arms over his chest, his fingers drumming against his biceps. "I've been running scenarios. Making plans. I want to get Luna back without sacrificing Nina or her crew."

The hair on the back of Gray's neck rose in warning. "Wait, you what?"

"You heard me. Luna's my priority, but I'm making contingency plans. We've handled hostage situations way more dangerous than this before."

"That's not a contingency," he argued. "A double cross? That's changing the game entirely. Did you come clean with Nina last night, or something?"

"No," Knox snapped. "And this isn't about the fucking. I *know* her now, and I know what she means to that neighborhood. This is about what she and her crew do for those people. It's all the reasons I couldn't obey the order to kill those organizers. The Protectorate stopped protecting them, Gray. She's what they have left."

None of it was untrue. And none of it mattered. "No."

Both of Knox's eyebrows shot up. "No?"

"No," he repeated firmly. "You don't get to make this call. Not this time, and not like this."

Genuine hurt tightened Knox's eyes. "So you don't trust me to put my squad first anymore?"

The truth was even more damning, and it would hurt far worse. "There is no squad, Knox, and you're not our captain. Not anymore. We left, remember? The Silver Devils are gone."

"I have to be your captain," Knox ground out. "I have to get you *out*. You're not out until you can walk away free and clear."

"Well, I didn't agree to that. Pretty sure Rafe and Con didn't, either." Gray clasped Knox's shoulder until the other man looked at him. "I'll still follow you—as your friend. But not if you're making bad calls. And this is a *bad call*."

Knox squeezed his eyes shut. "I know. I'm trying to find the least terrible thing to do, and I need you to tell me when I'm fucking it up."

"You're fucking it up right now. Ask me why." Without waiting for the question, Gray pressed on. "Because you're half-assing it. You haven't told Nina the truth, and you're not going to, are you?"

"If I do, chances are pretty high she'll turn around and haul ass right back to Atlanta, don't you think?"

It was a distinct possibility. Nina seemed to like a little danger, but not enough to compromise the rest of her crew if she could avoid it. She'd split, all right, if only to save Maya and Dani.

Unless she didn't. Unless they sat down together, discussed their options, and decided that saving Luna was worth the risk. Somewhere, deep in his gut, Gray suspected that outcome might be just as likely. Maybe more.

Then again, maybe Knox's hesitation wasn't entirely about that.

"I think telling her the truth is worth a shot," he said finally. "She's going to hate you no matter what, man. You're not getting out of this any other way."

Knox didn't flinch, but Gray felt the blow land in the tension of Knox's shoulder. "I know."

For a moment, Gray regretted the words. Not because they weren't necessary, but because they were weapons, and he'd been careless in wielding them. "We'll see, okay? We'll talk to the guys—"

A flurry of conversation cut through his words as Rafe and Conall emerged from the motel courtyard with Nina and her team. The women went straight to their vehicle and quickly began loading their bags into the back.

Nina didn't even look their way. Knox's frown, which had eased somewhat at the sight of her, returned. With a vengeance.

Rafe was casting covert gazes at the women, but he kept his mouth shut as he lifted Conall's bag from his shoulder and stowed it in the truck. Conall stopped next to Gray, his face tight, his fingers tapping restlessly on his thigh. "We should get on the road. Now."

"What happened?" Gray demanded.

Rafe choked on a laugh and hauled open the truck's door. "Oh, nothing much. Dani poisoned Boyd."

"Aw, shit." Gray grabbed Rafe's arm to stop him from climbing into the vehicle. "When? And how?"

"This morning. She popped him with a pellet of abrin."

At least it would take Boyd a few hours to notice anything was wrong. And by then it'd be too late. "That woman's got some nasty hobbies." Gray nudged Knox. "But she did you a solid."

Knox grunted. His gaze remained fixed on the women as they piled into their truck. "She definitely did. Anyone know why?"

"He was being skeezy at Nina," Conall rasped, easing into the backseat like his whole body ached. "I'd have poisoned him if I knew it was on the table."

Gray rounded the vehicle and climbed behind the wheel. "You wouldn't have gotten close, Conall. She probably took advantage of his stupidity by making big eyes at him. Not exactly an avenue of attack open to any of us. Not in Boyd's case."

Rafe let out another of those strangled-sounding laughs as he climbed in next to Conall. "You called it, Gray."

Gray snorted and started the truck. "She's perfect for you, Rafe."

"You trying to get me killed?" Rafe retorted. "Pretty sure she wants to poison me, too."

"Not if you play your cards right," Gray muttered. Knox was sitting in the passenger seat, the furrow between his brows deeper than ever, so Gray leaned toward him a little. "Are you upset about Boyd? Don't be. Even if his men realize what got him, I doubt they'll—"

"It's not that." Knox glanced at him, the indecision from earlier magnified a hundredfold. "Something's changed. Nina didn't even look at me."

Yeah, Gray had noticed. "Maybe she's worried you'll be upset that one of her team went rogue. Or maybe she was just in a hurry because of it." He shifted into reverse and began backing out of his parking spot. "Either way, best to find out."

"Yeah." He sighed and rolled his shoulders. "I better keep in mind that Dani's not just armed. She's packing poison, too."

"Not a bad idea, Garrett. Not a bad idea."

TECHCORPS PROPRIETARY DATA, L2 SECURITY CLEARANCE

66–615 managed to secure an unexpected victory by subverting several of the labor organizers and fracturing their alliance. Ending the strike without violence was vastly preferable, given the current state of discontent in the city.

We should consider how much more efficient he might become if afforded increased latitude and access to resources.

Recruit Analysis, November 2078

SEVENTEEN

Now that Knox was reluctant to make progress, they'd reached a clear patch of highway. Knox resented every mile of barely cracked asphalt and glared balefully at each easily avoided pothole. Gray had been making good time all day, driving them straight toward the point of no return.

Tonight or tomorrow, he had to make his final check-in, the one where he'd be given the exact GPS coordinates for the exchange. The longer he delayed, the more irritated Luna's kidnapper would become. If Knox was going to bring the women in and work out a plan that utilized all of their various skills, he had to do it soon.

It had almost seemed possible. For a few seconds after Gray said the words, Knox had thought it might be that easy. Even if Nina hated him for his lies, if he showed her the video of Luna, she'd help. She was *good*.

But she'd slipped out of his bed without a word and didn't want to look at him anymore. Maybe she could feel it already—the truth, seething between them. She wasn't just good. She was too good for him.

"Isn't Dalton coming up?" Conall asked from behind him. "Can we pull off and see if Eileen's is open? This implant is fucking me up, and I want some real food."

Knox glanced at Gray, who nodded his agreement. "We've been making good time," Knox said, reaching for the radio. "I'll see if the ladies are up for a pit stop."

Static crackled, and wary nervousness clawed up Knox's spine as he pressed the button. "Nina?"

After a few endless moments, he got a response. "Dani here. What do you need?"

He had enough self-control not to flinch. Barely. "There's a town coming up in a few miles. You guys okay stopping for a late lunch?"

Silence, for what seemed like an eternity. Then, "Sure. We're game if you are. Lead and we'll follow."

He waited for a moment, but nothing else was said. The soft static crackle felt damning in a way that chilled him.

Nina had tamed the lion, all right. One good petting, and he was panting for attention, frantic at being shut out, eager to prove himself. Rafe couldn't have played it better. Knox could see every move in this manipulative game like he was staring at his own seduction outlined as a tactical plan.

And his gut still insisted that Nina wasn't manipulating him at all.

A listing, rusted road sign warned them that Dalton was the next exit. Knox watched the kudzu-covered trees go by, their eerie shapes menacing in the overcast afternoon gloom. Someone had trimmed the growth back from the sign at the top of the exit—a weathered wooden door lashed to what was left of an old traffic light with DALTON painted in white block letters.

A century ago, tens of thousands of people had called this city home. Dalton had started to die long before the Flares, as its factories shut down and residents fled the contaminated rivers. They'd lived out their own private apocalypse while the world went on merrily around them. The people who'd remained were tough, the kind of tough that didn't buckle in the face of a mild inconvenience like the end of civilization.

Gray steered the truck down abandoned streets lined with crumbling factories and empty warehouses. Old fast-food restaurants dotted the sides of the road, their signs cracked or shattered, their interiors gutted by scavengers. Knox had rarely seen many people out and about at the edge of town, but even half a mile out from the center of town, the streets remained eerily silent.

He wasn't the only one to notice. Rafe leaned forward, bracing his arm on Knox's seat. "Where is everyone?"

"Still hunkered down after the storms?" Gray suggested.

"No," Conall said. "No, something's wrong."

Knox twisted to look at him. "What is it?"

A frustrated noise. Conall squeezed his eyes shut. "I don't know. My brain knows. But I don't know."

Gray's hands tightened on the wheel. "Should we circle back and keep moving?"

After another moment, Conall sighed explosively and shook his head. "No. Fuck, maybe I'm just hungry. I don't *know* what the fuck I'm feeling. Don't listen to me."

Conall might not trust his own instincts right now, but Knox always had. The implant might have short-circuited the connection between Conall's conscious and subconscious, but his genius brain was still taking in tiny clues and drawing conclusions from them.

Knox faced forward again. "We can get Conall his food, maybe stock up on a few things. But keep your eyes open. If we see trouble, be ready to move."

The radio crackled again. "Charming place you've brought us to, Captain," Dani drawled. "What gives?"

Before Knox could reach for the handset, Rafe lunged forward and grabbed it. "Hey, snickerdoodle. It's a little quieter than usual, but we're not going in hot. Keep the poison in your garter strap for the moment, eh?"

"Shows what you know, Morales. I don't wear garters under my clothes when I hunt." A pause. "I don't wear much of anything, actually."

"So where do you keep the—"

Knox snatched the handset. "We don't know if there's trouble or not. We're stopping in two blocks. Just stay on guard, and we'll get food to go."

Gray pulled the truck into one of the angled streetside spaces near Eileen's Diner, put it in park, unbuckled his seat belt, and glowered at Rafe. "Snickerdoodle?"

"What?" Rafe defended. "It's our thing."

Conall's dull voice came from next to him. "He's saying you shouldn't have a thing, Rafe. We weren't supposed to like them, remember?"

Shock rippled across Rafe's face, there and gone in a heartbeat, but it drove another shard of guilt into Knox's chest. Rafe *had* forgotten, just like Knox had known he would. The brash, focused soldier, blithely asserting that he would take down anyone for Luna's sake, had always been a lie. Rafe liked Dani. He liked Maya and Nina. Betraying them was going to break something in him.

Knox had set him up for this. It was his job to fix it. "Let's get our food and get back on the road," he said quietly. "And then we'll talk. Okay?"

"Fine," Rafe said, his voice forcibly cheerful. But he wouldn't meet Knox's eyes as he slipped from the truck.

That seemed to be going around.

By the time Knox exited the vehicle, Nina had parked the other truck and was climbing out of the driver's seat. When she closed the door and turned, their eyes met.

She froze.

She didn't look angry. She didn't look pleased at the game she'd played to tame him. Yearning softened her brown eyes, her lips parting as if to invite a kiss. Then she flinched almost imperceptibly and looked away.

Uneasy, Knox stepped up onto the neatly swept sidewalk and frowned at the hand-lettered CLOSED sign hanging just inside the diner door. He gave the handle a tug, just to see, but it was locked up tight.

Nina tapped the window where the placard indicating normal operating hours had been affixed and raised one eyebrow.

If the streets hadn't been so eerily silent, Knox might have assumed Eileen was just feeling under the weather. But even then, *someone* from the family would probably have opened up shop. In a town like this, the one real diner was a community gathering point, a place usually brimming with townsfolk grabbing a meal, charging their tech at one of the charging stations, or doing business over glasses of homebrew and Eileen's famous peach iced tea.

"That's weird," Rafe said from just behind Knox's shoulder. He had both backup fuel canisters dangling from one big hand—not a bad idea with the overcast weather eating through their solar batteries.

Knox caught Nina's eye and tilted his head to indicate the gas station and general trading post across the street. "Shall we?"

She nodded, and Dani and Maya climbed out of their truck and fell into step beside them, along with Gray and Conall. Instead of making conversation, everyone remained silent.

Halfway across the street, Nina nudged Knox in the side. "Don't look, but we have eyes. Top of the tower, two blocks down. I saw a muzzle."

Knox kept his movements casual and easy until he reached the door and could turn naturally while holding it open. He spotted the muzzle of the sniper rifle she'd mentioned, and let his gaze continue on, sweeping the upper floors of closer buildings. A curtain twitched, and another jerked shut.

They were definitely being watched.

Inside, a pale young woman behind the front counter started at the sound of the bell over the door. She returned Rafe's nod stiffly, then glanced down at the end of the counter, where a panel of one-way glass looked out over the store from the office.

A few moments later, the office door swung open, and a burly man walked out. He had cheap tattoos running up and down both arms, but he wore expensive leather—not to mention a pristine revolver on his hip.

"New management," Gray murmured.

Knox jerked his head toward the aisles, and his men obeyed the silent command and scattered. Rafe strolled toward the tattooed man with an easy, open smile and hefted one of the plastic containers. "You guys still sell biofuel out back?"

"We're out." The man hooked his thumb through his belt so that his fingers brushed his gun.

Rafe shrugged as if it didn't matter and strolled toward the aisle full of tools and tech gadgets. Maya was already there, poking through a shelf next to a stiff-shouldered shopper.

Nina slipped her arm through Knox's as they strolled down the center aisle. When they reached a turn, she swung around it, out of sight of the watchful man at the front of the store. "What do you think?"

"I think it would take something pretty bad to make Eileen shut down at lunchtime," he replied quietly. "And I think that cashier is scared to death."

Nina leaned closer, her mouth a scant inch from his ear. "Of strangers, or of—" Her words cut off as the bell over the door pealed again, and two more armed men entered the store.

They didn't even try to act casual. The weight of their gazes burned over Knox as he nuzzled Nina's cheek and studied them. Tall. Hard. They didn't move like soldiers, but they moved like men used to intimidating with their looks and their weapons. And they were comfortable with those weapons. They were the kinds of bullies who preferred easily cowed prey, but could still fight when they encountered resistance.

The kind of scum that had probably already marked Knox as military. Scum usually did.

Nina's hair tickled his cheek. He inhaled the clean, floral scent of her and exhaled on a whisper. "We have to get out of here."

Her hands tightened on his arms. "To leave or to regroup?"

"To assess the situation."

She nodded, pulled a handful of wrapped pastries from the shelf beside them, and raised her voice a little. "I have what I need."

Knox settled his hand at the small of her back as he steered her up to the counter. The nervous-looking cashier totaled Nina's purchases on a tablet and slid it over silently for a credit stick.

As Nina paid, the others lined up behind them. The cashier never spoke, even when Rafe offered her another open, friendly smile.

The silence followed them outside, where they wordlessly split up and piled into their vehicles.

Behind the wheel, Gray exhaled sharply. "What the *fuck*?"

Paper crinkled. As Gray started the engine, Rafe held out a crumpled scrap of receipt with two words scrawled on it in thick black marker.

Help us.

"The cashier's name is Sarah. I think her dad owns the shop. Last time we came through, I flirted with her a little. Mace gave her some meds for her brother." Rafe closed his fist around the paper. "She slipped me the note when she was handing me a bottle of liquor from behind the counter. Whatever's going on in there is *bad*."

No doubt about it. Knox started to reach for the radio but hesitated. If they had snipers with eyes on the street, they might have someone listening in for comms traffic. "Drive back toward the freeway," he told Gray. "Find a place to pull off. One of the old factories, something with some cover."

Gray obeyed, but it was with set teeth and a shake of his head. "This is not our problem. You realize that, right?"

Not a smart thing to say with Rafe's fist so close. He smacked it into Gray's shoulder. "Don't be an ass. The people need some fucking help."

"Rafe." Knox grasped the man's wrist and urged him to sit back. "We'll discuss the situation. But you need to remember what happens to Luna if a sniper takes you down and you bleed out in the street here in Dalton."

Gray pulled to a stop on the far side of an abandoned brick warehouse, underneath a sagging overhang. The building would shield them from the sniper's view, and the overhang would keep them out of sight of any potential drones. Dani followed, coming to a slow stop beside them, careful not to kick up any dust.

Nina exited the truck, already peeling off her jacket. "Recon. Who's on it?"

"Hang on a second," Gray protested.

Knox laid a hand on Gray's shoulder and pivoted to face Nina. "We don't know yet if this is a fight we can afford to pick."

Nina scoffed. "You're not serious."

"My men are on a clock, Nina. We only have so much time left. Conall may not—"

"No." Conall spoke, hoarse but firm. He had a heavy bag in one hand, which he dropped at Nina's feet. But his gaze clashed with Knox's, full of challenge. "If I only have one fight left, this is a good one. I don't want to live if the cost is letting innocent people die."

More than one message there. Knox saw the same sentiment reflected back at him from Rafe's eyes. When he finally looked at Gray, his second sighed deeply and bowed his head.

A tightness that had gripped Knox's chest from the first moment he'd met Nina eased. He took a full breath and saw the end of his deception, the end of this rift in his soul—

—the end of Nina looking at him with the satisfied smile that formed when he turned and nodded. "Rafe's good for recon. What about your team?"

Dani stepped forward. "I'll go."

Conall knelt and jerked open the bag. He didn't need help handing out reconnaissance equipment, so Knox stepped away, roiling with an anticipation that had nothing to do with the fight at hand.

Nina still wasn't quite looking at him. The playful physical affection they'd shared in the store had provided effective cover, but they were back to the careful, respectful distance of skilled colleagues. There was a wall between them, a wall he loathed and appreciated in equal measure. Maybe it would protect her heart when he laid out the stark, ugly truth for her. He didn't want to be the one who snuffed the light out of her. He wanted—

No. Too soon to think about those wants. *Reckless* to think about them. Saving this town might buy him back a little bit of his soul, but he couldn't pretend it was going to buy him forgiveness from Nina. Gray had been right about that. She was going to hate him.

But she'd still help him. Maybe not for him, but for his men. For Conall. For Luna. She'd help him pull off this impossible job, she'd help him save the people counting on him.

And her heart was so damn *big*. She might not hate him forever.

Someday, she might even save him.

EIGHTEEN

The reconnaissance was illuminating.

While they were planting surveillance devices and trying to get a head count on hostiles, Rafe and Dani had run across Eileen, the woman who ran the café. It hadn't taken her long to fill them in on what had happened to Dalton.

A self-professed trading caravan had stopped in a couple of weeks earlier, looking to make some business connections. Too late, the towns-people had realized that the traders' idea of *business* was more like thievery. They'd seized a handful of hostages, locked them away in the vault at the local bank, and used their safety as leverage to keep the rest of the town compliant.

By threatening their loved ones, twelve men had managed to maintain a stranglehold on an entire town. An effective bit of strategy, if you could overlook the cruelty of it. The greed.

Nina studied the 3-D holographic sand table Conall had set up. It mapped out the entire street, incorporating the intel Eileen had given them as well as the video and still shots from the cameras Rafe and Dani had managed to deploy.

"Time?" she asked aloud.

Dani finished buckling a sheath around her thigh and slid a knife into it with a snap. "Not quite nine."

"Perfect." In a little over a quarter of an hour, half of the men would be heading to Eileen's restaurant to start drinking, where Conall would take them out of play. "You know," Nina mused, "when you really break it down, we're not even close to outnumbered."

"We could pull this job alone." Maya had her braids up in a ponytail and was checking the stun-stick at her hip. "Should be a breeze with some supersoldiers tagging along."

Knox's lips twitched slightly at the characterization, but he didn't look up from the table.

"Here." Conall handed Nina a tiny earpiece. "I'll link these up with our subdural comms. We can all get cozy in each other's heads."

"I'm not sure I like the sound of that," Dani muttered.

"Don't worry," Rafe told her while strapping on his own hunting knife. "*You* get to take them back out. I'm stuck with Conall."

"Or he's stuck with you."

Nina slid her earpiece into place. "Is everyone clear on the mission?"

Maya shot Nina a thumbs-up. "Kill, kill, save, party."

"Overly simplistic, but accurate." Knox rose and swept up the tiny projector, disrupting the hologram. "I want open comms so we can hear what's going on. No one takes unnecessary risks."

"Fast and quiet," Nina added. "No guns if you can avoid them. And if you get in trouble, remember—"

"Help is on the way," everyone but Knox finished in unison.

Nina's cheeks heated, a flush that deepened when Knox stepped closer to help her secure her tactical harness. "I think I may have said that last thing one too many times," she murmured.

His lips curved. The backs of his fingers brushed her collarbone as he untwisted a strap. "Repetition is how they remember it with bullets flying at their heads."

"Or they get so annoyed they stop listening entirely."

"No. I see the way they watch you." He smoothed the strap down over her back and tugged it to test it. "They trust you. They'll always listen."

The words washed over her, warm and soothing, every syllable wreathed with sincerity. "Knox—"

Gray's voice cut through hers. "Target acquired."

The words elicited a burst of adrenaline that had her rocking up on the balls of her feet. "You all know what to do."

Rafe and Dani melted around the side of the warehouse, an offensive line ready to clear the path to the diner's back entrance. A heartbeat later, Conall followed them.

Nina went in the opposite direction, rounding the back of the building, with Maya and Knox at her heels. This time of year, the sun tended to set late, and the timing of their attack was crucial. This was perfect. There were shadows deep enough to hide in, but enough light left to see.

They made their way single file through the narrow alley that ran behind the row of shops lining the main street. Halfway down, a door opened, and a man stepped out with a two-way radio in one hand and an unlit cigarette in the other. Quickly, Nina waved the others back, and together they ducked into an alcove between two buildings.

The man lit his cigarette, took a deep drag, and raised the radio handset. "I don't like it," he grumbled. "That was the second group we've had to run out of town in the last few days, and this one could have caused us problems."

The speaker crackled, and whoever was on the other end snorted. "Since when are you scared of a couple of assholes?"

"They were armed, man."

"Barely. And they were more focused on their lady friends than anything. Besides, Henry had them on lock the whole time from his nest up in the tower."

Dani's voice whispered through Nina's earpiece. "Conall's in. Rafe and I are moving on to phase two."

The man at the back door took another long drag from his cigarette. "It's not worth it anymore. We should clean this place out, get rid of the witnesses, and split."

Maya grabbed Nina's arm, her face tense. Knox touched Maya's shoulder and held up a finger, then tapped his ear. The message was clear—when it was time to move, they'd hear it.

Maya's mouth flattened into a hard line, but she nodded, clutching her stun-stick in one hand.

In the alleyway, the smoking man was still griping. "The big man needs to take his head out of his ass, or maybe we'll have to get rid of him, too."

"You want a bullet in the head? Fuck off with that kind of talk. I'm gonna hit the bar before you get us both tossed in with the hostages."

A crackle of static ended the conversation. Over the comms, the faint clink of glass was followed by Conall's soft murmur. "The liquor's hot."

Knox met Nina's gaze, one eyebrow arched in silent query. She tilted her head in answer, and he slipped into the alley as the man holstered the walkie-talkie.

He was fifteen feet away. Knox covered it silently, in the space between heartbeats. The man turned after dropping his cigarette, and his eyes widened as Knox bore down on him. His mouth opened—

It was over before a sound emerged. Knox snapped his neck with one swift jerk and caught the body before it could slump noisily to the ground. He lowered the man, stripped away his gun and walkie, and melted back to Nina's side.

Nina steadied Maya. "How long did Dani say the poison would take?"

"Five minutes," she answered, matching Dani's inflection perfectly. "Ten if they're stubborn."

Then they only had a few minutes before the slower drinkers started watching their buddies drop—and raised one hell of an alarm. "When we get in there, head straight for the vault. Knox and I will handle the guards, but that keypad is all you."

Knox squeezed Maya's shoulder. "I'll take point. Nina will have your back."

"I'm fine," Maya promised. "Let's do this."

Knox slipped out into the alley again, leading the way through the shadows toward the little brick bank with its massive vault—and its hostages.

He burst through the locked back door, splintering the wooden jamb. There were two men just inside the back entrance. Knox hit the first one at full speed, knocking him back against the wall so hard the whole building shuddered.

The second guard reached for his radio. Nina slid across the floor on her knees and swept his legs out from under him. The radio tumbled from his fingers as he hit the cracked tile with a *thud*. Before he could regain his breath or his footing, Nina sank a blade deep into his chest.

He was dead by the time the radio crackled to life. "Hey, we heard a crash. Everything okay over there?"

Nina stepped over the handset. "Ninety seconds, Maya."

Maya stopped in front of the massive vault's numeric keypad and jabbed all nine keys in sequence. Each beeped with its own barely discernible tone, the difference so minuscule that Maya's task seemed impossible. But she tilted her head, her focus absolute, and waited for the vault to reject the code.

Then she started hitting keys.

They'd only heard the vault opened once during their surveillance, but for Maya's memory, once was enough. Her fingers flew over the keypad, matching each tone from her memory until she'd completed the fifteen-digit sequence.

The light on the lock flashed green. The door clicked.

Next to Nina, Knox whistled softly. "That is one hell of a party trick."

Maya twisted the handle and hauled open the door. Inside the vault, eight people huddled against the far wall—five adults and three kids, including one who looked like she was barely old enough to walk.

The fear on their faces squeezed tight around Nina's heart. "It's okay," she whispered. "You're going to be okay."

An older woman with a makeshift bandage wrapped around her head forced her way to her feet. Her dirty, bloodstained clothes were reminiscent of a uniform, and she had an empty holster on one hip. Her gaze shot straight to Knox. "I've seen you before."

"A time or two, Sheriff," Knox agreed, pulling the gun he'd lifted from the guard out of his belt. He handed it over to the woman. "Let's get your people to safety and we can talk all about it."

"Problem." Dani's voice came over the comms, clipped and harried. "We don't have a 20 on the leader."

Oh shit.

Nina looked at Knox, who nodded. She shoved another pistol at Maya, along with several spare magazines. "Keep them in the vault," she instructed. "It's good cover, and this could get ugly."

Maya braced herself next to the vault with line of sight on the door. "I'm on it. Go."

Outside, night had fallen completely. The only light in the street came from the moon . . . and the open door to the café, which was lodged open by two corpses lying in the doorway. Nina crept along the front of the bank beside Knox, trying to remain in the shadows as she scanned the street.

A gunshot rocked the stillness, and Nina moved instinctively, shoving Knox back against the wall. Scalding pain raked across her cheek as the bullet hit the brick and sent shards of it flying.

"Shit." Knox jerked her back into the shadows, wedging his body between her and the direction of the shots. "Stay behind me," he hissed.

"Knox—"

"Might as well come out," a rough voice roared. "I've got a gun to Eileen's head. You're gonna have to shoot through her to get me."

A woman screamed in pain, and Nina stepped forward, into the moonlight. "Stop."

The gang's leader, Mitchell, moved into the spill of light from the café. He was a tall man with wiry muscles and a mean face, and he had one arm locked under the woman—Eileen's—chin. It was a brutal grip, so tight she had to stay on her toes just to keep from choking, and her dark eyes shimmered with tears as she stared hopelessly at Nina.

Mitchell jabbed the gun into Eileen's side hard enough to make her cry out. "Where's the other one?"

"Here," Knox said, stepping up beside Nina. He lifted both empty hands. "We can negotiate. No one else has to get hurt."

"Let her go," Nina urged.

"Who do you think's giving the orders?" Mitchell roared. "You think I haven't planned for this? Put your face in the *fucking* dirt, or I'll tell my boy Henry to put it there for good."

Knox simply stared at him. "Do it, Gray."

A shot rang out from the sniper's nest in the tower, and Mitchell's head exploded, spraying Eileen with drops of blood and bits of brain and bone. She screamed, and Knox rushed forward to snatch her up in his arms.

Nina's knees wobbled. She slumped against the brick wall to steady herself as Dani, Rafe, and Conall rushed around the corner.

Dani frowned at the sight of Nina's blood-streaked face, but all she said was, "We have a firm count. All hostiles are down."

Sobbing filled the street and rattled across the comms. Eileen was clinging to Knox, who patted her shoulders in an awkwardly soothing gesture. His murmured reassurances should have been too soft for Nina to hear, but with the communications devices, they rumbled over her like he was whispering them against her ear.

She was spared that impossible intimacy when the sheriff rounded the corner of the bank and shouted Eileen's name. In moments, the woman was stumbling away from Knox, her sobs growing hysterical as she threw herself into the sheriff's embrace.

Rafe was dragging Mitchell's lifeless body out of the street, and Dani and Conall hurried to move the poisoned men back into the café, where the shades had been drawn to hide the carnage within.

Nina only had eyes for Knox, who was striding toward her, his gaze fixed on her face. When he reached her, he rubbed his thumb over her cheek. "We need to take care of this cut."

"Plenty of time for that." Her heart thudded painfully, harder and faster than it had in the middle of the damn fight. "Smile, Captain. We won, and we didn't even need contingency plans C through L."

His smile was slow to form, but when it hit her—

It felt like the first *real* smile she'd ever seen from him. Warm. Wry. No shadows or lingering pain, just pleasure as he stroked her cheek again. "We make a good team."

The air between them was charged. Knox leaned closer, and Nina stretched up—

Shouts from a few blocks away broke the spell. All up and down the street, doors were slowly opening, and in a matter of moments, the questions and confusion turned to cheers and sobs of relief.

The difference was instant, electric. The townspeople began to approach them, hesitantly at first, then in waves. Nina shook their hands and patted their backs, tried to take it all in, but it was too much.

Overwhelmed, she turned her face into Knox's shoulder and tried not to cry.

SECURITY MEMO

Franklin Center for Genetic Research

No sign of HS-Gen16-A. Our best intel indicates she headed south, presumably to Atlanta. Considering the delicate nature of current relations with the TechCorps, it would be better not to trespass in their territory unless we must.

Judging from her psych profile, she's unlikely to pose a problem to our operations. We should eschew capture in favor of defensive precautions. Our greatest imperative is to protect our future investments.

Dr. Baudin, May 2080

NINETEEN

Knox had never felt like a hero before.

He had, by most accountings, done heroic things. There was a tidy list of them in his file, and the Protectorate used to trot them out when they needed a pressure valve for the citizens' resentment. A public relations win. They'd make a glossy propaganda vid crediting the Silver Devils' achievements to the Protectorate as a whole, slap a medal on Knox's chest, and send him on his next morally dubious mission.

Every good thing he'd ever done had only been, at best, a double-edged victory. He'd threaded the miserable needle of expediency a hundred times. He'd found a way either to eke one good thing out of his orders or to blunt their damage as best he could. His heroism had been rooted in not being as terrible as he should have been.

That made it hard to feel good about a win.

Tonight, Knox felt it. How could he not? The party had spilled into the streets of Dalton. Music blared from the open windows of the bar. Someone had strung up little twinkling lights above the outdoor tables, like fireflies blinking in the night sky. Laughter filled the air as children up far past their bedtimes shrieked in glee and chased one another up and down the street.

People smiled at him. Thanked him. Rushed to refill his beer every time he took so much as a sip. Old ladies kissed his cheeks. Old men pumped his hand. He'd had to stop meeting the eyes of anyone young enough to flirt—it was apparently a good thing to be a mysterious stranger *and* a hero.

Conall had given in to the grateful flirtation of one of the hostages, a tall man with dark, serious eyes and a week's worth of scruff. They whirled wildly through the dancing, and Conall laughed in a way Knox hadn't heard in weeks.

It was all worth it, just for that.

Gray stepped up beside him, a tall mug of beer in one hand. "It's weird, isn't it?"

"It's pretty weird."

Gray chuckled. "You don't even know which part I'm talking about."

"It's *all* pretty weird," Knox retorted. "I mean, not Conall going straight for the guy who looks angry and damaged. That's reassuringly normal. But the rest of it? Weird."

"I guess." Gray sighed. "I owe you an apology."

It seemed impossible that the tough conversation in the car had only happened that morning. Knox felt like a lifetime had passed. Like he was a different person. "You don't. I need you to say the hard shit to me, the stuff no one else will say."

"What? No, not this morning. Hell, Knox—I'm talking about this place. Me wanting to leave at the first hint of trouble."

"You don't have to apologize for that, either." Knox sipped his beer. It was sweet and full, almost like a cider. Better than the usual homebrew the folks of Dalton brought out for tourists. "We still need to retrieve Luna, and this *was* a risk. You're the only one of us who's never lied to himself about this job."

"Yeah, but . . ." Gray waved his mug in the direction of the makeshift dance floor. "If you had listened to me—if we had left—then they'd all be dead. Gone. All of this . . . *life*."

As much as he'd depended on Gray as his second, Knox had never really crossed that invisible line between *captain* and *friend*. He knew his men. He understood them, could join in their banter, enjoy their company. But when it came time to make the hard decisions, the life-or-death calls over who could be saved and who became collateral damage . . .

That responsibility—that *misery*—he'd always kept for himself.

"It's not easy," he said softly, "having the kind of power we do. Do you know how many people I've left behind over the years, Gray? How many people I couldn't save? It was my call and my responsibility, but you were right today. I'm not your captain anymore. I don't have the right to decide who you save and who you don't. You're the only one who can decide what your life is worth or who you should risk it for. And you're gonna fuck it up sometimes. I sure as hell have."

"It's not my life I'm trying to pin a price tag to these days, Knox." Gray saluted him. "It's my conscience."

The salute had an air of finality. It was Gray, truly saying farewell to his captain. Knox returned it solemnly. "If we pull this off, maybe we'll all have time to figure that out."

"Even if we don't, it's been an honor. Sir."

Knox raised his beer. "Same to you, Gray."

Gray finished his beer and went in search of a refill. Knox sipped his own, letting his gaze drift over the crowd. Maya was near the edge of the square, knocking back moonshine with a steely-eyed older woman and two grizzled vets. Rafe went charging by, roaring, with two children clinging to his back and squealing with laughter. Even Dani had unbent enough to play darts with a few of the locals, and judging from their occasional groans, some amount of wagering was involved.

He drained his beer and made another sweep, finally admitting to himself that he wasn't checking up on his people.

He was looking for her.

Someone came by to top off his beer. He chatted briefly with the owner of the trading post, who promised to refill their biofuel stores tomorrow, on the house. Finally, as the music changed from a strong, energetic beat to something slower, Knox's patience was rewarded.

The crowd parted. Nina drifted into the opening, her face alight with joy as a gray-haired old man spun her through the steps of some old-fashioned dance.

She'd cleaned up at some point and changed her clothes. The simple sundress she wore left her toned arms bare and fluttered around her knees. She was like the fantasy of a simpler world come to life, a world of honest work and country dances and lazy nights under the stars, with no evil corporations waiting to destroy everything you'd ever loved.

He abandoned his beer and plotted an intercept course. As the old man spun Nina again, Knox stepped into their path. "Can I cut in?"

"If you insist." Nina pressed her lips together, but her eyes sparkled. "I'll save you another waltz, Enoch. I promise."

"See that you do, girl," he said, but he graciously handed Nina over to Knox.

Once he had her in his arms, Knox gave her a rueful smile. "I don't know how to waltz."

"Well, that's a problem, Captain. Neither do I." She wrapped her arms around his neck. "Enoch was leading."

Her fingers brushed the fine hairs at the base of his neck. A shiver worked through him, arousal coming on slow and hot. He let himself wrap his arms around her and pull her so close that their dance was nothing more than a lazy sway. "We're both highly trained athletes. We'll figure it out."

"I don't think that's how it works."

"I think it's working just fine."

"Because we're not waltzing." Her gaze fixed on his mouth, and her eyes went dark. Hungry. "I don't know *what* we're doing."

"Dancing, Nina." He splayed one hand wide on her hip, holding her close. Savoring the feel of her, for the little time he had left. As tempting as it was to steal another night with her, he owed her the truth. Tonight.

Soon.

"Can I ask you something?" she said suddenly.

"Of course."

She looked away, surveying the crowd. "If my team hadn't been here today, would you have left these people to fend for themselves?"

A serious question. It punctured a little bit of his heroic high, but he did her the courtesy of considering his answer seriously. "Maybe. I've spent a lot of years having to weigh what good I can afford to do against my mission objectives, not to mention what the TechCorps will do to the people under my protection if I step out of line. I would have wanted to help them. But I haven't always had the luxury of doing what I wanted."

"What changed?" she whispered.

"I didn't want to disappoint you," he admitted just as quietly. "And I'm tired of disappointing myself. I kept thinking if I could just get my men free, then I'd have time to worry about the rest. But some lines . . . If we cross them, we'll never be free."

Her thumb brushed the scar where he'd cut out his TechCorps tracker. "They don't own you—that was a lesson I had to learn. They may have made you, but what you do with that will always be your choice."

"I'm learning." He smiled at her and twirled her lazily toward the shadows. "Thank you for reminding me. I'm glad we did this. I needed to know what it feels like, to do something just because it's right."

"Are you trying to tell me you've never been a hero before?" The inside of her thigh rubbed the outside of his. "That's not what Boyd said about you."

It was the last thing he'd expected to hear. "Boyd . . . said something good about me? Was this before or after he was poisoned?"

"Oh, don't get me wrong. They weren't compliments. He had a little rant about how you always had to help people, save them. Do what was right." She bit her lip. "He said we deserve each other."

Then Boyd had done Nina a disservice. Knox had committed the least harm possible within the confines of his orders—which was a far cry from doing what was right. "Boyd was wrong," he warned her. "Nothing's changed, Nina. I've done some dark shit. Saving one town doesn't excuse that."

With a low, mirthless laugh, she stiffened in his arms. "Don't worry, I haven't forgotten all your warnings. I don't think I could. You keep giving them to me."

He couldn't seem to stop himself, even when it put distance between them—just not *too* much distance. As if he could find the right combination of warnings that would keep her close but blunt his impending betrayal.

He'd been a coward all along.

Her hands slid down to his shoulders, then to his upper arms, and she stopped swaying. "What am I doing?" Her voice cracked on the last syllable. "If you don't want me, Knox, you can just say it. I won't make a scene."

Fuck. "Nina—" he started, but there were no words that wouldn't make it worse. *I want you, but you won't want me. Not after—*

Anything he said to reassure her would just hurt her more in the long run. He had to tell her the truth.

Now.

Bracing himself, he took a step back. "Nina, can we—?"

"Sorry!" Maya appeared out of the darkness. She looped an arm through Nina's and tugged. "I'm stealing her. Sometimes girls just need to dance together."

Wordlessly, Nina slipped away with Maya. When she looked back at him, her brow was furrowed, and her eyes were bright with pain.

Knox watched her until she joined a circle with Dani and a few of the townsfolk. The music had changed back to something upbeat and cheerful, and the dancers soon swallowed Nina in their midst, leaving Knox torn between relief that he'd delayed the moment of truth and guilt that he'd hurt her.

Nothing to do about it now. Nothing but fortify himself with more beer and try to find the right words to break her heart.

Nina's room above the café was small, with only a narrow bed, a dresser, and an armchair beside the window. But the bed was soft, there was a tiny attached bathroom for her convenience, and everything was scrupulously clean.

She kicked off her boots and deposited them by the door. The rest of her things were still packed away where she'd left them earlier, and she paused only to dig out her toothbrush. She brushed her teeth, splashed water on her face, and collapsed on the bed, still clothed.

There was no air conditioning, just a lazily spinning fan on the ceiling. Nina watched it circle, wobbling just a tiny bit, until the room began to circle with it, and she squeezed her eyes shut. She wasn't drunk, though she should have been. Just a little tipsy, and even that pleasant buzzing sensation was fading.

She toyed with a piece of lace on her borrowed outfit, still unsure why she'd let Eileen press the frilly sundress into her hands in the first place. At the time, she'd told herself that she couldn't refuse a gift offered out of such desperate gratitude, but the truth was that she had wanted Knox to see it on her. She had wanted him to think she was pretty, wanted him to—

She had wanted him, full stop.

It didn't matter that she knew better, or that she'd promised Maya and Dani she wouldn't do this. It didn't matter that she knew he'd break her heart. Hell, it didn't even matter that he seemed determined to push her away as hard as he could.

She wouldn't chase him. She wasn't pathetic, and she knew how to take no for an answer. But none of that seemed to ease the longing that twisted in the pit of her stomach.

A muted knock sounded on the door, followed by the low rumble of Knox's voice. Because of course it was him. *Of course* it was. "Nina? Can I come in?"

If she stayed perfectly quiet and still, would he leave? Or would he think something was wrong? "The door's open."

He slipped in and shut the door softly behind him. He approached the bed tentatively, the shadows playing over his guarded expression as he held up a bottle of expensive imported bourbon. "I brought a peace offering."

She sat up and took the bottle. "I didn't know we were at war."

"Then consider it an apology." Knox hooked both thumbs in his belt, his gaze fixed on a spot just over her shoulder. "I blow hot and cold. I've been an asshole. But you *know* I want you, Nina. You have to know it. You're the only thing I've wanted for myself in . . ." A short, painful laugh. "Maybe my whole life."

Her heart was pounding so hard it felt like her sternum might shatter. "Me, too."

He took a cautious step closer, and his voice broke on a raw whisper. "I'm scared that when you really see me, you won't want me, after all."

There were no reassurances Nina could make, no promises he would hear, nothing she could say to chase away those shadows. All she could do was show him how much she needed him.

She held out her hand.

He hesitated. "Nina, I—"

"Words get in our way," she interrupted. "Not tonight. Please."

He stared at her hand for an endless moment, naked longing battling against some internal hesitation. The hesitation lost as he reached out and grasped her hand in his.

The bottle of bourbon rolled away, utterly forgotten, as she tugged Knox down to the bed. He stretched out over her, blocking out the rest of the world, and it felt *right*.

He framed her face with his hands, one thumb tracing gently over her cheek, where med-gel was already turning her cut into a thin scar. "No more words," he rumbled, his chest vibrating against hers.

Then he kissed her. Something in her heart shifted with a painful lurch, like a dislocated joint sliding back into place, and she knew.

She was in love with Captain Garrett Knox.

His kiss went on forever. Deep, starving, like he wanted to get lost in her. She was panting by the time he finally broke away, but she couldn't catch her breath, because he'd only shifted objectives. His mouth skipped over her jaw to her throat, then back again, his teeth and tongue grazing her skin.

She was arching against him by the time he reached for the lace ties on the bodice of her dress, and her hands bumped clumsily into his as she tried to help him.

"Shh," he soothed, pressing her hand gently back to the bed. Then his fingers returned, dexterous and sure, to untie the laces and trace hot, teasing patterns across the upper curves of her breasts.

He followed the same path with his lips, urging the loosened fabric open to bare her breasts. There, he brushed his open mouth over her— exploring, *tasting*. Nina focused on the sensations—his beard chafing her skin, his breath pebbling her nipples. The heat of his tongue.

Small things. Slight things. And they coalesced in a wild, unending throb of desire and denial. He could have slipped his hands under her dress and made her come in seconds. Instead, he undressed her slowly, spending the same amount of time on every inch of skin he uncovered.

It was as soothing as it was maddening, and Nina gave in to the slow burn. She was shaking by the time she was completely naked, and she twisted her fingers in his hair as he kissed his way back up her body.

His lips found hers. Deep, dreamy, still demanding that she *feel* even as he coaxed her hands to his shirt. He lifted his arms and broke away long enough to let her tug the fabric over his head, but before she could do more than press her trembling hands to the heat of his chest, he was touching her again. Stroking. Kissing.

Worshiping.

It felt . . . *different*. Desperate in a way that belied every leisurely caress. Intense. Breathtaking. Knox touched her as if he needed her more than the oxygen swimming in his blood, as if—

As if it was the last time.

Nina turned away from the thought. When she raked her teeth over the spot just below Knox's ear, he groaned her name, and the sound banished a little of her doubt. So she kept going, chasing that ardent groan with a sharp inhalation or a hiss and a sigh, until he gave in to the heat between them and drove into her body with a helpless moan.

They moved together—slowly at first, then faster. Harder. Soon, her entire world had been reduced to slick skin and grinding pleasure, whispered pleas and Knox's teeth on the back of her shoulder.

Whatever happened tomorrow, she would always have this.

TECHCORPS PROPRIETARY DATA,
L1 SECURITY CLEARANCE

Birgitte Skovgaard was critically injured during apprehension, but I have her data courier in custody. I'll handle the interrogation personally. You need to clear all our squads of involvement in her seditious activities.

Start with 66–615. She had someone following him.

Internal Memo, April 2081

TWENTY

Knox couldn't sleep.

He dozed for a few hours, soothed by the even tickle of Nina's breath on his throat and the warmth of her fingers resting over his heart. But real sleep eluded him. He could feel his stolen seconds ticking away. Each one was precious.

She slept in his arms, trusting and utterly exhausted. He'd driven her to the brink last night, as if he could prove himself with pleasure, make himself such an essential part of her that her need overrode her anger.

A pretty fantasy. No one was *that* good at fucking.

The sun was still teasing at the horizon when he slipped from her bed and from her room. The rooms they'd been given lined either side of the hallway, like an old-fashioned bed-and-breakfast. He crossed on silent feet and slipped into his own room, where his gear still sat untouched on the bed.

The satellite dish and his tablet were at the bottom of his pack. He'd scouted the path to the roof last night—down to the end of the hallway, up a narrow flight of stairs to the attic, and through a hatch in the roof. The neatly tended solar arrays took up most of the space, but he found enough room to assemble his parabolic dish and set up the connection.

Two terse messages were waiting for him after he connected to the GhostNet. The first was a simple demand for updated coordinates. The second was more sinister, implying that Luna's continued welfare depended on an immediate check-in.

He typed his carefully prepared response. *Delayed by storm. Currently in Dalton. Provide final coordinates for rendezvous.*

The tablet beeped almost immediately. *Incoming video request.*

Shit. Knox took two deep breaths and let emotion fade. The comfortable numbness he'd once embraced so easily came slowly now. It pinched in places. Emotion still surged beneath the thinnest of masks, and he briefly considered using the video software to anonymize his face. It would shroud any tells—but the choice to use it *was* a tell. The kidnapper already knew who he was. Trying to obscure his face would only indicate he had something to hide.

Bracing himself, he accepted the connection.

The kidnapper had no compunctions about hiding. The face that formed on his screen was a default avatar with generic features—neither masculine nor feminine, the skin a light brown, just like the short hair and perfectly symmetrical eyes. It hovered on the edge of the vast chasm between too real and not real enough, and unease crawled up Knox's spine as he met those blank, emotionless eyes.

"Captain Knox." The voice was shrouded too, faintly mechanical and utterly without accent or affect. "These continued delays have been most problematic. I thought you were professionals."

"I am," Knox replied blandly. "But few professionals do their best work under duress, and with insufficient intelligence. You left a great deal of information out of your brief."

A long pause. The avatar flickered, and Knox wished he knew what expression it was masking. "It was unnecessary," the kidnapper finally replied, and even the modulated voice sounded sharp. "You had the information you needed. I will accept no further delays. Once I transmit the final coordinates, I expect to see you there within thirty-six hours. Anything else would be unfortunate."

Knox hardened his heart against a spike of panic. "I want proof of life again. Now. Let me talk to Luna."

Another pause. "Fine," the kidnapper replied. "Thirty seconds. And then you'll receive the coordinates, and the clock starts. I wouldn't be late, Captain."

The avatar vanished. The screen stayed blank for so long that Knox wondered if he'd been disconnected. Then a bright light flashed, and the video swung down to frame Luna.

She looked exhausted. Her hair was scraped back from her face in a ponytail this time, and the light did the shadows under her eyes no favors. "Luna, are you okay?"

She swallowed a few times, like she was trying to work up the ability to speak. When she did, her voice was steady, but it held an edge of brittle defiance. "The food here sucks, but I'll make it."

"We're coming, okay? Just hold on. Everything's going to work out."

"Knox—" Her voice cracked, proving just how tenuous her bravado was. "Tia Ivonne. If I don't make it out of here, Rafe knows what to do."

If Luna didn't make it out of there, Rafe would be in no position to do anything. Then again, knowing Rafe's devotion to family, it was likely he'd set things in motion to protect Luna's aunt in any eventuality. "Don't worry. You know how Rafe is. And he's not leaving without—"

The screen went dark. A moment later, a set of coordinates appeared. Knox took a deep breath and plugged them into the GPS. It would take a solid day of driving to put them within striking distance of the rendezvous point, but if they made it most of the way by tonight, they'd have time to camp, strategize, and go in with a plan.

Knox packed away the parabolic dish and slipped back downstairs. But instead of going to his own room, he knocked quietly on Rafe's door, then Gray's. Within minutes, he had them all gathered in Conall's room, perched on the bed or leaning against the wall. Three sets of eyes stared at him in respectful silence.

Knox cleared his throat. "Gray pointed out to me yesterday that the squad doesn't exist anymore, and that I'm not your captain. He's right. I don't want to make these decisions for you anymore. Breaking free of the Protectorate means we get to decide when we fight. Why we fight. *How* we fight."

"Who we fight," Conall said quietly. "That's what this is about. We can't hand these women over to the asshole who kidnapped Luna."

Gray eyed Rafe. "What do you think, man? Is your little cream puff going to murder us all if she finds out we've been playing her and her boss?"

"Maybe," Rafe rumbled. "If she murders the kidnapper first, I don't know if I give a shit."

Knox tossed the tablet to Conall. "The rendezvous coordinates are on there. We have thirty-six hours. Get me everything you can about the location. We need a full tactical rundown before we take this to Nina." He hesitated, but only for a moment. "And look for anything you can find about the Franklin Center for Genetic Research. It's where Nina came from. It might be who's after her."

Conall nodded. "Connectivity will be sporadic while we drive, but I should be able to hit a few networks and pull down the latest satellite terrain."

"We need to be aware," Gray said. "No fooling ourselves. If we do this—if we tell Nina and her team the truth—it might be the end of us." He pointed to Rafe. "*And* Luna. Obviously, that's a worst-case scenario, but it's there."

Rafe scrubbed one hand over his head. "We're playing the odds, Gray. That's all we've been doing this whole damn time. If I had to carve out my soul to save Luna, I'd still do it. But I don't think I have to. Dani might poison us all before this is over . . . but I'd still put all my chips on her doing anything she can to get Luna out alive. They're better than us."

"Maybe," Gray admitted. "It's borrowed trouble, and those ladies seem to like that."

"That they do." Knox exhaled. "So we're doing this?"

"We're doing this," Rafe said.

Conall didn't look up from the tablet, but he flashed a thumbs-up. Knox looked to Gray, who just shrugged. "Why the hell not? May as well get started on that conscience thing."

TECHCORPS PROPRIETARY DATA,
L3 SECURITY CLEARANCE

Reward for the apprehension of DC–031 has been raised to 2 million credits. HIGHEST PRIORITY.

Dead or alive.

Internal Memo, November 2081

TWENTY-ONE

Dani parked the truck, cut the engine, and stared out through the windshield. "Your boyfriend takes us to all the *nicest* places, Nina."

"We are definitely going to get murdered here." Maya leaned up between the front seats. "Probably by angry ghosts."

Nina had to admit that the abandoned hospital's darkened façade was forbidding. It had once been white, though most of the paint had worn off the face of the cement structure. It had the blocky, distinctive architectural style typical of buildings erected during the Energy Wars; it was essentially an above-ground bunker, designed to pull double duty as a civilian shelter in case of enemy attack or severe weather.

Of course, that meant these types of buildings were sturdy, with specially designed walls and roofs, as well as windows that resisted blowing out or breaking. So they made excellent camping spots.

Provided you could get over the creep factor.

"Cheer up." She patted Maya's shoulder. "This time tomorrow, we should be in Chattanooga. We'll stay in some swank hotel on Broad Street, right near the river. The kind of place with room service."

"Uh-huh. I want a spa, too."

Knox's men had already dropped their gear in the lobby. It was a large, open space, with a few molded plastic chairs and even a stone bench arranged in a loose circle in the center of the room. Behind them sat a large, shallow tank with three massive columns of granite rising from it. An old, defunct fountain.

Instead of water sluicing over the granite, there were carvings—mainly sequences of letters and numbers that could only be initials and dates, along with a smattering of longer messages. A few were so smooth and neat they had to have been machine- or laser-engraved, but most had been laboriously etched into the hard surface by hand.

How many hours had travelers spent, scratching away at the rock, just to say *I existed, I was here*?

A hand on her shoulder made her jump. "Sorry," Knox said immediately, his voice a warm murmur. "I didn't mean to startle you."

"It wasn't you," she assured him. "I was . . . in another world."

"The place is a little eerie." He nodded to the fountain with its dozens of missives. "Seems like a popular pit stop, though. People can forgive a lot of creepy in exchange for solid walls and a roof."

"I know the feeling." Nina unclipped her flashlight from her belt. "We'll have to split up to check the place out. You take the east wing, we'll take the west?"

"Sounds good." His fingers brushed her shoulder again, a caress that felt almost yearning. Then, with a tight little smile, he was gone.

They'd been pushing so hard that they hadn't had much of a chance to breathe all day, let alone chat, and Nina couldn't figure out what was going on with Knox. Sure, he'd crept out of her bed before first light, but it seemed like he'd done it more out of necessity than payback or any need for distance. He was almost electrically charged with nervous anticipation, and she couldn't tell if it was because they were so close to the bunker coordinates . . .

Or if something was wrong, perhaps with his implant.

Promising herself that she'd watch him carefully, Nina quickly directed Dani and Maya on where to search and set off on her own.

The hospital's corridors were endlessly long and somehow managed to feel cavernous and claustrophobic, all at the same time. Worse, the darkness made it difficult for Nina to discern any rhyme or reason to the layout—some hallways circled around on themselves, while some branching paths did the same. Without the numbered rooms and suites set along the halls, it would have been impossible to keep her bearings.

And it *was* creepy. Her footsteps echoed off the tile in ways that made her think she was hearing another person. Her skin crawled with the sensation of being watched. And the rooms—

Most were empty save for a few chairs or shelves, basic office furniture. But others held pieces of old, unidentifiable medical equipment. In the darkness, cut through only by the brash glare of her flashlight beam, they looked . . . sinister.

Like they were waiting.

But she made it down the first hall without incident. She'd just reached a small room at the end of the second hallway when her beam passed over an object that glinted in the light. It was hanging from an old IV stand, something shiny and gently swaying, and Nina stepped forward.

It was her pendant, her chain. Her necklace.

Instinctively, she lifted her hand to her throat, expecting to encounter bare skin. It was the only explanation that made sense—somehow, she'd gotten turned around, had come this way already and lost her necklace.

But her pendant was right where it belonged, nestled into the hollow of her throat, warm against her flesh.

Panic bloomed, the kind of sheer, animal distress that came from encountering something that wasn't happening, that simply couldn't be. She reached out, expecting to close her fist around nothing, an illusion, but metal bit into her skin. She jerked the chain off the stand, which tipped to the cracked tile floor with a crash, and stared down at the three interlocking rings in the palm of her shaking hand.

A chill shivered up her spine, and she spun around, shining her light down the dark hallway. At the very end of it, nearly swallowed by the gloom, stood a woman.

"Zoey?" The word tore free of Nina, and she broke into a run, stumbling over the debris littering the floor. "Ava?"

The beam from her flashlight bounced wildly as she hurried down the hall. In the dizzying flashes of light, she watched the figure turn and disappear around the corner. "No, wait—"

Nina rounded the corner, and no one was there. For a moment, she stood there, panting, questioning her sanity more than anything else. Then she noticed the door at the end of the corridor swinging slightly. She rushed through it—her heart pounding, blood heavy in her ears—

And came face-to-face with a ghost. With the past that had haunted her for more than a decade of loneliness and regret and self-doubt and *pain*.

Her own face stared back at her, a shadow clad all in black with her hair hanging loose and curly around her shoulders. The vision watched her, her brown eyes coolly assessing. "Hello, Nina."

Of course—a ghost would always know your name. So would a solid hallucination. But Nina's other senses had started to catch up. She could smell soap and coffee, hear the gentle intake and exhale of breath.

Whatever—*whoever*—she was facing, it was a real live person.

Nina dropped her hand to the butt of her pistol. "Who are you?" She was ashamed to hear the pain wobbling in her voice. She sounded like she'd been kicked, punched, stabbed. Shot.

The other woman tilted her head in a certain way, a gesture so reminiscent of Ava that Nina's eyes burned. "I can't tell if you're earnestly confused or simply temporizing. I suppose you've become better at deception."

It couldn't be—and yet. "Ava?"

"Surprise, sister. It's been a few years."

Confusion and relief and sheer, utter *joy* warred with Nina's shock, but they couldn't overcome it. She stared at Ava, shaking her head. "What happened to you? *How?*"

"Does it matter?" Ava took a step forward, her heeled boots clicking sharply on the tile. "I finally got away from the Franklin Center."

"They—they told me you were *dead.*"

"I'm not." Another step. Ava opened her arms and folded them around Nina, and the familiar scent of lavender and vanilla curled around her. The memory hit her like a tangible thing—lounging around their shared room, idly picking through various bottles of oils as Ava mixed her own fragrances.

The joy finally broke through Nina's numb shock, and she exhaled with a sob. "You're here." She held Ava tighter. "You're *alive.*"

"I am." Ava's lips were so close that the whispered words fell against Nina's ear as a sigh. "And I hope you're telling the truth, Nina. I truly do."

A sharp stab of pain at the side of her neck made Nina jerk away. She tried to lift her hand, but a heavy warmth was already spreading through her, turning her limbs to lead. The necklace she'd found fell from her nerveless fingers, and she slumped to the floor.

The last thing she saw as dark oblivion spun up to claim her was Ava, bending down to retrieve the pendant.

Nina wasn't back from her perimeter check yet.

Knox rubbed at the back of his neck, as if that would settle the prickles. No one else seemed alarmed by Nina's tardiness. Maya had set up their clever little camp stove on a table Dani had righted, and the two of them were turning a series of those ever-present silver packets into dinner.

The scent filled the lobby—scalloped potatoes, thick slices of honey-glazed ham, and some sort of vegetables with a tangy citrus dressing that made Knox's mouth water. Lunch—and its bland nutritional bars—had been a long time ago.

The women were chatting easily as they prepared their feast. Conall straddled a chair on the other side of the table, his out-of-character silence the only evidence of the tension all the men shared. Gray was mostly hiding it, but Rafe had been digging through his pack for the last five minutes, shifting and rearranging things without purpose.

No one could relax until the truth was out in the open and they knew how the women were going to respond. And Knox couldn't broach the subject until Nina returned.

He was getting ready to go looking for her when footsteps sounded in the hallway. Nina paused on the threshold of the lobby, her gaze sweeping everyone's positions. He tried to catch her eye, but she avoided it and stepped into the lobby. "Dinner smells good."

"Sorry about the ham," Dani threw over her shoulder. "We made you extra vegetables, though."

Nina laughed, and the back of Knox's neck prickled again. Something was wrong. Something was *off*. The woman approaching the table looked like Nina and smiled like Nina. Laughed like Nina.

Trios of genetically engineered clones as far as the eye could see. That's where I grew up.

His gun was in his hand before Nina's words stopped echoing in his head. He pointed it at the newcomer as protective rage roiled up inside him. "Stop right there."

"Whoa, hey." Dani drew on Knox, her expression one of sheer outrage. "What the hell?"

Conall didn't say a word as he sprang from his chair and leveled his sidearm at Dani's head.

The woman who wasn't Nina raised both hands, her face the perfect picture of shocked concern. But the chilly hardness in her eyes betrayed her, even as she lowered the voice that could have been Nina's to a gentle murmur. "Knox, are you okay? What is it?"

"That isn't Nina," Knox ground out.

"Are you fucking high?" Maya's chair clattered to the floor as she rose and twisted, that dangerous little laser gun of hers pointing right at him. She drew a second pistol from her thigh holster and leveled it at Rafe before he could move. "You fuckers need to *back the hell up,* right now."

Gray popped a bit of freeze-dried apple into his mouth and studied the standoff with a critical eye, as if he hadn't moved yet because he hadn't decided who he would shoot. "If it's not Nina, who is it?"

Knox ignored the weapons pointed at him and stared into that beautiful face, so close to perfect and somehow utterly wrong. "What did you do to her? *Where is she?*"

The tense silence stretched out. Knox's pulse throbbed in his ears. Dani's finger hovered over the trigger, and he'd seen how fast she could move. Another second, another *fraction* of a moment—

The woman's entire demeanor changed. Her manufactured concern slipped away, melting into a look of cool exasperation that matched the ice in her eyes. "Honestly," she said. "You're supposed to be the best mercenaries money can't buy. The elite of the elite. And it took her all of a week to turn my rabid wolf into a lapdog. If she wasn't my sister, I suspect I'd hate her for that alone."

Dani inhaled sharply, then spun around so fast she was nothing more than a blur. She ended up with the barrel of her weapon pointed at the impostor. "The man asked you a question."

"Indeed, he did," the woman said. "My name is Ava. I'm Nina's extremely long-lost sister. She's currently safe in the company of some of my *other* well-paid mercenaries. Unfortunately, if I don't return within five minutes, I'm afraid they're under orders to shoot her. And Luna, as well." One perfectly shaped eyebrow rose as she studied Knox. "You remember her, right?"

Maya's gun, which had begun to waver, lifted toward Knox again. "Who the fuck is Luna?"

The suspicion in Maya's eyes was the tiniest pinprick of what was to come. Knox opened his mouth, but Ava cut him off. "Oh no, no spoiling the surprise. I'll need all of you to put your guns down. You too, Maya, darling. I don't necessarily *want* to turn you over to the TechCorps, but last I heard, the reward for your return was positively staggering. If you leave me no choice, I suppose I can find something to do with a few million credits."

Sick fury twisted Maya's face, but the terror tightening her gaze was stronger. After a miserable moment, she bent and placed both of her weapons on the floor.

"Good girl," the impostor murmured. "The rest of you, now. Disarm, if you please."

Knox wanted to believe it was a bluff. He wanted to believe that someone who shared Nina's face, who shared her *DNA*, would be incapable of the cold-blooded murder of a person she called sister.

But he'd stared into the eyes of too many killers. This woman was dangerous.

Moving slowly, he lowered his gun to the floor. "Disarm," he said softly, not taking his eyes off the woman as he stripped off his tactical belt and pulled the knives from his boots.

"Knox," Dani protested.

Nina's clone checked her watch. "Four minutes and nine seconds, Dani. I admit, you always were the wild card in my plans. Someone with your history isn't typically capable of loyalty—"

Dani cut her off with a literal hiss. "Someone with *my history* is going to peel your fucking face off and feed it to the wildlife, lady."

"*Dani.*" Knox pulled his last hunting knife from its sheath and flashed her a pointed look. "We need to get to Nina, okay?"

After a few more tense seconds, she relented and began to drop guns, knives, and even a small set of screwdrivers. "Fine. I do my best face-peeling with my bare hands anyway."

The woman only laughed. "I've been tortured by monsters who make your threats sound like a child's soothing nursery rhyme. But do feel free to continue. I'm charmed by plucky bluster."

Knox ignored the taunts and swept the room to ascertain everyone had dropped their weapons. "We did what you asked," he said, turning back. "Take us to the women."

"Such an eager puppy." The clone spun on her heel, so confident in the leverage she had over them that she presented them with her back with no apparent concern. "Come along. I'm looking forward to the big reveal."

Knox met Dani's eyes and nodded toward Maya, who still looked shaken. Dani wrapped her arm around Maya's shoulders and murmured to her as they followed the clone. Conall fell into step directly behind them as Rafe slipped up to walk next to Knox.

"She's nuts," Rafe whispered, the scuff of their boots almost covering the words. "And I'm not talking metaphorically, Knox. Someone broke that woman."

"I know."

"You can't predict that kind of damage."

"I *know*, Rafe." He kept his voice quiet. "Stick close to Conall. I don't know if that implant can compensate for this level of stress."

Gray glared at the woman's unprotected back. "If we want to move, I don't know if there'll be a better time."

"You don't," Ava replied without turning around. "You may share Dani's questionable morals, but you don't share her impulsivity. This isn't your moment, Gray, and you know it."

Gray clammed up, and Ava responded with chilling laughter as she led them down the darkened corridor. "Yes, I've researched you all. Not sufficiently, I suppose, since I underestimated Nina's ability to thoroughly corrupt your poor captain. It's the one disadvantage to being unwilling to employ a truly unsavory element. Luckily, the Center taught me to be flexible with my thinking. I don't *love* improvisation, but this might work out even better than I'd planned. For me, I mean. I anticipate it will be significantly worse for you and your men."

"Fucking hell," Maya groaned. "Just murder me, already. You know I'm going to remember every word of your second-rate villain monologue for the *rest of my life*?"

A snort of amusement came, unsurprisingly, from Conall. "Go easy on her," he murmured, deadpan. "Nobody really nails the evil monologue the first time."

Knox didn't find the situation particularly amusing, but their digs landed. The woman's posture stiffened, and the smart click of her boots on tile faltered for a heartbeat before she squared her shoulders. "Keep going," she said, struggling for—and failing to find—a casual tone. "I told you I find pluck charming."

"Oh, obviously," Dani muttered, grim amusement lighting her eyes.

The clone stopped in front of a door and shot Dani and Maya a cool look. "Maybe you two should focus on the important things," she said as she pulled the door open to reveal the floor of a cavernous, brightly lit room.

Knox's heart jackknifed into his throat.

Nina was sprawled on the floor inside, unconscious. Dani was kneeling by her side in what seemed like an instant, cradling her head. The clone had stripped Nina's clothes for her attempted ruse and re-dressed her in sweatpants and a tank top, but there was no blood, no obvious injuries. Knox still didn't take a breath until he saw her chest rise and fall.

"*Luna.*"

Rafe shot past him. Luna was on her knees a few feet from Nina, her hands zip-tied together in front of her. Shifting slightly to the side gave Knox an easy view of the rest of the room—and the mercenaries lined up in professional formation, guns fixed on their targets, their laser sights lighting up everyone Knox cared about.

Nina and Luna were the perfect bait in a perfect trap, displayed with such flair that Knox couldn't help but appreciate the artistry.

And the irony.

Maybe this was the cosmic justice he'd been waiting for. He'd lured Nina into a pretty trap that exploited all of her best impulses—her thirst for knowledge, her hunger to help people, her stubborn refusal to give up on thinking the world could be fundamentally good.

Ava's trap was exquisitely direct. She was exploiting the ragged pieces of his heart.

It worked. As Knox stepped into the room and watched the little red dots bloom on his chest, he wasn't sure if he was angry or relieved that enough of his heart remained to make this trap work. Maybe the Tech-Corps hadn't torn it out of him after all.

Too bad he hadn't figured that out a week ago.

Once they were all in the room, Ava stepped in and closed the door. She lifted a finger and gestured toward the front of the room, and one of the mercenaries holstered his weapon and pulled a handful of zip ties from his back pocket. "Let's all be polite about this, now."

Conall rose from his spot beside Luna and turned obediently, allowing a mercenary to frisk him for weapons before securing his wrists at the small of his back. Rafe snarled when the soldier tried to pull him to his feet, but a laser dot on Luna's forehead got him moving. Dani had to be dragged away from Nina's side, and her eyes burned with the promise of face-peeling vengeance as she submitted to a search—which turned up two more concealed knives.

"Fuck you," Maya exploded as the man approached her. She wheeled backward, panic in her eyes, and when the mercenary caught one wrist, she exploded into movement. Her nails raked the man's face and her knee drove up toward his balls so fast he barely twisted in time to take it on the hip.

Gray intervened, tugging Maya back before she could launch another attack. He folded his arms around her, held her head still, and whispered in her ear.

Maya dragged in one unsteady breath, then another. Squeezing her eyes shut, she turned in Gray's arms and buried her face against his chest. Knox braced himself, but the mercenary didn't exact revenge for his bleeding cheek or bruised thigh. He secured Maya's wrists with a dispassionate efficiency Knox recognized all too well.

These weren't desperate criminals or angry outlaws who had turned to killing. Ava had hired pros. Pros were not going to go down easy.

Once Maya was bound, Gray allowed the mercenary to secure him. The man approached Knox last, and he turned his back in silence for the search. The plastic tie went around his wrists and pulled tight, and he found himself staring into Ava's amused eyes as she gestured again. The mercenary forced him to his knees with one rough hand.

"Excellent." She slipped an injector from her pocket and crossed to kneel beside Nina. Dani jerked forward, but the woman had already held it to the side of Nina's neck and jammed the button.

Nothing happened. At Ava's direction, several of the hired guns put Nina into a chair and drew her arms around behind her. By the time she stirred, lifting her head, they had secured her wrists with the same plastic ties as everyone else.

Ava placed another chair a few feet away and sank gracefully into it. She crossed her legs and studied Nina. "Are you back with us?"

After a moment, Nina shook her head—not in denial, but as if to clear it. "What happened?"

"I had to take some precautions. Don't worry, your team hasn't been harmed." A bitter little smile twisted Ava's lips. "I know how much you care about them."

Nina's eyes finally focused, and she looked over at the six of them, bound and kneeling. Her chest heaved as she studied them, her distress growing.

Then her gaze landed on Knox. Her shoulders slumped as she tilted her head and mouthed, *I'm sorry.*

Ava could have stabbed him in the gut and hurt him less.

But the woman wasn't done. "Captain Knox has a confession to make, Nina."

"Let them go, Ava. None of them have anything to do with this."

"Are you going to correct her misconception, Captain? Or do I have to do it for you?"

"Nina—" he began, groping for the words. For the least painful way to deliver the truth before Ava laid it out in agonizing, bloody detail.

No, he'd waited too long for that. He'd rationalized over and over, found dozens of ways to cling to the way she made him feel for just one more day, one more hour, one more minute, one more *moment* . . .

"Captain," Ava warned.

Knox swallowed and met Nina's confused gaze. And he made the cut clean. "I've been lying to you from the beginning. The server was a trap. I was hired to retrieve you."

SECURITY MEMO

Franklin Center for Genetic Research

Subject HS-Gen16-B has gone missing. So has her employer.
She is going to be a problem.

Dr. Keller, March 2082

TWENTY-TWO

Nina was having a nightmare.

It was the only explanation for this horrendous turn of events. She'd spent too much time thinking about the past, pondering her ghosts, worrying about Knox—and it was all catching up with her. Any moment now, she'd jolt awake. The sudden movement would startle Maya all the way in the backseat, and Dani would make a dry joke about how being on the road made Nina twitchy.

Any moment now.

But Dani and Maya were still on the floor along with everyone else. Knox kept staring at her, the bright light casting the planes of his face in harsh relief, as his confession rang in her ears.

She stared back at him and jerked her wrists against her sharp plastic bindings until tears of pain welled up to blur her vision.

She still didn't wake up.

"I'm sorry," he told her, as if they were the only two people in the room. "I didn't know it was your sister. I just knew someone had kidnapped Luna, and she's the only one with a chance of saving my men. I was going to tell you tonight, I swear."

"Yes, first you betrayed her, and then you were going to betray me." Ava's chilly smile was vicious. "I have to say, you're not living up to your reputation on any front, Captain."

"Stop it," Nina whispered, her stomach twisting.

"You feel it, don't you?" Ava's voice trembled almost imperceptibly. "The stab of treachery. It hurts, doesn't it? Honestly, I didn't think I'd survive it. But you get past it, if you're lucky. You get angry."

For a heartbeat, Nina thought she was talking about whoever—probably some vaguely bored bureaucrat in a suit—had made the executive decision to separate them. But the words didn't sound like commiseration.

They sounded like accusation.

"You think I *left you*?" she demanded, anger driving back the pain for one blissful, relieved moment. "When I got you back to the Center, I waited outside the clinic for hours before someone came out. They told me you were dead, Ava. That you didn't make it."

"And you believed them." Ava's eyes held no understanding. No sympathy. "They told me you abandoned me. *I* didn't believe them. I had faith that my sister wouldn't give up on me. That's how I made it through the first year of torture, you know. I was so sure that if I just held it together, you'd come back for me. You'd get me out."

"I would *never* have abandoned you." Nina's throat swelled with an ache that threatened to choke off her breath as well as her words. "You were all I had left."

"You *did* abandon me," Ava snapped. "And why not? I was replaceable. When I finally figured out you weren't coming, I rescued myself. But you didn't need me by then, did you? You'd just picked out a new family."

The very idea would have been laughable if it wasn't so tragic. Nina loved Dani and Maya with all her heart, but they existed in addition to the ragged holes left behind by the loss of her sisters. They didn't fill them.

Ava would either believe that or she wouldn't. More words wouldn't convince her, so Nina steeled herself and returned her focus to Knox. "I want to hear what else the captain has to say."

Knox's face was a hard mask. He clenched his jaw, and the furrow between his brows deepened. "I have no excuse. I made a hard call to protect my people. I wish I could take it back."

"Why?" Nina tried to smile, but it felt more like a grimace, so she gave up. "You did your job, and you did it well. That's something to be proud of."

He flinched.

"Captain Knox is irrelevant," Ava said coolly. "If you truly believed I was dead, then now you have an inkling of how deep the rot goes at the Franklin Center. They took everything from us, Nina. They took Zoey. They took the last ten years of our lives. I'm going to take it back, and I'd much rather have you fighting with me than against me."

Nina twisted her wrists again, grounding herself with the bite of hard plastic into sore, sensitive skin. What Ava wanted couldn't be as simple as vengeance—if she'd known enough about Nina to send Knox and his team after her, then Ava could have just walked up to the warehouse anytime. She could have sent an electronic or voice message or a mediator or a goddamned carrier pigeon.

She hadn't *needed* to resort to kidnapping. But she had.

"All right." Nina refused to let her voice waver. "You win."

Maya made a noise of protest. "Nina, *no*."

"You win," Nina repeated. "I'll go with you. I'll do whatever you want."

Her sister's brown eyes narrowed with familiar shrewdness. Suspicion had run deep in Ava from the very beginning. She'd been obsessed with peeling back the layers of people's motivations, treating them like gadgets she could disassemble, lay out in a neat row of parts, and discern their innermost secrets.

Sometimes she could.

"You never were a good liar," Ava said softly. "Don't try to play me, sister. This isn't a surrender. You're initiating negotiations."

"That would imply that I want concessions."

"Don't you?"

Nina wet her lips. "Captain Knox did his job, so he and his people should be allowed to leave. He can take Dani and Maya with him—he owes me that much. And I'll stay."

"I'm not leaving you here with her," Dani growled.

Ava ignored her. She uncrossed her legs and leaned forward, her gaze burning into Nina's. "He lied to you. He betrayed you. And this is what you barter for? *His* safety? I'd be doing us both a favor if I put a bullet in his head right now."

Nina would not look at Knox. She would *not*. "How am I supposed to maintain a vengeance boner for the Franklin Center if I'm no better than them?"

Anger shuttered Ava's face. She rose in one smooth movement and dragged the chair out of the way. She walked to one of the mercenaries and pulled a knife from the sheath at his belt. "No, Nina. You don't get to save everyone. If you want to negotiate, here's my offer. I'll let one team go. Yours or Captain Knox's."

"Hers," Knox said without hesitation. "Let them go—"

"I'm not negotiating with you," Ava said without looking away from Nina. She approached a second mercenary and drew his knife as well, and the knot in the pit of Nina's stomach turned to ice. "You'll fight. The rules are simple. The winner saves the lives of their people."

It could have been a bluff, a strategic gamble carefully calculated to pay off. At one time, Nina would have sworn it had to be. Ava wouldn't have gone through all the trouble of acquiring Nina if she planned to leave her fate up to chance.

But nothing about that certainty would guarantee Knox's safety. And, honestly, Nina couldn't really be sure about her own. Not with that uncomfortable fire burning in her sister's eyes.

Something had changed Ava, something so profound and horrible that Nina barely recognized her—but maybe Nina could use that. After all, she wasn't the same idealistic kid Ava had known, either. There was a way out of this, despite her sister's insistence that Nina couldn't save everyone.

She just had to find it.

Being unbound and free to move around was a start. "I accept."

"I don't," Knox snarled, even as one of the mercenaries hauled him to his feet. "Fuck this, I'm not fighting you."

"Then she'll win," Ava replied, tossing both knives to the floor in the middle of the empty space. "Since you *did* bring Nina to me, I'll give you one concession. The girl is safe. A biochem hacker with knowledge of TechCorps infrastructure is too valuable to waste. The rest of your men? Well, given your current state of deterioration, it might be a mercy to put them down."

One of the mercenaries sliced through the zip tie binding Nina's wrists. Her body itched to move, to fight. To whirl around before he could react, snatch his sidearm, and end this whole stupid standoff.

Instead, she took a deep breath and rubbed her wrists as she rose. Two knives. Even if she threw them true and both found their marks, there would be a dozen mercenaries left to retaliate, plus Ava.

So she picked up one knife and kicked the other over to where Knox stood, his agonized gaze flitting over his men. The knife handle thudded against his boot, and he stared down at it. "No. No, Nina."

"Pick up the knife, Knox."

He scowled at her, swooped down, and came back up with the knife gripped in one hand. "This is insanity."

"Maybe." She circled him slowly. Her mind hurtled through the variables and possibilities at light speed, but she kept coming up empty. "But you have to do it. For your men."

"My men and I already had this conversation," he told her in a tight voice, pivoting slowly to watch her. "We're not sacrificing your lives for ours."

If he kept shutting her down, Ava would quickly realize she wasn't going to get the fight she wanted—and Nina would be out of time to think. So she darted forward, slashing her blade lightly across Knox's cheek.

As he hissed and recoiled, she danced back, adjusting her grip on the knife's hilt. "Focus, Captain."

His gaze locked with hers for just a moment. His jaw tightened. When he lashed out, it was with only a fraction of the speed she knew he possessed. Even that was still fast. His knife slashed toward her arm in a blur, and she whirled out of the way, unharmed.

"You'll have to do better than that," she admonished.

He snarled and lunged again. Nina sliced the front of his T-shirt this time, carefully controlling the force and angle of the blade so that it didn't bite into the skin beneath the cloth.

Ava watched, frowning. Nina could practically hear her voice, mildly disgusted, telling her to get on with things. She had Knox at a disadvantage already—

Just like that, the variables and possibilities clicked into place, and Nina knew what to do. It would be tricky. Ava could say no. Worse, it could make her suspicious. She could judge the risk too great. But she was running out of time and options.

Nina had to take the chance, and she had to make this *good*.

She worked up her best look of indignation—which wasn't difficult to do at this point—flipped her knife over in her hand, and gestured to Knox with the handle. "I'm not doing this. He's a mess—he can't even block or parry, much less move fast enough to strike. It's unfair to fight him while he's in this condition. I refuse."

Ava pinned her in place with a cool look. "I should think you'd appreciate a tactical advantage, given what's at stake."

"Well, I don't." Nina tossed the knife to the nearest mercenary, who caught it reflexively. "I'm a fighter, not a murderer."

"You and your damnable honor. You haven't changed a bit, have you?"

"Come on, Ava. You know better." Nina lowered her voice to a taunting croon. "What's that old saying about leopards and spots?"

Ava glared at her for another moment before waving at Luna. "Cut the girl free and get me a tablet."

The mercenaries leapt to obey. Luna eyed them warily but remained still as they removed her bonds, though she shoved one away when he attempted to help her to her feet.

Another man returned with an expensive folding tablet. Ava opened it and tapped in a code, then offered it to Luna. "This should be sufficient for your needs."

Luna stared at it for a moment, but even her obvious shock and confusion couldn't keep her hands off of it for long. She cradled the tablet like something precious and frowned. "You want me to optimize his implant?"

"I want you to fix him," Ava replied shortly. "After all, he's just one man. You may as well soothe my sister's overactive conscience."

Luna's fingers began flying over the screens. Hopefully, she was just as brilliant as Ava had claimed, and she'd find a way to get Knox back up to full fighting speed. Even then, Nina still wasn't sure they'd be able to plow their way through Ava's mercenaries.

It was a slim chance. But it was their only one.

SECURITY MEMO

Franklin Center for Genetic Research

HS-Gen16-B's employer has been found. Cause of death: asphyxiation. Forensics techs are still attempting to trace her digital activity over the past few months. We suspect she may have been embezzling assets from her employer's business for at least that long.

Even half of his money would make her one of the richest people in Washington. I don't like to imagine what she could do with those kinds of resources.

Dr. Keller, April 2082

TWENTY-THREE

Knox's cheek stung. His muscles trembled with the effort it had taken to check his instincts and not respond to Nina's attack with one of his own.

Letting someone slowly cut you to pieces was even harder than it sounded.

Maybe that was why it had taken him this long to recognize the glint in her eye. That perfectly arched eyebrow demanded that he stop. Think. *Understand.* It required the intimacy of knowing Nina. Knowing her team. Knowing what they were capable of risking.

Everything, always. Even for people who might not deserve it.

A tiny frisson of electricity snaked up his spine. Not from the realization, but because Luna had connected to his implant. It always felt like a prickle at first, mild and hardly painful, but still discomfiting. The doctors always swore it was psychosomatic, but the fact that there were no nerve endings in his brain to feel the implant didn't matter. Like Conall's brain overriding the anesthetic, Knox's brain understood what was happening and filled in the blanks.

In the heartbeat before the calibration kicked in, Knox caught Conall's flinch and Rafe's slightly widened eyes, and he knew.

He *knew.*

Luna, their glorious, ridiculously talented genius, was doing the impossible. She was fixing *all of them.*

The jolt hit him then, and Knox gave in to it with an unnecessarily dramatic groan. He hit his knees, drawing all of the attention in the room— just in time. Conall swayed, and Rafe jammed a shoulder against him to hold him up. Knox let out a roar that could have been agony, keeping all of the morbidly fascinated gazes in the room fixed on him.

Just a show. A good show. Because nothing hurt. Strength washed through him on a blissful wave, sweeping away a hundred aches and a bone-deep lethargy that had crept over him so slowly, he hadn't realized how far he'd fallen.

The wave broke inside him, and it wasn't just his body that was reborn. The cleansing feeling roared through the broken, agonized wreckage of his mind and erased the past week of tortured indecision. The misery of terrible choices fell away as he drew in an unsteady breath and released it on a laugh that must have sounded insane.

He'd never felt more stable in his life. He was Garrett Knox, commanding officer of the Silver Devils. The best damn soldier to ever come out of the Protectorate, operating at full strength and angry as hell.

He could take out a dozen assault-weapon-toting mercenaries with his bare hands.

But he didn't need to. He had Nina, who assessed him critically as he staggered back to his feet, his knife gripped in one hand. He flipped it in a showy move, caught it nimbly by the blade, then flipped it again before baring his teeth in a feral smile. "Let's do this."

After a cautious glance at Ava, the mercenary who'd caught Nina's knife slid it back across the floor. Nina bent slowly to retrieve it, never taking her eyes off Knox.

She straightened just as slowly, stretched her shoulders, and rolled her neck. "Remember what you're fighting for, Captain."

The same words she'd offered him before he stepped into Boyd's grimy cage. He'd thought then that he was fighting for his men, but he had started to wonder if he was partly fighting for her.

The truth seemed incredibly, starkly simple now. He was fighting for all of them, because that was the only way to fight for himself.

"I don't forget," he murmured, then lunged.

His body moved with exhilarating efficiency. He'd forgotten how *easy* it was supposed to be. The world sped by in a dizzy blur, and he had all the time in the world to contemplate the angle of his attack and Nina's reaction. She was as fast as he was, and her deflection and counterattack were perfectly timed to make a careful feint look like a vicious clash.

They were putting on a show again, but this time the audience was a ghost from her past. So Knox followed her lead as she broke apart and closed again, pushing his body to top speed to keep up.

The first time their fight trailed toward the side of the room, the mercenaries braced, swinging their weapons up at the ready. But Nina launched from Knox's next attack into an acrobatic roll that returned them to the center of the room, and the men relaxed.

He caught on and steered the fight in the other direction. When it was his turn to lunge to the floor to escape a slash that would have opened him from shoulder to shoulder, he twisted and came up facing his men.

Conall was breathing hard, his eyes glazed with adrenaline no doubt enhanced by the temporary implant. Gray was holding himself rigidly still. Rafe caught Knox's gaze and barely inclined his head.

At full strength, Rafe could snap those zip ties like useless string. They just needed the right moment.

Nina closed with him in the next heartbeat, their bodies slamming together, their violent dance bringing them in a circle before they broke apart. She drove him back toward the bulk of the mercenaries again, and he caught sight of Dani out of the corner of his eye. In his heightened state of awareness, the gentle tensing of her arm muscles told another story—behind her back, her hands were moving in the steady rhythm of someone sawing through plastic.

Almost ready.

The mercenaries scattered as Knox and Nina barreled toward them. But they didn't tense as much as they had the first few times. They were professionals, but even professionals could be lulled into a state of complacency.

Knox slashed close enough to slit the side of Nina's tank top, and she tumbled away again. He was there when she bounced to her feet, and she retaliated by slicing across his chest with such fine control that her knife split his shirt and stirred the hair on his chest.

He felt every move she was going to make before she made it, as in tune with her now as he'd ever been in bed. It was like the betrayal hadn't happened, like he'd never lied to her. They were the eye of their own private hurricane of flashing steel, and—for one painful second—he let himself hope.

They circled once more, each wordlessly angling the other to give them a chance to check in on their team members. Dani's furtive movements had stopped. Rafe's muscles were tensed. Gray seemed poised on the verge of exploding into movement.

Nina's gaze met Knox's. They didn't need to speak. He pivoted slightly and let the natural momentum of their fight drift toward the tightest knot of mercenaries again. Slash, dodge, retreat, spin, duck, parry—

Now.

Neither of them said a word, but they might as well have screamed it in unison. Because the room erupted into chaos.

Whatever Luna had done to configure his implant had jacked his cognitive processing speed up to maximum. Even as he flung his body toward the nearest mercenary, Knox marked the positions and opening moves of each person in the room.

Dani moved the fastest. A knife she'd produced from God-knew-where sliced through Maya's bonds, freeing her. Dani dove toward Conall as Rafe snapped free of his bonds with a roar and lunged at a startled mercenary.

Gray ignored his bonds and rolled to his feet close to another soldier. One vicious kick took the man's legs out from under him, the next snapped his neck on the way down.

Knox crashed into his first opponent—a mercenary whose gun was just coming up. He knocked it out of the way and used the momentum of his spin to pick the man up and hurl him at his comrades, who were only just beginning to react. Two lunged out of the way, but a third went down.

Before the first two could recover, Nina was on them, her knife flashing silver, her gracefully precise cuts now ruthlessly lethal. One soldier staggered back from her, straying too close to Luna. She swung a chair, crashing it into his chest. A grunt of pain was all they had time for before Rafe was there with a brutal punch that knocked the man out before he hit the floor.

Five seconds. Five seconds was all the time it had taken to unleash anarchy.

Five seconds was how long it took for the shooting to start.

He felt the first shot before he heard it, searing heat burning across his upper arm. The graze was minor, but it warned him to dive for Nina before the next shot exploded through the room.

He carried her to the floor as a bullet drove into the wall behind where they'd been standing, and Ava's voice rose over the madness. "No guns, *no guns.* Do *not* shoot at my sister!"

It had been a bluff, after all. All of Ava's blustering, all of her threats—frustration tore through him, but Knox was still intensely grateful. Not just because the mercenaries' confused hesitation would give the Devils a fighting chance.

Nina had weathered enough betrayal for one day.

Taking the guns off the table evened the odds. There were still too many men, but they couldn't stand toe-to-toe with the Devils, or with Dani or Nina. Even Maya was unexpectedly vicious, squirming out of the way of a man who tried to stun her before plunging a fork—a literal *fork*—into his neck. When he howled and reached up to claw at the utensil, she snatched his stun-stick from him and jammed it into his armpit.

He went down convulsing, and triumph surged through Knox.

They could do this. They could *win* this—

Agony exploded through him as a stun-stick hit him between the shoulders.

The pain was blinding. He lost momentary control of his body and went down hard, one knee smashing into the floor. Electricity coursed through him, enough to lay a normal human out. He wasn't normal, but it still *hurt*, the agony burning him from the inside out as he fought for mastery of his limbs, or even the strength to twist away.

He couldn't. Not even when he saw Ava using the chaos of the fight to slip out the door.

With a superhuman effort, Knox embraced the pain and locked his muscles before throwing himself back. It dislodged the stun-stick for a moment, and Knox took advantage of the respite by turning his body into a battering ram.

It wasn't pretty. Knox took an elbow to the cheek and a knee to his ribs as he took the mercenary behind him down. He couldn't get his arms to move right, but he didn't need finesse for this. Just a knee across the man's throat, cutting off his oxygen, and most of the rest was sheer gravity.

For the moment, it was all he was capable of—a truth he regretted deeply when he looked at the door again and saw Nina flying through it in pursuit of her sister.

"Nina!" His voice barely worked. The noise of the fight swallowed his cry, and the mercenary thrashing beneath him had a friend closing in fast. Knox flung himself to the side and rolled toward Rafe, and for the first time since a childhood he barely remembered, he prayed to whatever God might be up there to give him back control of his body before it was too late.

Nina shouldn't have to be the one to kill her sister.

SECURITY MEMO

Franklin Center for Genetic Research

I don't care if you think I'm overreacting. You *have* to give me the resources to find and eliminate HS-Gen16-B. If you think she won't succeed where we have failed and locate HS-Gen16-A, then you're not just naïve. You're a fool.

One of them is a threat. Together, and armed with the truth . . .

You have consistently underestimated this cluster, despite warnings from myself and Dr. Baudin. We will not be held responsible for the results of your negligence.

Dr. Keller, December 2082

TWENTY-FOUR

Nina ran.

The trees formed a canopy too thick for the moonlight to penetrate. She couldn't see through the darkness. Thorns raked at her bare feet and arms, and branches whipped stinging lines of pain across her cheeks.

But she ran anyway, blindly following the sound of her sister hurtling through the forest somewhere ahead of her. She counted time by the heavy thrum of blood in her ears; she measured distance by the volume of the sound as Ava's boots crashed through the underbrush.

Fifteen meters. Ten.

Five.

Nina burst into a clearing and spotted Ava. She pushed harder, faster, her legs and heart pumping like mad, closing the gap between them. *Almost.* Her lungs burned. Her muscles ached.

Two meters.

Nina dove at Ava, and they went down hard, tumbling through the grass and over sharp rocks. Before they slowed to a stop, Ava was already swinging. Nina avoided the first two punches, but Ava was fighting dirty. She drove her knee into Nina's rib cage, sending a splinter of pain snapping through her. Ava pressed her advantage, throwing an elbow that narrowly missed Nina's eye and catching her with the backhand that followed.

Nina tasted blood. Ava redoubled her efforts, her fingers digging into sensitive pressure points. Still, Nina held on, winding her hands into Ava's clothes to secure her grip.

She rolled them and tried to pin Ava to the ground, but Ava countered by bashing her forehead into Nina's nose. The world bloomed red with agony, and Nina struggled to focus on her breathing as Ava tried to wiggle away.

She almost made it. She might have, if Nina hadn't spent the first twenty years of her life having to fight through pain. It had been drilled into her by trainer after trainer—*suffering is no excuse*. She had to keep going. Anything less was failure.

She clutched blindly at Ava, dragging her back. She moved out of instinct now—drop a series of quick jabs to stun. Avoid retaliatory blows.

Wear down your opponent until you can move in for the kill.

Before she realized it, she had her forearm pressed tight across Ava's throat, cutting off her air, and Ava had stopped fighting back. Her face had gone dangerously red, and silent tears streamed out of her eyes.

Horrified, Nina scrambled back.

For one terrible moment, the darkness of training, of *memory*, warred with Ava's desperate, rasping breathing. The sound won out, each breath accompanied by a sob that seemed to wrack Ava's entire body.

Nina licked her dry lips. Relaxed her clenched fists. "Ava, I—"

The words cut off with an anguished jerk as Ava hit her with a stunstick, and electrical current surged through Nina. Her jaws snapped together as every muscle contracted and pain expanded, and all she could do was ride the agony.

"I'm sorry, Nina. I do wish this had gone differently."

Nina was trembling by the time the waves finally subsided and her muscles unlocked. She lifted her head just in time to glimpse Ava's retreating form reach the edge of the clearing.

Instinct. Muscle memory. Nina drew the gun she'd stolen from one of the mercenaries and aimed as she rose. Her arm was still shaking, but not enough to affect her marksmanship.

Another thing she'd learned at the Franklin Center—how to hold a weapon at the ready as minutes bled into hours, unaffected by things like fatigue or distraction or agony.

Ava paused at the edge of the clearing and looked back.

Nina's index finger tightened on the trigger.

A million memories flashed through her mind. Whispers and giggles after lights-out. Debates and laughter and screaming fights. Ava's brows drawn together as she considered a complicated equation. Zoey, laboring over a pendant until every curve and twist of metal was exactly the way she wanted it. Impromptu dance parties and melancholy that didn't seem so bad when someone was there to share it.

Family.

Nina lowered the gun.

By the broken moonlight spilling across her sister's face, she thought she caught a hint of surprise—and disappointment.

Then Ava vanished, melting into the tree line like a shadow or a wisp of smoke.

Like a ghost.

Nina stared blankly at the darkness between the pines, too numb to cry as she sank to her knees in the grass.

The sound of footfalls crashing through the trees came from behind her. By the time she turned, Knox had burst into the clearing. He stopped half a dozen paces away, his gaze sweeping over the crushed grass where she'd fought with Ava before fixing on her face. "Nina?"

She clung to her careful detachment, wrapping it around her like a blanket. A shield.

He holstered his gun as he took another step forward, every movement slow. The way you'd approach a wild creature. "Is she gone?"

She was stone.

"Nina?"

She was ice.

"Nina, are you—?"

The ice fractured. "How long did it take?" she rasped, clambering back to her bare feet. "Did you even put your pants back on before you started laughing at how *easily distracted* I was?"

Knox recoiled. "I never *laughed* at you. It wasn't like that."

"I should have known. I should have *known*." She spun away from him. "You spent all that time warning me not to get mixed up with you, but you let me crawl into your bed anyway. Because that's exactly what I was supposed to do."

"No—" The word cut off in a growl that moved closer. "Damn it, Nina. I wasn't trying to play you. I just . . . I fucked up."

"No. No, you were brilliant." Nina backed away, keeping a precise amount of distance between them. "It doesn't matter anyway. Not anymore. You have what you want."

"Nina . . ." He stopped, both hands held placatingly at his sides. "It's more complicated than that."

A wry, humorless laugh shredded its way out of her throat. "It always is, isn't it, Captain?"

"I was going to tell you." His fingers curled toward his palms. "I know it doesn't mean shit now, but I was going to tell you tonight. I couldn't hand you over. Any of you."

Looking at him felt like sandpaper over a new burn, fresh and raw. She pressed her bare foot harder against the earth, counting the stones beneath her sole to distract herself from the pain.

But the anger remained.

What do you want, a medal? The caustic words died on her tongue, but their taste lingered as she stared at him. "It's a little late for confessions, Knox. You crossed the line, and don't pretend you don't know what I mean."

"I know."

"You know." Nina's throat ached, and no amount of blinking seemed to ease her burning eyes. "Well, then. In that case, we have nothing more to say, do we?" She walked past him, careful not to let her bare skin brush his.

"Nina, *wait*—"

He caught her arm, and her nerve endings screamed. They *sang*. Fury and lust and heartbreak battled for supremacy, tumbling end over end until they seemed to meld together.

She wanted to lash out, hurt him.

She wanted to cry.

She wanted to ask him why.

The only constant was that she *wanted*.

"You deserved better than this," he said quietly. Implacably. "Better than me."

The soft confession did what none of his apologies and assurances could. The dam inside her broke, and the words rushed out of her. "Why didn't you ask for my help? You didn't even *try*."

"I thought I couldn't. People aren't like that. The *world* isn't like that." He lifted a hand, but stopped short of touching her. "But you . . . You made me wonder if I was wrong."

"No." Ava had kidnapped an innocent person in her quest to wreak vengeance on Nina. And Knox had lied to her with more than words—with every soft touch, every rough whisper in the dark. "No, I think you were right."

He sucked in a breath as if she'd slapped him.

She'd hurt him. They could go in circles like this, wounding each other, biting and bleeding until there was nothing left but anger and resentment.

Or one of them could make the break, and make it clean.

She pulled her arm free of his grasp. "I'll make sure to get word to you about how and where you can pick up your truck—"

"Fuck it," he said roughly. "You can keep it."

She ignored the words. "I'm not sure when it'll be, but you have my word. Otherwise—" The lump in her throat threatened to choke her, and she had to swallow hard to speak again. "Leave me alone, Knox."

He stared at her in silence as protest seethed in his dark eyes. She was sure he was about to open his mouth to argue, to make this bloody and messy.

But he only inclined his head. "That's what you want?"

"It's how it has to be." Misery washed over her, and she finally stopped trying to modulate her voice or hold back her tears. "You told me that if I ever *really* saw you, I wouldn't want you anymore."

Somehow, the pain digging lines into his face intensified.

"I still do," she confessed. "I want you more than anything. But this— this would always be there between us. You'd always feel guilty, and I'd never know if I could trust you."

"I should feel guilty," he replied harshly. "And I don't deserve your trust."

"See?" She closed the distance between them. The moment her hands touched his face, a visceral longing seized her, and she wavered. All she had to do was take it all back, tell him she forgave him.

Tell him it was all right.

But she couldn't bring herself to say it. Oh, she could forgive him someday. She knew that already, felt it in the pit of her stomach.

But she didn't know if she would ever be able to forget.

She kissed him. But the heat that unfurled when he groaned and reached for her was edged with bitter heartache, and she quickly pulled away.

"Good-bye, Knox." The moment the words left her lips, she turned around—180 perfect degrees—and walked away.

**TECHCORPS PROPRIETARY DATA,
L1 SECURITY CLEARANCE**

The skeletal remains have been verified as those of DC–031.
Cancel the reward.

Security Memo, February 2082

TWENTY-FIVE

Nina loved her home.

Her neighborhood wasn't the fanciest or safest or cleanest, but it was hers, which would have made her love it anyway. But it was also the nicest—she knew all the people hanging out on the front stoops and street corners.

And they knew her.

That all changed when she left Five Points. When she ventured out into other parts of Atlanta, she became something worse than invisible. People's long-neglected lizard brains jolted, their creaky instincts came to life—and somehow, *some way,* they knew they were in the presence of a predator. They smiled tight little smiles that didn't light their eyes, and they skirted around her in wide arcs. Like if they somehow came too close, they'd get sucked into whatever troublesome orbit had brought her into their territory. Sure, she could smile and dispel their tension to varying degrees of success, but that took energy.

Energy she didn't seem to have these days.

No wonder she preferred night drops. Dani might have decried the dangers, but Nina would take her chances. She'd take *anything,* so long as she didn't have to look into one more stranger's fearful eyes.

So when the Professor had requested a daytime exchange, it had given Nina pause. Not because it might be a TechCorps trap—the setup for a perfect ambush, one that would leave her dead or worse—but because she'd have to venture up on the Hill, where skyscrapers and high-rises spiked up between estates that could have housed dozens of families. The waste of space nauseated Nina.

Worst of all, smiling didn't work on the people up on the Hill. *All* of their predators smiled, so it only made them more nervous.

She found the Professor right where he said he'd be, sitting on a bench outside one of the area's many research facilities. This one apparently specialized in developing synthetic substitutes for plant-based pharmacological agents, and for a moment she wondered if this was where he worked.

Probably not. Even the Professor wouldn't be *that* sloppy.

But even Nina had to admit it was a nice place—lush and well manicured, with tall trees shading the cobblestone paths. Places like this got hard to find when you strayed too far from the Hill.

The Professor barely looked up when she slid onto the bench beside him. He was preoccupied with scattering birdseed from a rumpled paper bag in his hand.

She let the silence hang for a few seconds before cracking it open. "What are you doing?"

Instead of answering, he pushed his horn-rimmed glasses up the bridge of his nose with the knuckle of his index finger. The damn things had been old-fashioned even before the Flares, but the Professor was like that. Sweater-vests and bow ties and heavy optical frames that kept sliding down his nose.

A black-and-white photo of him would be indistinguishable from an image of a mid-twentieth-century Cold War operative, right down to the bench and the fucking brown bag of birdseed. Maybe he'd seen too many spy movies. Or maybe he was just a lonely, bored scientist who got off on the idea of a little danger.

She waited.

Finally, he spoke. "I was feeding the pigeons."

Nina looked around. Verdant as it was, the area around the bench was decidedly bereft of wildlife. "There are no pigeons."

He shrugged, as if that had no bearing on anything he'd said, and set the bag aside. "I heard you had a bit of excitement recently."

Shit. "Just a job," she demurred. "It took us out of town for a few days."

"Eleven days, to be specific."

Eleven days. Not even two weeks. No time at all, really. But if lives could change in a heartbeat, what could happen in eleven days? You could fall in love, have your entire world turned upside down.

You could get your heart broken. Your *soul* broken.

She shook off the wave of pain. "Just a job."

"Hmm."

She sighed. "Who's been talking?"

"Besides everyone?" He shrugged again. "You're more blasé about partnering up with a rogue Protectorate squad than most people would be, Nina. I like that about you."

Partnering. His choice of words led her to believe he didn't know the truth about what had really happened. The way he was watching her, on the other hand, like he was waiting for her to correct him . . .

He knew, maybe everything.

For the first time, she wondered who he really was. She'd always figured he was a researcher with decent TechCorps security clearance. Overworked and underappreciated, padding his bank account and catching a few thrills by selling trade secrets on the side.

But the man sitting beside her now was no lonely lab rat with a hard-on for the nostalgic 1950s. He was too well informed. And too interested in her reactions.

"Cut the shit and tell me what you want, John." Her hands were already in her pockets, and she closed her right one around the butterfly knife she kept stowed there. "If that's even your real name."

"Oh, it's as real as most other things." He didn't seem upset at having been made. On the contrary, he accepted it with the same unflappable calm as everything else. "I have information, and I thought you might be interested."

"How much?"

That raised his hackles. His brows drew together in a stern line. "Don't be crass, Nina. This is a friendly heads-up."

"Be still, my beating heart."

He chuckled. "TechCorps execs want Garrett Knox's head on a platter. The rest of his team too, but mostly him. They've authorized the Protectorate to use lethal force."

"Obviously," she muttered.

"Obviously. But more importantly . . ." He turned toward her on the bench. "They've authorized them to use *resources.*"

TechCorps executives would spill blood at the drop of a hat—especially if they didn't have to get their own hands dirty doing it. But getting them to open their wallets was a whole different story. If they were prepared to spend big to hunt down and reacquire the Silver Devils . . .

She swallowed past the lump in her throat. "How long?"

"I'd expect the first strike any day now."

Maybe this was a TechCorps trap, after all . . . only she wasn't the prey, she was the bait. "Uh-huh. And what do you *expect* me to do with this information?"

"I wouldn't dare to presume. But your options seem somewhat limited."

They were, in fact, precisely three.

One: she could turn them in. High-profile deserters often commanded hefty rewards for capture. If the bounty on the Silver Devils was anything like Maya's had been, Nina and her crew could retire. After Knox and his men had been executed, she could take Maya and Dani and split. They could sail down to the western coast of Mexico, live like kings, and hate themselves forever.

Option one wasn't an option at all.

Two: she could ignore the Professor's warning. Knox and his men were on their own, and whatever happened . . . happened.

As choices went, it was barely better than the first.

Three: she could pass on the warning. Knox was a smart man. He'd probably already figured out that he and his squad needed to get the hell out of Atlanta. Out of Georgia. But, just in case he was being stubborn, she could let him know that the Protectorate wasn't going to give up on finding him, and going on the run was his only rational move.

She knew which option she could live with. Now she just had to figure out how to survive another encounter with Garrett Knox.

SECURITY MEMO

Franklin Center for Genetic Research

Dr. Keller has been stripped of her security clearance and reassigned to our research division. All memos on B-designation subjects should be sent to Dr. Phillips.

Dr. Reed, February 2083

TWENTY-SIX

Knox stared at the bare concrete wall and ignored the impossible tickle inside his head. Luna's third attempt to find a way to disable the degradation fail-safe in his implant had started off as their most optimistic effort yet, but her enthusiasm had faded into dull, tense silence.

Knox was trying to ignore that, too.

He was getting good at ignoring things. He ignored the hollow, helpless guilt that opened up inside him every time he thought of Nina, standing in that clearing, telling him he was right. That the world was bad. People were bad.

He ignored the knowledge that he'd broken her.

He ignored the exquisite pain of being back here, staring at the wall where Conall had first projected her image, an inescapable reminder of the first shitty choice he'd made—the decision to give her lies instead of the truth.

He ignored the fact that constantly reviewing his list of transgressions was like poking an endless row of bruises, the literal opposite of ignoring anything.

"Great news," Luna muttered. "I managed to figure out the final layer of encryption."

Knox glanced at Luna. She had her dark brown hair pulled back from her face and her eyes narrowed in concentration, and nothing about the tension in her body said *great news*. "So why don't you sound happier?"

She blew out a breath. "Because if I try to actually decrypt it, your head will explode."

"Figuratively or literally?"

"Do you really need me to answer that?"

"No." Knox rubbed at the back of his neck, his fingers lingering over the scar from his tracker. "So what does—"

Before he could finish the question, the warehouse door crashed open. Knox was on his feet with his gun in hand before the door finished rebounding off the wall. Conall practically bounced in, his eyes alight with a giddy, familiar amusement. It hadn't taken much to set Conall's world right—a swift surgery to remove Boyd's hack job and an afternoon with Luna fine-tuning his implant, and Conall was walking on air, joyously embracing his second chance at life.

Seeing it dulled the sharp pain in Knox's chest to a softer ache. "What's got you grinning today?"

"Rafe."

Conall ducked out of the way as Rafe stormed in, looking decidedly less amused. He glared at Conall, stomped to the table with a decided limp, and stripped off his shirt. "We tried to stop in at Clementine's to get a drink." Rafe twisted to poke at his side. "And now I have buckshot in my ass."

Unable to contain himself anymore, Conall collapsed into a chair, laughing.

"Very funny," Rafe growled, jerking at his belt. He shoved down the edge of his slightly shredded pants and glared at his hip. "You're not the one she tried to murder."

"Eh, she wasn't trying to murder you." Gray retrieved the medical bag from its spot in the corner and hefted it onto the table. "Miss Clementine doesn't strike me as a lady who misses too many shots. If she'd wanted to hit you square, she'd have hit you."

"She got enough of me," he grumbled.

Luna eyed Rafe dubiously. "What did you do to her?"

"Like I said, I tried to order a drink." Rafe winced as Gray probed at one of his wounds. "I'm guessing word has gotten around."

"Yeah." Conall's mirth mellowed a little. "I don't think we're going to be very popular in this neighborhood. Not until tempers cool."

No, they likely wouldn't be. Knox doubted that Nina had told anyone the whole truth—they'd have been greeted with worse than buckshot in that case—but she didn't need to share the details to be damning. The people she'd helped so much would close ranks around her.

In a perverse way, he was glad. Nina deserved that loyalty.

Knox exhaled roughly and glanced at Luna. "What's the prognosis on the implant? Is there a way around the encryption?"

"Sure. All we have to do is go to TechCorps headquarters, find a lab with Level One security, and steal an administrative log-in." She shrugged. "Piece of cake. Except for the part where we all die about thirty seconds in."

"They're geo-blocked. Of fucking course they are." Conall drove both hands into his hair and curled them into fists, like he was trying to pull out a solution along with his hair. "No one can get into the L1 labs. You basically have to be a VP just to empty the trash. And the network is a completely closed intranet. Tobias Richter manages all access *personally*."

Even if Knox could have bribed his way through enough support staff to get them inside, even if he could have somehow traversed the maze of surveillance that intensified the deeper you went into the heart of the TechCorps research division, no one subverted or betrayed the vice president of security. The only thing more legendary than Richter's loyalty was the punishment he bestowed upon traitors.

Definitely *not* a person Knox wanted to see right now.

"It's not the end of the world—hey!" Rafe yelped and shot Gray a glare as the man dug another piece of buckshot from his skin. "Be gentle with my fine ass, would you?"

Gray rolled his eyes and reached for the anesthetic spray. "I've watched you shrug off worse. Why are you being such a baby about this?"

"Because I'm not used to being shot by ladies I've already laid my best smile on." He grimaced. "As I was about to say, it's not ideal, but we have another month or two on the clock now, and Luna can just tune us up if we start to feel rough."

"It buys us some breathing room," Knox said. "We have time to figure out where we're going to go."

"Uhh, go?" Conall's eyes widened in alarm. "Is leaving really a question? We won't find any permanent fixes out in some backwater village running on generator power."

Gray snorted. "And if we stay here with people who want to shoot us, then sooner or later, someone's going to turn our asses in to the Protectorate brass."

Rafe wasn't looking at either of them. "Do you *want* to go, Luna?"

"I don't want to completely uproot Tia Ivonne," she admitted, "but her safety is my priority. I'll do whatever I have to do to guarantee that."

And Luna's safety had to be a priority. If the Devils left her behind, there was a high probability the TechCorps would eventually unearth the connection between them. After all, Ava had managed it.

So she and Tia Ivonne would have to come, too. Just a band of rogue supersoldiers, their biohacker sidekick, and her elderly aunt.

What could go wrong?

It would be a disaster . . . and it was still their best shot. "If we stay, they'll come at us. And they won't stop coming. All it's going to take is one pissed-off local venting to the wrong person, and the countdown will start."

"I don't want to spend my life running," Gray said. "I'm not judging anyone who wants to split, but I think I'll stay right here. Enjoy the time I have left."

"It's not hard to lose yourself down here on the south side of the city. Too many people, no facial recognition infrastructure, the locals' charming tendency to shoot down drones . . ." Rafe scratched at his stubble. "Maybe I'll grow a beard."

"You'd look hot with a beard," Conall said approvingly. "Gray would probably look like the kind of guy who hides in cabins and builds bombs, though."

Gray stifled a yawn and held up his middle finger.

Knox rose and gripped the back of his chair, as if he could hide his tension when the wood groaned in protest under his fingers. "I'm not joking, Conall."

"Neither am I," he retorted. "I mean, about the reclusive bomber thing, yeah. Gray already looks like one of those. But I don't want to go die on a farm somewhere, Knox. Give me the rest of the day. I'll scramble our trail a little. Lay a few false bread crumbs. I can play cat and mouse better than anyone in the Protectorate."

"And I still have contacts who can help us," Rafe added. "Even people on the inside. And since when has any other squad ever been a match for us, anyway?"

They were so earnest. So *hopeful.* Even Gray's cynicism had taken a peculiar twist toward embracing life. Knox had fought and bled and carved out his own heart to buy their futures, and they planned to gamble them on the irrational hope that they could outmaneuver the inevitable.

He wanted to forbid it, to load them all up into a truck and leave the dust of Atlanta behind. They could find their remote little farm. Hell, they could go back to Dalton. The place made him think of peach iced tea and country dances under the sweltering night sky. He'd been happy there, twirling under the twinkling lights and the distant stars.

Of course, Nina had been with him then.

The chair back creaked under his grip, and the wood split with a crack. Knox blew out a breath and stared at the broken pieces.

He'd bought their lives with his pain, but he didn't own their futures. That had been the whole fucking point. He wasn't their commanding officer anymore.

"All right," he said quietly. "We stay."

RAFE

The dream was nice. He always enjoyed a warm body, a husky laugh, the scent of clean hair and subtle perfume. Fingers flexing, lips touching . . . When a delicate weight settled over his hips, it felt like part of the dream.

The blade against his throat did not.

Rafe jerked into full consciousness, every muscle in his body tensed against the need to move. The weight on him was light enough to be easily dislodged, but any movement would get him cut to ribbons.

Especially since it was Dani straddling his hips. "Well," he breathed. "Fancy meeting you here."

"I came in the window." Her words were casual, but she didn't move her knife. "Your security here could use some work."

Their security was admittedly laxer than it could have been—Conall was still making do with the supplies Rafe had been able to procure—but they had motion sensors and cameras. Plus, Rafe's room was on the third floor of the warehouse, with a perfectly smooth wall and no convenient trees or cover nearby.

Not exactly a rational thing to ponder with an armed assassin straddling his quasi-interested dick. "Did you stop in to give me security pointers, or did you just miss me?"

Her eyes went dark, more stormy gray than blue, and she leaned forward. "You're still here."

"In my bed? Yeah, it's where I tend to spend my nights. If I don't get any better offers."

"You're still *here*." Her frown deepened. "In Atlanta."

"Yes." He settled his hands on her waist carefully, freezing when the blade seemed to tremble against his throat. "Are you here for an apology?"

"What? No." She flipped the knife up and slid it into a sheath strapped to her thigh. "I thought you were smart."

"That is not the impression you gave me."

She made a soft noise in the back of her throat and climbed off of him. For someone wired to move fast, she took her time as she wandered slowly around his room, silently trailing her hands over the boxes of supplies stacked against the far wall.

He could almost feel her fingertips as she ghosted them up the side of the painting Tessa had made for him. The moody landscape showed a collapsed building being swallowed by kudzu under a night sky blazing with the greens and purples of a particularly brilliant aurora. There were no identifying geographic details, no way to trace the artwork back to his baby sister in her safe, anonymous little corner of Atlanta . . .

He still wanted to tear the painting off the wall and hide it. Dani always saw *too much*.

Instead, he threw back the covers and forced himself to be casual as he hauled on his discarded jeans. "This is the oddest break-in I've ever experienced. Did you want something? To borrow a book? To shiv me?"

She didn't answer, just continued her circuit around his room.

"If you're looking for the valuables, I keep them under my pillow."

She idly flipped the cover of a book on his desk open and shut as she studied the painting on his wall again from a distance.

A thread of frustration unfurled. Rafe was usually good with people. And he'd fallen into a rhythm with Dani—a give-and-take of friendly insults, a glorious game they were playing together. Under any other circumstances, the game would have ended in his bed.

Instead, their game had been abruptly cut off by betrayal.

Maybe there was only one way to come back from that. Trust.

"My baby sister painted it for me," he said softly. "Her name is Tessa. It's not safe for me to have pictures of my family, or anything that might lead the Protectorate back to them, but she wanted me to have something to remember her by." Rafe swallowed hard. "Not even Knox knows their names or where they are. He just knows I send everything I can back to them."

Dani hopped up to sit on his desk and finally looked at him. "So you're not smart. Not at all."

It was so bluntly *her* that a reluctant smile tugged at his lips. No, Dani wasn't going to melt at a display of vulnerability, even if it was earnest. If anything, vulnerability would piss her off. She was made of hard edges and feral protectiveness . . .

And she was here, getting irritated at his lack of self-preservation.

Oh, *shit*.

Dani was feeling protective of *him*.

Rafe hooked his thumbs through his belt loops and relaxed into a lazy smile. "If I didn't know better, cupcake, I'd think you were worried about me."

"Of course I am." She said it without a hint of shame or embarrassment. "Staying here is suicide, Morales. I thought you wanted to *survive*. Otherwise, why would you have bothered burning my crew? Burning *me*?"

"To save Luna's life," he shot back. "Which apparently was only in danger because of some fucked-up family drama. And hey, I'm sorry for your boss—"

"Do not," she cut in, her voice utterly devoid of inflection, "talk about Nina. She's a better person than either of us."

"No argument there." Rafe sighed and leaned one shoulder against the wall. "This thing in my head is a ticking bomb, Dani. We thought Luna could fix us, but all she can do is keep buying us more time. So I have to stay here and try to find a solution. I can't accept my fate and go count down my days on a peanut farm somewhere. I don't want to be a farmer."

Her fingers curled around the edge of the desk so hard that her knuckles turned white. "Your odds aren't any better here. The Protectorate is already after you. That's what I came to tell you."

Not exactly news, and not remotely surprising. The fact that she'd worried enough to warn him was, though. "We'll be careful. I promise. And we won't do anything to lead them back to you guys."

"The thought never crossed my mind."

"Because you were too busy being worried about me."

"It's not funny." She leaned back a little, almost reclining on his desk. "I might not be around to save your ass when your old buddies finally catch up with you."

Rafe was sure she had very good points. He might have been able to focus on them, too, if her break-in clothes hadn't been so . . . formfitting.

And if she hadn't been deliberately angling herself to display her very, very well-formed . . . form.

Professionally, from one player to another, he had to respect her game.

He'd be *suicidal* to let himself get distracted by it, of course. And to forget that she'd been wearing that same deadly shade of red lipstick the night she'd pumped poor, dumb Boyd full of abrin.

Relaxing his muscles, Rafe let his gaze drift down her body in a lazy perusal, then worked his way back up to her face. "Just tell me one thing, Dani."

"What's that, *cupcake*?"

His lips curved in his most seductive smile, the one that melted knees. "Where *do* you keep the poison?"

"Don't be lazy, Morales." She held both arms out wide. "You want it? You have to *find it*."

Yes, please.

He'd only taken one step toward her when his door rattled. Only one person knocked that damn hard—Conall. "Hey, Rafe, you awake?"

Grinding his teeth, he held up a finger to Dani and spun toward the door. If he didn't open it fast enough, Conall was fully capable of sticking his head in. Instead, Rafe cracked it open a few inches, angling his body to block the view inside. "Hey. You need something?"

Conall held up a tablet. "I have a new list of supplies. Can you hit up your contacts?"

"Everyone's asleep. Like you should be."

Conall huffed out a laugh. "Man, I feel too *good* to sleep. Besides, I thought all your criminal friends did business at night. Just give me five—"

Rafe could feel Dani's presence behind him like a blazing heat at his back. "*Tomorrow*, Con."

"Fine, fine!" Conall threw up his hands. "God, you're grumpy. Go get your damn beauty sleep."

"I plan on it." Rafe closed the door. Then, for good measure, he locked it. "Sorry," he murmured as he started to turn. "He's just really excited to not be falling apart . . ."

He was talking to an empty room.

For a few seconds, he wondered if it had all been a dream. He'd certainly had more outlandish fantasies about beautiful women. Hell, he'd had more outlandish fantasies about Dani. Though maybe nothing as revealing as her showing up, worried about him in spite of all of the bad blood between them.

But when he approached his desk, the light, floral scent of her perfume lingered. And next to the book she'd been toying with, he found a battered and creased cardboard coaster bearing the logo and address of a dive bar popular with scavengers. The ink was faded and imperfect, the way it looked coming off a cheap chemical printer instead of one of the smooth print shops up on the Hill. Alcohol stained the cardboard, and it smelled like cheap moonshine.

There were several potential messages to be inferred from the gift. The most obvious was that she'd heard what happened when he'd tried to buy a drink from Clem. Getting his ass pumped full of buckshot had been a humbling moment, and he didn't necessarily love having Dani know about it. But maybe this was her way of showing him a place to drink safely.

A place where she might join him?

Probably best not to hope for that yet. It was enough to know that she worried about him. That she wanted him alive, his fine ass intact.

She *wanted* him.

Rafe could work with that. If he could manage to stay alive.

SECURITY MEMO

Franklin Center for Genetic Research

EF-Gen14-B's employer is dead. Autopsy indicates poison. The techs have only just begun their forensic accounting, but it's already apparent that the employer's business holdings and the vast majority of their material wealth has been diverted in a manner similar to what we saw with HS-Gen16-B's employer.

Dr. Keller's termination may have been premature.

Dr. Phillips, November 2083

TWENTY-SEVEN

The pitying looks were coming from inside the house now.

Nina sighed as she finished washing lettuce for their salad. "Stop looking at me like that, Dani."

The blonde didn't lift her chin from her hands, but she did raise both eyebrows. "Like what?"

Nina set the bowl on the table and began gathering silverware. "Like I'm some horribly sad book you can't stop reading."

"That's not . . ." Dani trailed off. "Okay, that's not a bad metaphor, actually. You're breaking my *heart*, Nina. Just call the man, for fuck's sake."

"You don't have to." Maya perched on one of the stools at the island, juicing lemons. "We're Team Nina, all the way. But, as a member of Team Nina, can I just say that you've been looking . . . kind of yearny?"

Nina's cheeks went hot, and she avoided their gazes. She'd spent the first few days after their return to Atlanta just trying to keep her head above water. She'd thrown herself into work, because if she wasn't ready to process everything that had happened, she could at least use the desperate shallowness of her thoughts to her advantage.

And once she felt steadier, like she could cope with things again, she had other things to think about—the fact that Ava was *alive*, along with the revelations about the Franklin Center. Knox's betrayal was low on the list.

But circumstances kept conspiring to bring her attention back around to him, anyway.

Nina wiped her hands on her jeans and took a single deep, careful breath. She tried to sound casual, but she overplayed it *hard*, and she fought a wince when she heard her own voice. "Did you pass along the message?"

Dani hummed. "I paid Rafe a friendly visit last night."

Maya froze with a lemon hovering in the air. "How friendly? Like actual friendly, murder-friendly, or *friendly*-friendly?"

"Oh, he was revved and ready to go." Dani sighed. "Too bad we were interrupted. Anyway, I didn't have to tell him about the Protectorate. They know the score. They'd have to be stupid not to."

But they hadn't left town yet. Nina worried her lower lip with her teeth as she considered the implications. Knowing what she did of Captain Knox, it wasn't hubris that kept them from running.

It was exhaustion.

Sympathy tugged at her. She'd known people who were being hunted by the Protectorate. Most hadn't survived the experience. Some had . . . but only with help.

When she glanced up, her gaze locked with Maya's, and Nina knew she was thinking the same damn thing.

"We know what they're up against," Maya said softly. "I know they're assholes, but maybe we should—"

"Put yourselves in the line of fire? Honestly, I thought Dani, at least, was more pragmatic."

By the time Nina registered Ava's voice, Dani was already out of her chair and across the kitchen. She knocked Ava against the wall and held her there with a blade to her throat.

"Yes, exactly," Ava said, as if the knife wasn't even there. "Pragmatic. I appreciate that about you, Dani."

Maya hopped out of her chair, a stun-stick in one hand. "If you like her pragmatism, wait until you see her face-peeling."

"No one's peeling any faces," Nina countered.

Dani groaned in protest, her muscles trembling. "Come *on*, Nina. You have to give me this."

"*Dani.*"

She relented with another groan. "Fine. But I'm keeping the knife handy. One wrong move . . ."

Ava quirked one eyebrow. "If I had come here to hurt you, I wouldn't have announced my presence."

"Not helping your case," Dani shot back through gritted teeth.

Nina stepped between them. "Excuse us for a few minutes."

"Nina—"

"Just . . . wait here, okay?"

Nina led her sister through the back door and into the warehouse, where they'd set up the staging area for the freeze-dryers. They only had two, and the machines were plenty small enough to fit in the utility room off the kitchen, but they were loud. With that, plus the space needed to prepare and package the food, it was easier to do it out here.

A small window up near the ceiling was open, just a crack. It must have been Ava's access point. "I hope you were planning on closing that before you left. It's supposed to rain tonight."

"Of course." Ava walked the length of the table, running her fingers over crates piled to the brim with fresh peaches. "You didn't shoot me. In the clearing. You had a clear shot, but you didn't take it."

"Jumping right in with both feet, huh?"

Ava picked up a peach and turned it over, examining its pristine skin. "I never had much use for small talk."

"Okay." Nina crossed her arms over her chest and waited.

After a brief, tense silence, Ava set the fruit aside and squared her shoulders. "I've been thinking about how different our training was. You and the other A-designations were taught never to question orders. Chain of command, obedience to authority . . . Those things were beaten into you from the cradle."

Beaten. The word evoked a flash of somatic memory—standing for hours, arms outstretched, muscles burning. The agonizing lash across the delicate bones of your wrist when you wavered or broke form.

Nina blinked it away. "We were ground troops, Ava. Any thinking we learned to do, we had to figure out on our own."

"Being a B-designation was different. We were dangerous." Ava's short laugh was bitter. "They had to make us smart and suspicious in order to make us effective. But smart, suspicious trainees cause problems. That's why you got a job offer after we lost Zoey, and I got . . ." Her eyes darkened for one haunted, furious moment, then the expression vanished.

"Decommissioned." Nina whispered the word. "I didn't know. You understand that now, don't you, Ava?"

"They told you I was dead, and you had been conditioned to believe them. Intellectually, I know that. Accepting what they said at face value would have been logically consistent with your training and your personality."

If Nina closed her eyes, she could still see Knox, bemusement tilting his brows into severe angles as he called her an idealist. "I didn't know that they would lie. Not about something like that."

Ava's fingers curled into helpless fists. "Believing you should make it stop hurting. It's irrational to still feel betrayed."

"Feelings aren't always rational. Sometimes, they just *are*."

"I don't like irrational feelings." The words came out on a snarl, and Ava blinked, as if shocked at her own loss of control. Then her lips quirked into a rueful smile. "No. I don't like when feelings make me act irrationally. Which they have clearly done recently."

"But you're here." It meant more than Nina had known. She hadn't gone looking for her sister—if Ava didn't want to be found, she wouldn't be found—but she only just now realized how much of her had been arrested, *waiting* for Ava to show up. "That means something."

"It means I'm still behaving irrationally." Ava reached out, her fingers hovering close to Nina's temple, touching her hair. Zoey had been the nurturing one, the one who expressed her feelings with hugs and easy contact. Ava's love had been less direct. She'd solved problems, or acquired coveted contraband as gifts. Her one tactile expression of affection had been to spend her evenings twisting her sisters' hair into impossibly intricate braids.

"I missed you," Ava whispered. "Even when I thought I hated you. You're part of me. A better part of me."

The vague pressure that had lived in Nina's chest for the last few days twisted suddenly, sharpening into a bolt of breathtaking pain. She breathed through it, then tried to smile. "Then you already know why I didn't pull the trigger."

"It might have been easier on me if you had. I could have kept hating you." Ava exhaled shakily and let her hand fall away. "But you didn't, so I can't."

As admissions went, it was small. Except that it had come from Ava. "Does that mean you'll stay? There isn't a spare room upstairs, but you can have mine, and I'll sleep in the gym or the study—"

"Nina, don't." Ava shoved her hands in her pockets, her expression carefully, heart-wrenchingly blank. "You have your new family. It's all very cozy and domestic, but I don't know how to live like this. Besides, I already have my next mission."

"Mission?" The phrasing startled Nina. "Are you working for someone? I just assumed—"

Ava cut her off with a perturbed noise so familiar it echoed through Nina's bones. So did the words, their rhythm and cadence carved into her heart. "Assumptions are for people who don't have facts." Ava's lips curved in a reluctant smile. "You used to hate it when I told you that."

Nina didn't have facts, but she had feelings. Things she knew on such a visceral level that they might as well be enshrined truth. "You wouldn't work for anyone, not willingly. Not once you were free."

"You're right. You usually are—and I used to hate that about you." Ava inclined her head. "I work for myself. I plan my own missions. Maybe next time we meet, I'll tell you about a few of them."

"Wait." Nina took a single, careful step toward Ava. "You don't have to go. Really. If you need privacy, there's room in the basement. We'll make you your own little space. Just . . . please stay a while."

Fear spiked through Ava's eyes, a flash of raw, naked vulnerability. But by the next heartbeat, she'd locked her expression down again. She stood stiffly, a chilly stranger clad in heeled boots and a designer coat that was too warm for the summer evening.

"I can't," she said quietly. "I'm sorry."

"Where will you go?"

"I have business up in Virginia." Her sudden smile was vicious. "I've got to see a very bad man about his continued insistence on breathing."

"Will you come back?"

"I'll try." Ava turned to leave, but stopped after a few steps and looked back. "I'm glad you have this cozy, domestic life, Nina. Zoey would be so proud of you."

Some things were familiar, but not this. The words and sentiment were so jarring that Nina closed her eyes. By the time she managed to breathe through the pain and open them again, Ava was gone, and the window near the top of the wall shut tight.

Nina leaned against the prep table. Part of her wished that Ava had promised to stay, but that would have been a lie. Oh, she would have tried, but she would have wound up leaving the same way—silently, through a window, with her farewells disguised as emotional confessions.

This way was better. Honest. And they needed that if they ever had a hope in hell of rebuilding their relationship.

Of being sisters.

TECHCORPS PROPRIETARY DATA, L2 SECURITY CLEARANCE

Recruit 66–615's habit of altering his mission objectives has become more pronounced. While he continues to navigate conflicts to successful, nonviolent resolutions, some members of the Board have expressed concern about his ultimate loyalties.

The VP of Security has requested a comprehensive psych evaluation on Knox's entire squad the next time they come back to Atlanta. Given the lingering tensions over Skovgaard's activities, I advise we comply.

Recruit Analysis, February 2084

TWENTY-EIGHT

The bar wasn't as nice as Clem's, but at least no one had shot them.

Yet.

Knox traced his fingers over the obscenities someone had carved into the table and pretended the entire bar wasn't studiously avoiding their gazes.

It wasn't working. Even Conall's enthusiasm had dimmed slightly in the fifteen minutes they'd been nursing their beers.

No one was willing to be caught looking at them, but the glares directed at their backs were sharp enough to slice bone-deep. This bar was situated on the very edge of Nina's neighborhood, not to mention filled with the sorts of toughs and criminals he couldn't imagine her associating with, so the distrust probably wasn't personal.

This time.

Knox sighed. "How much longer do we wait for this guy?"

"I don't know." Rafe fiddled with one of Conall's clever little folding tablets, snapping the thin screens open and shut in an uncharacteristically nervous gesture. "McClain's never really been punctual, but he always shows up."

Knox imagined that being perpetually high on the most exclusive proprietary drugs in the TechCorps' dispensaries tended to warp one's sense of time. But the inside connections that got him access to those drugs made him an invaluable resource when it came to countering implant-related side effects. "I suppose we can give him another ten minutes."

"Can we? We've already been out in the open too long." Despite the doom and gloom of his words, Gray casually sipped his beer. "Plenty of time for someone to make us."

True enough. Fifteen minutes was probably ten minutes too long—a grim fucking assessment of their futures. Conall had spent days laying false trails and scrambling any evidence of their passage. He'd mapped every TechCorps camera within a dozen miles and set alarms for incoming drones. He'd bent every scrap of intelligence in his brain, the best tech brain the Protectorate had ever produced, toward the singular goal of covering their tracks.

And if they still couldn't spend an hour outside without getting tagged, it was all for nothing. A hopeless delusion.

"I'm trying to crack the Protectorate tracking system," Conall muttered. His open beer sat untouched in front of him, and he had a large tablet unfolded. His fingers tapped in hypnotic patterns, gliding over the surface as text flickered past too fast for Knox to even read. "I basically rebuilt it a decade ago, but they must have let Charlie in there to lock me out." His face twisted into a scowl. "I beat her out for the top spot in our cohort by a thousandth of a percent. I bet she's loving finally being number one."

There were shadows under Conall's eyes. Even his perfectly calibrated implant couldn't eliminate his need for sleep. He was one person, fighting everything the TechCorps could throw at them. He couldn't sustain this for long.

"Fuck this." Rafe suddenly exploded. He slapped the tablet open and pulled up his messages. "Let me see if I can—"

His tablet *pinged* softly.

A shiver of warning clawed its way up Knox's spine.

Something was *wrong*.

He assessed the room. He'd done it upon entering, marking the grungy windows in the front, the bar, the swinging door that led to the kitchen, and the narrow hallway that led out the back. The kitchen shared a wall with the sketchy secondhand tech shop next door.

The seventeen civilians he'd counted on arrival had grown to twenty-three. Twenty-three people who could have sent covert messages. Twenty-three people who could turn into collateral damage if a fight broke out.

A Protectorate squad wouldn't care about civilian casualties. They weren't trained to. Neither was Knox, except that he had to. Otherwise, what the fuck was the point?

"Shit," Rafe ground out, voice spiking with panic. "Shit, shit, *shit*. It's from McClain's sister. A Protectorate squad picked him up two hours ago."

"Plenty of time to torture someone for information *and* deploy a couple of squads." Gray finished his beer. "We're surrounded, of course."

An odd peace settled over Knox at the certainty. At least this was a battle he was equipped to fight. "That's a safe assumption."

"Well, fuck." Conall snapped his tablet shut with a sigh. "We should probably get out of here before they get bored and blow up the whole block."

Rafe still looked stricken. Luna's kidnapping was still a fresh wound. It couldn't be easy for him to find out that another of his contacts was in Protectorate custody because of him.

Knox reached across the table to grip Rafe's wrist. "We get out. *Then* we deal with the fallout."

Gray was already on his feet, his beer bottle grasped loosely in one hand. Knox jerked his head at Rafe as he hauled Conall from the booth and started for that narrow corridor.

A typical Protectorate squad was five to eight men. Knox's team was down a man, but none of them were typical. He'd recruited the best men the Protectorate had to offer, and year after year of difficult missions had given them an edge. No other squad stood a chance against them, one-on-one.

"Like that time in Memphis," Knox murmured as they approached the back door. "On three."

Conall pulled his sidearm—a deceptively modest small-caliber pistol with rounds that could burrow through armor—and thumbed the biometrics.

"One."

Rafe closed his hand around the doorknob, the muscles in his arms and shoulders flexing.

"Two."

Gray smashed his empty bottle against the wall, leaving behind only the jagged neck in his fist.

"*Three.*"

With a snarl, Rafe tore the door off the hinges and charged into the alley, holding the door in front of him like a combination shield and battering ram. He'd barely cleared the doorframe when Gray lunged through, slashing a startled Protectorate soldier across the face.

66–987. Knox identified the man's ID number automatically as he dove through the doorway. This was what it felt like to operate at peak performance. To have every muscle move in concert as the world slowed to a blur around him, the space between each heartbeat stretched out into enough time to analyze, extrapolate, and act.

Thump.

66–987 was a member of the Lucky Sixes, a squad led by Captain Patel. Efficient, dangerous, but inflexible. Patel was meticulous and methodical, but he couldn't adapt when a situation changed.

Like when the targets he'd been closing in on burst into his midst.

Thump.

Knox cleared the doorway and swung around. Shocked blue eyes stared back at him from a grizzled face. 66–591. Carl. Carl liked to cheat at pool, sulked when assigned any task he considered menial, and resented the fact that he'd never risen above a basic rank even though he'd never bothered to put in the work.

Knox's reinforced fist connected with Carl's throat. The force was sufficient to break his hyoid bone and crush the cartilage of his larynx, collapsing his airway. He went down wheezing and clawing at his neck, never to cheat or sulk or resent again.

Thump.

The alley ended in a dead end just three meters to Knox's left. It opened to the street fifteen meters to his right. Six men still filled the crate-strewn space, men whose strength and speed matched his own. Men who were already shaking off their surprise and lifting their rifles.

Knox could name them all. He knew their vices and their habits. He'd trained them and worked alongside them and sometimes even laughed with them.

He would regret taking them down, but not enough to let them kill him.

Thump.

Knox gave in to the tempo of the fight, and the sound of his heart beating melted away in a surge of adrenaline. He dove out of the path of a bullet and came up with his gun in hand. It was dangerous to fire in such close quarters, but dangerous was all they had. He took his shot, winging Patel on the cheek.

Conall's voice rose above the fight, "Captain, *down*," and Knox hit the pavement. One of Conall's clever little rounds whizzed over his head and sank into Patel's armor, transforming the man's expression from anger to horror as it burrowed through and into his chest.

Knox rolled and came up in time to see Rafe swinging the door like a bat. It crashed a man back against the wall, clearing a path for Gray to swipe his broken bottle viciously across another man's throat. 66–831, Knox's brain noted against his will. Hooper. Always hungry as a new recruit. He'd stabbed someone over extra rations and earned himself time in the stockade.

He was going to bleed out in a grungy alley.

Knox took 66–771 down with a bullet to the knee and cracked his skull with one solid blow to the temple. Rafe bashed 66–627's face in with his own gun. Gray killed 66–737.

Simmons. Kelvin. Roberts. Knox couldn't stop his brain from reciting a neat list of facts about each fallen man, like items on an obsolete dossier. Simmons would never again favor his left side in a fight. Kelvin's tendency to question orders wouldn't plague another commander. Roberts's collection of pre-Flare magazines would probably end up in the recycling incinerators.

Rafe finished off the squad with a series of swiftly cracked necks, and Knox wondered how high the cost of their freedom would grow before the end of this.

A crackle from the radio on Patel's hip answered him. "Hold on, Sixes. Hellcats have your 20 and are en route. ETA, less than two minutes."

Gray picked up Roberts's rifle and swore. "Definitely locked to biometrics. Time to load up on ammo and start ripping the thumbs off our buddies, the Lucky Sixes, here."

"No." Knox crouched to check the nearest soldier's pockets. "Two minutes is enough time to give you guys a head start." He pulled out two grenades, their color-coded bands promising smoke and fire, respectively. "I'll stall them for as long as I can. Pick up Luna and get the hell out of town."

Nobody moved to obey. "Not our captain anymore, remember?" Gray said.

"God *damn* it, Gray—"

A duffel bag hit the asphalt in front of him. Knox spun, his heart rocketing into his throat as he swung his pistol toward a familiar face that left him staring in shock.

"Put it away, you twitchy bastard." Dani vaulted over the edge of the building and rappelled to the ground beside him. "We thought you could use some help."

Maya poked her head over the edge of the roof. "Hey, Conall. This is an awkward situation. Good thing we brought presents."

"Maya?" Conall's eyes popped wide. "What the hell—"

"*Damn it,* woman." Rafe gripped Dani's upper arm. "Are you fucking crazy? Do you know what's coming for us? You shouldn't be here."

She glared back at him, affronted. "Of course I know. That's *why* I'm here. Nina sent us."

While Rafe gaped at her, Maya made a more controlled descent and landed lightly next to Knox. "Hey," she said, snapping a finger in front of his face. "If there was ever a time to embrace your inner evil genius, Captain . . ."

Reality snapped back into place, but Knox couldn't stop himself from scanning the rooftop one last time.

Nina had *sent* them to help. She hadn't come with them.

He didn't have time for the sting of disappointment. His team was still handing out weapons when Maya whistled and held up one arm in silent communication.

Enemy incoming.

"Hey, Knox." Dani had already taken cover behind one of the crates, and she threw two more grenades at him—one smoke and one unidentifiable gas. "Dealer's choice."

The first bullet whistled over his head as he ducked behind the steel door Rafe had wedged across a corner for cover. Knox pulled the pin on the smoke grenade, ticked off two seconds in his head, and chucked it over the barrier.

It exploded midair, spewing smoke that quickly obscured their position. Knox caught the rifle Maya tossed him and checked the magazine to find it had been loaded with incendiary rounds.

It was a good thing these women were in a forgiving mood, because they didn't fuck around.

"Spray and pray," Rafe muttered.

Knox rose above the cover of the door and began firing. Screams mingled with the sounds of bullets pinging off of brick as the smoke seemed to thicken. Rounds whizzed past Knox's head, some so close he could feel them splitting the air, but he focused on firing. Again and again and again—

When it finally penetrated that no one was shooting back, Knox braced his back against the wall and watched the smoke from the grenade and the guns dissipate on the afternoon breeze.

Seven Hellcats lay sprawled in the mouth of the alley, blood pooling beneath them, their unseeing eyes open to the bright blue sky.

Their names started to materialize on his tongue. Another list of ID numbers, another list of facts that would never matter again. Knox pushed it all down and turned to his men.

Conall had a superficial wound on his cheek. Rafe was nursing a graze to his shoulder. Gray looked as untouched and unruffled as always. And Maya—

"No. *Shit*, no."

Maya tore at Dani's sleeve, her fingers covered with blood. She'd barely pulled the fabric away from the wound when Rafe was suddenly *there*, trembling with the effort it must have taken him not to elbow Maya out of his way.

Dani tried to break away from them both. "It's just a scratch. Jesus."

"You always think it's just a scratch," Maya growled, using the torn fabric to wipe away blood.

From where Knox was standing, it didn't look like a critical injury. The bullet had entered and exited the muscle, bypassing the bone, and it wasn't bleeding enough to have involved the larger vessels. But Rafe was all but vibrating with tension as he tore his shirt over his head and ripped it into shreds. "Stay still," he snarled.

Dani sighed and let him lift her arm above her heart and apply pressure to the wound. "Relax, Morales. I'm not dying." She grinned wickedly. "It doesn't even hurt."

Knox had watched Nina and Maya take turns checking Dani after a fight, but the *reason* had never fully registered. Now, he realized with a start that she wasn't joking or playing tough.

She really couldn't feel the pain.

Christ. The TechCorps couldn't have been happy to have her slip through their fingers. If she got caught up in the next attack on the Devils, there was every chance they'd cart her back to a lab where they could take her apart at their leisure.

Too high. That was the cost of Knox's freedom. Too fucking high.

"There," Rafe muttered, cinching the bandage tight. "You'd better put med-gel on that the *second* you get home."

"Hey." Maya's voice was almost sympathetic as she shoved the tattered remains of Rafe's shirt back at him. "We take care of her. You don't need to worry."

But Rafe would—even more if he had to watch Dani walk away, not knowing whether she'd made it back to safety. "Gray," Knox said quietly. "Can you three get them home?"

Gray eyed him sharply. "What about you?"

"I'll meet you back at the warehouse. I have plans to consider."

"Knox . . ."

Knox squeezed Gray's shoulder. "I'm not going to be stupid."

"I don't think I believe you." But he turned away anyway, following Maya as she guided Dani toward the mouth of the alley. Rafe followed close on their heels, practically hovering over Dani, but Conall hesitated.

"You did what you had to do." He jerked his head toward the tangled sprawl of bodies. "All these men knew the Protectorate. They made their choice."

"I know," Knox lied.

Conall stared at him for a few seconds, but didn't call him on it. "Don't stick around here, brooding," he said as he turned to follow Rafe and Gray. "The place will be crawling with more squads in another ten minutes. If that."

An unnecessary reminder. For years, Knox would have been the one deployed to clean up a clusterfuck like this. He would have questioned the witnesses he could find, pulled whatever spotty or irregular camera footage was available. He would have been the one crouching in this dirty alley, meticulously examining the carnage for what it could tell him.

Grenade fragments, shell casings, and over a dozen dead Protectorate soldiers. What *did* it tell him?

That the prey was too dangerous to be captured or contained. That when *he* came for them, he wouldn't risk the chaos and unpredictability of a shootout. If Knox were sent to clean up this mess, he knew what he'd do next.

It wouldn't happen immediately. The Protectorate always responded to a bloodied nose the same way. A step back, a calm, methodical evaluation.

They wouldn't take another swing until they knew *exactly* where they were aiming, and who might be standing in their way.

But when they swung, it would be with a force overwhelming enough to devastate everything in its path.

Somehow, Knox had to cut all ties with Atlanta and have his team long gone before the Protectorate punched back.

SECURITY MEMO

Franklin Center for Genetic Research

Authorization granted to terminate the HS strain with Generation 17.

Dr. Reed, July 2084

TWENTY-NINE

"It's nearly healed already."

"Told you, Nina." Dani stretched her arm out, then flexed her biceps experimentally. "I'll be weaker on this side until the muscles heal, but I can compensate for that."

"Great." Now, if only Nina could compensate for the stress. Sending Dani and Maya out on their own had been a mistake. It didn't matter if the bullet that hit Dani had been a lucky shot, or that Nina likely couldn't have prevented the injury.

She should have *been* there.

Panic fluttered in Nina's belly. She carefully counted through it, three counts of three, until the dizziness subsided.

Dani's vague smile vanished as she studied Nina. "Hey, don't look like that, okay? Maya and I knew the score when we said we'd do this."

"I know, I just—" The empty med-gel applicator in Nina's hand snapped. "I wish I had my shit together, that's all. If I did, I could have gone with you. Backed you up."

"You're not ready to see him again," Dani said matter-of-factly. "It's understandable. I mean, here you are, beating yourself up for not having a handle on your broken fucking heart yet, and it's been . . . what? Two weeks? Give me a break, Nina. You bounce back fast, but not *that* fast."

It didn't feel like she was bouncing back at all. The whole goddamn situation had knocked something loose inside her head, and she had to wait for it to stop bumping around before she could do anything else.

Before she could even *begin* to start dealing with it.

"Now, that said . . ." Dani slid off the prep table and hauled a fresh tank top over her head. "I'm really going to need you to make a choice. Either we help them, or we don't. No more cinematic warnings and last-minute

Hail Marys, all right? My arm may not hurt, but I still don't like having bullet holes in me."

She was right. *Of course* she was right. "I hear you. I promise that I will get over my bullshit long enough to figure it out." Nina carefully closed the lid on the medical kit. "Will you do me a favor? Go see what Maya wants for dinner?"

"Sure." Dani crossed the room but lingered by the door, her hand on the push bar. "If we're not going to help them out . . . I could do it."

There was a hint of something utterly foreign in her voice, so unexpected that it took Nina a moment to identify it as dread. "Do what?"

"Kill them." Dani stared at her, unblinking. "I could make it quick. Painless. It'd be merciful, compared to letting the TechCorps get their hands on them. I know that for a fact."

Three counts of three wasn't enough to stave off the blackness swimming at the edges of Nina's vision this time. "We're not killing anyone, Dani."

"Could've fooled me." She pushed through the door, and it slammed behind her with a sharp snap that twisted Nina's stomach.

"She's unpredictable, isn't she?"

Ava's voice echoing through the warehouse *should* have startled Nina. Instead, she felt like some part of her had known her sister was there all along, listening. "Not really. Dani is Dani. She's a hammer, so everything looks like a nail. It's not her fault, and her heart's in the right place."

Ava stepped out of the shadows. Her perfectly tailored suit was unrelieved black today, with a silver necklace shining brightly against her vest. She carried her sleek leather bag to the table and set it down with a soft thump. "I've been doing my mission prep. I picked up a couple things for your girls while I was shopping."

"We don't need gifts, Ava."

Ava ignored her and pulled a small case out of her bag. "For Maya. Those earbuds she's using are outdated. She can connect her watch to these ear cuffs. They use bone conduction. They're impossible to buy on the open market and extremely stylish. She seems to appreciate style. And these . . ."

"Ava, stop." Nina shoved the items back in the bag and pushed it toward her sister. "*Stuff* won't help. What they need is for me to make a decision. And I'm not sure I can this time."

Ava gripped the handle of her bag for a moment, her muscles tense. Then she exhaled. "Do you remember Beth? EF-Gen14-B?"

"Only vaguely." She mainly remembered the A-designation from that cluster, the fighter who had been in some of Nina's training groups. That girl had been focused, driven. Harsh, at times.

"Beth was soft, especially for a B. The trainers were terrible to her in class sometimes. I think she might have been the smartest of all of us, but she refused to strip scenarios down to logic. She always said humans were variables that couldn't be simplified. She sounded like . . ."

"Zoey," Nina supplied.

"Yeah. Her sisters went down on a mission about a year after you left. I didn't know at the time because I was still being . . ." She trailed off and took a deep breath. "They didn't want her after that, so they sold her to the highest bidder—some asshole up in Virginia who made his money in the black market. He kept her in the basement, fitted with a shock collar, running books for him."

Nina closed her eyes, as if that could block out Ava's words.

"I got her out," Ava continued. "Three years ago. Dumped that asshole in the Potomac, but only after I stole his entire empire out from under him. Beth's been running it for me ever since."

"Congratulations." Nina didn't drink often, but she'd never wished harder for a bottle in her hand than at that moment. "Why'd you do it? Rescue her?"

"Because I *was* her," Ava said in a flat voice. "Because after they broke me down far enough, the Center contracted me out to the biggest criminal in D.C."

Nina's eyes burned. Knox had told her—over and over, in a million different ways—that the world was a hard place. That people only really cared about themselves. In retrospect, she could see that he'd been warning her. Indulging his guilt. Hating himself.

None of those things made him wrong.

There was something clawing at Nina's throat and gut, a pressure that she could barely contain, much less categorize. Rage and pain and loss and a helplessness so deep it felt like she could fall into it.

All the agony in her life, and she'd never felt *hopeless* before.

Tears burned down her cheeks. When she spoke, she tasted salt. "I've spent the years since I left the Center trying to be more like Zoey. Should I have been trying to be more like you?"

"*Christ,* no." Ava's voice sounded as hollow as Nina's chest felt. "I killed the man they gave me to, you know. You or Zoey would have found a better way out, but I manipulated him for years. I played all sorts of twisted games to get close enough to take everything he owned before destroying him."

Her brown eyes glittered as she continued, and Nina couldn't tell if it was with rage or tears. "I might be the richest person on the Eastern Seaboard by now. And I almost took it all and left. Left Beth behind, not to mention all the other people the Center gave away like broken toys. But even when I hated you, I wanted to be like you." Her lips curved in a pained, bitter smile. "I never could quite manage it. I saved Beth for the wrong reasons. I do everything for the wrong reasons. Without you and Zoey, maybe I'm just bad."

"That . . . or you were right all along."

"Is that what you think? Is that why you can't decide what to do?"

"Oh, please." Nina clenched the edge of the stool so tightly the metal rim bent in her grip. "I know what I have to do. What I don't know anymore is why I should bother. Helping people, doing the right thing—it's not the way the world works. Knox told me that, but both of you drove the point home."

"Nina—"

"*No.*" She turned and pinned Ava with a glare. She didn't know if she looked angry or pleading or desperate—or all three. "Instead of contacting me, you kidnapped someone so you could blackmail the Devils. And instead of asking for my help, Knox lied to me. He set me up. Everyone has an agenda, Ava, and if I don't face up to that, I'm going to get my crew killed. I can't afford to do this anymore. I can't afford to be *me.*"

"You don't even understand what it's like to be around you," Ava whispered. "Knox lied to you. He set you up. I gave him every reason in the world to betray you. His agenda was a tactical certainty before he met you. But you made him want to change the way the world works. And you weren't even *trying.* You're like a star, Nina. Everyone who gets too close ends up drawn into your orbit."

With Knox, it had been more like a collision course. "It hurts too much, Ava. Believing in people."

"I know." The shimmer was back in her sister's eyes, but Ava squeezed them tight before tears could fall. "I don't know how to apologize. The words would be empty if I said them now. I'm still too angry. But you're the only one left who can make me want to believe."

Maybe words were always empty. Maybe that was the problem. "So don't apologize. Help me. Make *me* want to believe, too."

Ava's eyes popped open. It only took a moment for shock to turn into a thoughtful assessment so achingly familiar Nina's breath caught. "You want to save the Silver Devils."

"It's what I do, right?" Nina pulled out the stool, slid onto it, and reached for the notebook Maya kept stashed near the freeze-dryers. "I know a guy in Druid Hills who can get us what we need, as far as materials go. Benny owes me. But I can't collect without more information. Biomed records. Can you get them?"

"From the TechCorps?" Ava hooked the other stool with a booted toe and dragged it to her. "You wouldn't believe how many of those L1 and L2 pigs barter proprietary trade secrets for access to their favorite vices. I may be lightly blackmailing a few of them. Give me twenty-four hours."

There were so many pieces she needed to line up. Nina would have to contact the Professor, see how much time they had left before the Protectorate's final strike. And Benny was just the start. He'd supply the raw materials, sure, but he never got involved in any processing that could be traced back to him. She and her crew would have to do the heavy lifting.

They needed more help. They needed the Devils. Besides, it was only right to let the men have a hand in their potential salvation. A chance to save themselves.

"I'll have to face him, you know," Nina whispered. "Knox. And I haven't figured out *how* yet."

Ava wet her lips, uncharacteristically hesitant. "How do you feel about him?"

She felt . . . pity. Admiration. Fear. Lust. Hatred.

Love.

"I miss him," she admitted. "Which is difficult to say out loud, because I should be smarter than that, right?"

"Logically?" Ava tilted her head. "He wouldn't have done any of it if I hadn't threatened him. Of course, he still made his own choices. But there at the end . . . He wasn't lying about that, Nina. He was going to betray me. I know it."

"The fact that it would have benefited me doesn't turn it into a ringing endorsement, Ava."

"Debatable. For all my irritation with Captain Knox, it's difficult to claim the moral high ground over a betrayal when you opened the relationship with hostage-taking." Ava sighed softly. "It wasn't the easiest method, you know. I have the money to hire mercenaries, whole armies of them. I chose him because there's something exhaustingly noble about him. I thought I could trust him not to hurt you."

How wrong she had been. "He *did* hurt me, but that's not on you. You couldn't have seen it coming. So you can take that off your list of things to atone for."

"It's still a significant list." Silence fell, and Ava traced her finger along a stain in the table. "Am I the only one waiting for Zoey to tell you what to do about him? I know she's been gone for a long time, but sitting here with you again . . . It feels like we're off-balance."

"I know what Zoey would say." Nina could hear her voice—so like hers and Ava's, but lighter somehow. Brighter. "I have to forgive him. For my own sake, not his."

"Can you?"

"I'm not angry with him." Her voice broke on a fresh wave of tears. "I'm just *sad*."

Ava folded her into a hug, and the years melted away. She was fifteen years old again, sobbing out her pain and frustrations and *rage* in the protective circle of her sisters' arms.

It felt . . . like home. Not the tears, but the comfort. It didn't matter that all Ava could do was murmur nonsense and stroke her hair. She was there, and it was enough.

MAYA

Maya took her new stun gun to the meeting.

It wasn't like she thought she was walking into a trap. The Silver Devils were low-grade backstabbing jackasses, granted, but they hadn't seemed like extra-strength evil. And you'd have to be extra-strength evil to fuck over someone who'd just graciously saved your not-entirely-deserving asses.

If she'd suspected a trap, she would have brought Dani, at least, as backup. But when Conall's message had popped up on her tablet that morning, something had stirred in her. A terrifying weakness.

Maya kind of missed him. And that made Conall dangerous.

It had been a long time since she'd been around someone else who understood the unique mindfuck of being raised as a petted and prized TechCorps genius. Conall's training as an elite computer specialist had been different from hers as a data courier, but there was an impossible-to-explain camaraderie between kids who'd breathed that rarefied air.

He understood the way you could hate the TechCorps to the depths of your being and still not be able to banish the nostalgia. The bright, shiny memories, forever edged with guilt, of excitedly receiving expensive gifts to celebrate every achievement. Of having unlimited access to chefs and personal shoppers. Clothes, movies, video games, new gadgets . . . They'd grown up in the most fantastical of gilded cages, and it had taken them years to fully feel the bars.

So when Conall asked her for a private meeting, Maya showed up.

At a place she'd chosen. With a stun gun.

The table was outside a little grocer that served sandwiches and sweet tea for lunch. Maya bypassed both for a huge slice of fresh peach pie, which she took to her seat under a tattered umbrella. It had a perfect view of Clem's bar across the street, and she'd already popped in to let Clem know what was going down.

Nina might still kick her ass later, but she wouldn't be able to say Maya hadn't taken precautions.

A hand fell on her shoulder, and Maya tightened her grip on her fork as she twisted. She had closed her other hand around her stun gun before her gaze followed the muscular arm up to an impossibly hard shoulder and then a pair of brooding, Gothic hero eyes.

Her heart jumped into her throat. Part of her shoulder was bared by the wide strap of her tank top, and his fingers burned on her skin. She knew he was a liar, and probably a dead man walking to boot, and his touch still burned. "You shouldn't sneak up on people," she told Gray stiffly. "That's a good way to get a fork in the face."

"Right, how could I forget?" He didn't withdraw his hand so much as it slipped away as he moved around the table to the seat across from hers. "You and your lethal utensils."

"Improvised weaponry." Conall slid into the third chair. "Nothing but respect for that."

"Uh-huh." After a moment, Maya released the stun gun and resumed eating her pie. "So. You're still alive."

"For the moment."

"And still in Atlanta."

"For the moment."

Maya scrunched up her nose at him. "If I were in your boots, I'd be halfway to the Mississippi by now."

"That's kind of why we're here." Conall pulled a compact data pad from his pocket and slid it across the table.

Maya drew it closer and tapped the screen to activate it. The RLOC logo stared back at her, along with a set of vault schematics.

It was her goddamn wheelbarrow full of money.

"I unlocked it," Conall said nervously, "and stripped the encryption. You should probably lock it to your own biometrics. It's not exactly info you want hanging around, unsecured."

Maya looked up at them, her mind still reeling. "Is this real?"

"It's not a bribe," Gray rumbled. "Just what your team was promised at the outset of this whole fucking mess."

"Good, because absolution isn't something you can buy." She glared at them both, but only for the few seconds before her eyes were drawn back down to the tablet as if by gravity. Her fingers almost trembled as she paged through the first few files and found the coordinates.

Shit. The damn thing was in Atlanta. It had been under their feet the whole time.

"Knox wants Nina to have it," Conall said. "My uncle was a member of the RLOC. Protecting this was his life's mission, but I think he'd agree with Knox. Nina will do right by it. Give it back to the people."

Still stunned, Maya glanced at Conall. He shot her a jittery smile before bouncing to his feet. "And I am going to go get some of that pie. It smells amazing."

Maya watched him stroll into the shop, conflicted emotions churning through her. Conall looked like he'd been reborn, all traces of neural overload and pain stripped away, his steps light even though the target on his back should be weighing him down.

Gray, on the other hand, looked exactly the same. Solid, implacable, unreadable. Either the degradation of his implant hadn't impacted him, or he simply hadn't shown the discomfort. Somehow, she guessed it was the latter.

"How are you?"

It could have been small talk, but Gray didn't seem like the small-talk type. The memory came too easily, still tinged with terror and embarrassment. The mercenary approaching her to tie her hands. Panic shredding through her. And Gray's arms closing around her, his chest hard at her back, his dreamy voice a low, urgent warning against her ear.

Lock it down, or bad things are going to happen.

It took supreme self-control not to rub at her wrists. Med-gel had long since healed the evidence of her bonds, but she could still feel the cool plastic digging into her skin. "I'm okay. I never thanked you for—for what you did. I mean, you don't deserve a lot of thanks because you kind of got me kidnapped. But thanks for helping me keep it together."

"It was the least I could do." His gaze roved over her, and it felt like he was actually looking at her. Seeing her.

It felt like he'd wrapped himself around her again, and she refused to like it. "Listen, I know what it's like to have someone you care about held against you. I had someone I would have done almost anything to save. So I get it. But I'm Team Nina. Like, I would ride the express train to hell for her. And I may have shown up to save your sorry asses, but I still want to take my stun-stick to your boss's balls for how bad he hurt her."

He inclined his head. "That's fair."

The sheer reasonableness of it irritated her. Anger would have been a convenient shield against her annoying, frustrating *awareness* of him. Maybe she wouldn't need to hold out for long. "Just tell me you're getting the hell out of town soon."

Instead of answering, Gray smiled. A slow smile, a knowing one, the kind of smile that made Rafe's flirtation seem as shallow as a stone skipping across a reservoir. The kind of smile Gothic heroes didn't bestow until the ends of books, when they wanted the hapless heroines to forget how scary they were.

Oh, that was a *bad* smile. The warm velvet of his voice was worse. "Why? Are you worried about me, Maya?"

No, right now she was worried about her pants. And not falling out of them. Frantically, she tried to recall every damning thing Birgitte had ever said about the possibility of Gray being a psycho serial killer.

It didn't help. God *damn* it, why didn't it help?

Without waiting for an answer, he rose and headed toward the café, barely hesitating beside her chair. "Thanks for your help the other day. I owe you. May not be around much longer for you to collect, but I owe you, just the same."

Maya waited until the café door shut behind him. Then she snatched up the tablet and her stun gun and bolted without regard for dignity. She made it two blocks before she felt steady enough to stop and slip in her earbuds. FlowMac Pop filled her ears, drowning out the chaos of the city.

The tablet felt like a grenade clutched against her chest. So much possibility—but she couldn't drop it on Nina like this, not when she was still struggling to get through the day. This was some suicidal, final-gestures shit. Whatever precarious mental balance Nina was trying to find would be shot to hell if she thought Knox was over there giving away his earthly belongings in preparation for meeting his maker.

Maya could quietly investigate the contents of the tablet. There'd be plenty of time to consider what to do once Knox and the Silver Devils were a distant memory. Maya had her own information network, a sprawling, invisible web of people scattered across Atlanta, each one a survivor of the TechCorps' violent purge of their internal revolution. Maya knew the names, vital stats, and personal histories of every one. And when she asked for help, they dropped everything to give it.

After all, the TechCorps had tortured Maya's first and only lover to a slow and painful death right in front of her, and she hadn't broken. She hadn't betrayed their names.

They all owed her.

TECHCORPS PROPRIETARY DATA, L1 SECURITY CLEARANCE

Send Knox to deal with the situation at the Villa Rica research facility. Make it clear the entire facility—including staff—must be decommissioned.

If he deviates from his orders in the slightest, I'll be stepping in to resolve this situation.

Internal Memo, July 2085

THIRTY

The comforting thing about planning for disaster was the numbing routine of it.

Knox knew the rhythm of a crisis. He knew how to set aside emotion and make a dispassionate assessment of the situation. Each day was carved into hours. Each hour assigned a list of action items. Each item could be broken down into rote tasks.

Rafe and Gray had been busy assembling the supplies they'd need to go off the grid. Conall was locked in his room, spending every waking moment struggling to buy them a few more days. Luna was explaining the hard truth to her aunt.

Knox was doing inventory.

It was mindless, monotonous work, the kind he should have been able to lose himself in. He knew what they'd need to settle somewhere. Meds. Tech. High-value barter items. Biohacked seeds, cultivation guides. Tools.

He was going to be a truly shitty farmer.

He kicked the thought away and forced himself to focus. To feel nothing. To think nothing. To *want* nothing.

Check the crates.

Count the items.

Cross it off his list.

Stack the box against the wall.

The silence inside his head was *torture*.

He hadn't heard from Nina. Not that he'd really expected to—the fact that she'd sent Dani and Maya to help them without showing up herself was an eloquent statement of her feelings. But part of him had hoped that knowing about the RLOC server might spark . . . something. Excitement. Happiness. Maybe even forgiveness.

He'd known better. He'd made his devil's bargain the day he'd agreed to kidnap her. All those brazen promises in the dark of the night, his claims that he'd sacrifice anything to see his men safe . . .

Someone with a sense of humor had taken him up on them.

Knox started to hoist a box of seeds, but dropped them and went for his sidearm when a harsh *buzz* tore through the warehouse.

Conall's perimeter warning.

The wail cut off as quickly as it had started, and Conall's voice came over comms. "I checked the cameras. It's safe to open the door."

Too quick. Too casual. There was only one reason Conall wouldn't just *tell* him who was on the other side. Knox's heart kicked, and all that hope he thought he'd snuffed out roared up in one brutal attempt to flood through him.

He struggled against it as he opened the door.

Nina stood on the other side. She was dressed casually—jeans and a plain black tank top, her hair pulled back into a ponytail—and cradled a tablet in one arm. "Good afternoon, Captain."

"Nina." Her name came out hoarse, and he cleared his throat. "Is everything all right?"

"Everything's fine." She arched one eyebrow and gestured inside. "May I?"

She didn't seem angry, or particularly eager. She didn't seem *anything* except relaxed and coolly proficient. Uncertain but unwilling to close the door on her, Knox stepped back and waved her in.

She looked around as she walked in, surveying the main room of the warehouse with a decisive nod. "Your bays are clear. Good. Dani's on her way with a truck, so you'll need to open one of the doors."

"A truck—" Knox started, but jerked when one of the far bay doors groaned softly and began creaking upward.

"Sorry." Conall's voice came inside his head. "I'll stop eavesdropping."

Knox tapped behind his ear to make *sure* Conall couldn't keep listening. "This may not be a good time, Nina. I don't know how long we have before they hit us. We're getting organized to leave."

"*We* have sixty-eight hours." She activated the tablet. "In three days, Protectorate squads will be deployed for a door-to-door search of west Atlanta."

Ice clarity flooded him. "You have a contact inside, I take it?"

She didn't answer. "Only one order supersedes that one—if they receive credible intel regarding your whereabouts, they'll scramble drones for an airstrike. So that's what we're going to do." Nina handed him the tablet. "They want the Silver Devils, dead or alive? Then that's what we'll give them."

Knox scanned the orders, one eyebrow raising in spite of himself. Whoever Nina had on the inside had access to internal security memos. This one came from the desk of Tobias Richter himself, and the anger seethed in every coldly precise word.

"This isn't as simple as whatever you did with Maya," he said, glancing up. "She was a sheltered kid who'd never been off the Hill. It was easy for them to believe she ended up dead. But a squad of Protectorate soldiers—"

"Give me a little credit, Knox." Nina pulled the tablet from his hands. "Maya was a high-level target, but they weren't actively searching for her. I was able to use that to my advantage. I'm pretty good at that, you know. Using things to my advantage."

She turned away to lay the tablet on the nearest stack of crates. "The Protectorate would never believe that someone had gotten the drop on your entire squad. Unless . . ."

"Unless it was them."

"Exactly. So we'll let it be them. If they're so hot to blow you guys up?" With a flick of her fingers, she pulled up a holographic schematic. "We'll let them blow you up."

Knox stared at . . . himself. All the parts that made him *him*—his frequently broken bones, his biochemical implant, his reconstructed hands, and all the rest that had been regenerated and restored so many times; none of it was the flesh he'd been born with by this point.

"These are internal medical scans," he said flatly. "L1 classification. They're impossible to get."

"Next to impossible, Captain," Ava said.

Knox didn't think. His gun was in his hand and he whirled, finger already caressing the trigger as he leveled the pistol at their new arrival.

She wasn't trying to pass as Nina today. In fact, she was dressed like a TechCorps VP, in an expensive fitted suit. Even the severe twist of her hair and the ostentatious sparkle of diamonds on her ears wouldn't have been out of place at a meeting of the board.

She quirked one elegant eyebrow in amused condescension, and it truly was a mindfuck that the same DNA had produced this chilly cyni-cism *and* Nina's aggressive optimism. "If you're not going to shoot me," she said, "you should really put that away."

"I'm still deciding," he retorted. "Is there a pressing reason I shouldn't?"

"Just that I'm currently saving your life." She tilted her head. "Not out of any particular affection for you, so don't let it sway you too much. If you want to play rough, I'll let you take the first shot. Might not want to miss, though."

"When I take a shot, I don't miss."

"I'm in absolute awe of your virility." Ava crossed her arms and tapped her fingers idly against her elbow. "Shall we cut through all the posturing? My sister wants you alive, and we both owe her a rather sizable debt at the moment. So stop waving your gun and let her save your life."

He still wanted to shoot her. Hell, that smug expression made him want to shoot her *more*. But she was right. Knox held up the gun, engaged the biometric safety, and carefully holstered it.

Then he turned to Nina. "Are you *sure* she's your sister? Honestly, I don't see the resemblance."

"Very funny." Nina shoved her hands in her back pockets and slowly circled the crate—and the projection above it. "We'll get updated scans and go from there. Even taking into account the destructive nature of airstrikes and fires, we'll have to make it good. I'm talking 3-D-printed biologics, DNA replicated in cellular matrix . . . The works." She paused. "Ava, can you go find out what the holdup is with the truck?"

"Of course." Ava inclined her head to Knox and slipped out the door.

When she was gone, Knox raised both eyebrows. "So . . . she came back, I guess."

Nina stared back at him, unblinking. "Is that really what you want to say to me?"

"I don't know what to say to you." It was true. The words wedged them-selves in his chest until he wanted to rub at it to soothe the ache, but he didn't know how to start. If he *should* start.

No, there was one thing he could say. "I'm sorry."

"You told me that already."

He had. The ache expanded into a sharp pain. "Then . . . thank you. For helping us, even though we didn't earn and don't deserve it."

She kept staring at him, her eyes wide, her expression inscrutable.

Finally, she opened her mouth, but the intermittent *beep* signaling a truck backing into the docking bay cut her off.

She took a step back instead. "Better gather the troops, Captain. It's time to fake some deaths."

Knox's first problem was keeping Rafe from killing Ava.

Or more realistically, given the fact that Ava was Nina without Nina's capacity for affection and morality, keeping Rafe from getting murdered while trying to kill Ava.

The group spread out around the warehouse, perched on crates, straddling chairs, and leaning against walls, as temperament dictated. Rafe was seated at the table, pointedly sharpening his meanest knife and casting menacing glares at an unconcerned Ava. Conall and Maya had claimed cross-legged positions on the table, tablets spread out around them.

"So tell me how this is going to work," Conall said, looking back and forth from Maya to Nina. "Because I've never heard of *anyone* pulling off something like this."

"I'm not sure anyone has," Nina allowed. "You nervous?"

"Fuck, no. We're gonna do absolutely impossible, totally illegal, questionably sane science? I'm *pumped*."

"Conall," Knox chided. "Nina, can you break down the basics for me?"

"The basics are easy—we replicate your bodies so the Protectorate will have something to find in the wreckage after they use drones to drop bombs on this place."

"It's the details that are going to be rough." Dani hopped off her crate. "They won't just trust finding four crispy corpses. They'll want positive ID. So when Nina says replicate—"

"I *mean* replicate." Nina nodded, and Maya activated one of the tablets. "First, we'll do full-body scans of you so we can start 3-D-printing skeletons."

Gray shook his head. "And the minute they take a tissue sample, the whole thing falls apart."

Nina tilted her head. "This isn't amateur hour, Gray. The skeletons won't just look real, they will *be* real. Printed with a matrix of osseous cells."

Knox glanced at Maya. "Is that how she faked your death?"

Maya wrinkled her nose at Conall. "Really? You found my file?"

"Hey, in my defense, for all I knew, you were a psycho."

"Still, it's rude."

"Faking Maya's death was easy compared to this," Nina explained. "In her case, I figured they'd follow protocol for finding skeletal remains in the field—a quick dental scan and a bone marrow sample—and move along. I printed Maya's skeleton out of the same stuff they use to make surgical replacements, then filled the long bones with replicated marrow."

Yep, Knox had been right that first day on the road. Her casual description of efficiently faking a death and fooling the most powerful corporation on the Eastern Seaboard *was* unbearably attractive.

"Of course, with Maya, I only had to fool a squad CO." She looked around. "Your bodies? They'll drag them to a lab, no doubt. Subject them to numerous tests to make absolutely certain the Silver Devils are dead."

"And that will be their mistake." Ava slid a tablet across the table toward Conall, who caught it and studied it with a frown that vanished as his mouth fell open.

"No fucking *way*," he breathed. "Is this . . . ?"

"Mm-hmm."

"And you just encode it . . ."

"Right into the DNA."

"And it *works*?"

"It did the last time."

Genuine awe filled Conall's eyes. "You are basically an evil fucking genius."

Ava's chilly, vicious smile sent a shiver of atavistic fear through Knox. He rubbed at the goose bumps on his arms and pinned Conall with an expectant stare. "Care to share with the rest of us, Con?"

"Oh, you know. Nothing big." Conall waved the tablet. "Just a sexy bit of malware that will give us a back door into the TechCorps. She encoded it in the DNA, so when they haul everything back to the lab to lovingly scan it, they'll be handing me access to . . . Hell, almost everything."

"Security? Protectorate orders?"

"We'll know what they're doing almost before they do."

So Nina wasn't just faking their deaths. She was giving them the tools to stay one step ahead of the TechCorps. To stay, for as long as they needed.

For as long as they *wanted*.

He swallowed down the sudden surge of *wanting* and cleared his throat. "So. Real bones, our DNA. What else do we need to make them buy this?"

Nina met his gaze. "Everything, down to your implants and the polymers and alloys they used to rebuild your hands. We can't copy those exactly, but we don't have to. The fire will do enough damage to cover our tracks."

Dani grinned. "The last step is the best one. We vacuum-seal a gel matrix around the skeletons. The gel's there to approximate flesh and organs. When they're finished, they'll look like ballistics dummies. Or giant gummy bears. It's pretty gross, actually."

"Charming," Rafe drawled. "Good to know you're even bloodthirsty about fake carnage, honeybun."

"It's a lot of work," Nina said, "but we have almost everything we need. We just have to get it done."

Knox frowned. "Almost?"

"I can get them here, but I can't convince them you're inside," she explained. "Conall will have to handle that part."

"Hmm." Conall leaned forward, resting his elbows on his knees. "They'll scan for heat signatures, for sure. Check to see if there's any Tech-Corps tech they can connect to. If they dragged Charlie into this, she could probably program a drone to pick up the signals from implants. She'd have to practically park the drone on top of the roof to do it, but if they're that serious . . ."

"Let's assume they're that serious," Knox said. "Can you counterfeit that?"

"Someone toss me one of those implants."

Ava picked up a slim foil packet and slid it across the table. Conall swept it up and tipped the contents into his hand. "Okay, it's the latest version. We all have this. If Luna will help me, I should be able to make this work."

Luna moved from her spot in the corner to lean over his shoulder. "We can spoof the signals, but only at half strength. Make it seem like you tried to suppress the broadcast."

"First things first." Nina started handing out tablets. "Dani, you get started on scans. Maya, you handle DNA samples while Ava and I get the equipment up and running."

Dani plucked the knife from Rafe's hand. "Ready to strip down, Morales?"

"Always." Rafe grinned. "You planning to cut my clothes off?"

"Stab me first," Maya groaned.

People began to scatter, but Nina lingered by the table, staring at the schematics. "Not much of an end for Captain Garrett Knox, is it? Firebombed in a warehouse in West End."

"I can imagine worse." Knox couldn't look away from the tiny intricate designs mapping out his reconstructed hands. "I should count myself lucky I only made them mad enough to kill me."

"They get angrier than airstrikes?"

"They get meaner. Firebombed is better than locked in a cell, being tortured and experimented on."

Nina slid her hand across the table, sympathy softening her gaze. But she stopped shy of touching him and pulled away, and Knox curled his fingers toward his palm to keep from reaching for her.

She cleared her throat. "It's going to be a long few days. You might want to get some sleep now. You may not have another chance."

"Nina?"

"Yeah?"

"Thank you."

That seemed to startle her into movement, and she began to turn away. "I don't want you to—"

"Not for this." It was Knox's turn to clear his throat. "For reminding me of who I used to be. It doesn't have to matter to you, but it matters to me. You've made me want to fight again. Whatever happens, even if this is my last few days, this is how I want to go out. Believing."

She exhaled slowly, softly, her gaze locked with his. "In people in general? Or in me?"

In people. In her. But mostly in himself.

Before he could say it out loud, Dani called Nina's name from across the warehouse, breaking the spell.

"I have to go." She retrieved one of the tablets from the table, then hesitated. "But maybe we can talk later."

"Sure." There was that hope again. A faint flutter in his gut. Fucking *hell*, he was too old to have nervous fucking butterflies in his stomach because a girl wanted to talk to him.

Getting firebombed might be a mercy at this point.

PROTECTORATE INTERNAL MEMO

Oversight of 66–615's squad has been transferred to Tobias Richter. All Protectorate employees should defer and report to him on matters pertaining to the Silver Devils.

September 2085

THIRTY-ONE

The whole thing felt like a vigil.

Nina cupped her hands around the steaming mug in her hand and surveyed the warehouse's open main room. Along with the night, a strange sort of hush had fallen over everything. It wasn't silent, by any means—machinery hummed near the loading dock, busily replicating and coding the Devils' DNA in raw organic material, and murmuring voices echoed strangely off the high ceiling and bare walls.

But it felt peaceful, somehow. Serene. Or maybe that was just her, her conscience and her heart both appeased by the fact that she'd finally gotten off her ass and *done something*.

Conall and Luna were hard at work, making the necessary modifications to the implants Ava had procured, while Maya looked on, observing and offering suggestions. Gray sat nearby, silent and watchful. Rafe had retired to his room for some sleep, and Dani had claimed a battered reclining chair not far from the stairs. She had the footrest up, and was staring at exposed beams overhead.

Only Knox was in constant motion, pacing beside the DNA vats as they churned. Nina filled a second mug and carried it to him.

"Coffee," she said as he glanced down at her offering. "Normally, I'd say you don't need it. But desperate times call for desperate measures."

He accepted the mug with a tight smile. "Smells like the real stuff."

"I figured we could use it." God, she sounded breathless. "Just like you could use a break."

"I could." He hesitated, glancing around the room. His gaze caught on Ava, who was seated in the corner, seemingly absorbed in the tablet balanced on her crossed legs. "You want to step outside?"

"Lead the way."

He moved with that same restrained energy, pacing to the door on the far wall. He held it open for Nina, then followed her out into the humid night air.

There was a covered patio outside, just big enough for a rickety wooden table and a few chairs. Nina sank into one and looked around, trying to shake the chill that raised goose bumps on her arms.

Finally, she gave up. "It's strange, isn't it? Being in a place you know won't exist in a few days? It's like walking over graves."

"In more ways than one." Knox settled into the chair next to her and set his mug on the edge of the rickety table. "I'm okay burying Captain Garrett Knox in there, though. Maybe all of us need that."

"I don't know, I kind of liked him. What I knew, anyway."

Knox was silent for a long time before he shook his head. "You never really met him. The Protectorate captain, I mean. Rafe told me to lie to you with the truth, and that was what I did. I pretended to be the man I used to be . . . until I realized I wasn't pretending anymore."

"So tell me about him." *Help me understand.*

Knox shifted. Exhaled softly. "My father's name was Gregor. He was a contractor who worked in real estate development. Those first years after the Flares hit him hard. His mother died of heatstroke the first summer, and he lost his sister in the food riots. His husband—" Knox's voice hitched. "I don't really remember my other dad. I was only a few years old when he died. Gregor Knox could have turned into a bitter man, but he didn't. He was like you. He believed people could be good, and it was our job to put goodness out into the world. To help others."

Nina clenched her fingers around her mug to still their trembling. "What happened to him?"

"Bandits." The word was flat with anger, barely repressed after all this time. "Not even an organized gang like the one in Dalton. Just a couple toughs with stolen guns and big ideas. They tried to rob the butcher while my dad was there fixing her solar generator. He got in front of her and . . ."

"I'm sorry." It was a common story, violence rendered casual and unremarkable because of its regularity. Devastating to the lives it touched, and a mere curiosity to those it didn't. A cautionary tale. "How old were you?"

"Fifteen." Knox's sudden laugh was pained. "The perfect age. Young enough to feel lost without him, old enough to feel like I should have been there to save him."

"So you joined the Protectorate." Her heart ached as she considered it—a kid, desperate for someone to make him strong, turn him into the kind of hero who could have saved his father. "When did you realize heroics weren't high on their list of priorities?"

"Not at first." He shrugged uncomfortably. "I was one of the first they used the latest generation of implants on. I responded remarkably well, better than they expected, I guess. For the first few years, they were just excited to see what I could do. But it became clear pretty fast when I started going on missions under my first captain."

Nina fell silent. She hadn't meant to interrogate him, but it felt like everything she'd learned about him on their trip north had been distorted, skewed as much by half-truths as outright lies.

On some level, this was more than important. It was *vital* that she figure out who the hell he really was.

But it couldn't happen in one conversation over coffee. Hell, it might not happen at all, and she had to reconcile herself to that possibility. "Sorry. You didn't come out here to play Twenty Questions."

"That was only four." Knox reached for his coffee and took a sip before offering her a tired smile over the rim of his mug. "I'll give you one more for free."

His eyes crinkled at the corners when he smiled. It was such a tiny thing, but it hit her with the force of a sucker punch, stealing her breath. It made her want and it made her *hurt,* and she didn't know which emotion would win out until an errant tear slipped down her cheek.

Knox made a pained noise. "Nina."

Fuck. "Sorry. I'm sorry. It's just—" She pressed the heels of her hands against her eyes until the burning subsided. "This is . . . a lot."

"Then why are you doing it?"

Because she had to. Because her sister, at the very least, owed him and his team. Because Nina could, and they needed her help, and somehow, *somehow*—

She'd lost the ability to imagine the world without him in it.

But she gave him a shaky smile and the blithe, easy answer. "It's who I am, remember? The lady who doesn't understand how the world works."

"That's right." Knox sipped his coffee again. "You know, I've been thinking—"

Nina's vision wavered, and she rose so abruptly that her chair scraped over the pitted concrete floor of the patio. "I have to check on the replication vats," she blurted. "It's a tricky process. If something goes wrong . . ."

"I understand. If you need any help—"

"I can handle it." She stood there for one more miserable moment, then tossed her rapidly cooling coffee into the scrub beside the side door and fled.

She stumbled blindly through the warehouse, up the stairs. She didn't stop until she was alone, clutching her chest in the dark solitude of a dim hallway.

One, two, three.

One, two, three.

One, two, three.

She'd assumed that seeing him again would be the hard part. That if she could only get past that initial meeting, she could handle the rest. She could save him and then send him off with polite courtesy to live the rest of his life. But every minute that ticked over into hours drove home a truth she'd hoped to escape.

When Garrett Knox finally walked out of her life, he was going to take her heart with him.

Twenty-four hours of forced proximity wasn't making Ava less unsettling.

At least, it wasn't for Knox and his team. Incredibly, Dani and Maya seemed to be getting used to her. Knox couldn't tell if it was her resemblance to Nina, or if they both just respected violent, potentially deadly women, but they had unbent enough to welcome Ava into the poker game Rafe started.

Civility took a marked downturn immediately.

"She's cheating," Conall protested as Ava swept the makeshift chits toward her and started organizing her pile. "She must be using superpowers."

"It's not cheating if everyone has them," Maya shot back. "You don't see them over here, whining that our brains are so fast we can calculate the odds in our heads."

"Which really *is* cheating, since the rest of us can't do it," Rafe grumbled. "You're just pissed off that you're losing for once."

"Obviously," Conall said loftily. "*Why* am I losing? That's what I want to know."

"Because you're riddled with tells." Ava didn't look up from her stacks of chits. "You're so used to thinking faster than everyone else at the table, you haven't bothered to cultivate a disciplined game face."

Dani raised both eyebrows as she threw her hand into the discard pile. "She's not lying."

"Excuse me, I am *extremely* disciplined." Conall swept the cards toward himself and began shuffling. "And don't think I'm not watching you and your ridiculous reflexes."

Maya snorted. "You *can't* watch Dani. That's the point. If she wants to look at your hand or switch cards around, you won't notice her doing it."

"I don't cheat," Dani declared. "I don't have to."

Gray waved off Conall's attempt to deal him in for another hand. "As much as I enjoy getting my ass whipped, I think I'll sit this one out."

"If you want to practice discipline, you should watch him," Ava murmured, tipping her head to indicate Gray. "He's the only one of you without a single tell."

Maya rested one elbow on the table and propped her chin on her hand, studying Gray with curious eyes. "Can I ask you a question?"

"Sure, why not?"

"So, like . . . Are you a secret serial killer with bodies buried all over Atlanta?"

Conall choked on his beer. "Is he *what*?"

Maya kept her attention on Gray. "I worked for the VP of Behavior, and she *really* thought you were trouble. Granted, she also thought Knox was a company man, yet here we are."

Gray smiled—rare, unrestrained. "Your boss seriously overestimated my industriousness."

Dani laughed. "Wait, your defense is that you're too *lazy* to be guilty of this?"

"Says the *actual* serial killer," Luna muttered behind her cards.

"Hey," Maya said, straightening. "Dani is something else, entirely. She's an energetic vigilante."

"I might qualify as a serial killer," Ava mused.

"Oh, we're all *so* surprised," Rafe snapped, glaring at his cards. "Who do you murder, orphans and grandmas?"

"Only if they run the top criminal organizations in the D.C. area." Ava tilted her head. "There are two who are grandmothers, now that I think about it, but neither is currently on my list of potential targets."

Rafe groaned and leaned forward, smacking his forehead lightly against the table. Dani rubbed his back with a soothing noise, then offered him her flask.

"Wait—" Maya started.

It was too late. Rafe took a giant swig, then spit it out all over the table. Maya held up her arms with a squeal as everyone else at the table ducked—except Ava, who watched Dani with renewed interest.

"What the *hell* is that?" Rafe roared.

"Grain alcohol and spiced rum." Dani glanced around the table. "What? It's good."

Gray grimaced. "It's *lighter fluid*."

"Rookie mistake, man." Maya shook her head and tried to wipe the liquor from her cards. "Never drink from Dani's flask. She doesn't feel pain, remember?"

"Apparently," Rafe said before draining half his beer.

The banter continued as they started the next hand, but they'd settled into an easy rhythm. Knox left them and paced back to check the machines, which were churning away with agonizing slowness. There was nothing he needed to check. Nothing for him to *do*. There were no contingencies to consider. No files he could pore over a third or fourth time. Nothing to plan. No concrete actions to take.

Nina had arrived with her mission laid out with admirable precision, but her aggressive confidence had left Knox . . .

Lost.

He paced the warehouse to check the various machines again, then circled back toward the table. No one seemed to notice Gray as he pushed silently away from the table and came to stand next to Knox.

"Not in the mood to lose your shirt?" he asked.

Knox snorted. "I've gambled enough with Ava, I'd say. I don't like my odds."

"It's just as well." He paused. "I heard Nina tell Maya she was heading upstairs. The roof."

"Did she seem okay?"

"Not really." Gray slanted him a look. "You know she's in love with you, right?"

Knox froze. The words, delivered in Gray's casual, unhurried drawl, were so unexpected that all he could do was stare. "She . . . what?"

Gray let his head fall back with a groan. "Look, I know you think Nina's a saint and everything, but even saints don't mount million-dollar rescue missions for assholes they hate—or, worse, don't give a fuck about."

As far as Knox could tell, Ava was footing most of the expense—a penance she most certainly owed, in Knox's opinion. But Ava's money didn't change the effort involved, or the risk. Or the fact that Nina could have asked Ava for *anything*—all the supplies she wanted for her library, everything she needed to help her neighborhood . . .

Instead, she was here. Saving his life. Saving all their lives.

"Oh," he said.

"Oh," Gray agreed. "So—if you don't mind me asking—what the hell are you doing?"

"Honestly, Gray? I don't fucking know anymore."

He snorted. "At least you can admit it now, I guess."

He could. Knox didn't know what the hell was going on. There was no briefing file to read, no research tasks to assign Conall. No mission objectives, no rules, no way to collect intelligence and make plans. He wasn't in control of this moment.

"So." Knox exhaled roughly. "I guess I'm going up to the roof."

"Only if you've figured out what the hell to say." Gray tapped his chin. "If I were you, I'd start with a heartfelt declaration. You've apologized enough, so just move right in on how you can't sleep, can't eat, can't—"

"*Gray.*" Knox rolled his eyes at him. "Maybe I'll just start with how she's doing and go from there."

Gray grinned. "Fine, don't listen to me."

"I always listen to you," Knox told him seriously. "You know that, Gray."

"Of course I do." He jerked his head toward the stairs that led up to the roof. "Go on. Go be where you need to be."

Knox stopped on his way to the stairs to grab a bottle from a crate of liquor they'd been using to barter. Eleven more bottles rested in the crate, each one emblazoned with an increasingly coveted label—a skull over a

pair of crossed guns. The liquor, supposedly distilled by some distant bar-
barian king, had started trickling across the Mississippi last year, its rarity
making it wildly popular up on the Hill.

Rich people loved anything that no one else could get.

He carried it up the stairs, nerves and hope twisting so tight he couldn't
feel anything but an odd buzzing anticipation.

Knox had no idea what to dream about for his future. He'd honestly
never really believed he deserved one, much less might survive to have
one.

Maybe with Nina, he could start to dream.

TECHCORPS PROPRIETARY DATA,
L1 SECURITY CLEARANCE

Upgrade C-block detention with the strongest clear polycarbonate we have. We'll need five cells. Expect an extended stay.

Internal Memo, November 2085

THIRTY-TWO

Nina didn't have much use for the TechCorps. Not for their fancy high-rises up on the Hill or for the posh neighborhoods surrounding them, where their executives lived in isolated, luxurious comfort. She didn't like their methods, their goals, or the way they did business.

But she had to admit that the lights were very pretty.

Most of the space on their roof at home was occupied, whether by their water cistern or trellises and planters, but they'd managed to carve out a little space for a few deck chairs.

The roof of the warehouse the Silver Devils had commandeered was empty, save for a single folding chair. Nina had dragged it to the edge of the roof so she could sit, her arms folded on the ledge, her attention fixed on the lights blazing up on the Hill.

Compared to the rest of the city, especially West End, it was brilliant, a bright spot in the gloom. But all that beauty was paid for with its own sort of darkness. With secrets and blood.

The door to the roof opened. Nina didn't move. After sixteen seconds that she counted off out of habit, Knox moved into her field of vision, a bottle full of amber liquid in one hand.

"The kids are getting along fine, more or less." He held up the bottle. "Mind some company?"

"Suit yourself." She took the bottle, shivering when her fingers brushed his, and sat back. "What are they doing?"

There wasn't a second chair, so Knox cleared a bit of the rooftop with his boot and sat facing her, his back against the wall. "They're down there debating what makes someone a serial killer while your sister clears them out at poker."

Nina closed her eyes as the memories washed over her. Ava had been utterly convinced that poker could be mastered with a solid understanding of the fundamentals and some basic statistical math. Zoey, on the other hand, knew better than to discount the human element.

"Zoey taught us how to play," she said finally. "How to bluff, how to read tells, and how to keep from giving anything away ourselves. Basically, nobody downstairs stands a chance."

Knox's voice lowered to a gentle rumble. "Do you want to talk about her?"

"*No.*" The word came out too forcefully, and Nina fought a wince. "No, I mean . . . I was just thinking about the past, but not the good parts. And Zoey was a good part." She met his gaze with a helpless shrug. "Does that make any sense?"

"It does."

He didn't say anything else, just let the silence stand. Nina swallowed the first stirrings of panic and tightened her fingers around the whiskey bottle. She wanted to be like the cool glass beneath her palms—solid, unmoving. Unbroken. But the truth was already shredding her from the inside out, and she had to start somewhere.

Anywhere.

She took a deep breath. "Finding out that Ava's alive—that the administrators lied to me? It's made me ask myself a lot of questions about the Center, and the way we were raised. About my memories." She met his eyes. "I don't know if I can trust the things I think I remember."

He studied her. "Like what?"

She had to count to three before she dared to open her mouth. "Sometimes, during combat training, kids would get hurt. It happened often enough, but a few times . . . A few times, they never came back. The instructors always told us they'd been transferred."

"Nina." Knox's tone was gentle. "You had no reason to doubt that."

"Didn't I?" The lights in the distance blurred. "I don't remember. It seems so obvious now—those kids died, Knox. They were beaten to death right in front of me, and I *don't remember questioning it.*"

"I'm sorry. That's a terrible thing to do to children."

There were more memories. They flashed through Nina's mind when she least expected them, leaving bruises that felt physical. Ice cream. Movie nights. Her ears ringing during a live-fire exercise. Laughing in the cafeteria. Hot breath on her cheek as an instructor screamed at her. Zoey drawing on the wall with paint she made after hours in one of the science labs. Blacking out in the pool because the top time for a breath-holding drill was four minutes and seventeen seconds, and she had to beat that, she had to—

"I have nightmares," Nina whispered. "I think it's all the things I *don't* remember. And I'm scared to open the door any farther."

"You don't have to, if you're not ready." His fingers brushed her clenched fist, and he laid his hand on hers. "But you're not alone, either. If you want to talk, you have lots of people who will be here to help you. Dani, Maya. Me."

She shook her head to counter the sudden flutter in the pit of her stomach. "You don't have to do that."

"I want to." He stroked his thumb over the backs of her fingers, soothing and maddening, all at once. "I care about you, Nina. I know I broke your trust, and I'll agree to any boundary you set. But if you let me . . ."

"No, I mean—" She pulled her hand away. "In a couple of days, you'll be free. And you can go anywhere you want. Do anything."

"That's true." He retrieved the bottle and took a slow sip. "I haven't considered it much. From the day I cut that tracker out of my neck, I never thought I'd have a future. I figured the best I could hope for was getting my men free and safe."

"What will you do?"

"I don't know for sure. I never really learned how to have dreams." His leg bounced nervously. "But—if you don't mind us sticking around—I'd like to do something to help this neighborhood. I had this idea . . . I don't know, maybe it's stupid."

"Knox." She nudged his leg to stop its jittery movement, but she found herself reluctant to give up the warm, solid pressure, so she kept her leg pressed against his. "Just tell me."

"A clinic." He touched the dog tags she could see outlined beneath his shirt. "That's what Mace would have wanted more than anything. I'd have to find people with medical training to run it, cultivate new connections to get the meds and tech. But Mace used to say the best way to treat people was to make sure they didn't get sick in the first place."

Nina's throat ached. "We have a doctor—Dr. Wells. He does what he can, but he's mostly a last resort. He can't really afford to take care of everyone, so he focuses on the ones who need him most."

"Triage," Knox murmured.

So much of life in Atlanta boiled down to it—medically, economically. Mentally. It was a constant struggle to meet too many needs with too few resources. Nina had been juggling enough of it on her own to understand the consequences of failure. When she dropped a ball, people weren't just disappointed. Sometimes they died.

It was *exhausting*.

But Knox was familiar with that level of responsibility. Maybe, if he stuck around, if he helped—

The possibility stretched out before her like a mirage, hazy and dream-like. She was tempted to throw herself into its warmth, sink into it until she didn't feel so cold and alone anymore. But she wouldn't be doing any of them any favors—not herself, not Knox, and not the people of Five Points.

"You have time," she told him. "If a clinic is what you want, you'll make it happen. And it'll be the best damn clinic anyone's ever seen. For Mace."

"For Mace," he echoed, holding up the bottle. He took another sip before holding it out to her. "So it's okay with you? If we stick around?"

She took a long swallow, then set the bottle aside. "It's not up to me what you do, Knox."

"No, I know." He tilted his head back against the wall and closed his eyes. "But I care how it makes you feel. I don't want to hurt you again."

She rose and stepped away from the edge of the roof. Away from him. "Let me worry about my feelings, okay? It's not your job."

His gaze followed her. "What do you want?"

"What?"

"You keep telling me all the things I don't have to do." He rose gracefully, but didn't step toward her. Just watched her, patient. Intense. "What do *you* want?"

It was a reasonable question, one she'd asked him on more than one occasion. A normal person would have been able to answer.

Nina, on the other hand, didn't have a goddamn clue.

TECHCORPS PROPRIETARY DATA,
L1 SECURITY CLEARANCE

MD–701 has reached critical implant degradation. Seizures should prove fatal in a matter of days.

66–615's damaged hands present a unique opportunity. Tell the reconstruction lab that we should have a candidate for their new project within a week.

Internal Memo, January 2086

THIRTY-THREE

What do you want?

Nina shook the echo out of her head and tried to focus on the plate in front of her. Everyone else had already eaten and cleared the table, but she'd been running at half speed all day. Especially since she'd spent a sleepless night pondering Knox's question.

What do you want?

"Oh, is this what we're doing?" Dani nudged the cloth Gray had spread out over one end of the table in preparation for cleaning his rifle.

He barely glanced up. "Got something you want me to clean?"

"Me? I don't let anyone get grabby with my equipment. I handle it myself."

Luna squinted at them both. "I can't decide if this sounds dirty or not."

"Dani's dirty isn't really subtext. It's usually just text." Maya dropped into the chair across from Gray and examined the rifle. "Can I touch it?"

"Nope. Get your own."

Nina gave up on eating and carried her plate to the makeshift kitchen in the corner. She washed up on autopilot, lulled by the growing noise of the conversation around the table and words pounding a drumbeat in her head.

What do you want?

The answer was simple—and terrifying. Since the night Knox had shown up at her door, all fake smiles and very real determination, she'd wanted *him*. What had started as a purely physical attraction had deepened once they hit the road, weaving through her until it felt like an intrinsic part of her existence: *brown eyes, brown hair, 1.78 meters tall.*

Fascinated by Captain Garrett Knox.

If it had ended there, she might have been able to walk away for good.

But it didn't matter that he'd lied to her or pushed her away. She'd *seen* him, his strengths as well as his weaknesses, everything. Scattered between the half-truths and the open, unguarded conversations were a thousand tiny moments—each one insignificant, perhaps, but when you put them all together . . .

She loved him. That hadn't changed. She didn't think it could. But what she hadn't anticipated was that she would *need* him this much. Now that she'd crashed back into his life to defend him from the Protectorate once and for all, she could feel it so sharply, the hole he'd left in her chest. In her life.

And it *hurt*. Dear God, it hurt.

She made her way back to the trestle table, where Gray was shaking his head at Rafe. "That's a terrible trade. She's pulling one over on you."

Dani waved a pistol at him—an M1911 that she'd bought off a traveling dealer and painstakingly refurbished. "Hey, you shut up. This isn't a replica, okay? It's the real deal."

"No shit?"

"Yeah, no shit."

Maya had abandoned Gray for Conall, who had spread an impressive array of specialty weapons out in front of him. "EMP, shock wave, Taser, flamethrower," he listed, touching each one in sequence before picking up a shiny silver handgun so delicate it looked like a toy. "You'll like this one. Tiny, poison-tipped darts with just enough velocity to pierce clothing. Half the time, they can't even figure out what happened before they drop."

"Ooooh." Maya reached out, wiggling her fingers in excitement. "Gimme, gimme."

"*No.*" Dani intercepted the dart gun. "What if you shoot yourself in the foot? What if you shoot *me* in the foot?"

"Hey, I'm a good shot!"

"Let's not test that with little poison darts," Rafe drawled. "Here, I have something better for you." He rummaged through one of his bags and resurfaced with a smooth cylinder. "This stun-stick hasn't even hit the market yet. Makes the ones that Ava's mercs were wielding look like kiddie versions."

He slid it to Maya, who beamed at him in delight as she swept it up. Rafe glanced at Dani, clearly eager for her approval, because he broke out in a brilliant smile when she winked at him.

"Someone's going to get worse than shot," Knox growled, stopping next to the table with his most fearsome glare. "Could at least one of you pretend you have some weapons training and stop *throwing them around*?"

Dani shot him her most innocent look. "Relax, Dad. We're professionals."

Knox raised both eyebrows. "Sloppy thinking leads to—"

"Sloppy deaths," everyone finished for him in unison. Even Dani and Maya joined in, while Luna stifled a snicker and hid behind Conall's back.

Knox glowered at them, and Nina's pulse hitched.

What do you want?

"Settle down, all right?" she said firmly. "There's plenty of printing to monitor, and someone should go ahead and set up the vacuum-sealer. So get to work." They started to scatter, and Nina jerked her head at Knox. "Can I talk to you for a minute?"

"Sure."

He fell into step with her, but he wasn't moving fast enough. She had to get these words past the lump in her throat now, or she never would. So she grabbed his wrist and pulled him into the nearest room with a door—a supply closet with nothing in it but two broken brooms, an ancient sink in the corner, and a bare light bulb hanging from the ceiling.

Not the most romantic location for a heartfelt speech, but it was so *them* that Nina swallowed a nervous laugh.

Knox looked around, then down at her. His eyebrow quirked up. He looked on the verge of a smile. "This is an odd place for a chat."

"I can wait," she lied.

"Can you?" he murmured.

No, not even close. "I want this," she confessed in a rush. "You and me and our crews, working together. Even when it gets hard or we fight, I want the last forty-eight hours, all the time." She finally paused to drag in a breath. "I want *this*."

"You want us." His smile was beautiful, riveting. Everything she'd imagined it would be, and *real* for the first time, with no lies between them. "You want me."

She reached for him, sliding her hands up his arms. "If you'll have me."

"If?" Knox gripped her hips and dragged her against him. "*If?* Being with you is the only thing I've ever wanted for myself. Before I met you,

I didn't even remember *how* to want, and now I can't stop. I want everything."

She twined her arms around his neck and closed the distance between them to capture his mouth. He met her kiss with a groan, lips parted, head tilted, his fingers flexing on her hips before sliding down to cup her ass. Then he hauled her up, urging her to wrap her legs around his waist.

Nina tore her mouth from his and kissed her way to his ear. "Here?"

"Everywhere." Two steps and her back hit the wall. He leaned into her, his teeth teasing along her jaw. "Unless you want me to stop . . ."

"Don't." She reached up and gripped a shelf for leverage so she could rock against him. "Don't stop."

He murmured something unintelligible against her throat, his beard rasping over her skin. Nina shuddered as his fingers slipped under the hem of her tank top and up, stroking her sides as he guided the fabric higher.

She twisted, trying to arch into his touch. "Say it again."

"Which part?" His thumb traced the lower curve of her breast. "That I've never wanted anything as much as I want you?" He plied her nipple through the soft fabric of her bra with just enough pressure to make her gasp. "Or that I'm going to spend the next year figuring out how many different ways I can have you?"

"Why wait?" she whispered. "We have a sink. Walls. There's even a bed upstairs—I hope."

"Oh, I'm not waiting." Knox hauled her away from the wall and spun to balance her on the edge of the sink. Before she'd caught her balance, he was coaxing her tank top up over her head, his gaze drinking her in. "But it's going to take more than one night. Maybe more than a year, now that I think about it."

"Sweet-talker." She hauled his shirt over his head and kissed him again, threading her fingers through his hair.

He moaned against her lips and wedged his hips between her thighs. "Off," he murmured, hooking one finger beneath her bra strap. "Everything, off."

Her shoes hit the floor. She and Knox moved in concert, tugging at buttons, pushing and pulling fabric, their fingers meeting only to part again, sliding and seeking. There was as much discovery as memory in the reunion, a thousand sighs and moans and secret places neither of them had ever had time to touch before.

When she was naked, caged in his arms, trapped between the cool ceramic and the heat of his body, she stopped. Each panting breath pushed her breasts against his chest as she traced his jaw, the bow of his mouth, even his tongue when he parted his lips. "Don't move."

He tensed beneath her touch, his fingers curling around the shelf behind her until it groaned, as she pushed her thumb deeper into his mouth and reached for his belt buckle with her free hand.

"Nina," he rumbled.

She slipped her thumb free and dragged it down the center of his chest. "Hmm?"

His muscles flexed beneath her hand. "Can I move yet?"

"No." His belt fell open, and she caressed the warm leather for a moment before unbuttoning his jeans. "Kind of busy here."

She held his gaze with a challenging stare as she pushed the denim down, sliding the fabric and his underwear off his hips, freeing his cock. But she only brushed the back of her hand over his hip bone, then dragged her nails across his stomach.

Knox sucked in a breath. The shelf creaked dangerously. His eyes all but commanded her to touch him, but he stood rigidly unmoving. Just as she'd asked.

She wrapped her fingers around him.

"Fuck." His hips jerked, a tiny fracture in control before he froze in place again. "You like this game, don't you?"

Even as he uttered the words, his erection grew hotter, harder. More insistent. Nina stroked him once, then lingered to circle her thumb around the head. "Do you need a safe word, Captain, or just a little mercy?"

"I need *you*," he growled.

Desire pulsed through her, as if his words had elicited an echo from her core, and she gave in. She braced her arms on his shoulders, gripped his sides with her legs, and slowly levered herself up until the head of his cock nudged between her thighs. She hovered there, trembling more from denial than strain, then whispered one single word against his temple. "*Yes.*"

The shelf behind her snapped. Knox lifted her before the wood hit the floor, spinning to press her back against the wall.

With a groan of naked gratitude, he drove into her. The intensity of it stole her breath, and she managed a single ragged gasp before he did it again, and again, and *again*, until Nina decided she didn't need oxygen, after all. Just this.

His mouth found her ear. He rasped her name with every thrust. A chant. A plea. The rough wood paneling bit into her back, but she could barely feel it over the mounting pleasure. She clung to him, her nails pricking his shoulders as he fucked her harder, faster—

She came with a hoarse cry, every muscle clenching so tight it almost hurt.

His hand slammed into the wall next to her head, cracking the paneling. He buried his face against her throat, the sting of his teeth closing sharply over her pulse twisting with the pleasure as he drove into her once, again, and then—

"*Yes.*"

It shouldn't have been possible for it to get *better*, but it did. Nina wrapped Knox in her arms and held him as he shuddered. She rubbed her cheek against his jaw until he slowed and stilled, his fingers sliding over the sweat-slicked skin at the small of her back. They stood there, locked together, breathing each other in.

For the first time, it didn't feel like a stolen moment. It felt like . . .

"Do you believe in fate, Knox?"

He smiled against her cheek, and held her tighter. "I might be starting to."

Looking at his own soon-to-be-firebombed doppelganger should have been a somber and morbid affair. Instead, Knox found himself digging his teeth into his lower lip to hold back utterly out-of-character laughter.

"I know it looks ridiculous now," Nina muttered. "But give it forty-five minutes at eleven hundred degrees Celsius. It would probably convince *you*, even though you know it's fake."

"I'm not doubting you," he soothed, but his lips kept twitching.

The body they'd constructed was sprawled out on his bed, his 3-D-printed skeleton—complete with a replica of his rebuilt hands—surrounding enough internal organ–ish material to keep the TechCorps busy for a while. All of it was encased in a clear gel that matched the general shape and mass of his body.

Dani was right. It looked like the world's most disgusting gummy bear.

Impressive logistically, if not visually. But the fact that every scrap of it carried his DNA elevated the whole thing from macabre art project to work of evil genius.

"Did I ever tell you what I thought when I saw Maya's file for the first time?" he asked.

"Was it something along the lines of *oh fuck, I just coercively kidnapped the wrong set of ladies*?"

"That would have been a lot smarter," he conceded. "No, I thought whoever faked her death instead of walking away with two million credits was a ridiculous idealist *and* highly ingenious. And I found both of those things uncomfortably appealing."

"That's sweet." Nina wrapped her arms around his waist. "But you can stop trying to butter me up."

"Oh, I haven't even gotten to the flattery." Being able to touch her was a heady thing. He stroked his fingers over her cheek and brushed her hair back from her temple. "I always knew you were brilliant, but I have to be honest. This whole new level of advanced technological deception is extremely sexy."

She laughed, then sobered as she leaned her head against his shoulder. "Will you miss him?"

"Who, Captain Knox?" He'd expected to. Had been dreading this moment, in fact. Then Nina had pulled him into a closet and set the entire world on its side. "I thought I might. I may not have loved who I'd become, but that was all I had. A rank and my crew."

"But?"

"But I still have a crew. And they haven't followed me just because of the rank in a long time." He threaded his fingers gently through her hair and tilted her head back. "And you gave me something better than a rank. You gave me back my purpose. I have a future now."

Her eyes fluttered shut, and she made a soft noise in the back of her throat. "Does that mean you've made your peace with this?"

Peace sounded too passive. The feeling churning inside him was closer to sharp anticipation, a roiling desire to be done with the past. "I'm mostly feeling impatient." He brushed his lips over hers, soft and sweet. Quick, because if he really started kissing her, he wouldn't want to stop. "I'm ready to start my new life now."

"Hey, we're almost—oh." Gray caught the doorjamb, halting his forward momentum with a jerk. "Right, this is a thing that's happening now."

"What's up?" Nina asked.

Immediately, Gray straightened, unconsciously assuming the posture of a soldier giving report. "Everything's ready. We've placed the decoys, along with the explosives and the accelerants."

"And Conall double-checked the calculations?"

"Twice. It's all exactly where it needs to be for maximum damage and conflagration."

"Good." Knox drew back and slipped his dog tags from beneath his shirt. The final piece of the deception. "Make sure Conall and Rafe left their tags on the bodies, and that everything we need is packed into the trucks. We'll be down in a second."

Nina checked the time as Gray pounded down the stairs. "We'd better hurry. Only half an hour left before Clem makes the call."

Knox stared at the little bits of metal in his hand. Almost three decades of his life were tied up in those tags. Three decades of his life—and one death that would haunt him, no matter how many decades he had left.

After a moment, he snapped the chain and freed Mace's tag. It sat in his palm for a moment, warming against his skin, the only thing that hurt to let go. Conall and Rafe and Gray would be a part of whatever new life he built, but Mace . . .

Nina closed his fingers around the tag. "You can keep it. It's not something they would expect to find. They won't miss it . . . but you would."

"I would." He held it for another moment, making a silent promise—to himself and to Mace. He'd find a way to open that clinic, to do all the things Mace would have done if Knox had just gotten them out a few months sooner.

Mace would live on, even if only through the men who had been his brothers.

Swallowing hard, Knox slipped the memento into his pocket. His dog tags went onto the counterfeit body, to melt into whatever was left by the fire and give the TechCorps the death they so heartily craved.

Then he turned his back on the whole mess of it and held out his hand to Nina. "Are you ready?"

Smiling, she slipped her hand into his. "Let's go home."

**TECHCORPS PROPRIETARY DATA,
L2 SECURITY CLEARANCE**

66–615's tracker went inactive at 0500 hours, followed shortly by 66–793, 66–942, and TE–815.

By all appearances, the Silver Devils have gone AWOL.

They must be either contained or destroyed.

Internal Memo, July 2086

THIRTY-FOUR

Nina's plan worked smoothly—maybe too smoothly. It barely felt real as they stood on her roof and watched the West End warehouse explode, killing Captain Garrett Knox and what remained of his Silver Devils.

They toasted with champagne—which Ava pointedly explained failed to meet the qualifications for *real* champagne, as it had not been imported from France—and took the celebrations inside. To their new home.

Instead of two crews, now they had one. One crew that laughed and drank and groaned in mock horror when Nina grabbed Knox by the back of the shirt and hauled him up the stairs. He followed her to her bedroom trailed by joking pleas to get her room thoroughly soundproofed, and then he fell into bed and into her until they were both too exhausted to move.

Something woke him just before dawn.

Nina's body was a warm weight against his side. Her lips were curved in a soft smile free of lingering sadness. He added that to his mental list of things to do—keep sadness firmly away from Nina at all times.

Her steady breathing didn't falter as he slipped from her bed and pulled on his jeans. Out on the landing, he lingered in the shadows, scanning the remnants of the night's celebrations—empty beer bottles and bowls of snacks, an upended deck of cards, and a knife plunged into the table from Rafe and Dani's game of chicken.

That last one had almost ended in bloodshed, but both participants had given every indication of enjoying the hell out of it.

Awareness pricked up his spine, and Knox shifted deeper into the shadows. A moment later, he was rewarded with movement below.

Ava.

She was dressed in her usual black, with a bag swung across her shoulder.

Her heeled boots were somehow soundless as she stopped at the kitchen counter and slipped several packages from her bag. She spoke without turning her head, her soft words drifting up to him. "Are you going to wake her?"

No point to lurking in the shadows, then. Knox walked down the stairs and crossed his arms over his chest. "Are you really going to leave without telling her good-bye?"

Ava shifted the box she'd left on the counter until it was perfectly straight. "She'd ask me to stay, and I'd have to disappoint her. This is easier on both of us."

"If you say so."

She stiffened and turned to face Knox. Rationally, he *knew* that Nina shared those same dramatic cheekbones, the dark brown eyes, the full lips—but she looked nothing like the woman in front of him. And it was more than just the way Ava used makeup to accentuate the sharp angles of her face and frame her eyes with smoky shadows.

All of Nina's warmth was missing from Ava. There was none of the joy, the ready smiles and teasing affection, none of the things that made Nina who she was. This hard, brittle woman with pain shadowing her eyes was a stranger.

Maybe his pity showed, because her lips pressed tightly together. "I assume you realize this celebration tonight was premature. The Protectorate may have snapped up the bait, but it will take weeks for them to fully process that scene. My sister is inarguably brilliant, but there are still a thousand things that could go wrong. And even if it works flawlessly, your life is over. You can never be Captain Garrett Knox again."

"No, I can be *myself*." They all could. The Silver Devils finally had a chance to become whoever they might have been if circumstances and need hadn't brought them to the Protectorate. To start fresh. There would always be risk—the danger of discovery, the uncertain stability of their implants, the daily insecurities that came along with living in a place where the strong preyed on the weak . . .

But they *were* strong. They could be protectors instead of predators. Like Nina.

And that was the secret he was beginning to understand about her. It wasn't that she couldn't fathom the darkness of the world, or the cruelty of the people in it. She knew every day that she was living on borrowed time.

She'd simply decided to embrace that time. To make the most of every hour. Of every second.

To live.

Ava sighed. "I know that look. You belong to her now. Don't feel bad, Captain. It's happened to better people. As long as you never forget that you don't remotely deserve her."

Knox bared his teeth at her in a mockery of a smile. "Neither of us do."

Ava's eyes froze over. "You had better live up to what she thinks you are," she whispered, the threat somehow more chilling in that soft, husky voice. "I'll be paying attention. And if I find out that you've hurt her, I'll come back here and cut you into pieces so small, even the TechCorps hasn't invented the technology to see them yet."

"Fair enough," Knox replied easily. "But *you* had better plan to come back here and be a part of her life. Because you're about to hurt her again by disappearing, and I won't put up with that too many more times."

Ava stiffened. But, after a moment, her lips twitched. "Fair enough," she echoed. She dipped into her purse and withdrew a data card the size of her thumb. "I don't like you, Knox. I imagine you feel the same way about me. But we have one thing in common."

She flicked the data card at him, and he caught it out of the air and turned it over in his hand. "Another gift?"

"Conall will know what to do with it. If Nina is ever in trouble, if she needs *anything* . . ." Ava's composure cracked for a moment, revealing the wildness in her eyes, and a well of emotions that went so deep—

Crazy, some people would call it.

And maybe she was. The love Ava felt for Nina was a feral, unpredictable thing. She might fight with her sister, might hurt her, but Knox had no trouble believing that Ava would burn the TechCorps and everything in Atlanta to the ground, and not care how many thousands of bodies were strewn amongst the rubble.

Just to keep Nina safe.

He closed his fingers around the data card and nodded. "Take care of yourself, Ava. I'll take care of her until you come back."

"You'd better, Captain."

"I'm not a captain anymore."

"Time will tell, won't it?"

She turned and disappeared down the darkened hallway. Knox listened for a while, but he didn't hear anything. Not the scuff of her boots, not doors or windows opening. Just the distant hum of the solar generator and the softer drone of the kitchen appliances.

Ava might as well have been a ghost.

He checked the locks on the doors before going back up to Nina's room. He left the data card on her bedside table and shed his pants. Sliding back into her bed shouldn't have felt like coming home. It was the first night he'd ever slept there, but the scent of that sweet shampoo permeated the pillow, and she murmured something and curled into him, her legs tangling with his, her silky hair spilling across his chest.

He could have so easily become Ava. Feral and broken, so filled with pain and rage and hatred that he couldn't accept an open hand, couldn't settle beneath a welcoming roof and breathe in the comfort of being safe. Of belonging.

His men had held him back from the brink, and then Nina had pulled him into the light. She'd forgiven him, let him back into her life and her bed. She was the reason he was here, warm and content. No, not just content. *Happy.* Nina had given him a future.

He owed her too much to waste it.

With Nina's soft breath tickling his throat and her heart thumping beneath his fingers, Garrett Knox, no longer captain of anything, began laying out his next mission. His most important mission. One that would likely take the rest of his life.

He was going to make every last one of Nina's noble, idealistic dreams come true.

EPILOGUE

Nina dropped into the darkness.

With their available intel, Conall had estimated a ten-meter distance to the bottom. She counted off half that, then gave the command. "Halt."

She stopped almost immediately as the brakes inside the mechanism attached to her harness engaged. She flicked on her flashlight, illuminating the cavernous space, and activated her comms. "It's more like twelve meters to the floor."

"Got it," Knox replied.

"Slow." The single-syllable command resumed her descent, and she readied her knife. The moment the soles of her boots touched the concrete, she cut the line, and the proximate end retracted automatically into the housing embedded in her harness.

The stale air tasted bitter and musty, so Nina tossed out an oxygenation canister. It rolled across the floor, hissing as it began to disperse its contents, just as Knox touched down behind her.

He unslung the huge solar battery backup from his shoulder and lowered it to the floor. Instead of his usual pistol, the holster at his hip held a clever little gun loaded with putty-like pellets. Each one he discharged hit the wall and spread into a three-inch disc that began to glow brightly as it reacted with the air, slowly bringing the room into illuminated focus.

They were in a large, bare room filled with rack after rack, each one loaded with dozens of hard drives. Everything had been wired together, the cables hastily gathered and secured to each rack, with a single terminal in the middle of it all.

Nina swept up the bag Knox had deposited and started toward the terminal. "I'll hook up the battery, and we can see if any of this stuff works."

"I'll clear the rest of the place." He stopped next to her, leaning in until his mouth hovered teasingly close to hers. A smile curved his lips as he dipped a hand into her bag and pulled out another oxygenation canister. "I'll be right back."

The power supply for the terminal was meant to plug into an outlet, not interface with a solar battery, so Nina pulled out her knife again and got to work stripping the cord so she could hook up an inverter. She'd nearly finished separating out the necessary wires when Knox called her name from the next room over.

She abandoned her task and followed the sound of his voice. He was standing in a room stacked high with boxes and shelves, holding a book in his hand.

"Look at this." He tilted the book into the spill of light from a lamp he'd affixed to the wall. It was a children's book, the cover illustration bright and colorful, though the dings and dents along the edges suggested it had passed through plenty of hands. He flipped it over and showed her the bar code on the back, affixed with a sticker that said PROPERTY OF KIRKWOOD BRANCH LIBRARY.

"They're all like this," he said, passing her the book and pulling out another. "The room goes back forever. There must be thousands of boxes in here. Maybe tens of thousands."

Nina reached out, her finger trembling as she traced one bright red sweep of color on the cover. "They saved more than the files."

"I think it's a whole library." He nudged one massive shelf with his foot. It didn't even budge under the weight of hundreds of boxes. "Maybe more than one."

Her heart started to pound. "We'll have to expand."

"You can." Knox smiled at her. "*We* can."

Giddy joy flooded her as she wrapped her arms around his neck and kissed him once, twice. "We can." The third time, the kiss went on and on, her absolute, utter focus on *Knox*.

Until their comms crackled again. "It got quiet," Dani observed. "Are you guys dead or making out?"

Knox broke away with a noise that was half laughter, half groan, and activated his communication device. "It would serve you right if I didn't answer."

"I mean, anything's better than the Great Dirty Talk Fiasco of last week," came Conall's voice. "You and Maya should be glad you don't have these things in your heads. We all got a show until I cut the feed and changed his activation protocols. Do you know how weird it is to get porn *inside your head*?"

Nina's entire face was flaming. "That's it. The subdural comms have got to go."

Maya's voice cut through Knox's laughter. "Put your pants back on. Dani's on her way down, and Gray's fixing up the ladder."

Nina replaced the book in the box and stole one last kiss. "Why do we keep them around?"

"Because we love them." Knox caught her and pulled her against him. "And because we're about to be really, *really* rich."

As if he gave a damn about the money. "They're family," she agreed.

And if the last month had taught her anything, it had taught her that family was as ever-evolving as it was eternal. It went deeper than blood or DNA. It was a promise that, no matter what you did, there would always be someone who loved you, missed you. Someone who had your back.

"I love you." Knox's whisper was barely audible beneath the sudden flurry of activity and sound in the bunker's main chamber.

Smiling, Nina echoed the words, and it didn't matter if he could hear her or not. She'd tell him again later, when she could show him, too.

MACE

Mace was in hell.

It felt like a cliché, but it was the only explanation that made sense. He couldn't escape, and nothing felt real anymore, but it didn't have the dreamy, detached quality of a nightmare, either.

He'd never expected hell to be so damn *cold*.

Mace tried to mark the passage of time by the artificial lights in his cell. Twenty-seven times, they had clicked on, harsh and blinding. And twenty-six times, they had gone out, plunging him into utter darkness. But he didn't know if those were hours or days or years.

He experienced the world in flashes—words that drove him to catatonia or blistering rage, cold water sluicing over his skin, food he could barely taste.

Hot blood gushing under his bare hands.

No, that last one was wrong. Familiar, yes, but *wrong*. His brain stuttered, and his fingers began to move from muscle memory.

Isolate the artery. No clamps, so I'll have to apply manual pressure. Fuck, where is all this blood coming from—

"He's doing it again." The flat voice made Mace jerk. Shudder.

Another man sighed. "I don't get it. He'll make it halfway through a kill, and then a switch flips, and he starts trying to save them. It's like he can't help himself."

"He can't. It's how he was wired." The voice slithered through the room. Mace knew that voice. He *loathed* that voice. "You're supposed to fix that. He's no fucking good to me if he can't properly eliminate a target. We might as well let him rot here."

Yes. Mace grabbed at the words, clutched them close. Cold comfort, the idea of dying alone in a box, but he didn't mind. Because somewhere, deep down, in the sick, cold knot in his gut, the one that never eased, he knew it was better than what the man with the flat voice wanted him to do.

"Let me die," he croaked.

"We might as well, Richter," the second man said. "What's the point now that the rest of the Silver Devils have been killed?"

"The point, in fact, is that I'm not so sure they have." Silence. Then, "Clean it up. We'll start again fresh tomorrow."

ACKNOWLEDGMENTS

Every book is a journey, and this one was especially epic. After a decade in the business, trying something new can be scary. We are deeply grateful to our agent, Sarah E. Younger, who held our hands every step of the way and turned scary into fun. Thank you for every excited dancing gif.

Working with a new editor for the first time in years can be daunting, too. But from the first moment we talked to Claire Eddy, we knew she got us. It's thrilling to have an editor who wants *more* of all your favorite parts of the story. The questions she asked made this book so much better.

Alyssa Cole listened to a million versions of this book's pitch, read a million versions of the synopsis, and offered endless support as we sat down to write it. It is no exaggeration to say it exists in great part because of her. (Just the good parts, though.)

Eternal thanks go to the people who have helped us get this far: Lillie Applegarth, keeper of bibles and timelines. Sharon Muha, eagle-eyed proofreader of legend. Angie Ramey, the most patient assistant in the world. Jay and Tracy, our wonderful community moderators. And to all our friends on Patreon, whose support gives us a little breathing room to concentrate on writing. Special thanks to Packy and Nikki for reading an earlier version of this book and cheering us on through revisions.

Thank you to every librarian who has helped connect a child with a book. Librarians are why we're here today.

And, as always, thank you to our readers. From the old school O'Kane VIPs who have been with us from the beginning to any new readers joining us for this book: we wouldn't be here without you.

Finally: our sincerest apologies to Ms. Rosalind Franklin. When we originally named the Franklin Center, it was supposed to be a relatively friendly place, an homage to a woman whose vital, fundamental work in the field of genetics was tragically obscured by ambitious, predatory colleagues. As the book evolved, so did the Center bearing her name. I suppose it's oddly appropriate that bad men came into our book and messed up her legacy *again*, but please don't hold that against her.